Bettina Selby was born in London, and as a very young child was evacuated to a coal-mining village in South Wales at the beginning of the war. She left school at fifteen and joined the WRAC. After some years as a freelance photographer, she studied for a degree in world religions at London University. She is married and has three grown-up children.

The author has written two previous books – RIDING THE MOUNTAINS DOWN and RIDING TO JERUSALEM – and has written for the *Independent*, the *Sunday Telegraph*, the *Traveller*, many cycling publications and other newspapers and magazines.

D0258431

Riding
the Desert Trail

BETTINA SELBY

SPHERE BOOKS LTD

Published by the Penguin Group
27 Wrights Lane, London w8 5tz, England
Viking Penguin Inc., 40 West 23rd Street, New York, New York 10010, USA
Penguin Books Australia Ltd, Ringwood, Victoria, Australia
Penguin Books Canada Ltd, 2801 John Street, Markham, Ontario, Canada l3r 1b4
Penguin Books (NZ) Ltd, 182–190 Wairau Road, Auckland 10, New Zealand

Penguin Books Ltd, Registered Offices: Harmondsworth, Middlesex, England

First published in Great Britain by Chatto and Windus Ltd in 1988
Published by Sphere Books in 1989
1 3 5 7 9 10 8 6 4 2

Printed and bound in Great Britain by
Richard Clay Ltd, Bungay, Suffolk

*This book is dedicated to Vimto, Michael, and Fatima,
and to all the young survivors of Africa*

Contents

List of Illustrations

Maps

Acknowledgements

Writing the account of this journey has been a strange experience, bringing to light difficulties and dramas that I wasn't always fully conscious of at the time, which was perhaps just as well. Without the friendly support, encouragement and humour of a great number of people whom I met along the way, often in the most remote of places, I might not have survived to tell the tale. To these people who fed me, provided me with shelter and found ways of my getting to impossible destinations I owe a special debt. Not everyone can be mentioned by name since to do so might bring repercussions down upon their heads. I must therefore include them all under the umbrella of my African friends.

Acknowledgements and thanks are also due for the practical help and encouragement I received from: The Egyptian State Tourist Office, The Egyptian Cultural Centre, The Egyptian Exploration Society, The British Council, The Sudan Cultural Centre, OXFAM, UNICEF, Euro Action ACCORD, The Ugandan Embassy Khartoum, Uganda National Parks, The Rt Rev. John Baker, Bishop of Salisbury, The Rt Rev. John Neale, Bishop of Ramsbury and Hilly Janes of the *Independent*, and my family and friends.

I must also acknowledge my indebtedness to all the African explorers who opened up the way and whose courage and resourcefulness were such an inspiration for the journey. I think particularly of Dr Livingstone, John Speke, Samuel and Florence Baker, Burton, Stanley and especially Amelia B. Edwards who began it all for me.

Foreword

In all this extraordinary panorama so wild, so weird, so desolate, there is nothing really beautiful, except the colour. Never even in Egypt have I seen anything so tender, so transparent, so harmonious. I shut my eyes and it all comes before me. I see the amber of the sands; the Cataract rocks all black and purple and polished; the Nile a greenish brown flecked with yeasty foam; over all the blue and burning sky permeated with light and palpitating with sunshine.

It has an interest however, beyond and apart from that of beauty. It rouses one's imagination to a sense of the greatness of the Nile. We look across a world of desert and see the river still coming from afar. There is no sail on those dangerous waters, no moving creature on those pathless sands, it would seem as if we had touched the limit of civilization and were standing on the threshold of a land unexplored.

Yet for all this we feel as if we were only at the beginning of the mighty river. We have journeyed well nigh a thousand miles against the stream; but what is that to the distance which still lies between us and the Great Lakes? and how far beyond the Great Lakes must we seek for the Source that is even yet undiscovered?

Amelia B. Edwards, 1877

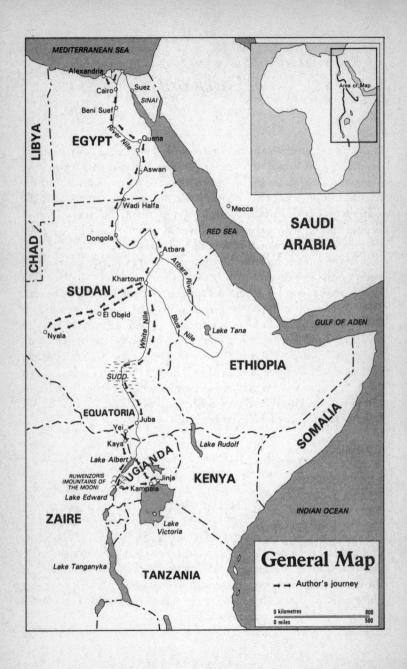

MEDITERRANEAN SEA

Alexandria

Cairo   Suez

Beni Suef   SINAI

LIBYA

EGYPT   Quena

Aswan

Wadi Halfa   Mecca

CHAD   Dongola   RED SEA   SAUDI ARABIA

Atbara

Khartoum   GULF OF ADEN

SUDAN

El Obeid   Lake Tana

Nyala   ETHIOPIA

SUDD   SOMALIA

EQUATORIA   Juba

Yei   Lake Rudolf

Kaya

Lake Albert   KENYA

RUWENZORIS   Jinja
(MOUNTAINS OF   Kampala
THE MOON)

Lake Edward

ZAIRE   INDIAN OCEAN

Lake Victoria

Lake Tanganyka   General Map

TANZANIA   Author's journey

0 kilometres   800
0 miles   500

River Nile

Atbara River

White Nile

Blue Nile

UGANDA

Area of Map

CHAPTER ONE

The Inspiration

When I landed in Cairo in early November I was met at the airport by three men bearing placards with the legend WELCOME MRS BETTINA. With its well-developed tourist industry, Egypt values visiting writers, but to provide a reception committee at four in the morning, with the aeroplane two hours behind schedule, was impressive. It also meant that I was spared the normal laborious entry formalities and the necessity to change a large sum of money at an unfavourable rate, so it was very much appreciated, and predisposed me to react favourably to the country. But kind though it was, it made not a jot of difference because what really set the tone of Egypt – and, indeed, of the whole journey – was the moment when, only a few hours later, I was awoken in my hotel room by the infernal din of Cairo's traffic. I'd gone over to the window feeling jet-lagged and irritable and had seen beyond the Corniche, in splendid contrast to the six lanes of frenetically weaving, horn-blaring vehicles, a very broad body of sparkling water calmly and majestically flowing past. It was spanned by many bridges and flanked by the tall buildings of the modern city, and yet it seemed astonishingly untamed and immensely and effortlessly powerful. It dwarfed everything man-made, making the concrete tower blocks look just a touch ridiculous, and reducing the endless streams of cars on the bridges to lines of clockwork toys. Somehow it seemed wonderful that a river which had had such a profound effect upon the history of mankind for so many ages should still be bowling along with its energies unimpaired, while the civilisations that it had nourished had long since crumbled into dust and been carried down on its waters to the sea. It gave a refreshingly different scale to time and events, reducing the importance of both. In the months that followed, there was no occasion on which a sudden glimpse of the Nile didn't result in the same lifting of the heart and a falling away of petty concerns and irritations.

The idea of making a four-and-a-half-thousand-mile journey to the source of the Nile had come to me one winter's day nearly a year before in the British Museum. It had happened on the sort of soaking wet grey day when the last of autumn's leaves are still choking the gutters and making black, slippery patches on the pavements; when traffic is throwing up gouts of dirty water over bicyclists and over the pedestrians standing too near the kerbs, and London is at its least attractive. On such a day I find it a delight to escape for a while, chain my bicycle to the railings and drop in at the Museum for a brief look at old favourites like the stone tablets of fierce Assyrians doing despiteful things to long-forgotten conquered cities, or the wealth of lovely pilfered marbles that the Greeks are so eager for us to return. Until this particular day, however, the Egyptian collection had never really attracted me; I found the rows of mummies depressing, and the massive statuary rather dull and lifeless.

What changed my attitude to things Egyptian was a book that caught my eye as I passed through the Museum shop, damp and chilled on my way to hot soup at the cafeteria. The painting on the cover showed a sunny river scene with palm trees and golden ruins which was the absolute antithesis of the vile weather outside and on the spur of the moment I bought it to dip into over lunch. It was a re-issue of a work written 110 years before by a Victorian novelist named Amelia B. Edwards, who had travelled a thousand miles up the Nile by sailing boat in a most delightful and leisurely manner. Her enthusiasm for the hot dry land of Egypt and for its antiquities was infectious, especially in the august setting of the British Museum. As I walked back through the familiar galleries packed with the spoils of other nineteenth-century Nile journeys I began to look with new eyes at the huge statues of blank-faced pharaohs, the animal-headed gods, the inscrutable lions with crossed paws and the yards and yards of stone inscribed with strange hieroglyphs. And quite suddenly I wanted to go to Egypt and see for myself the part of the world that had produced it all.

Once the idea had taken root it grew rapidly, until the journey I was planning was not to be just the last thousand miles of the Nile which waters Egypt, but the whole length of that great and fascinating river, right up to its source, deep in the heartlands of Africa, where the Rift Valley cradles vast equatorial lakes and the Mountains of the Moon raise their mysterious snow-covered heads behind wreaths of mist and cloud. It was a journey which would take me from the sites of one of the world's most ancient civilisations to some of the last discovered places on the planet. When Amelia B. Edwards was sailing up the lower reaches of the Nile, making caustic comments about Thomas Cook steamers and packaged tours, the upper reaches of the river were still largely unexplored. Barely a decade had passed since Burton, Speke, Baker, Dr Livingstone and Stanley had all striven to be the first to settle the question of the Nile's source – something Ptolemy had already decided (quite accurately as it turned out) 2,000 years before. The existence of the Mountains of the Moon was not even suspected by those competing explorers, for who would expect to find Ptolemy's 'eternal snows' barely a dozen miles from the equator?

It was an immensely exciting prospect, but formidable too. Deserts, swamps and jungles still presented no small challenge, just as they had in the great days of Nile exploration; and once past Egypt there were few roads other than the imprint of tyres in the sand. There were questions of security as well, for Uganda and the Sudan could not be counted among the most stable of countries, and to judge by their histories it seems that they never were. But there are few journeys that the long distance traveller can make without passing through some trouble-spots. The world is seldom peaceful in all places at once, and if I decided to wait until it was I would never get anywhere. If one sees the chief aim of life as travel, then the only thing to do is to leave what can't be solved and take decisions affecting one's personal safety later, in the light of local knowledge.

Planning the practical aspects of the journey was far easier than worrying about political problems, and a lot more enjoyable. The means of travel had already been decided on: I would go by bicycle. I did toy with the idea of a camel as it would have been more at home in the deserts, but I doubted my ability to handle one alone and I couldn't afford the services of a camel driver. Bicycles I do know something about, and I enjoy riding them very much. I also value the flexibility they give me, as I can convey my bicycle by aeroplane, boat, car or train and even carry it for short distances on my shoulder. It makes me independent in a way no other form of transport can – it needs no fuel, no documents and very little maintenance. Most importantly, it goes along at the right speed for seeing everything, and as it doesn't cut me off from my surroundings, it also makes me lots of friends.

I decided that I should have an 'all terrain' bicycle for the Nile journey, as the wider wheels and stronger construction of this type of machine were more suited to the arduous conditions it would have to stand up to. Evans, the shop that has made previous wide-ranging bicycles for me, allowed me to design this one myself. It turned out very well and had steeper frame angles and a shorter wheelbase than most ATBs and was fast and lively in spite of its extra weight. It was sprayed a glowing pillar-box red and I thought of it affectionately as 'the firecracker', but only until I reached Egypt, when it became the 'Agala' which is Arabic for bicycle, or the 'Ah Agala' which was how Arabs rapturously greeted its appearance – for it was much admired in countries where bicycles are as numerous as donkeys, but are always painted a dull black and are single-geared. The shining red 'Ah Agala' had eighteen gears, sealed bearings to keep out the sand and dust and very superior equipment, including a set of four smart new pannier bags into which all my equipment for the four and a half months was to be stowed.

Travelling by bicycle does present one major problem, namely the weight that can be comfortably carried, and a firm line has to be taken about what is essential and what can be done without. Having made other long bicycle journeys through the Middle East, the Himalayas and Turkey, I had some previous experience upon which to draw, but it was still no easy task. After lots of list-making, and scratchings out and addings on, I decided to sacrifice clothing and took only the absolute minimum, planning to replace worn-out items en route. Because of Moslem sensitivity to human flesh it was necessary to have long-sleeved shirts and trousers reaching the ankle, which are in any case sensible clothes to wear under burning skies. I assembled as lightweight a basic survival kit as possible, consisting of tent, sleeping bag, stove, pans and some dehydrated food. Water could prove to be the biggest single problem, both getting sufficient supplies in the desert and removing dangerous matter from it – bilharzia and gardia are just two of the horrors that teem in Nile waters. I collected enough plastic containers to hold two and a half gallons – more than I could actually carry – and I also tracked down a Swiss-made water filter pump with a solid ceramic core. It weighed over a pound but was well proven, and guaranteed to take out all harmful bacteria from contaminated water. I chose it in preference to purifying tablets because I hate the taste of these and would need far too many to deal with the gallon or two of water a day which is easily consumed in the tropics.

Tools were weighty items, even the rather horrid lightweight ones I keep for travelling, and I also had to pack one spare tyre and an inner tube – further spare tyres I sent on ahead to Khartoum. Then there were the necessary antibiotics and other drugs and the first aid equipment to deal with most medical eventualities short of snakebite or amputation. Writing materials and essential guide books, a camera and ten rolls of film, a petrol stove and a flask of fuel for it, increased the weight alarmingly. I economised by taking only a plastic mug and two horn spoons for any meals I cooked – I could always eat out of a pan. Reading material, like music, I would just have to do without, making do with the snatches I had stored away in my mind. I was fortunate in having had the sort of old-fashioned education that believed in committing large chunks of prose and poetry to memory – a habit that served me well on long solitary bicycle rides. A plethora of small items – penknife, lithium torch, miniature compass, a net bag for covering my head to keep off plagues of insects, an ingenious 'long life' match, a slow burning candle, insect repellent, sun cream, a sewing kit, and jet amulets given me by a learned friend who said that travellers had always taken such things with them in classical times to keep them safe – all added to the burden, bringing the final loaded tally to 65 pounds. I was profoundly glad that the prevailing winds of Africa were expected to blow from behind me when I headed up-river; I also wondered how much I'd be charged in excess baggage on the flight to Cairo.

While happily engaged in assembling all this equipment, I was also finding out about visas, attempting to find out what I could about the route, and following up useful introductions. People with experience of any of the Nile countries were loud in their praises of the inhabitants and nostalgic for the lifestyle, but vague about the sort of practical details I wanted to know – not surprisingly really, since none of them had ever travelled around those countries by bicycle. It didn't seem as if the available information about some parts of my route had increased all that much from the days when map-makers filled in the blank spaces with whatever came to mind; the thought that I might be pedalling through virgin territory gave me an anticipatory shiver of excitement.

I did not need a visa for Uganda, but it was hinted darkly that with Britain demanding visas for members of the Commonwealth, reciprocation might be operating by the time I reached that country's borders. There seemed to be no point in applying for further help or information to an embassy whose country had had its latest coup only a few months previously. The Sudan was also experiencing considerable internal problems and did not seem keen to encourage tourism; the difficulty of obtaining a visa from the Sudanese loomed large. I could be issued with one valid for just thirty days but only if I could produce an air ticket in and out of Khartoum. As the idea was to bicycle there this seemed unreasonable, but eventually I had to do just that, and being innocent of such matters I did not realise that I could cash the ticket in after obtaining the visa, and so wasted a lot of money over it.

The Egyptians, on the other hand, said they were delighted that I was going to visit their country. They would be only too happy to do what they could to help, and invited me to attend a series of forthcoming lectures to be given by eminent Egyptologists. These took place at the Egyptian Cultural Centre, an elegant eighteenth-century house in Mayfair that has become slightly seedy and chaotic, which the Egyptians were convinced had been built for King Farouk. (Dates are not an essential element of Egyptian history – a couple of hundred years seems neither here nor there to people dealing in dynasties.) It was here that I began to get to know some Egyptians, and I liked them very much. They seemed to like me too, especially when they discovered that I could operate the eccentric slide projector that caused such problems to the visiting professors.

Hours were spent in libraries, consulting atlases and reading accounts of African journeys of exploration. These accounts always included harrowing details of extreme privation and hardship and difficult encounters with 'the natives'. Malaria and other afflictions had laid all the explorers low for months at a time. The awful difficulties of forcing a way over the broken trackless terrain had made them dependent upon endless strings of porters, who were notoriously unreliable. Worn out by hunger and disease they had at length struggled back to an ecstatic homecoming, mere skeletons of their former selves. My dreams began to be peopled by long trains of porters bearing Fortnum and Mason hampers. Armies of fanatical 'Fuzzy Wuzzies' boiled out of the desert behind their Mahdi, hurling themselves against 'thin red lines' of pith-helmeted soldiers with Kitchener moustaches. Crocodiles lurked around every bend of the river, blinking back hypocritical tears while they waited to devour explorers shipwrecked in leaky native canoes. T. S. Eliot's hippo-potamus, multiplied a thousand times over, ascended from the damp savannas like a skyful of captive barrage balloons. Perhaps my overfed imagination was being further inflamed by all the injections I was having against typhoid, yellow fever, tetanus, cholera, meningitis, hepatitis, and rabies.

As I had been indoors throughout so much of the spring and summer, poring over books, I did not feel in particularly good physical shape as the time to leave drew near. It was far too demanding a journey to rely upon the first few weeks of riding to get me fit, and so a month before departure, when most of my preparations were completed, I took a job as a bicycle messenger with the 'On Yer Bike Despatch Company', situated conveniently near the Egyptian Cultural Centre in Mayfair. Never have I worked so hard for so little monetary reward, or enjoyed myself more in the process. Fitness I certainly achieved, and my reflexes speeded up tremendously – otherwise I'd not have survived long in the cut and thrust of the capital's aggressive driving techniques. The heady delights of anarchic riding around streets where all other traffic had wound itself into a snarling chaos was an additional bonus that was to hold me in good stead for my entry into Africa.

CHAPTER TWO

Stress of Weather

Cairo stands at the head of the Nile delta. A little way north of it the great river divides into two streams which take separate routes to the sea, enclosing a huge fan-shaped area which has been one of the most fertile stretches of land in the world since the dawn of civilisation. Three crops a year can be grown there, and it was on its surplus food production that the greatness of Egypt grew. From near the western outlet at Rosetta came the stone tablet, closely inscribed in three scripts, which provided the key for deciphering Egyptian hieroglyphs and uncovering 6,000 years of the dynastic history of the pharaohs. Up through the mouth of the eastern branch, past Damietta, the Crusaders had sailed to challenge the new Arab masters of Egypt. The fate of the Holy Land was sealed there, when the Christian armies perished, defeated by disease and the superior forces of Saladin, as well as by the yearly falling of the river which left their transports high and dry.

In 1869 Christians were back again at the eastern edge of the Nile delta, this time cutting a channel through the narrow piece of land that separated the Mediterranean from the Red Sea, opening up a route which was to take months off voyages to India and the Orient. The importance of the Suez Canal to a great maritime nation like Britain ensured her interest and her influence in Egypt, an influence which would inevitably spread throughout the lands through which the Nile flowed, and along which danger might come to threaten Britain's expanding trade and empire. By 1899 Queen Victoria, in fact if not in name, ruled all the Nile from the Mountains of the Moon down to the Mediterranean Sea.

It was from this Mediterranean coast that I planned to start my journey. I thought I would ride in a leisurely manner along the seaboard of the delta, from Alexandria to Port Said, seeing all the famous places that had been a legend to me for so long. Only after that would I head south to begin the 4500-mile trek which would eventually take me deep into the heart of Africa, where the Nile has its high, remote beginnings. So I did not linger in Cairo, for I could explore it later when my route led me back to it in a week or two. Instead I headed straight down to Alexandria on the desert road – and suddenly, from a pleasant temperature of 80°F I was plunged into a cold wet world, no better than that which I had left behind in England. The winter storms were early. Huge waves came crashing in over the Corniche; the sky was a lowering dark greyish purple; water flowed dankly down the sides of buildings and gushed out of broken drainpipes and blocked gutters. It was all depressingly monochrome; only at night was the greyness relieved, when the sky was lit up along the seaward horizon with noisy displays of forked lightning.

Somewhere beneath the wet cobblestones lay the lost remains of Alexander the Great. 'Uneasy will be the city where this body lies,' had said the chief priest of Memphis, refusing it burial and instructing the bearers to return with it to Alexander's own city. It is not the only treasure that lies beneath the nineteenth-century frenchified town. Cleopatra's fabulous library had been housed here, and one of the seven wonders of the ancient world, the Tower of Pharos, had lighted the way for ships sailing into its two fine harbours. It was a city that had vied in greatness and scholarship with Athens and Byzantium. From here Ptolemy had mapped the world and decided upon the source of the Nile, and here Euclid had founded his school of mathematics. Art, philosophy, and theology had all flourished here for centuries until the tide of barbarism swept over it and its splendid buildings were broken up to become quarries for lesser ones. Now, occasionally, a crack opens and a remnant of the Graeco-Roman world breaks surface. One of these, a small pretty Roman theatre, had recently been unearthed and as I stood looking at it from the shelter of an open shed where the excavators' shovels were kept, I realised that in this dismal wintry weather I could get no feeling at all of that brilliant vanished world; it needs sunshine to dream of Alexander.

My thoughts turned instead to the Victorian novelist and traveller, Amelia B. Edwards, whose Nile journey of a hundred years before had in no small way influenced my being here. She had not planned to visit Egypt at all, but had been driven south by 'stress of weather' during a particularly wet painting expedition in Europe. The effect of her

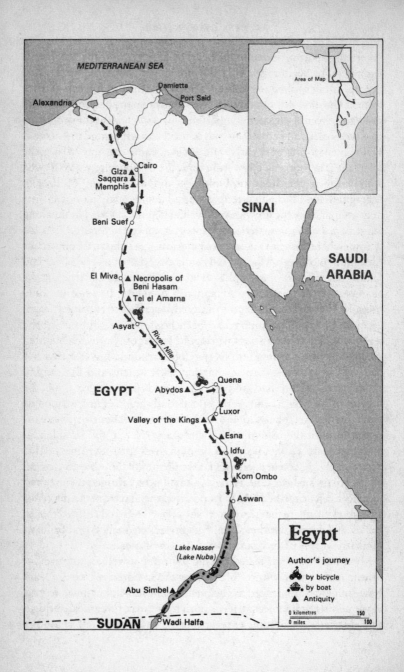

MEDITERRANEAN SEA

Damietta
Port Said
Alexandria

Area of Map

Cairo
Giza ▲
Saqqara ▲
Memphis ▲

SINAI

Beni Suef ○

SAUDI
ARABIA

El Miva ○ ▲ Necropolis of
Beni Hasam
▲ Tel el Amarna

Asyat ○

River Nile

EGYPT   Abydos ▲   Quena

Luxor
Valley of the Kings ▲

▲ Esna

Idfu

▲ Kom Ombo

Aswan ○

Lake Nasser
(Lake Nuba)

Abu Simbel ▲

SUDAN   ○ Wadi Halfa

Egypt

Author's journey

🚲 by bicycle
⛵ by boat
▲ Antiquity

| 0 kilometres | 150 |
| 0 miles | 100 |

chance visit was momentous. She gave up writing romantic fiction and became an ardent and indefatigable Egyptologist, mugging up on hieroglyphics and hieratic script and thinking nothing of riding for hours in her long voluminous clothes, through burning deserts, to visit distant, obscure temples. I had no intention of emulating this formidable lady's scholarship, but in the matter of 'stress of weather' I could certainly take a leaf from her book. I decided to abandon the coast forthwith and hurry back south to Cairo with the last of Europe's swallows. Cairo has desert on either side of it, and it rains there on average for only five days a year.

I could have kept pace with the swallows by going up to Cairo on the train. I seriously considered doing so, as neither I nor the bicycle was equipped for riding in these wet conditions; I had planned for heat and drought and had even taken the mudguards off the bicycle before I left, to save weight. But the delighted cries of 'Ah Agala' that greeted the shiny new, bright-red bicycle at the station, followed by talk of 'You leave him here. He follow maybe tomorrow, maybe next day', changed my mind. Since landing in Egypt I had received so many requests to sell 'that so lovely Agala' that I rather feared for 'his' safety. If we couldn't travel together on the same train I decided I'd better ride back and have the benefit of a closer look at the rich agricultural landscape.

I fully expected the rain to stop once I was clear of Alexandria but I soon discovered that it was not only an incessant downpour that I had to contend with. The whole of the delta was also awash. This was not because the Nile was bringing down its age-old bounty of rich silt in the annual floods, for it no longer does this since the building of the Aswan high dam. Chemicals have replaced the 'gift of the Nile', and the silt builds up in the enormous man-made lake behind the dam, where it breeds monstrous fish which cause havoc to the turbines of the hydro-electric plant, resulting in breakdowns and power failures; while the huge shoals of sardines that once gathered off the delta to feed on the residue of the silt have now disappeared altogether. The Aswan dam was thought to be responsible for the present floods, however: the water table has risen throughout North Africa since it was built, so that most of the rain that had fallen in the last few days remained on the surface.

The rain continued to fall; without the restraint of a mudguard, the back wheel directed a continuous fountain of muddy water up my back, while the bow waves of passing lorries drenched any part of me not already reached by what was descending from above or splashing up from below. The road surface left a lot to be desired, with frequent large, deep potholes into which I plunged, as I could not see them under the general covering of water. Occasionally a bridge crossed overhead, and where the road dipped to pass beneath it, the water was as deep as two or three feet. These depressions had to be taken at a rush, pedalling as fast as I could with my submerged feet in order to overcome the tremendous resistance of the water against the pannier bags. Eventually I was as wet as it was possible to be – at which point I stopped worrying about it and began to take an interest in the scenes around me.

I was passing an almost continuous chain of broken-down lorries and trailers. Some had left the road altogether and lay peacefully on their sides – their drivers over-bold on an excess of hashish. Others had simply sighed to a halt, their electrics saturated. Beyond them lay a world which was seemingly quite unrelated to these mechanical failures, or indeed to the present century at all. In primitive mud-brick villages, flocks of grubby children in long gowns chased scrawny chickens around huge steaming middens. Men in long biblical gellabiyahs and head-dresses followed behind their water buffalo in the rice fields. Donkeys trudged an endless circle around archaic water-wheels, and everywhere women and girls clustered in colourful chattering groups, doing their washing or filling clay water jars beside the overflowing irrigation canals. Everyone seemed happy, rejoicing in the mud as though it was still a cause for celebration. It was all delightfully like Herodotus had described it 2,500 years ago, when 'the land is transformed into a sea and only the towns remain above water like islands in the Aegean'. I half-expected to see a flotilla of ancient fellucas sweeping past full of noisy revellers singing bawdy fertility songs and indulging in the even bawdier gestures which Herodotus had carefully noted as a feature of these annual festivities.

It was probably such thoughts that distracted my attention and caused me to mistime my efforts at the next depression in the road. Suddenly I ran out of momentum and slewed to a halt, thigh-deep in the murky water. As I extricated myself from the bicycle and started to wade out with it, a pick-up van came alongside. The driver put out his head and said, 'Oh Madam, you are very wet.' He sounded most concerned, and when he asked, 'Will you ride with me and get dry?' I needed no second invitation; soon the bicycle was in the back and the windscreen was steaming up as the heater began to act upon my saturated clothing. My rescuer was a very kind man who found it difficult to understand what I was doing on the flooded delta road with a bicycle – still more so as Egyptian women don't ride cycles, even in suitable conditions. After a while he abandoned the problem and talked to me instead about his fruit and vegetables, which he was beginning to export to Britain. He also told me about his three houses, to reassure me, I think, that he was a man of substance.

After a short while we stopped at a small hovel on the edge of a mud-brick village, which served as a transport café. It was also a family home, with a couple of beds in a dark corner, and a few chairs and a rickety table. A fire burned in a shallow metal bowl on the floor, from which coals were taken in a pair of metal tongs to light the hubble bubble pipe, which was kept constantly on the go for the drivers who called in. Coarse straw absorbed some of the debris on the ground, and light and flies came in through the open doorway. Two grubby-gowned, grubby-handed children served tea and tended the hubble bubbles. I refused the pipe and the hashish and accepted the tea – though not without some misgivings. One of the most difficult aspects of my kind of travel is to keep healthy, and eating or drinking in such insanitary conditions is clearly not the best way of doing this. However there are other even more important considerations, such as meeting people and not offending them, so a compromise has nearly always to be practised.

When the two children had overcome their shyness they brought out 'Welcome to English' textbooks from under one of the beds and began to chant 'Sit down class', 'Good morning, teacher', 'How are you?', 'How old are you?', 'What is your name?' and other such utterances that afflict today's traveller in emergent nations. After several hundred exchanges on this model I began to feel more like a speaking robot than a human being, and longed for a little inhibition or for some creative divergence on the part of these infant linguists. Even a preamble like 'Please' or 'Would you mind' or perhaps 'Excuse me, may I ask you?' would have softened the bluntness of it, or at least have given the victim a chance to flee. The fault, of course, lies with the compilers of the boring, unimaginative textbooks, and they, I fear, are British. This was only the beginning of the journey, however, so on this occasion I was charmed rather than irritated by the bright-eyed, tousle-haired pair.

Before we left I was honoured by being shown the household's prized possession. Concealed beneath a sheet of plastic was a television set. There was no power supply for it to be connected to; it simply sat there blankly on a rickety box, like an inscrutable presence in a shrine. I took it to be the new household god, a symbol of progress that had replaced the ancient forces. Perhaps it promised an entirely predictable world which would no longer flood.

Before my benefactor left me a little way outside Cairo he dropped a banknote worth about £6 into my lap. 'You have need. Take. Take,' he urged, brushing aside my protestations and adding a packet of Tutti Frutti bubble gum to the gift. I understood by this that he had solved the puzzle of why I was riding a bicycle through the flooded Delta. I must be poor and needy and he felt moved to exercise charity, as directed by the Koran. There was no way I could persuade him that I was not in need or refuse the alms without a rude abuse of his generosity. I rode on into Cairo still wet and incredibly muddy but warmed by the encounters of the day, and the realisation that I had completed the first stage of the journey with much enjoyment in spite of the weather. Things could only get better now that the rain had at last quite stopped and the skies were clear.

CHAPTER THREE

Cairo

I was only ever run into in the streets of Cairo by drivers reversing, at which they were particularly inept. When going forward they behaved more like bicyclists, weaving in and out wherever they saw a gap, but although they also kept up a continuous blaring of horns, they did not seem to have any real malice towards other road users. This was a comfort, for even if the effect is much the same, I prefer to be knocked down as a result of someone's lack of skill, rather than their aggression. Parking was often three deep and a large number of men were kept employed juggling vehicles around so that those trapped against the kerbs could be released. To keep the pavements free of cars, the kerbs had been raised to a height which made them practically unscaleable, so pedestrians joined the traffic in the narrow space left in the centre of the road. It says much for the vigilance of my guardian angel that I cycled around Cairo, day and night, for a couple of weeks without adding to the city's prodigal accident figures.

I settled first in a small family hotel near the modern centre of the city, where the management was willing to accommodate the bicycle. It was eight floors up by a small eccentric lift, which required someone to stand outside it and lean against the door before it would start. The only way I could get the bicycle into the lift was to rear it upright and balance it on its back wheel; I had then to squeeze myself in alongside and maintain a most contorted position until a leaner came to start us off. It was not easy. Various offices and businesses occupied the lower floors of the building, which was the pattern for many of the more modest of Cairo's hotels and a good thing in one way, because the noise of motor horns even from the top floors was quite deafening. I only managed to sleep by stuffing my ears with the wax plugs I'd had the forethought to pack. In another way it was an alarming arrangement, for there seemed to be no way out other than by the unreliable lift – there were no stairs and no fire escape.

Like much of Cairo this hotel had seen better days, and although it retained an echo of faded gentility, it was decidedly shabby around the edges. It was still good value, however, as two long-term residents testified. One of these, a pale, sandy-haired lady with pebble glasses, had been living in Egypt for thirty years as a governess without ever losing her Dundee accent. She was retired now, but she said her blood had thinned and she could no longer cope with the cold of Scotland. She had a snappish manner but was a romantic at heart and could wax lyrical when the conversation turned to the past splendours of Egyptian society. The other resident was an elderly Egyptian who had married a Greek woman and nearly died of homesickness in the peace and quiet of an Aegean island. There is a widely-held belief that Egyptians have such a special relationship with the Nile that they are seldom happy away from it, but Mr Beirum said it was the sounds of Cairo for which he had pined. He had taken the noisiest room in the hotel and kept both the windows wide open all the time. Life, he informed me, was a sad business, for he missed his wife sorely, but neither could live where the other thrived. The two long-termers enjoyed preferential rates and conditions, as – to a lesser extent – did guests on package tours from Israel. There was a notice saying that these packaged tourists could ask for an egg to accompany their sparse Continental breakfasts, and this made me wonder if I too could claim some preference, perhaps as a lone bicyclist. I showed the management the letter given to me by the Ministry of Tourism – a few short lines in Arabic, stamped with a small pale eagle. Clearly it was more impressive than it looked, for my terms were immediately reduced, albeit by a minute amount. I was not offered the egg; nor did hot water ever materialise, although it was frequently promised.

There were also preferential rates available for the conversion of currency if the exchange was made in the street rather than the bank. 'Change dollar?' was the hopeful cry that greeted foreigners everywhere, even in the mosques. Otherwise it was 'You like look at . . . ?' followed by offers of every imaginable commodity in the souvenir line, with flower essences far in the lead. It was all very relaxed and friendly, however, with none of the heavy importuning of many oriental cities, and I grew to like Cairo more each day I spent there.

The famous Egyptian Museum was conveniently near at hand, a huge building closely packed with colossal dusty statuary; a major tourist attraction, but daunting to most people who were not dedicated Egyptologists. I was fortunate in having been given a card admitting me without charge to such places, so I could retire at frequent intervals for rest and refreshment. I find there is a limit to what can be absorbed and enjoyed in museums at any one time; an hour is really quite enough. But when a large entry fee has been paid the poor visitor feels obliged to struggle on and try to see everything at one go and I think this is one of the most important arguments for keeping Britain's museums and galleries non-fee-paying.

The chief attraction of the Egyptian Museum is the magnificent funerary treasure of Tutankhamun. Some of the pieces in this fabulous collection are exquisite, like the solid gold and enamel mask and the jewellery that had adorned the mummy; but it is the sheer quantity and richness of it all that is so impressive. There are magnificent chariots, thrones, beds, and carved and gilded containers for every imaginable necessity of life in the next world, and the three highly decorated crates into which it had all been packed are each large enough to use as a garage. Everything is worked with superb artistry and craftsmanship, and is worth no less than a very great king's ransom. Later, when I saw the rock chamber from which it had come, in the Valley of the Kings at Luxor, it was hard to see how it could all have been fitted in there. Tutankhamun had been only a very minor king who had died young and been thrust hurriedly into a small unfinished tomb. The extent of what the huge tombs of the great pharaohs had contained can only be imagined, for all, except Tutankhamun's, had been discovered and looted long ago by grave robbers – sometimes, apparently, at the direction of later pharaohs, who had the golden artifacts melted down and recycled, possibly for use in their own funerary trappings.

Egypt is the repository of so much of such sheer magnitude that the prospect of viewing more mammoth monuments can sometimes seem a trifle daunting. I felt rather this way about those most exalted of all royal tombs, the pyramids. Moreover their form has become so over-familiar, adorning chocolate boxes, biscuit tins and a host of other trivial things – quite unsuitable really, considering the nature of the monuments – that I was uninspired by the idea of them, and it was more in the nature of duty that I rode out to Giza to see the pyramids for the first time. The way there was once a pleasant country drive, which was later made into a processional route for the state visit of the Empress Eugenie. Now the city has spread to the very edge of the limestone ridge on which the pyramids stand, so I didn't have the experience, reported by many early travellers, of seeing the familiar triangular shapes from afar, made small and insignificant by distance. My first glimpse of them was from close-to and took me by surprise – I was negotiating the hazards of a busy road and just happened to glance up and see a great tawny flank of the Pyramid of Cheops slide suddenly into view from behind a tall, drab apartment block. The sight was so arresting that I had to pull out of the traffic and stop at the kerb and stare at it. Like the Nile, it reduced everything else to insignificance. This was not simply a question of its size and bulk or of its immense age – I had read up on the statistics, and knew that it had been standing there for more than two thousand years before Christ was born, that it was over a hundred feet higher than the cross on St Paul's Cathedral, and that many of the great Cairo mosques had been built with its stones and facing blocks without making any significant difference to its mass. But all of these facts were quite irrelevant to the impact that it made – to its extraordinary qualities of power and sublimity. Later, when I learnt that it was meant to represent the primal hill that had first risen up out of the waters of chaos, it seemed to me that that is exactly how it first appeared to me on the busy Cairo street – as the most tremendous symbol of the Creation.

On the ridge itself the sense of unbelievable weight and mass is even more overwhelming, but it is not easy to preserve a sense of wonder while constantly beset by the importunings of an army of licentious camel boys, donkey boys, horse boys, and boys selling dirty postcards, souvenirs, fake antiquities and other services. These 'pyramid Bedouin' have been complained of since Victorian times and are still, as Mark Twain remarked, 'as numerous and annoying as flies' and their attentions just as often 'accompanied by leers and lewd gestures'. I soon learned that it was a great mistake to ride with one of them on the same animal, or to be out of sight of other tourists for a moment. Even small boys of nine or so made a sport of pinching the bottoms of foreign females, or thrusting offensive pictures under their noses. The wind was quite strong up there too, filling the air with swirling sand

and flying rubbish. With all these annoyances, it shows how great an attraction the pyramids possess that so many people return to them again and again.

I achieved some peace by hiring a quite repulsive Arab youth who seemed to be in a permanent state of sexual arousal. By insisting on riding alone upon his camel, unsuitably named Mickey Mouse, I not only escaped his unwelcome attentions but also those of the other touts. From the smelly back of Mickey Mouse I viewed the sphinx and all the mortuary temples and rode all round the three main pyramids. Then, while the camel sat and rested with his legs folded demurely beneath him, ruminating and hissing at passers-by (at whom his owner uncouthly leered), I toured the indoor sites and saw the most ancient ship in the world – the huge and beautiful high-prowed solar barge excavated from one of the five boat pits around the great pyramid. Such boats bore the bodies of the pharaohs along the Nile to be mummified and prepared for their final resting-place; and in the even more elaborate ones that were buried with them they were supposed to make their ghostly journey to the sun, after passing through the lands of the dead. The labour of building such craft – and this one was over a hundred feet long – only to bury it and four others like it was beyond my comprehension. I found myself instead thinking of the much later Cleopatra, and of Shakespeare's lines 'The barge she sat in like a burnished throne burned on the water.'

Struggling with incipient claustrophobia I also climbed, bent double, through hot airless shafts and corridors, so cleverly contrived, into the interior of the great pyramid, to stand at last in the royal tomb at the centre, where there is nothing but an empty granite sarcophagus and a sense of unimaginable weight overhead. I did not attempt the exterior climb to the top of Cheops' pyramid, as it is strongly discouraged these days because too many people have fallen in the attempt, dashing themselves to pieces on the corners of the blocks – a fate that Mark Twain had earnestly hoped would befall the pestering Arab who had followed him up there.

I often returned to Giza in the late afternoon, to ride out a little way into the desert and see the three main pyramids from different angles. Nowhere was their grouping less than superb, and the immense lengthening shadow they cast at sunset stretched so far into the desert that it seemed like the ancient myth of night devouring the land.

Cairo itself is not an ancient city in the reckoning of this part of the world; the Romans first built there, calling their fortress Babylon, which suggests that their geography might have been a little shaky. On the ruins of the fortress Old Cairo was built, a small town which was not incorporated into the later Islamic city. As a result, Old Cairo has retained much of its early Christian flavour and is a place of narrow, roughly cobbled alleyways and fourth- and fifth-century Coptic churches. Many Moslems claim that the cleanliness of people of other faiths is inferior to those who have embraced Islam, but although there is not often much discernible difference, this is not the case with Old Cairo, which is quite noticeably filthier than any other area of Cairo – no part of which could exactly be called clean. One of the primitive little churches has the proud tradition of being built over the resting place of the Holy Family on its flight into Egypt, but unfortunately I found that this grotto is now drowned beneath the infiltrating waters of the Nile. The Coptic statuary and architecture which could be visited seemed a rather lumpish and provincial reflection of the glories of Byzantine art, and Old Cairo itself appeared unnaturally arrested and almost moribund in its antique dirt. The medieval Islamic city was infinitely more beautiful and exciting.

Although I had previously travelled in Moslem countries, it was not until I reached Cairo that I conceived a passion for Islamic architecture. In many countries Islam, a late religion, has built over earlier cultures, to its own detriment. In Istanbul I had been blind to everything but the glories of the Byzantine Empire, beside which even the splendours of the Blue Mosque seemed a little banal and over-stated. In the tense atmosphere of modern Jerusalem it is not easy to divorce the Dome of the Rock from 3,000 years of contentious history – a Jew or a Christian can be forgiven for seeing it more as a late accretion upon the Holy City than as the pearl it undoubtedly is. Even in Damascus the Great Mosque is built on a greater Christian foundation. But Cairo, the true setting of the Arabian Nights, is all of a piece, a city built from scratch at the very height of Islam's swift, dramatic conquest, when its wealth was limitless and its science and art were flourishing as never before or since. There is a magnificent mosque on every corner of the walled, medieval city, over five hundred of them, many far larger than European cathedrals, all jostling for space with Koranic schools, public fountains and merchants' fine houses, the ornately carved wooden screens of which once hid the women of the harem while they looked out on the life in the streets below.

To wander through the narrow winding alleyways at night, with a thousand slender minarets outlined against the stars in the velvety blue darkness; the slightest of crescent moons hanging there in improbable perfection, was to glimpse the Cairo of legend, to touch the very fabric of a fabled city. By day, although the souks pulsed with life, the galloping decay of that fabric was very apparent, and from lofty viewpoints on minarets and medieval gates, the flat roofs could be seen to be covered with rubble, and dust lay thickly on every horizontal surface. Even so it was still splendid, and I decided to move into the area, so as to get to know it more intimately.

I found a hotel that was especially for Moslems of modest means, where each room was provided with a woven plastic prayer mat, to be rolled up when not in use. It was a large modern building like a Salvation Army hostel, with no pretensions about emulating its architectural heritage or pampering its guests with effete comforts. I stayed there because it was during the time of the Feast of the Prophet's Birthday, and this was the only place that wasn't full. However, I must give it credit for providing constant hot water for washing, a most infrequent luxury in Egypt, even in five-star hotels. Actually, apart from the dreadful cream and green decor and the unrelenting noise from the brass beaters' workshops, only yards away across a narrow alley, I rather liked it there and the management was most kind, putting up the Agala in a downstairs cupboard with a less aristocratic cycle of Indian extraction, and sending out to the souk for my breakfast each day. Other guests made their own breakfasts, sitting in large groups on rush mats in the wide tiled corridors eating foul, the field beans which are the ubiquitous food of Nile dwellers. They cooked on simple charcoal stoves, scooping up the foul from a large communal bowl with bits of flat unleavened bread. I would invariably be invited to share these meals as Arabs are kind and hospitable, but at this stage of the journey I hadn't yet come to terms with foul – later it would be my staple diet.

I met all sorts of people as I wandered through the souks and seldom felt lonely – which is not often the case in a large and strange city. There were the few persistent nuisances, but they were rare; usually it was quite all right to strike up a casual acquaintance in a coffee house, or to accept assistance without having to pay highly for the privilege. People would willingly go far out of their way to direct me to places: once a young man spent a couple of hours helping me through the lengthy frustrations of making a telephone call, and when I invited him to a modest beer and kebab, as a small recompense for his trouble, he accepted but then insisted on paying because he said he was in my debt as he had enjoyed talking to me about his girl friend.

Only once was this pleasant atmosphere shattered, when I was taking photographs in the souk and was set upon by three very large, very black women in brilliantly coloured clothes, who had suddenly materialised from nowhere, their eyes flashing fire, screaming 'Who say you can take our picture? Who give you permission?' The small camera was on a cord around my neck and the women were determined to get it off me, even if it meant removing my head in the process. 'We have to break it,' they chanted in unison, as though it was some kind of ritual, while each one clutched and heaved at a different part of me. I saved my breath, for I needed every ounce of strength I had to hold onto the camera. I could not have been heard above the noise they were making in any case, and I don't think they were in the mood to heed my protests. Men from the open-fronted souk shops rushed to the rescue, but it seemed to take a long time and a lot of men to prise the women off me, and I thought both my arms would be dislocated in the process. It had all happened too fast for me to be scared at the time, but once it was all over I felt quite weak from reaction and thought I was going to faint. I was helped into a tiny shop and given tea while the winning tug-of-war team stood round and tried to make me smile, patting me on the back and pinching my cheeks as though I was a child. 'Not Egyptians these women,' they reassured me. 'No Egyptians would do this thing. All Egyptians good. All Africans very good, only from Nigeria and Zaire come big trouble, like these mad women.' Warming to this decidedly racist theme, they went on to claim that 'They eat people,' with a great show of biting forearms to illustrate the point. 'Cannibals! We all very frightened!

But you not worry, here is Big Ali – Big Ali not let them hurt nobody here. Any trouble you come, find Big Ali,' and so on, until I was weak with laughter instead of shock.

I needed no excuse for lingering in Cairo, for I had planned my journey with plenty of time in hand so as to be as free as possible to follow my inclinations, which is what independent travel is all about. Even if I had been anxious to get away, however, I could not have done so, as I had to attend to the tiresome business of permits and visas and of trying to obtain information about the difficulties that lay ahead along the Nile. Many frustrating hours were spent gathering conflicting facts and advice in the dusty avenues of bureaucratic muddle, but as few offices stayed open for long each day, and never on Fridays as that was the Moslem sabbath, nor on Sundays as that was the Christian one, while Saturday being sandwiched between the two was also a day of rest, it left plenty of time for doing more pleasant things.

Only for a short time, late in its long history, has the Nile been a completely open river with free and relatively easy passage along its entire length – that was from 1899 when the British effectively took control over all the lands through which it flows. Whatever one may think about colonialism, it did make life very much easier for travellers. Nowadays, with all the three countries of the Nile under autonomous rule, Uganda, the Sudan, and to a lesser extent Egypt, all present difficulties to free movement and as I was beginning to discover, some of these are considerable, if not actually insurmountable. I decided to ignore the minor concerns which the authorities worried more about than I did, such as local feuding and lawlessness in Middle Egypt, since I could do nothing about them, short of carrying a gun. But I could not dispense with permission to ride through the two hundred miles of desert above the first cataract and the High Dam, where the man-made lake spreads far into the Sudan, as it is now a military area, and I did not want to run the risk of being shot for not having the correct piece of paper. I spent a lot of time pursuing this elusive permit and eventually I had no option but to leave it and try again when I got to Aswan. I had also hoped to find out more about the situation in the Sudan, for when I left England it wasn't clear whether up-river of Khartoum was a total 'no go' area, with most of the south in the hands of the Sudanese People's Liberation Army, or whether the rebels were being pushed back. There were also ominous rumours about renewed fighting in Uganda which I wished to verify or dispel. Such information as I gleaned on all these points only confused the picture even further, and most of the people I contacted tried to dissuade me from making the journey at all. It seemed to me that the situation further south was so volatile that it might have changed completely by the time I got there, and with so many prophets of doom shaking their heads over my prospects for survival, I decided I'd better make a start before their prognostications of doom wore me down. I set a date for departure and then started on a final tour of all my favourite places.

I spent the last day checking over the bicycle, oiling and greasing it and generally making sure that there was nothing that had suffered in the floods. I then laid out all my equipment on the bed like an army kit inspection and packed and repacked it in the four pannier bags until I was satisfied that I knew where everything was stowed and that I could find anything I needed without a lengthy search. Items I used frequently I put in a bag on the handlebars – things like the camera, sun-cream, the day's vitamin tablets and anti-malaria pills, the torch, my notebook, a pen, money, documents and sun-glasses. When I left the bicycle for short periods I could detach this bag and take it with me, so if the bicycle did get stolen I should still have my passport and not be destitute. I did not carry a cycle lock, partly to save weight and partly because such things are not a lot of use, except as a temporary deterrent. I found it was much safer to give the bicycle into someone's keeping and there always seemed to be plenty of people about eager to perform this service. In any case, the bicycle was too distinctive to render it likely to be stolen; even re-painted it would be instantly recognisable. There was a small pouch on the outside of the handlebar bag, in which I kept the aerosol can for dealing with savage dogs. It only worked if the contents were squirted into their eyes at close range, at which they were supposed to retire in discomfort until the smarting stopped and the quarry had made good her escape. I had no faith at all in this device nor in my ability to use it, but I carried it anyway. My small Swiss army penknife was the only other thing I had that could be construed as a weapon, and this I kept in my pocket attached to a lanyard to prevent it getting lost.

When I had done all I could to prepare for my departure, I took a last walk through the long central street of the medieval city I had grown to love. It was quite late and the souk shops were all shuttered, but the courts and alleyways were still full of families sitting around their thresholds among the tethered sheep, goats and donkeys, while chickens scratched around in the dirt at their feet. As I walked on into the silversmiths' quarter I was startled by a sudden flurry of pistol shots, followed by the blaring of a trumpet and drumbeats – and all at once a procession burst upon the dimly-lit scene, and the street had become a stage. I could see at once that it was a wedding, for there was the bridal couple, he in a faultlessly cut white lounge suit, she in a white Western-style gown, all nylon flounces and several inches too long, so that she was having difficulty walking. Around them a circle of young men, also in white, with red sashes and red bands around their foreheads, leaped and whirled, stamping and clapping in time to a drum which one of them played as he danced. Occasionally the dancing stopped and people came forward to shake hands with the bridal pair. Women in black shawls stood behind the dancers throwing back their heads to produce the high-pitched and unearthly ululations that are a feature of all celebrations in the Middle East and seem to be made by holding a single long high note while the tongue is moved rapidly from side to side.

I hadn't realised until then how responsive Egyptians are to music and rhythm: every wide ledge and car roof had its complement of small boys swaying and turning in time to the dance; even babies in their parents' arms jiggled and bounced up and down, crowing with pleasure. One fat jolly man with a little boy on his arm linked his free arm with mine and drew me into the swaying crowd. 'Welcome, welcome,' he beamed, proudly introducing his infant son, Mustafa. At the next pause I was pulled forward to shake hands with the bridal couple and wish them good luck. I was now part of the celebrations, and lots of people came to ask my name and shake hands. With many stops for pistol shots and trumpet calls, the dance slowly worked its way into one of the four-hundred-year-old courts in the centre of the tenement that housed the silversmiths. Here at last the bride could relax from her preoccupation with not tripping over the too-long dress. She was seated with the groom on a raised platform and dark-eyed, flushed young women fanned them both, while the young men continued to dance before them, and the rest of the guests sat in rows facing them. Baby Mustafa had fallen asleep on my lap while his father had gone in search of a Coca Cola, the strongest drink that would be served at this Moslem wedding.

Another day had started as I made my way back to the hotel, after toasting the bride and groom in Coca Cola and delivering up dear little Mustafa to a large black-clad lady who looked as though she was not pleased at finding her son in the arms of an infidel. The last shouted farewells of other guests followed me down past the fairy-tale minarets crowned with stars. It was all as romantic and improbable as could be, and a most satisfactory way to be leaving the city for the last time before setting off upriver.

CHAPTER FOUR

Middle Egypt

Finding a safe shelter before darkness falls is a cardinal rule of survival for the lone traveller, but Egyptian towns with hotels of any kind are few and far between and not always within the daily reach of a bicyclist. I had my tent, of course, but that was intended for use in the desert, far away from human habitation. Apart from proper camp sites, of which I saw only one in Egypt, there are few places where it is sensible for a woman to camp alone. On the first day out of Cairo, however, I had no such worries for I thought I was assured of my night's lodging. I was heading for Saqqara, the necropolis of Memphis – the oldest city of ancient Egypt and possibly of the world – and I was very much looking forward to visiting it. On a clear day it
is visible from Cairo, for the Giza ridge continues for many miles running parallel to the east bank of the Nile, with a skein of exotic pyramids along its length. The Step Pyramid of King Djoser at Saqqara is the prototype of them all and very distinctive, for it is built in a series of stepped layers of decreasing size, like a giant child's tower of building blocks. Nearby is the 'English House' for visiting British archaeologists, one of whom was an acquaintance of mine and had kindly brought out some dehydrated food and a spare tyre for me to pick up on my way south. I had understood that, at the very worst, there would be sufficient floor space for me to spread my sleeping bag.

So it came as a nasty shock to be turned away by the professor in charge when I arrived just as night was about to fall, in an area where the valuable antiquities are protected by armed guards with twitchy trigger fingers, who think anything that moves is a modern tomb robber.

'Quite welcome to a cup of tea,' the professor said, looking anything but welcoming, 'but I can't have you here. Very sorry and all that. Question of security you see. Wouldn't do at all, I'm afraid; certainly not.'

Other members of the party were shocked too and pointed out to the professor that apart from the lack of hospitality, it would not look at all good if headlines back home read 'BRITISH WOMAN SHOT DEAD AFTER BEING TURNED FROM DOOR BY MUMMY MAN' – especially when the universities were trying hard to present a favourable image in their fight against financial cutbacks.

The professor was not to be moved, however. He claimed that the security clearance of the expedition would be jeopardised by my presence and the more the others pooh-poohed the notion and the more I produced my bona fides to show how keen the Egyptians were to have me in the country, the more adamant he became. He was not a flexible man.

'I was afraid you'd have problems when I received your letter some months ago,' he continued, in tones of satisfaction at being proved right – though he didn't explain why he hadn't communicated his fears to me. 'Cycling through Egypt? Oh, no, virtually impossible, I would say. Hardly anywhere to stay you know. So sorry I can't help you.'

As it was generally agreed that there was nowhere else to stay in Saqqara, it seemed the only thing left to do was to walk out cheerfully to certain death as Titus Oates had done on Scott's Antarctic expedition, and this would almost certainly have been the case had I followed the professor's advice to bicycle back in the dark to Cairo, alongside the wild, eccentric traffic. In the end, however, under pressure from the rest of the party, an alternative was proposed, and the expedition's jeep set off with me pedalling furiously behind it, like an over-worked piston engine. We finally arrived in a village three miles away, where two other resident archaeologists were asked to take me in for the night – which they did, though with a certain lack of enthusiasm. I was reminded of being a very small child at the beginning of the Second World War, with a label pinned to my coat and a gas mask on a string around my neck, like an unwanted parcel, waiting with other bewildered evacuees in a strange village hall until someone came forward to claim us.

Although my reluctant hosts had unbent somewhat towards me by morning, I still felt a social outcast and was determined that whatever happened I would not be beholden to anyone else for a night's lodging; far better, I decided, to pitch the tent by the side of the road and hang the consequences. This resolve, I am pleased to say, was constantly broken throughout the journey – indeed the difficulty was often one of too much hospitality. Perhaps it was just as well that this single sour note was struck early on, and by people from my own country.

The next town was eighty miles away – a hard day's ride which would leave little time for exploring Saqqara. I had had only a glimpse of it the night before and in the grey twilight, with a thin cold drizzle falling, it had seemed a desolate place. Archaeologists' diggings and spoilheaps were everywhere; cavernous pits gaped deep enough to swallow up an army, and bits of bone and skulls were lying all around. It had looked exactly what it was – an ancient desecrated cemetery. Under scintillating blue skies and a sun which had had time to make the steep climb back up to the ridge uncomfortably hot by eight in the morning, it seemed an altogether different and more exciting place.

A tall camel came swiftly and silently from the far side of Djoser's Pyramid, riding out of the sun like a mirage, kicking out its huge feet as it ran and holding its disdainful head to one side, the upper lip raised in a permanent sneer. An old man sat on the brightly coloured, many-tasselled saddle-cloth, straight-backed and proud in flowing robes and turban. He looked both noble and romantic, as do most Bedouin riding camels, and bore little resemblance to the importunate rabble at Giza. I wished I had come across him the previous evening, for he seemed much taken by me and the Agala, and almost at once invited me to stay at his house. Had I accepted it would have given me time to see Saqqara properly, but after the events of yesterday I was feeling generally disaffected and was unwilling to respond to his friendliness. I remembered my resolve to accept favours from no one, and said I was on a journey up-river and in a hurry. Courteously ignoring my abruptness, he said he would pray for me and would ask his God to help me because I was only a woman and such a journey as I was making was hard, even for a man. All this solicitude, albeit rather sexist, went a long way towards restoring my spirits.

His tall camel was called Ramesses the Second – many Egyptian male camels are so called on account of the pharaoh of that name having had so many colossal statues of himself made that his name is the best remembered of all the pharaohs. With Ramesses the Second's help I was able to see something of the wonders of Saqqara in the one brief hour I could spare. I rode him to the elaborate and beautifully decorated tomb of Ti, a high-ranking official of the Old Kingdom who had survived three pharaohs and married a princess. His titles read like a litany – Overseer of Pyramids and Sun Temples, Royal Counsellor, Scribe of the Court, Lord of Secrets; and the walls of his tomb are a pictorial encyclopaedia of what life was like for the privileged classes in ancient Egypt, from hippopotamus-hunting to dealing with tax-defaulters.

Afterwards I rode on across the sand to the Serapeum, where the sacred Apis Bulls were once interred in catacombs as vast as the labyrinth of the Minotaur on Crete. For some obscure reason all but one of the grisly relics have been stolen, and only the enormous empty sarcophagi now remain, the lids slid half-way back as though they had but recently been vacated. The Apis Bull was believed to be the animal in which the god Ptah, Lord of Memphis, had his being upon earth; when an Apis Bull died, its body was mummified in the same lengthy and elaborate procedure as that of a pharaoh, and another bull of the same breed took its place, living out its earthly existence in a large luxurious temple complex full of giant statuary. The practice continued for at least 2000 years, though even in the pagan world of Herodotus's day, 500 B C, it was considered a pretty bizarre belief, and numbers of ancient Greek tourists travelled to Memphis especially to see it for themselves. Alone in these still catacombs, the monotony of the gargantuan repetition was oppressive. The monstrous empty coffins, each identically carved from a single huge block of granite, and the endless, dimly-lit corridors hollowed out of the solid limestone were like a nightmare, a mindless Herculean labour going on for ever.

Of Memphis, the great vanished capital of Lower Egypt, I saw nothing at all, for there was no time and, in any case, there is little there now but low shapeless brick mounds. What was built in enduring stone was long ago carried away to build many of the mosques and houses I had so admired in Islamic Cairo, while those of its statues and monuments that are not also in Cairo are scattered among the museums of Europe and America.

I had the long line of the pyramids close on my right hand all that first day as I rode south; there are a dozen of them, set at intervals on the ridge for about a hundred miles, no two alike except in the basic idea. One is called the Bent Pyramid because the angle of its construction was altered half-way up, causing a most peculiar kink in the middle; another, built at a particularly steep angle and without proper footings, collapsed in upon itself and for a long time was thought to be a tower rather than a pyramid. It has been suggested that each of these pyramids was an experiment, an attempt, an outreach towards the perfection which was finally achieved at Giza, after which pyramid-building declined. Imperfect they might be, but they still stir the imagination and they took my mind off the minor aches and pains I was beginning to experience, as the first long hot day in the saddle over a rough surface began to take its toll. It occurred to me as I rode that about the same time as the ancient Egyptian architects were working out the complicated mathematics of pyramid construction, our northern ancestors were dragging huge shafts of stone to set upright, so creating Stonehenge and other such monuments. Though quite different in form, both these tremendous labours, so extremely costly in resources, seem to share the same intention, and both point to a need for a focus that transcends mere everyday existence, for something that expresses the idea of eternity. For the Nile-dwellers the pyramids must also have seemed like sentinel forces, holding back the hostile desert.

A coloured map of Egypt's Nile valley looks like a green flower with a long curved stem lying in a waste of yellow sand. The fan-shaped delta forms the flower and the stem is the narrow strip of intensively cultivated land bordering the river in the flat-bottomed valley that floods have carved out over the millennia. This fertile river belt, together with the delta and a few oases adds up to only about one twenty-fifth of the total area of Egypt: the rest is barren desert. The one meets the other in a line as sharp as if it had been drawn with a ruler, and there is nowhere in this riverine valley from which the desert cannot be seen.

Riding through this narrow ribbon of land, I thought that I would always have the Nile in sight too, but this was not the case. Although only a little way off, it was usually invisible. At first I was disappointed and wished that, like Amelia B. Edwards, I had taken a boat; but then I realised that from the water the high river banks would have obscured everything, except perhaps the waving tops of the palm trees. All in all, I was much better placed for seeing the country where I was.

The road followed a much straighter line than the twisting sinuous course of the river, and had a wide canal bordering it. Bedouin villages were strung out on the farther side of this canal, the small, primitive mud-brick dwellings leaning drunkenly against each other in picturesque squalor. Herds of goats browsed on the rubbish thrown over the near-vertical banks, which were exposed for about eight feet because of the low level of the water in the Nile. Old women dressed all in black and younger women and girls in brilliantly coloured dresses washed pots and clothes and babies in the thick green water. In the smaller irrigation canals which criss-crossed the fields, wet brown flesh gleamed in the sun where the men bathed, their straight square shoulders and lean bodies looking like the ancient frescoes on the walls of the tombs. Clothed, they wore graceful gellabiyahs in pastel shades, of which blue was the most common and looked the most romantic against the brilliant green of the fields and the dark, statuesque palms.

Since land is so precious in Egypt, little of it is wasted in building roads, and often my minor lane would debouch me onto the main north-south highway, which was neither pleasant nor safe. Fortunately my rarity value ensured that I was at least noticed by the drivers of the endless line of trucks, and so avoided being crushed underwheel, a fate which befell innumerable sheep, goats, donkeys, cattle, camels, dogs and, presumably, people too – though human corpses were not left to rot by the side of the road like the others. The main road was also horrid in other ways, especially the blaring motor horns, and the dirt – not just the organic dirt of primitive village life but the sordid effluvium that accompanies old and poorly maintained transport of the twentieth century. The air was full of dense black exhaust fumes and the road and its surroundings were thickly coated in oil and grime. Fragments of tyres, scraps of ruptured metal and a quite amazing number of large nuts and bolts that had parted company with their parent bodies lay about everywhere, waiting to undo the unwary.

At intervals the highway passed through small unlovely towns, where the tarmac suddenly ceased and a surface of broken cobblestones and bare earth with large holes and depressions took its place. Here the squalor multiplied and a mêlée of carts, donkeys, ancient sagging buses and a crush of humanity brought everything, even bicycles, to a jangling, horn-blaring standstill. I stopped in such places to eat, and soon learned that it was best to get away from the main road and ask around in the souk for a good café. Once I had found someone who could understand my few words of Arabic, or as happened more frequently, someone who knew a little English, I would be escorted through colourful, narrow streets lined with stalls to the best eating-house the place had to offer, while one, two or even three ragged male escorts would guard the bicycle until I had finished my meal and given them a tip. Without their help it would have been difficult to eat, as large crowds gathered immediately and had to be kept at bay. The escorts did this efficiently, often giving impromptu talks about the bicycle at the same time to entertain the crowd. Whereas I was merely a curiosity, the Agala continued to be greatly admired. People were puzzled by its various levers, gears and other sophistications and seemed to have no idea what they were for; I wished I knew enough Arabic to understand the ad-lib explanations given by the lecturers, who I am sure knew no more about it than their audience.

The cafés I was taken to were mostly simple open-fronted shacks which could not have been nearly as insanitary as they appeared, because I had only the most minor of stomach upsets the whole time I was in Egypt. Being Moslem places, there was always a tap to wash at before eating and in the towns the water was usually heavily chlorinated. I ate fried aubergines, felafel and the ubiquitous foul. Sometimes the foul was stewed with onions, tomatoes and herbs and sprinkled with chopped green leaves, which was very good. At other times the beans swam in a pool of oil which was vile, but still sustaining. I avoided meat at first, having been put off by the slaughter at the roadsides, both intentional and unintentional. The intentional slaughter consisted of an enthusiastic hacking and slashing with knives after the ritual throat-cutting and required period of bleeding, and seemed a more barbaric affair than the accidental killings; but the Western world carries out this unsavoury act in abattoirs, possibly with even greater cruelty. By the time I had reached the border I was hardened to butchery done in the open air – as long as I didn't look – and could once more eat meat without thinking too much about the animal it came from. The flat pitta bread which accompanied all meals was subsidised by the government and an average meal, including Egyptian Coca Cola, seldom came to more than the equivalent of 35p.

The fears of the inhospitable professor had proved groundless and I always found somewhere to stay, even if I had to cycle further than I would have chosen to in a single day. The furthest I had to ride was about a hundred and thirty miles, but with the wind behind me and on a totally flat road it was arduous but not impossible. It is true that most of the 'hotels' were very basic – the size and boldness of the resident cockroaches was the rough guide I applied. I picked up no fleas, however, and the squalor was more than made up for by the friendliness of the people. Everyone in Egypt, it seemed, was eager to practise their English, and there was no evening in which I did not end up sharing my dinner-table with several earnest young men, discussing such subjects as why America gives so much money to Egypt to promote birth control, or how to obtain a visa to live, study or work in England or America or anywhere other than Egypt. With all this intellectual effort coming at the end of a hard day of physical exercise I seldom found trouble in sleeping, though without my own sleeping-bag, ear-plugs and insect repellent, I would not have fared quite so well.

What made for difficulties was trying to see the sights as well as simply riding on to the next town. The antiquities were usually some way from the road, and often a visit entailed crossing the Nile by ferry, after a lengthy wait for some piece of aged machinery to be repaired. Then came the haggling over donkey hire and the donkey ride itself, on some poor undernourished creature with only an old sack thrown over its boney back and a bit of rope twisted round its jaw. Having finally arrived at the site there could be a further delay while the custodian of the keys was tracked down – as like as not asleep in a patch of shade somewhere. The whole thing could take several hours: and sometimes the prospect seemed altogether too much and I tried to adopt the blasé attitude towards temples of 'seen one seen them all'; but I always regretted what I missed out, for like Amelia B. Edwards, I found Egyptian ruins increasingly addictive. I'm not quite sure why; I didn't find their massiveness attractive, or moving in the accepted sense. Nonetheless, they were seldom less than magnificent, and there was an air of mystery about them and a sense of the sublime that was most compelling. They gave me the feeling that they held some sort of puzzle that needed to be unravelled.

Sometimes a visit would coincide with the arrival of a well-heeled party from one of the Nile cruises. Nowadays these consist of Nile-Hilton or Sheraton steamers, and I think Amelia B. Edwards would disapprove of them quite as much as she did of the Thomas Cook steamers of the 1870s. She was always pointing out the superior merits of her own independent mode of travel in a traditional wooden sailing boat. Steamers, she noted with satisfaction, frequently went aground on the sandbanks. She would certainly have had more disparaging remarks to make had she arrived at the Beni Hassan tombs on the same day I did.

I had met up with a young Englishman while we were both waiting for the ferry; he was studying Arabic at Alexandria and was currently spending a week touring around the archaeological sites of Egypt on his ancient motor bicycle. We arrived together at the tombs just as a large French party from a huge three-decker steamer came ashore. They were all clad in skimpy cruise clothing, which is anathema to Moslems who consider even shorts of the generous British Raj cut to be indecent for both sexes. All the local women had a fold of their shawls drawn across their face to express horror, but not so completely as to hide their view of the 'shameless infidels'; the local men gawped openly, making no attempt to conceal their interest in the generous expanses of female flesh toiling up the flights of steps in the cliff face.

The custodian of the tombs of Beni Hassan was a surly type, not in the least interested in dress, but only in the size of the tip he expected; and since the large French party was clearly more likely to distribute largesse than a solitary English pair, we found ourselves hustled around at the rear of the group, and when they had had their cursory look, we were chivvied out too and the door locked against us. Nor were we allowed to exchange a single word in the tombs. The cruise supplied a guide who talked away incessantly and loudly in French, and if we forgot ourselves and addressed a remark to each other, she frowned heavily in our direction, at which the custodian sycophantic-ally hissed at us to be quiet. After that excursion I was prepared to wait until cruise parties had returned to their deck-chairs before making my tour.

In ancient times Egypt was divided into two kingdoms: Memphis was the capital of Lower Egypt, and Upper Egypt was ruled from Thebes. Historically, the most interesting thing, about the part in the middle, was the reign of the Pharaoh Akhenaten and his equally famous wife Nefertiti who, in the fourteenth century BC, challenged the whole complex structure of ancient Egyptian religion and the pantheistic worship of huge numbers of gods. He proclaimed that only one god existed – Aton, whose symbol was the sun, and who could only be truly worshipped through the pharaoh himself. Some scholars consider that his reign constituted Egypt's first essay in monotheism, and marked a true religious advance; others see it, more cynically, as an attempt to elevate further the divine status of kingship.

Akhenaten moved his capital south from Thebes to virgin ground at Amarna, 50 miles from modern Beni Hassan, where a whole new style of art was created to match the new worship. It was a magnificent but brief flowering. He had taken on the might of a powerful priesthood, who by this time owned a tenth of all the arable land in Egypt. Akhenaten's brave new order barely survived him and came to an end altogether when his descendant, the boy King Tutankhamun, restored the old worship before his own early death. The priests of the old order took their revenge by destroying Akhenaten's capital, and hacking out his name and that of his queen and immediate successors from the lists of kings inscribed on stone tablets at the royal cities of Thebes and Memphis – a sentence of total annihilation, for with their names expunged it was as if they had never existed. Immortality in ancient Egypt was linked to solid matter, to things considered to have special power: the spirit needed tangible objects like written names, statues, a mummified body and funerary trappings to continue its existence. The reign of Akhenaten, 'the heretic', however, had such a distinctive influence upon the prolific art of his day that he still exerts a hold on the imagination shared by few other pharaohs, and the head from a broken statue of Nefertiti in the Berlin Museum is one of the most exquisite treasures from any period of Egypt's long history.

Sometimes, coming back from these visits, I got lost among the maze of small dirt lanes in the fertile strip between the road and the Nile and found myself in another world, quite separate and seemingly uncon-nected with the twentieth century as embodied in the ribbon of tarmac, or the cosmopolitan Nile steamers and tourist attractions. It was a shaded, green place, muted but intensely active, where seventy per cent of the population, the fellaheen, live a rural existence substantially unaltered since ancient times. Every inch of land was cultivated, irrigated by a complex system of small canals and drains which were opened up by kicking out a segment of banking and closed again with a spadeful of earth. It was a labour-intensive way of life where mechanisation was rare – and not really needed in a country which is said to increase by a million every ten months.

Some villages practised a corporate trade such as pottery or brick-making, working together in groups, using age-old methods and the ubiquitous Nile mud, dried in the sun. It was in these villages, where I'd stop sometimes to watch the activity, that the desperate extent of Egypt's poverty really showed. It could be seen in all aspects of daily life – in the insanitary housing, in the babies covered with flies, in the children suffering from untreated ailments, and in their parents, men and women old long before their time. I was seldom pestered in these rural villages: only on the banks of the Nile, where tourists had traditionally been accosted, would children sometimes become im-portunate and strident in their demands for 'baksheesh', the women occasionally joining them and, more rarely, old men too.

But it was on the roads in the afternoons that I felt really intimidated. When the schools closed for the day, an endless stream of children and young people poured out of them to line the road for miles. There was no escaping them. Sometimes, when the traffic was sparse, they formed a human chain across my path trying to force me to stop. The boldest of them had their hands out, shouting, 'Money, you give us money.' Some of them had stones ready to hurl and sticks to thrust through the spokes, and the further south I went the fiercer the children became. There was little I could do except hope for the protection of passing traffic, for the young fiends ahead were alerted by the ones behind and were always waiting for me. Stopping was fatal – I tried that and had the utmost difficulty in getting away again – so I always tried to keep going no matter how many stones were flying over my head, sometimes waving my penknife about in a threatening manner. I began to think with horror of those million new Egyptians produced every ten months; it seemed an awful prospect that they should all pass through this unattractive phase before metamorphosing into Egyptian adults, who were on the whole so very charming.

CHAPTER FIVE

Falling among Thieves in Upper Egypt

At Asyut I had been warned to take particular care on the way ahead, as armed feuding and general lawlessness was said to be common-place. As with most warnings about which I can do nothing I forgot all about this one until after the event – a robbery which came about because of my desire to take photographs. All morning I had been riding along a spectacular road, flanked by the golden limestone cliffs of the Eastern Desert, honeycombed with caves and tombs. The sky had never seemed more perfectly blue nor the fields a more vivid green. Stands of stately date palms were dotted all around, single trees even sprouting from the centre of houses or from the flat roofs of the mud-brick villages that lined the route. Every so often the road would touch upon the edge of the Nile which at this point was so wide that the further banks were imagined rather than seen. Graceful fellucas were moving upstream on the same gentle wind that was helping me, and in the fields egrets echoed the white wings of the sails. It was all as idyllic a landscape as could be wished for and simply cried out to be photographed. Each possible picture however was blighted in the bud by the endless small children, full of animation, pouring into the road the moment they saw me, screaming like banshees – 'Hello Mis-terrrrr . . . How arrrrre . . . you?' Dozens of hands would thrust forward for the 'Baksheesh, Misterrrr . . .' (I had to be Mister since women don't ride agalas). In their other hands they clutched their stones or sticks ready to use in the event of a failure in generosity – even
Croesus would have been beggared by dropping the smallest coin into all the hands that were held out to me in Egypt.

Then, in one particular village, a man beckoned me to stop. I was not sure what he had in mind, but he shook hands and seemed friendly enough. He certainly didn't object to my taking out the camera, in fact he seemed flattered and summoned his whole family – somewhere around twenty or thirty persons, as he appeared to have the four wives allowed him under Islamic law. I took a few photographs while they held the bicycle and then they pointed out some other scenes of interest, like two old men mending a fishing net. When I turned back from taking the photograph, I found that the bicycle had disappeared beneath a sea of bodies. Wading in to rescue it I saw that one individual had taken my journal from the handlebar bag, while another was busy removing the tools and luggage straps. While I repossessed these items, hands were thrust at me from all directions and voices were raised in the familiar demand. One woman seized my hand and tried to prise a ring off my finger. It began to seem a rather alarming situation and I suddenly realised what a tough and sinewy lot they were, as well as extremely uninhibited. They offered no real resistance, however, as I pushed my way out from their clutching and importuning hands, and a few stones clattered harmlessly after me as I made my escape.

I was a good half-mile from the scene before I discovered that they had purloined my sun hat. It was of no great value in itself, but it could mean the difference between life and death in the deserts of Sudan which lay ahead. Already I was far enough south to find its protection essential in the hot afternoon sun. I realised I had to do something about it, but it was another half-mile before I plucked up the necessary courage. With my small Swiss army penknife in my hand I slogged back against the wind, practising suitable gestures and grimaces to make my weapon appear more formidable and to get me in the mood for battle. As I neared the offending place, a small boy on a donkey spotted me. With a look of panic he turned his mount and clattered back to the village yelling a warning. I pounded after him shouting 'Police! Police!' at the top of my voice, hoping that the Arabic word sounded similar and brandishing my knife over my head. I felt rather like Don Quixote tilting at windmills.

The whole tribe was bunched together in the space between two of the hovels and there was my hat, clutched in the hand of a very grimy small boy. Several people were finishing off my picnic lunch. Guilt was written on every face. They looked for all the world like a bunch of naughty schoolboys caught red-handed raiding the larder. I found it impossible to feel intimidated by them; in fact I had the utmost difficulty in keeping a straight face as I strode sternly forward to pick up the hat. The sandwiches, or what was left of them, were past retrieving.

   In the next village a group of puzzled men who were now seeing me
pass for the third time, beckoned me to stop. Full of confidence after
my successful encounter I did so and sat down to drink tea with them.
The village elder, who had a little English, asked me about the knife
and I explained what had happened, miming where words failed. By
the time the incident had been acted out to everyone's satisfaction, we
were all friends and they were laughing uproariously, especially over
the modest dimensions of my knife. Before I continued on my way,
they solemnly presented me with a large stick of sugar cane. 'Not for
eat,' they told me. 'Hit!, hit!' – indicating how I should bring it down
on the heads of any other would-be robbers. I kept it for a long while
and it was very useful, even putting to flight a troupe of bold young
women on donkeys who tried to knock my hat off as they trotted past.
Later I took to having the occasional gnaw at it when my energy had
run low, and I found it very refreshing. It was quite gone by about
half-way up through Egypt, just before the great bend of Qena, where
the Nile takes a ninety-degree sweep to the east.
   A little way before this point lies what is possibly the most ancient
place of worship anywhere in the world – Abydos, the cult centre of
Osiris, God of the Underworld. It had once been the desire of every
Egyptian, noble and commoner alike, to make a pilgrimage to Abydos
in his lifetime and to be buried there, or for his mummified corpse to be
taken there by barge before being interred elsewhere. The site has gone
a very long way downhill since the days of its greatness; even the Nile
has turned its back upon it and taken a new course several miles to the
east. Rough villages huddle on mounds that were once temple
complexes of unimaginable antiquity, and now only a small shadow of
the New Kingdom period, circa 1560–1080 BC remains, in two
temples built by Seti the First and his son, the prolific Ramesses the
Second. It is still a most important site however, though no one ever
stays there; tourist coaches stop by on their way between Cairo and
Aswan, while other visitors come down for the day from their
comfortable hotels at Luxor or from their Nile steamers, and leave
again before nightfall.
   As overnight visitors were not catered for, I was able to find shelter
at Abydos only in a sort of garden shed, thanks to the good offices of a
young man named Waleed, an itinerant pharmacist whom I'd met two

days before and who happened to be doing his weekly stint at Abydos when I arrived there. My shed was next door to the one he slept in. It had a bed in it, of sorts, also a fly-blown bulb hanging from a frayed flex and a pipe jutting out from the wall at head height which might have been intended for a shower; but as there was neither power nor water, only the bed appeared to serve any purpose. In this I was mistaken however, as the thin cotton-stuffed mattress proved to be in such an advanced state of decay that I decided to spread my inflatable mattress on the floor instead and take my chance with the beetles, cockroaches and possible rodents. I had my slow burning candle so the only serious problem was the absence of water – which was ironic at a site where large pools and tanks for purifying the pilgrims had once been such a feature and where Herodotus had claimed that the priests had bathed four times a day. Cycling in temperatures which were now never below the high seventies, and often considerably higher, I too would have relished four baths a day and perpetually yearned for large quantities of water to wash the encrustations of sweat and dirt from both my skin and my clothes. Apart from a very few hotels in which the shower actually worked, I had to make do for the most part with half a bucket of murky liquid sluiced over myself from a plastic mug. Sometimes, when the road met the banks of the Nile, the temptation to plunge headlong into the sparkling expanse of it was almost too much to resist; it was only the stern warnings about bilharzia that held me back.

There were nonetheless many compensations for the poor standard of Abydos's accommodation, not least the pleasure of spending a night in the country instead of in the usual noisy town. The shed stood in a garden where drinks and ice-cream were served to tourists by day, when it possessed little charm. But night lent it an air of mystery, hiding the scattered rubbish and accentuating the pleasant scents of shrubs and plants. Without the interference of street lighting the stars were enormous, their light strong enough to illumine the pylons and walls of Seti's temple. It was all most satisfactorily romantic, as ruins ought to be, and although there was no dinner, there was good Egyptian beer and the emergency fruit and peanuts I had with me supplemented the felafel sandwiches from a village stall.

An additional attraction was that of being taken round the temples by Waleed's friend Abdel, an archaeology graduate now working for his doctorate. Abdel had grown up at Abydos, where the courtyards of the temples had been his playground and the high walls covered with coloured reliefs his first 'books'. A clever child of a poor family, compulsory education had been Abdel's chance to break free from a peasant's life. It could not have been easy for him, for although proud of their son's abilities, his family had put pressure on him to study something more obviously useful. Now they had given up on him, except for his mother – and all she cared about, said Abdel, was getting him married, a fate he seemed determined to avoid.

One of the fascinations of ancient Egyptian religion is that scholars disagree so profoundly about it. Some argue that the evidence points to a high religion of one eternal God, pre-existent and all-powerful, of whom the numerous deities are merely symbols; others see it as totally pagan, a complex, extended polytheism with local gods of limited power, the whole structure underpinned by sun worship. Abdel was passionately of the first opinion and advanced the Osiris myth itself as the clearest proof of a very early monotheistic faith, pre-dating by far Akhenaten's reign. He took me to the inner chambers of Seti's shrine where the sacred mysteries of the resurrection of Osiris were celebrated at the annual festival. Here a rather poorly preserved relief depicts Osiris lying upon a bed after being hacked into pieces by his brother Seth – the power of evil. The various pieces of Osiris's body, except the phallus which has been eaten by a fish, have been gathered together again and imbued with life through the love of his wife Isis. She hovers above his head in the form of a bird, at what is meant to be the very moment when Osiris is mysteriously able to beget upon her his son Horus, before passing out of this life to take up his duties as Lord of the Dead. Horus grows up to avenge his father's death and to destroy evil. The 'divinity' of pharaohs was based upon their association with Horus as 'Punishers of Wickedness'.

What further arguments Abdel advanced to support his theory have become confused in my mind with all the many things about Egyptian religion that other scholars have told me or that I've read about. The subject seems to be so enormously complicated, although at its centre is the theme of good versus evil which is common to all religions. It is the incidental things that Abdel told me which I best remember because they are what always captures the imagination – like the fact that Hathor, the consort of Horus, is meant to be the most beautiful female imaginable, so she is given cow's ears because ancient Egyptians thought more highly of cows than of anything else. There was also a sacred, underground pool which he showed me, a dark place approached down a few ancient broken steps. Barren women came to bathe in this pool and to beg the god for a son, and as the woman prayed a hidden priest would toss a stone into the water, which so startled her – supposing the splash to be the god answering her – that she went away and conceived the very next time she lay with her husband. I gathered from several sources that the pool is still visited for the same purpose today and is so noted for its success that it has been the subject of several serious scientific studies.

With the help of Abdel's explanations and of his enthusiasm, I could begin to picture the colossal temples, with their forests of thickly-set massive columns as the setting for the ancient priestly rites. I could see how the sun's rays would strike the inner sanctuary so startlingly in those dark halls, waking what lay within. Processions of robed figures bearing the stiff statue of the 'awoken god' became momentarily detached from their places on the walls and took on flesh. The statue they carried was clearly more than its form – it was an object of power that held the Ka, the essence of the god, and had therefore to be served like any great lord with wine and meat, dancing and singing. It made a great difference to see it like that, even for a little while; it softened the stark emptiness of the abandoned buildings and made a temporary bridge back through the centuries to the people who had worshipped there.

I arrived at Qena where the river swings back to its southward course again, after a hard day's riding against a strong easterly wind. It was now three days since I'd had anything but the most cursory of washes, and my clothes felt stiff with the salt of perspiration. Nor had my diet of fruit and beer been particularly conducive to hard, prolonged physical effort, so I was feeling a little out of sorts and not enthusiastic about the more than usually indifferent accommodation on offer.

After traipsing round the town and finding only a succession of dirty hotels, I went into a travel agency to see if they knew of somewhere better. They didn't, but the young man in charge made enquiries and escorted me to a place which turned out to be rather cleaner than average and did at least have water coming out of the taps. I had no sooner washed myself and rinsed out my clothes, than the young man, Deesa returned with an invitation from his parents for me to spend the evening at their home.

It was an average, middle-class Egyptian family. The father a primary school teacher, with Deesa and two other grown up sons and a daughter still at school. The mother waited lovingly and cheerfully on all of them, a model of devotion who looked rather ill to me and coughed incessantly. They lived in a small, neat apartment on the first floor of a narrow, roughly built, unfinished house on a rough dirt street. I gathered that eventually another two floors would be built on above them and these would be let to other people. This seemed to be the pattern of most new housing in Egypt – lots and lots of half-finished, raw building, none of it of a high standard. Even rudimentary building techniques seemed absent: for instance, the brickwork was never pointed at all, and I often wondered why many of these buildings didn't just collapse like rows of playing cards. It was all so at variance with the massive historical structures built to endure for eternity. The same sloppy standards prevailed inside buildings too, and I stayed in many three- and four-star hotels where good materials had been ruined by really shoddy workmanship. The plumbing often looked as though it had been beaten into place with a sledge-hammer, and tiling appeared to have had gangs of people throwing wet concrete at it after it had been hung. Cramped and simple though it was, Deesa's family home with its neat little shower room and the absence of lumps of concrete disfiguring the walls and floors, was a model of good order.

That the family could afford even such a basic little home of their own was because all the grown-up children contributed their earnings to the family coffer. This was not unusual Deesa told me, but it meant that young people could not afford to be married much before thirty. He had himself been engaged for five years and doubted whether he would be able to get married before another five years had elapsed. As too much contact between the sexes before marriage was discouraged, these protracted engagements helped to explain why there were so many delightful young men about in Egypt with time to spend talking to a middle-aged English woman.

Deesa's parents could not have been more welcoming if I had been royalty, and they insisted that I stayed with them instead of returning to the hotel. The whole family's sleeping arrangements were turned around, so that I finished up alone in the large bedroom which contained both the rock-hard marriage bed and the daughter's bed. Despite my protests the occupants of these bivouacked elsewhere as best they could. The graciousness of the hospitality was such that they tried to make me feel that it was I who was conferring the favour upon them.

The seven of us had supper seated around a low, circular brass table with lots of individual dishes into which we dipped as we chose, using our fingers and pieces of bread. There was rabbit, spinach, stuffed pigeon, an omelette, chips, a minced meat dish, pickled lemons and cheese. It was all quite delicious, though some things, like the mince and the spinach, were not easy to eat without cutlery. Afterwards local dates were served, and tea was drunk from thin tulip-shaped glasses. Everyone smiled a good deal and laughed outright at my ineptness at eating with my fingers. They were the warmest, kindest people I had met in Egypt, and I was only too happy to spend the next day with them as they urged.

They wanted me to see the famous Qena pottery, so after breakfast the following morning I was taken to the country by Deesa, who had borrowed a bicycle for the outing. I had seen village potteries before, but this was something strange and different; a huge area of rubble and pits where great primitive kilns fired by charcoal were constructed – a stone-age pottery producing a world of amphora-like pots, acres and acres of them all the same shape and size, stacked up everywhere in large mounds. The rejects were built into garden walls and lavatories for the workers' houses and were the most substantial parts of the primitive dwellings. Qena was famous for these particular pots apparently and they had been made there since time immemorial by the ancestors of the present potters. There was no one around who could tell me what particular use they served or who bought them and the whole place had a strange surrealist air about it, as though it was beyond the common world of functions.

Afterwards we walked through the beautiful surrounding fields on paths so narrow they could barely take one foot placed carefully in front of the other. Every inch of ground was as eat and ordered as could be and in great contrast to the sprawling ramshackle villages, with their spreading middens and ragged children. There was one field that had just been harvested and ploughed and three old women were grubbing up the remaining roots by hand, squatting in the dirt like huge black crows. They called out to us as we passed, and Deesa told me that they were complaining about how hard the work was and teasing him, 'a city man', by pretending to ask for his help. The owner of the land met us and sent a beautiful boy in a green gellabiyah running off to bring tea in a tall narrow metal pot from his house; and he then entertained us, sitting on a small patch of grass where two paths met and mango and fig trees joined branches overhead and provided shade. We each drank from the single small glass, which was then refilled for the next person.

Deesa's cousin's home, where we were to have lunch was at the far end of the village, a substantial Arab house which he shared with his brother. Neither man was a farmer, but worked in government offices in town, and the house had come to them through one of the wives. There were small children everywhere, their faces covered with flies – Egypt is without doubt the land of flies, and Egyptian children seem able to bear having them crawl all over them without trying to brush them away. The rooms were dark and high-ceilinged, with very thick walls and small windows. They rambled into one another haphazardly, with courtyards and hallways in unexpected places as though the house had simply gone on growing without any cohesive plan. The kitchen had nothing in it but a calor gas stove and a few pots on the floor in a corner. The rest of the house was sparsely furnished with settles and beds on the bare earthen floors. The best rooms had distempered walls with a stencilled pattern, and beamed ceilings. Some of the rooms had been abandoned to mice and pigeons and the whole place had an air of dilapidation and rather lacked charm. In spite of its look of great antiquity it had been built just sixty years before.

Only one child was allowed in to eat lunch with us, the rest being kept firmly outside with the women. This child was the four-year-old son of our host and clearly the favourite. He clung about his father's knee and scowled at us, and later, when he realised that his father was leaving to come back to town with us, he spat out the orange he was eating, hurled it at his father and howled as though his heart would break. 'He do this always when I go, he love me so very much,' said Deesa's cousin with an air of pride, making no effort at all to console the child.

That evening a succession of nephews and nieces came to visit Deesa's parents, sitting in an eager, bright-eyed row on a hard wooden settle, plucking up the courage to try out their English phrases. I had spent the afternoon helping Deesa's mother, Hanna, prepare vegetables for the evening meal and in spite of the frustration of having no one to translate for us, as Deesa was back at his travel agency, we had enjoyed a sort of silent communication of smiles and gestures, both undemanding and restful. Although Hanna and I were much of an age, we could not have been more different, she with her horizons bounded by her family and I a solitary traveller far from home, and yet we found ourselves somehow very much in sympathy. She was one of those rare women who seemed utterly content with her lot and radiated happiness so that it was a pleasure just to be with her.

Nonetheless she was ill, as I had suspected from the first. She had had an operation on the glands of her throat and it had not been successful; the swelling had returned and there was nothing more that could be done. The positive acceptance with which the family faced the fact that she did not have much longer to live was far removed from a dull fatalism. Perhaps their religion helped them in this; they were all practising Moslems in an unobtrusive yet serious way – for example Deesa could not bear hearing me mention my travel plans without prefacing them with a 'God willing' and ending them with 'Thanks be to God.' But I thought it was really mostly due to Hanna herself and the way she so whole-heartedly accepted life and what it had to offer, that the rest of the family had the courage to bear the thought of her death with such equanimity.

I left them all with a wrench that seemed strange considering how short a time I had spent there. It was as though I was leaving a family of which I was now a part; once Deesa, on his borrowed bike had waved a last goodbye to me on the road to Luxor, I was almost glad to have the hassle of the young baksheesh hunters to take my mind off the parting.

CHAPTER SIX

The City of a Hundred Gates

In all Egypt, it is Thebes that most nearly matches the expectations of the Nile traveller, for even in its vast and sprawling ruins it remains what it has been since the dawn of civilisation – a wonder of the world, an incredible awe-inspiring magnificence. It was Homer's 'first of all cities' – 'Egyptian Thebes' he has Achilles say in the *Iliad*, 'where the houses are full of treasure, and through every one of a hundred gates two hundred warriors with their chariots and horses come.' Although Homer's many-gated city has quite vanished beneath the dull architecture of modern Luxor, the sober little town is quite dwarfed by the immense extent of the ruins of Karnak, which tower over it on the southern side. The four temples with their gigantic columnar halls, courts of colossal sculptures and towering pylons are the most staggering collection of ruins to be found anywhere in the world. The remains of a mile-long avenue of ram-headed sphinxes link the vast complex of Karnak to the Great Temple of Luxor, restored by a century of reconstruction to a mammoth jewel at the Nile's edge.

Coming into Luxor from the north, after forty eventful miles evading the attentions of the baksheesh hunters and trying to ignore the meaningless flurries of horn blaring from eccentric motorists, I was suddenly confronted with all this overwhelming splendour; and could well understand the reaction of the French army, which while pursuing the Mameluke, Murad Bey in 1799, also came suddenly upon this same scene, and to a man and without any orders being given, presented arms to the accompaniment of pipes and drums. Later, Verdi set his exotic opera *Aida* here and had my journey taken place the following year, I might have seen its first ever staging in the Temple of Luxor. I can imagine nothing more appropriate to the place than grand opera, with horsemen, chariots, lions led around on golden chains and a cast of thousands. It really needs all that, for on closer acquaintance there is more than a hint of the grandiose and even a touch of the absurd in these towering forests of masonry. So very much magnificence underpinning the might of the pharaohs cannot be taken completely seriously – which is what made it so enjoyable a place, I think. It never seemed to me in the least bit like one of Rose Macaulay's 'sites of gentle melancholy'. In its superb setting, with the honey-coloured cliffs behind and the Nile flowing so expansively past under blue enamel skies – the felaheen crossing and recrossing with their baskets of produce and their ducks and chickens – the remains of ancient Egyptian Thebes was like a celebration of life; too beautiful and full of colour and interest to dwell on anything but the pleasure of it all.

A comfortable hotel, the first since Cairo, added considerably to my enjoyment and happily was not ruinously expensive, since Egypt was experiencing a sparse tourist season and hotel prices were consequently a matter for negotiation. I had no sooner settled on the terrace to enjoy the view, than I was hailed by 'Tennessee Madge', whom I had met briefly at Saqqara. She was a woman of my own age, who like Amelia B. Edwards, had been smitten with egyptology in her middle years and was now reading for a degree in the subject. Since Memphis USA contributes to the research funding at ancient Memphis, the university is entitled to send two students to Egypt each year for a few weeks of their course. Madge had been one of these students and had proved most useful to the expedition, being the only member who could handle the jeep which had escorted me away from the 'English House' on the night I had been denied shelter there. She had finished her spell at Saqqara and was about to embark on a luxurious Nile cruise before flying home to the States. In the meantime she was spending a few days exploring Luxor. Not having been away from her home state before, she was somewhat naive about foreign travel and was worried about a follower she had picked up.

She told me all about it over tea, and her tale was all too familiar. A personable man of about thirty-five had approached her in the museum, claiming to be an official there, knowledgeable in matters relating to ancient Egypt. He had invited her for a coffee, over the drinking of which he had professed to be altogether smitten by her charms and had persuaded her to meet him later for a meal, followed by a visit to see some belly-dancing at a night club. Madge was not so naive that she did not suspect both his motives and his protestations of affection, but even so she did not want to hurt his feelings – Egyptian men can give a very convincing display of being hurt by suspicions of unworthy motives. They even imply, ever so subtly, that only the perverted minds of Western women could possibly imagine such unpleasant things. The upshot was that Madge had agreed to the evening's entertainment, and now wanted me to come along as a safety measure, a sort of chaperone.

I do not enjoy being gooseberry and Madge's man, one Mohammed Yosef was even less pleasant than I had imagined he would be and so patently 'on the make' that I was surprised anyone would think twice about his motives. He appeared equally unimpressed with me, and was understandably put out that Madge hadn't come alone. The belly-dancing took place in the dimly-lit but rather clinical surroundings of one of the modern hotels and was very sparsely attended. Madge was persuaded to go up on stage and gyrate her corduroy-clad hips around in company with the Egyptian girl's white and mobile stomach; it was not at all edifying, and Mohammed Yosef watched with cold and calculating eyes. Afterwards he invited us both to spend the following day at his house on the other side of the river – the chance to fleece two silly middle-aged women instead of one, I took that to mean, and had absolutely no intention of going. However, as it is indeed so curiously difficult to refuse invitations in Egypt I murmured a tacit acceptance simply in order to get away. During my week at Luxor I accepted so many invitations to tea, lunch, dinner and so forth that in the end I couldn't remember where I had promised to be, and which places I should consequently avoid, with the result that I kept meeting my would-be entertainers when out and about, and had to plead loss of memory. Mohammed Yosef was the only one who had the temerity to phone my hotel room and demand to know why I hadn't shown up, after which the staff kept giving me annoyingly knowing looks.

Poor Madge, in the meantime was getting into ever deeper water with Mohammed Yosef, culminating dramatically one evening in fisticuffs aboard one of the luxury Nile steamers. I was, perhaps, partly to blame, as I had realised that Madge wasn't fit to be wandering around the ruins on her own and needed a minder. But whereas I was perfectly happy trundling about by myself on the bicycle, Madge wanted a proper guided tour by car, so Mohammed Yosef organised one for her. Madge had continued to discuss endlessly the possible motivation behind his interest; she had discovered that he had nothing to do with the museum, as he had claimed, so it was not, after all, a shared passion for egyptology. She said she was sure it wasn't pure affection, but secretly, in her romantic Tennessee heart, I was certain she hoped it might be.

She took the guided tour on the day she checked out of her hotel, just before boarding her Nile steamer and she was carrying all her luggage and valuables with her. 'No problem' Mohammed Yosef told her, 'you can leave everything safely in my house and pick it up later.' Madge, setting her desire not to hurt him with false suspicions against her natural common sense, turned her back on sense and left everything, including her passport, money and traveller's cheques. After the trip, which had cost far more than Mohammed Yosef had quoted, they returned to his house for lunch. 'Count all your money,' said Mohammed Yosef. 'Make sure nothing is missing, and then we can go into the next room and eat lunch. You can leave your bag there, now you know that it is safe.'

I was told the details over dinner aboard the steamer before it sailed. Madge was dry-eyed and out for revenge – hell knows no fury like a woman robbed it seemed. She hadn't noticed Mohammed Yosef going back into the room to help himself to a few traveller's cheques and the money and she had only discovered the loss later, when she was in the American Express office cashing a cheque. It was a stupid theft because he would be sure to be caught if he tried to cash the cheques. The clerk in the American Express office had advised her not to go to the police but to try and persuade Mohammed Yosef to return what he had stolen. By this stage I don't think Madge cared a hoot if Mohammed Yosef was locked up for life, but she was afraid of the possible consequences to herself of becoming embroiled with a foreign police force. If I came with her to corroborate some of the facts, she thought she could tell the story to the ship's agent and let him deal with it.

The agent was a sleek, prosperous-looking, over-fed man, with an ill-concealed contempt for women travelling alone. He asked the sort of overt sexual questions about the affair that I didn't think were in the

least relevant but which Madge answered as if to her father confessor –
Yes, he had kissed her and yes he had tried to touch her all the time . . .
The interview took place in the bar, with the barmen leaning over the
counter in unconcealed, open-mouthed interest. When drinks were
ordered I was the only one who wanted alcohol, but the whisky was
automatically set before Madge – clearly the debauched one. It was
while the agent, who came from Cairo, was verbally castigating all local
men as 'scum' and 'filth', alienating me in the process since I found most
of the local men both kind and helpful, that Mohammed Yosef calmly
walked in on the scene, greeting Madge as though nothing untoward
had happened. By this time Madge was totally into her role of the weak,
helpless, abused female in need of male protection, and she shrank back
into her chair casting an imploring glance upwards at the ship's agent,
who sprang to his feet very nimbly for so heavy a man, and roaring like a
bull sprang at the startled Mohammed Yosef, slapping and pushing him
all the way back down the gangplank. 'He will not bother you now, you
will not need to be anymore afraid,' the agent said as he returned in
triumph, symbolically wiping his hands of the matter and settling his
crisp cuffs back into place.

But the matter wasn't by any means over. 'What about my money and
the cheques?' asked Madge, suddenly very brisk. The agent retired and
came back in a very short time with two men in ordinary dress whom he
introduced as detectives, but whom I thought were more probably
members of the crew. After a further brief interview and a half-hearted
show of note-taking, the three men, Madge and I went off on a brief tour
of the hotel bars to try to find Mohammed Yosef. By playing on Madge's
tender womanly feelings, together with veiled hints of the unpleasant-
ness that might ensue, the agent had persuaded her not to bring charges;
the last thing he wanted was adverse publicity that would reflect
unfavourably on the profitable cruise business. It was, I decided, all an
elaborate charade. 'We will beat up him a little,' said the agent, clearly in
charge. The 'policemen' nodded their heads in cheerful agreement. 'Not
too much, just so he not do it again and so he give back your money.'

I didn't see Madge again after that night and I don't know if she
recovered her money, but early next morning the hotel staff put a call
through to my room, contrary to instructions. It was Mohammed
Yosef, who wanted me to meet him so that he could return 'the

somethings belonging to your friend'. He sounded just a little less confident than usual, but I didn't want to become involved any further; I told him to take whatever it was to the American Express office, and that same day I changed my hotel. I saw him once more across the road as I cycled past a few days later; he spotted me and waved cheerfully, so I gathered that nothing too drastic had overtaken him.

Even without all these distractions I would have found it hard work to gain more than a cursory oversight of Luxor, for there was just too much of it. It took the best part of a day just to walk around the temple complex of Karnak on the East Bank, without looking at it in any detail. There were also elaborate *son et lumière* shows in the evenings at Karnak, while Luxor Temple was floodlighted so beautifully that it took on a mystery it lacked by day, so that hours could be spent wandering through its courts simply soaking up the atmosphere. The West Bank, with its legendary necropolis, was even more daunting; and it was here that visitors spent most of their time, with two ferry boats plying continuously to and fro across the Nile. One of these boats was especially for tourists and was besieged immediately on both sides by the taxi men, donkey boys and other touts. The 'people's ferry' was a quarter the price and full of folk with their miscellany of wares going to market; it landed a little way downstream, away from the worst of the crush.

Bicycles were a common way of exploring the West Bank, but there were none about like the 'Ah Agala'. As usual it was much admired, which helped considerably in the way I was treated around the necropolis; that and the fact that I was alone. Groups were much more pressurised to buy goods and services, and I heard many people complaining that the place was ruined for them by the unending hassle. From the first morning in the Valley of the Kings I found it nearly all a sheer delight. I had left the Agala in the care of the souvenir sellers, at the temple of Hatshepsut – a suitable place, as Hatshepsut was a woman who had held on to power in the face of male opposition and became, in around 1500 BC the only female pharaoh in history. She had suffered the same fate as Ahkenaten, having her name hacked off the King Lists by her successor, but her magnificent mortuary temple, like no other in Egypt, has remained largely intact. It rises in an exuberant sweep of colonnaded terraces against a great natural amphitheatre in the cliffs of Deir el Bahri in the Theban hills. With its delicate proportions, it looks more Greek than Egyptian.

There is a short cut over the hills from the temple of Hatshepsut to the Valley of the Kings, and a young souvenir seller named Achmed volunteered to lead me up the cliffs, along the same paths that Egyptian artisans had trodden since time immemorial, when they had been fashioning the royal tombs. Every inch of these bare rocky slopes was thick with modern Thebans selling fake antiquities which they drew from the folds of their gowns with a conspiratorial hiss: 'Psst, psst, I know you not tourist my friend, therefore I show. I dig it up myself, only look!' There were genuine antiquities for sale too, at a price, as there always have been since the eighteenth century, but they were proffered with greater discretion, since the traffic is strictly illegal. Many of the fakes are beautifully made, possibly by the descendants of those distant artists who worked here, father and son, down through all the ages it took to construct the tombs. Just as ancient Egyptians didn't think of themselves as artists but simply as workers on the payroll of the State, so these modern souvenir makers don't make any claim about artistic expression – they are merely poor men trying to earn a living. Achmed let no one bother me and escorted me down the precipitous paths, out of the dry powdery hills, and into the narrow winding Valley of the Kings, that had once housed more treasure to the square inch than anywhere else on earth.

There are 62 known tombs in the Valley of the Kings. Only a dozen of these are lit by electricity, and only about six of them are normally visited. They are without doubt marvellous, and maybe one day I will return to see them again – but I doubt it for I do not think I possess the necessary dedication. Had I attempted only one tomb it would perhaps have struck a more vibrant chord, left a richer memory, but after so many deep hot descents down endless steps and processions through long airless corridors, the bright wonderfully-preserved reliefs began all to look alike. Coachload after coachload of visitors converged on the Valley, with queues forming to ascend and to descend past walls bearing the familiar dynastic boasts and the same instructions from the Book of the Dead. It creates a dilemma for the visitor: it has to be seen, but who has the year or two needed to see it properly?

I remember Tutankhamun's tomb best because I had already seen his treasure in Cairo, and although the tomb was so small and comparatively simple it had all the drama attached to it of having remained undiscovered until this century. Of all the tombs in the Valley of the Kings, only Tutankhamun's has the body of the pharaoh still in situ; and this too makes a difference, giving it more a feeling of its original purpose. I had also been reading Thomas Hoving's recent exposé about the opening of Tutankhamun's tomb, which revealed that the much-publicised day on which Howard Carter and his patron Lord Caernarvon had broken through the last barrier and entered the chamber in the presence of eagerly waiting museum staff and newspaper men had been a sham. Apparently the two of them had sneaked in there secretly several days earlier and stolen thirty-five items before walling the tomb up again in preparation for the elaborate public hoax.

In a different part of the necropolis there were other tombs to which I returned happily many times – those of the nobles, the pharaohs' officials. It was these exquisitely decorated rooms which moved me more than anything I saw in Egypt. The delicacy and freedom with which the reliefs had been carved and painted suggested a delight on the part of the artists at having been released from the straitjacket of decorating imperial walls. The invention was endless, so that no two tombs were remotely alike. One I especially enjoyed was the tomb of Sennofer, overseer of the royal gardens of Amon in the reign of Amenhophis the Second, around 1500 BC. It is also known as the Tomb of the Vines because the ceiling is covered with a painted trellis, heavy with great bunches of purple grapes – the most fluid and natural painting in all the tombs I saw. But the tomb I visited most of all was that of Ramose, who was preparing his burial chamber at the time of the takeover by Akhenaten, the 'monotheistic heretic' pharaoh, in about 1400 BC and there is a distinct change from one wall decorated with a marvellous Old Kingdom-style relief to a scene on another wall of the new worship of the sun disk, executed in the revolutionary elongated manner of Akhenaten's reign – a style something akin to the modern sculptures of Modigliani.

Ramose's tomb was just outside the home of a family who became my friends – Ibrahim and Zenab and their children, Gebal, Fatin and Mohammed. The village of Gurna had grown up over and around the tombs of the nobles, clustered so closely together on the hillside. For centuries the fellaheen had built their houses so as to incorporate the burial chambers as a sort of basement room, into which they could retire for warmth in winter and for relief from the burning temperatures in summer. Once the worth of the tombs had been recognised – when Egyptology had become all the rage, houses were torn down from around the important decorated tombs, and several attempts were made to remove the villagers away from the area altogether. A fresh site was made available to them nearer to their fields by the side of the Nile, but no amount of piped water and electricity has made this new village attractive to the people of Gurna. They like it where they are, on their dusty, amenity-free hillside where the tourists come to provide their second or even first incomes. The men of Gurna continue to wander about the tombs like kings in their graceful, biblical robes and the women continue to haul water for miles every day, while their children tumble about the spoil heaps of the excavations, the toughest of them surviving into adulthood.

I usually left the Agala at Ibrahim's house. He had invited me to lunch the first time I met him and I almost forgot about it, just as I had with all the other invitations, but fortunately he came to meet me, and I found that an elaborate banquet had been prepared. Ibrahim lived in a superior two-storey house built just over a hundred years ago by his grandfather, the local sheikh. It was spacious and cool with high ceilings and shuttered windows in the thick walls. The rooms were very long and narrow with carved double doors and tiled floors. Over the years the upper floor had fallen into disuse, and the whole building was well past its prime. The furniture was sparse – a few rush mats, wooden benches with cushions to recline against and a very rough home-made dresser – but it was nonetheless a pleasant home. Ibrahim's grandfather had been a wealthy man with much land, but too many surviving children claiming their portion had led to a very different state of affairs for Ibrahim's generation. This is the tragedy of much of the third world – a big increase in the population without an accompanying increase in ways of making a living. Ibrahim was rare in limiting his family to just three, but he seemed more intelligent than most men I met in Egypt and could clearly see how disastrous a large family could be. He was helped too in having an unusually close and warm relationship with his wife Zenab, who was also very intelligent and much more liberated than most Egyptian women appear to be.

I visited other houses in the village which were considerably poorer, where the cockroaches ran freely and plentifully around even in daylight. Such was the house of Tya, a young man home on leave from his national service, who wanted my help in writing a love letter to a forty-five-year-old French woman. He was far more typical of the men of Gurna than Ibrahim. 'You ever try it with hashish?' he asked me, a dreamy far away look in his eyes as I read through the impassioned airmail letter he'd handed me. I had to admit that I hadn't. 'You make love, maybe it last ten minutes. All over. But with hashish, one hour, two hour, maybe all night. Never she forget you!'

Many of the men of Gurna had their biscuit tins of love letters from Western women and the glimpses these epistles afforded into 'the wilder shores of love' were fascinating: things have not changed much since Victorian times, it seems, but I suppose love never does change really, only places and partners. All the letters were written by sensitive, educated women, many of whom seemed prepared to leave everything to come and settle in Gurna with their Arab lovers. Few of the Gurna men matched this devotion. Only Tya seemed to be contemplating a future with his French lady, brushing aside the twenty years difference in ages and the wife he already had – 'What matter? we love, we will be happy.' For most of the others it was a light-hearted game and the letters were tokens of their success. It was not that they were insensitive or unkind, simply that their ideas about Western women, or women in general perhaps, gave them double standards. They were graceful, attractive, hot-blooded men who simply lived for the day. Like Hamdy Hassan, a seller of head scarves, with whom I once gently remonstrated over a letter in which a woman was threatening to leave her husband because of him, and who replied with genuine puzzlement, 'But I tell her I find other women when she gone. I am young man. I want do everything. Later, maybe thirty-five I stop, go mosque like my father.'

Because of my friendship with Ibrahim's family I wasn't pestered as much as I might have been and I found most of the men would accept a firm and unequivocal no. Only Hamdy Hassan, in between selling his tatty Arab scarves to coach parties, continued to pursue me with undiminished enthusiasm, which I took in the nature of a friendly compliment. Once I had become the unofficial scribe, composing answers to the Gurna men's love-letters, I could do no wrong and they even defended me from other tourists at need – like the time at the Ramesseum. In Ramesses the Second's flamboyant mortuary temple is the colossal fallen statue of himself that was misrepresented in Shelley's poem, and became – 'Ozymandias, King of Kings' of 'Look on my works ye Mighty and despair' fame – a change of character which would certainly not have amused the vainglorious Ramesses the Second. Americans in particular flocked there, panting to get 'a shot' before they tore off breathlessly to the next 'must' on their itinerary, and they could be most rude and peremptory to any innocent bystander whom they considered was in the way of their pictures. Like most people, I found this annoying and tended to ignore their shouts. One day I was bellowed at several times by a woman with a Biblebelt accent. Hamdy Hassan, who had been lurking in readiness with his scarves, sprang his cover prematurely to deliver a lecture – 'You not boss here. She our friend. You not tell her what she do.'

When I left the bland comforts of East Bank Luxor, I had moved into a no-star hotel just below Gurna, where the bare stony sand changes dramatically to fertile fields. It was a thick walled two-storey building, ochre-washed and enclosing a tree-shaded garden. It was owned by a very old man called Sheikh Ali and he had decorated the dim interior with photographs of himself as a superlatively handsome young man, and kept strings of cheap beads to give to female visitors, although he was barely able to shuffle the few steps from his room to the garden. I was the only guest and was looked after by a great-grandson of the sheikh, another Ali of about eleven, who promised to be as handsome as his aged relative. My room was on the first floor, tolerably clean and like a Provençal interior painted by Van Gogh. The window was covered with gauze to keep out the flies and looked towards the two seated figures of the sixty-foot-high Colossi of Memnon, rising in battered awesomeness from a sea of bright green sugar cane.

It was an excellent base for all the West Bank sites. In the evenings the villagers came in to drink beer and smoke and talk, and it was then I struggled with my duties as unofficial scribe, trying to compose answers to the women who had not chosen to resist these men. Sometimes there was music with a drum and fife and the men danced, one or two at a time, a long scarf tied around their hips, sinuous and graceful and totally unselfconscious. At such times, with the scent hanging heavy from the flowering shrubs and the stars huge and bright overhead in the desert sky, it would indeed be an unromantic heart that did not understand the attraction.

CHAPTER SEVEN

The Desert Closes In

A marvellous wind blew me along through the fields of Upper Egypt as though I was sailing through the fields of tall gilded sugar cane. It was the most effortless and pleasant bicycling so far, and the faster I went the more the air was stirred around me, blowing the hair back from my forehead and fanning my face with a welcome coolness. It was one of those rare days when the presence of a secondary road allowed me to enjoy the tenderness of the landscape without the distractions of noisy traffic or threatening children. This idyllic state continued for the thirty-five miles to the small town of Esna where the first of a string of Ptolemaic temples lurks at the bottom of a deep pit in the centre of the suq.

All the grand temples south of Luxor were built by the Ptolemys, following Alexander the Great's conquest of Egypt in 332 BC. They were rebuilt or re-embellished again by the Romans, after the death of Cleopatra in 30 BC had brought the age of the Ptolemys to an end. The temple at Esna was dedicated to one of the most ancient of the Egyptian gods, Khnum, who made man on his potter's wheel, but all that remains of it is the elegant hypostyle hall credited to the Emperor Claudius, who engaged in a flurry of building activity in these parts in the first century AD to advertise the might of the Roman Empire. Neither Romans nor Greeks had the least interest in provoking the native population or the powerful priesthood by interfering with their religion, so all their temples were built on ancient sites, in the established style of the country. The most striking thing about the temple of Esna is its sunken position in a town that has grown fifty feet above it on the accumulation of centuries of rubbish. As her drawings show, it looked very odd when Amelia B. Edwards was here, for it had been only partially dug out and just the top few feet of the columns and the lovely varied capitals were exposed. Far more dedicated than I, she had spent a whole day sketching the scene, forgetting in her interest to eat the elaborate luncheon brought over for her from the ship. Drifting slowly up the Nile, she could not have been expending the same amount of energy as I was on the Agala; I was only too pleased to tuck into my pitta bread and felafel while I admired the forest of the now fully revealed columns.

When I climbed up to street level again, the temple guardian pointed out that the back tyre of the bicycle was flat. Temple guardians were often rather impressed by the pink card that admitted me gratis to the antiquities, and assumed that I must be a learned Egyptologist. Such was the case now. The 'Professor' – the only visitor of the day moreover – had suffered a puncture while her Agala had been in his care, it was a major catastrophe and he had already summoned a mechanic from a nearby garage to deal with it. With difficulty I convinced both gentlemen that I needed no help – though in fact I did: they were very useful in holding back the crowds that gathered as soon as I had the bicycle turned upside down and was taking out the back wheel. A large nail still firmly embedded in the tyre made it easy to locate the leak. Normally I would put in the spare inner tube and leave the repair until evening when I had both time and something heavy, like a table leg, to apply pressure to the patch while the glue was setting. But so large an audience deserved rather more entertainment I decided, and I did the complete puncture repair treatment for them and was rewarded by their awed respect and one man's remark that he didn't know a woman could be an engineer. For a city that had once been a noted centre for dancing girls and ladies of pleasure catering to the camel caravans, mending a puncture seemed to me a very tame substitute.

I did not linger in Esna as I had another thirty-five miles to make to Edfu, where I intended to spend the night – a poor choice as it transpired. Edfu is traditionally the place where Horus met Seth in immortal combat, and there is a temple to commemorate this triumph of good over evil built by Ptolemy the Third in the 2nd century BC in an antique style designed to outdo the ancient Egyptians at their most grandiose. To call it monumental would be an understatement; it is certainly one of the largest and best preserved of all Egypt's temples but after such a wealth of the massive, size alone no longer impresses. No doubt it provided a splendid Cecil B. De Mille setting for the annual festivities held here to celebrate the victory of Horus, at which

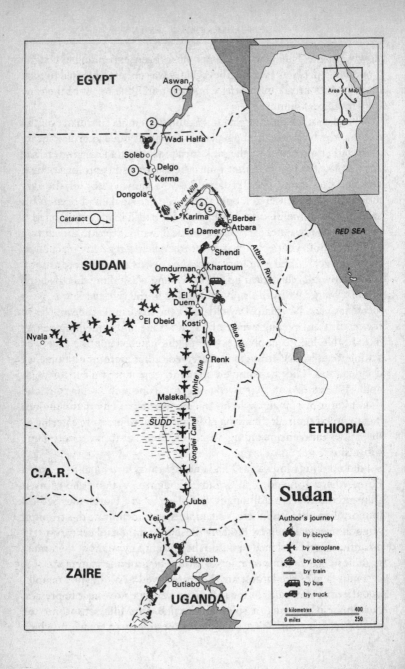

EGYPT

Aswan ①

② Wadi Halfa

Soleb

③ Delgo
Kerma

Dongola

Cataract ○→

River Nile

④ ⑤

Karima
Berber
Ed Damer Atbara

RED SEA

SUDAN

Shendi

Omdurman Khartoum

El Duem

Nyala

El Obeid

Kosti

Blue Nile

Atbara River

Renk

White Nile

Malakal

SUDD

Jonglei Canal

ETHIOPIA

C.A.R.

Juba

Yei

Kaya

Pakwach

ZAIRE

Butiabo

UGANDA

Area of Map

Sudan

Author's journey

🚲 by bicycle
✈ by aeroplane
⛵ by boat
by train
🚌 by bus
🚐 by truck

0 kilometres 400
0 miles 250

his statue was paraded with that of his bride, Hathor of the cow's ears, which had sailed up the Nile from Denderah in a magnificent sacred barque. Without all this colourful panoply – brought to an end after the Roman Empire went Christian and forbade pagan worship – Edfu is a chill place like an empty gutted cinema.

Perhaps I saw it at an unfortunate time, at the end of a long day in the saddle, when the sun's rays were low, so that the high walls and the gigantic pylon cast gloomy shadows over the immense courtyard from which the sky seemed almost completely cut off. The walk through the endless dark halls was far too long and reminded me of subterranean vaults. The only things that relieved the massive dreariness were four monstrous birds, carved in granite and wearing the double crown of Upper and Lower Egypt, which guarded the entrances. One had keeled over and lay there still rigidly watchful, with one baleful eye pointed heavenward. These enormous birds were Horus in his falcon guise, but they looked to me like something very nasty from a worm's nightmare. 'Beware the Jabberwock my son,' quoted the guide book with a fine degree of aptness.

Edfu would have come bottom of the league as a place to stay had I not met up with two of the town's police officers, who took me under their wing. They had been posted to Edfu without having had any say in the matter, which I gather is what happens in the Egyptian police service, run as it is rather on military lines. It was not considered a plum position, and they were sympathetic to anyone else with the misfortune to be benighted there. The best accommodation they had been able to find was a hotel opposite the police station, a rather solid mansion that had fallen upon hard times. Its imposing staircase, panelled wainscotting and nice brass handles were covered in layers of impacted grime and thick cobwebs – the sort of place where one is careful to avoid contact with the walls. The officers spoke very firmly to the owner, demanding that a room be cleaned, hot water prepared and so forth, but they could not achieve the same degree of authority as they had with their own men, whom they had left at the station swilling everything down with buckets of heavily disinfected water. None of the requests were actually met, though there was a tremendous show of willingness. 'Never mind,' said one officer consolingly, 'you will have us next door to protect you.'

They were more successful at producing food, as they had an arrangement with a widow in the town who prepared their evening meal, and her elderly father brought it over and hung about while it was eaten, for fear, the police said, that they took it into their heads to make off with the chipped bowls and the tin spoons and forks, which the old man thought were of great value. We ate together in the room which had been prepared for me, in which there were three beds, a table, a chair held together with string and the bicycle which had been carried up the staircase by a traince policeman. I had the chair and the police sat opposite on one of the beds with the table between us, covered with the newspaper in which the bread had been wrapped. The food was a speciality of the place, and worthy of a better setting – fried Nile perch and liver cooked with garlic and a green herb like coriander. Both dishes were delicious, and I realised half-way through the meal that although it had been intended for their supper, the policemen had made sure that I had had the largest share; they really were very kind.

One of them, the captain, was a Moslem, his lieutenant, a somewhat younger man, was a Copt, and very interested in religious matters. No one knows quite how many Copts there are in Egypt, though they may constitute about ten per cent of the population, the majority of whom live in Upper Egypt. This young Copt tackled me on the subject of Western Christianity the moment the last piece of bread had disappeared. Having ascertained that I was Protestant and not Catholic he demanded, 'Why do you not like the Virgin Mary?' I could see that there was no answer that I could give him which would be satisfactory, since he had already decided what I thought on the subject. The Coptic Church is the oldest branch of Christianity but because its doctrine of the Holy Trinity is different to that of the Roman and the Greek churches, in that the person of God the Father is considered to be above and superior to Christ the Son, it is considered heretical by the others. Moslems on the other hand, being so very particular about the One God, have been able to rub along more or less equably with the Copts, just as they used to with Jews, before the vexed question of Palestine arose. With their belief in the three persons of the Trinity, other Christians, according to Moslems, Jews and Copts alike, are practising a form of plural belief little better than outright paganism. Few people in the West seem to worry any more about such fine points of doctrine, though not so long ago many were prepared to go to the stake over them, as I felt this young man might well do. So in the discussions that ensued I was at a disadvantage, and could only admire the strength of feeling and the devotion that the details of religion aroused in this particular policeman.

That night I spread my inflatable mattress on what I took to be the least obnoxious of the beds, which seemed preferable to laying it on a floor covered with the dirt of ages. I left the light on in the hope that it would discourage the cockroaches, which in the awesome lavatory across the corridor were of a size to feature in nightmares alongside the Jabberwocks. I did not sleep well, and before I left in the first uncertain light of morning, the amiable, greasy old hotelier napping on a bench across the threshold demanded extra on top of the trifling bill to compensate for the excessive use of the fifteen-watt light bulb.

My last day's ride through Upper Egypt saw a dramatic closing in of the bare flanking cliffs and the disappearance of the green fertile strip. The desert fell back again for a short space around the temple of Kom Ombo, built for Horus and Sobek the crocodile god, where a few bright acres of cultivation supply sugar cane for a nearby refinery. Kom Ombo is in a more ruinous state than Edfu and Esna, having been used as a quarry for other buildings – including the refinery, and this gives it a poignancy that the other two lack. Its walls are almost gone and its courts and columns are open to the sky and sun, like a Greek temple. In its splendid setting on a bluff overlooking the Nile, with desert hills all round the horizon and the great span of brownish green water flowing serenely past, it has a delicacy and a unity with its surroundings that is absent in many Egyptian temples. There are unexpected touches too, like the stiff mummified crocodiles stacked up in a dusty chapel like hugely grinning planks and a relief carved on a fragment of wall showing the instruments of sophisticated brain surgery and dentistry that were in use here 2,000 years ago.

Beyond Kom Ombo the desert closes in once more on the Nile, and here I had my last Egyptian picnic sitting on a wall beside the strongly flowing water. The waves had a distinct slope where the wind fought the current and a felluca drifting mid-stream with its gear dismantled in the manner in which sailing boats have always dropped down the

Nile, made only slow progress, broadside on to the wind. That the river flows as strongly as it does indicates what unimaginable volumes of water are pushing it on, for the rise in the level here, nearly a thousand miles from the sea, is only eighty-six metres.

After lunch the day deteriorated in the now established pattern of assaults by ever increasing numbers of belligerent juveniles coming out of school. Intrepid though she was, Amelia B. Edwards had a rule never to set foot ashore without one of her boat's crew in attendance. At times like these I could have wished for similar protection. The harassment had been getting worse with every mile I made southward, and from the concentration of impoverished-looking villages in the now barren surroundings, it was not really surprising. Many people had been settled here in recent years after their homes had been destroyed by the building of the High Dam. Nubia, the land that lay beyond the first cataract, has now largely disappeared under the waters of the biggest man-made lake in the world. Fortunately, during this last onslaught I met up with a motor-cycle policeman and proceeded under escort for the last few miles into Aswan.

At Aswan the long oasis of Egypt finally comes to an end. Sand stretches out east and west from the banks of the Nile, and the first cataract bars the river to the south. Aswan was always a frontier town and trading post to which the exotic wealth of the interior came – wild animals, slaves and ivory from the far south, gold from the land of Nub, spices and perfumes from Punt. Here the camel trains lurched in across the desert trails to link up with the great river highway to the sea, and military expeditions unshipped and marched forth to subdue the far territories. Jews fleeing from Nebuchadnezzar in the diaspora of the sixth century BC had found this the end of their road and had settled here on the island of Elephantine. The 'gift of the Nile' ceased here. Above the cataract, the fertile silt brought down on the flood waters was deposited in only very small and occasional patches. Temples like Abu Simbel, which were built into the cliffs beyond Aswan were in the nature of a reminder to others of the great might of Egypt, a warning in the wilderness to any danger that might threaten from the wild and hungry lands of the Sudan.

I went straight to the Old Cataract Hotel where mail and supplies of dehydrated food and spare tyres awaited me. It is Aswan's most famous hotel, the place where Agatha Christie wrote *Murder on the Nile* and where anyone who was anyone had always stayed before the requirements of today's jet travellers produced the obtrusive tasteless structures of the modern luxury hotels. The discerning still put up at the Old Cataract, largely because its terrace enjoys the best views in Aswan, across the Nile and the island of Elephantine and also because its interior is individual and memorable, redolent of a more leisured and cultured clientele. I wasn't considering staying there myself as it was far outside the limits of my budget, but the management very kindly offered me free accommodation in their new Kalabsha Hotel, a hundred yards up the road. I cannot honestly say I liked the Kalabsha, but a little four-star luxury, no matter how tasteless, was not unwelcome after my recent lodgings and I slept there, when not jerked awake by the baying and barking of packs of roving dogs and the noisy 4 a.m. calls to prayer from a nearby mosque. All my leisure moments I spent on the terrace of the Old Cataract, drinking turkish coffee brought by Nubian servants in red fezzes.

Not that there was much time for leisure. Aswan was the jumping off place for the next stage of the journey, where once more I had to wrestle with officialdom for the necessary permission to bicycle on above the High Dam. I didn't want to take the crowded tacky boat to Wadi Halfa. Quite apart from the fact that it had a poor record of safety, and shipwreck in the crocodile-infested waters of the Nuba Lake tended to be a serious and terminal affair, I wanted to travel alone through the desert into Sudan, visiting Abu Simbel on the way.

It took me days simply to locate the relevant offices and find a time when they were open. I then explained what I wanted, and showed my powerful letter and my pink card, which were duly admired, but got me nowhere beyond offers of guided tours to far-flung temples, free trips to *son et lumières* and invitations to dinner. The whole area around the lake was a military zone, a no-go area – mined too, they hinted, in case I should take it into my head to dispense with permission. Successful travel is often a question of compromise, and this particular journey was no exception, with all the uncertainties that lay ahead. The important thing was to reach the great basin of the Nile and to see as much as possible on the way there. If it was the boat or nothing, I would take the boat; and with the political climate deteriorating daily in the Sudan, the sooner I got there the better, before travellers were refused entry altogether.

That capitulation promised no easy passage, was made clear by the mile-long queue of jostling Sudanese trying to make it back to their sandy wastes after voyages of acquisition to the fleshpots of Egypt. Sudan, I was told, lacked many consumer commodities: rich people flew to Europe to obtain them, while those less affluent made the long laborious journey to Cairo, which for them was like El Dorado. A colonial mentality still prevailed in Aswan however, and if any employee of the Nile Navigation Company – which operated the Wadi Halfa steamer – spotted a Western face in this daunting queue they removed the person to an office inside the building to allow him or her to purchase a ticket in a more becoming privacy. No cabins were available, for these were booked months ahead – not a cause for concern according to the booking clerk – 'No problem madam, boat take only two days now. Not so long.'

The young man who made out my ticket said he would be there at the quay when the boat departed in order to help me get the Agala aboard. 'You will give me then address in England?' he asked, betraying his true motive. I asked him why he wanted it though I knew well enough. 'Maybe I visit you? Stay some, find work huh?' England was still an alternative Mecca for many young men of the third world.

With my departure only days away I took up the offers to see two of the great sights of Egypt which I certainly could not miss – the temples of Philae and Abu Simbel. Both of them had been victims of the floods: in fact Philae, the sacred island of Isis had become so as long ago as 1902, when the British built the first dam at Aswan. After that it was under water for six months of every year, and tourists used to take boat trips out over the island, looking down at the submerged pillars undulating in the green translucent water. The High Dam would have finally drowned Philae for ever, so in a multi-billion dollar project all the buildings were dismantled and rebuilt on another island nearby which had been carved and bulldozed so as to resemble the original as closely as possible. There are about four temples in the complex; the whole place used to be the most tremendous tourist attraction for ancient Romans because of the cult of Isis who came to be associated with the Mediterranean and Near Eastern mother goddess figures. It lingered the longest of all the pagan cults. Two hundred years after the rest of the Roman Empire had officially become Christian, Isis was still wrshipped at Philae. Not until the Emperor Justinian put his foot down in the sixth century AD was the place converted into a Christian church, dedicated appropriately to the Virgin Mary. Philae was a great attraction for Victorian tourists too because it was so pretty and romantic on its low island, which made it appear as though the pillars were floating on the water. It was Amelia B. Edwards' favourite place and judging by her sketches of it, with lots of greenery softening the heavy lines of the masonry, it was a more attractive ruin then than now.

I made my visit there one evening to see the *son et lumière* and unfortunately an Egyptian school group came too. It didn't improve the atmosphere to be with a large number of uninhibited teenagers of both sexes who were far more interested in each other than in their country's ancient history. But that aside, I felt as though I was visiting a well-endowed, well-lit museum, and try as I might, Amelia B. Edwards' ecstatic descriptions did nothing to make me see it differently. The soul of the place was no longer there: it was simply a beautifully executed engineering feat, a large group of venerable buildings which had once been temples and had now been rebuilt on profane ground. Miss Edwards half expected 'a sound of antique chanting and a procession of white-robed priests bearing aloft the veiled ark of God'. The *son et lumière* practically achieved that, but – alas – it made absolutely no difference.

I saw Abu Simbel in the full light of day. I drove the two hundred miles there and back in a comfortable coach, travelling on a brand new highway that will one day go right on to Khartoum, or so they say – but they have been saying the same thing for at least fifty years. As far as one could see on either side of this new smooth tarmac strip was desert, with here and there the skeleton of a camel, lying neatly where the animal had fallen for the last time, too far from water to make it any further. The kites had come and picked the bones bare, leaving them with the austere dignity of abstract art forms. For the space of about fifty miles there were thousands and thousands of pyramids of varying sizes. They were a natural phenomenon, created by the wind from the sand but so perfectly formed that it was hard to believe they were not man-made. I found them more awe-inspiring than the temple of Abu Simbel.

Abu Simbel is another multi-billion dollar engineering marvel. As the waters of the new lake rose, the whole colossal structure of Egypt's most famous temple was injected with resin and sawn into a thousand blocks, which were put back together three hundred yards away from the original cliff-face site. A huge dome disguised as a mountain was specially constructed to receive them. The visitor can walk about inside this hollow hill and wonder at the feat. He can walk around the four colossi of Ramesses the Second at the entrance and stroll through the halls and never find a trace of where it was all stuck together again; all is exactly as it was. He can then do the same with the great companion temple of Nefertari, Ramesses the Second's wife, and if he is as keen on engineering feats as my guide Mousa Mohammed was, he will be amply rewarded for the two-hundred mile journey there. If however, he has gone to see a great temple, he might well be disappointed. Abu Simbel is now yet another well-preserved museum; as at Philae, the spirit of the place is buried beneath the waters.

Mousa insisted that the modern spirit of Aswan is the High Dam, and that no visit to Egypt would be complete without paying homage to it. He had the dimensions of it by heart and reeled them off as we stood on the viewing platform staring at the huge concrete mass. There were enough materials in it, Mousa claimed, to build the Great Pyramid seventeen times over, and enough steel for 15 Eiffel Towers. But it really has nothing at all in common with those other structures. It points to nothing beyond itself, and makes no statement other than one of immense power and expediency. For some, like Mousa, it is a symbol of man's coming of age, taking responsible control of his environment; for others it is an unjustifiable tampering with the forces of nature, which are as yet beyond his understanding – 'flinging back the "gift of the Nile" in the teeth of the giver' as one critic wrote.

The High Dam was completed in 1971 and it was from the first a controversial undertaking, the pros and cons of which are still being hotly disputed. Egypt's rapidly growing population needed huge reserves of water to reclaim desert land for cultivation, as well as vast new resources of power, and the dam provided both, but the price to be paid for these benefits is not yet fully known. The people who lost their homes beneath the three-hundred mile lake and the ancient temples which have been severed from their roots are purely local tragedies, but the effects upon the ecology of at least half of Africa are only just beginning to be assessed. The water table is rising throughout the Sahara and all the life-giving silt of the Nile is now confined in the lake, to be replaced by chemicals produced by the power from the dam. An awful lot of the precious water is lost in evaporation, 5,000 million cubic metres annually according to some sources. It is also estimated that the lakes will have silted up completely in five hundred years. On the other hand, the arable land of Egypt has increased by thirty per cent, and even in the recent droughts that brought devastating famine to Ethiopia and the Sudan, stocks of water have kept Egypt growing its three crops a year. Electrical power has also doubled – but of course none of these benefits will go far if Egypt's population continues to increase at the rate of a million every ten months.

As the new barrier to Egypt's southern border the High Dam is certainly impressive and more than a little frightening in its sense of limitless power. I could well understand why it was a military zone – with terrorism such a feature of today's world, a breach in this dam could unleash a torrent of pent up water that would destroy the whole country.

I spent my last afternoon in Egypt appropriately afloat on the Nile in a small felucca with a tall mast, the sail of which was held together with a hundred patches and caught every puff of breeze that fluked about the islands. The boatman was called Saiyid. He wore a blue gown and said he was torn between friendship and making a living, which meant that we compromised on the price of the trip. His talk seemed to be all about the difficulties of life; the difficulty of sex and the single devout Moslem who prays five times a day but cannot resist temptation ('I am good, I try, I try, but my body need and if the woman wants I do it'). Marriage was also difficult: 'Money is not enough, much money for marry. I am thirty-two, have many sisters and small brothers, not time yet for marry.' Only his family was not a difficulty and his voice softened as he spoke of it: 'We have need with our families. I must see my mother every day and if one of my brothers is not there I miss him.' Not far beneath the surface was a sense of deep contentment that belied all the talk of difficulties. He was rooted to the place where his family had been for as far back as anyone could remember and he knew every eddy, every rock and every trick of the wind on this island-studded stretch of the Nile.

We glided back to the rocks below the hotel just as the sun was going down and the evening sky turned violet. I felt a sudden pang at the thought of tomorrow's departure, and realised how fond of Egypt I had become. As with Saiyid, the difficulties of the country had all been on the surface, like the hassles with the baksheesh seekers, annoying but never really menacing. I had found it essentially a gentle country where I had been treated with much courtesy and friendliness. I thought of the eighty-year-old Sheikh Ali shuffling through the gardens of his no-star hotel by the necropolis of ancient Thebes. When I left he had pressed a few strings of cheap beads into my hands and said 'Good you, you are nice missus. I love you. I love you like my mother.'

CHAPTER EIGHT

Beyond the First Cataract

Most of the deck space of the Wadi Halfa steamer was reserved for prayers. Only the men prayed, standing in a line shoulder to shoulder on the mats spread out specially for them, their shoes and sandals placed neatly around the edges. They went through the prescribed Moslem ritual making the deep obeisances, foreheads touching the ground while trying not to look at the distracting sight of young Western men and women lounging about the periphery in scanty clothing. The bikinis and bare torsos were not unsuitable for the weather, which was growing noticeably hotter by the hour, but were insensitive in this part of the world, where people consider bare flesh to be immoral and even the men keep their legs covered. There were about thirty of these sun-worshipping whites, mostly fairly young Britons and Australians on a bus tour through Africa. I had seen their vehicle, looking rather like a moon buggy, with its wide smooth tyres. It was lashed onto a barge steaming up the lake ahead of us, and I think that it may have sunk somewhere in the middle because although I spent three days in Wadi Halfa, it had still not arrived when I left. By then the passengers were becoming extremely irritated with one another as well as with the local people.

There were five other independent Western travellers. Two, like me, were travelling alone – a middle-aged German called Heinz, who was making for the game parks of Kenya, and a younger German, Andy, who was travelling where the fancy took him. Three young Americans – Mark, Tom and Judy were going overland at great speed to visit the young men's parents, who were missionaries in Uganda. The six of us had gravitated together at the dockside and were attempting to disassociate ourselves from the half naked bus people, who seemed keen for us to swell their ranks. There was little space to manoeuvre, however, as the ancient craft was filled to bursting point with returning Sudanese and their mountains of baggage.

Conditions below decks were grim. Every inch of space was

occupied and I feared for the safety of the bicycle which had been placed by the helpful ticket clerk in a bay against the exit doors, and was now being used by some large Sudanese ladies and their children as a leaning post. The hot airless saloons, with their walls and upholstery worn to an overall brown colour and wreathed in tobacco fumes, were a bewildering tangle of bodies camping on and around the seats. Within hours the decks were littered with all manner of things squelching and crunching underfoot as one slowly wormed a way through the crowds. There was far too great a crush for the ground to be visible; if something was dropped it was lost forever. To enter the lavatories required a considerable effort of will, or a really pressing need. When Judy and I finally overcame our reluctance to go into the place clearly marked LADIES a squatting man was occupying it. We complained of this to a passing crew member who rushed in and dragged the offending person out with his robes still hitched up about his middle.

All in all, the small area of the deck not used for prayer was the only place to be, and we laid out our sleeping bags and mats to stake our claim to it, hoping that the black looks directed at the bare limbs of the bus folk would not result in us all being sent below.

At some point in the night we crossed the Tropic of Capricorn, which has moved slightly south since the second century BC, when Eratosthenes of the Alexandrian School, observing that the sun's rays dropped perpendicularly into a well at Aswan exactly at midday on the summer solstice deduced that the earth was round. He also worked out the earth's diameter and was correct to within fifty miles. I thought about this brilliant piece of deduction as I lay in my sleeping bag on the metal deck, one of a line of shrouded shapes laid out as neatly as a display of mummies in the British Museum and stared up at the velvety darkness and the undimmed brilliance of the stars. The invisible barrier marked the final parting from Egypt, and the severing of the last link with the Mediterranean world. Maybe I only imagined a different feel in the air, but the constellations had certainly become strange and disorientating, denizens of unfamiliar skies. Everything seemed in the wrong place. The Plough, which is never absent from the night skies of Britain, was invisible somewhere below the northern horizon, whereas Orion, usually a low-profile presence, was almost overhead. Constellations I had never seen before crowded the southern hemisphere and I fell asleep trying to put a name to some of them.

The second day was harder as the desire for soap and water and clean clothes increased, and the thought of sitting in a chair rather than reclining on metal decks began to seem like a luxury. Hunger finally drove us to exchange our issued vouchers for food slopped out into bowls that had first to be collected from people who had finished their meal. It was not easy to tell what one was eating. Beans seemed rather better than the amorphous chunks of gristly meat, but there wasn't really a choice; people just took what was ladled out. We independent travellers had brought our own supplies of drinking water; the bus folk hadn't and drank what was available, with the result that many of them had upset stomachs. I gave up even thinking about going to the boat's lavatories. The Sudanese seemed to be sticking to Coca Cola and tea, using water only for their ritual ablutions before prayers.

There was little to see beyond the confines of the boat – just the flat expanse of the lake, a far away line of desert hills on the western side and an occasional bird passing overhead. It did not seem like a natural stretch of water, perhaps because of a distant glimpse of the re-sited Abu Simbel, and the knowledge of all the drowned places passing beneath the hull. It was a strange and unmomentous voyage, like being suspended in a vacuum with nothing to mark the passage of time. I decided that I was not cruise material.

The worst time came when we docked and I went below to protect the bicycle – which was very necessary as I do not think it would have survived intact in front of the exit. A few officials came aboard and after that the doors were closed again and stayed closed for several hours while the pressure of bodies built up behind, all steadily pushing forward. The temperature climbed, the smell of unwashed flesh intensified and the Agala and I became ever more closely emmeshed. Several women began to look as ill as I was feeling and one appeared to faint, though the crowd was too dense for anyone actually to fall. This distress appeared to cause amusement rather than concern among the other passengers, with several young girls dissolving into fits of giggles. Later I decided this was just a sort of nervous reaction, but at the time I began to wonder if I was going to like Sudan. Fortunately before the crush completely welded me into the bicycle frame, some members of the crew forced the crowd back and got the doors open, and we were able at last to go ashore.

The lovely feeling of liberation at getting away from the confines of the ship and all those bodies made the desolate shore seem like a sort of paradise and after the limited palette of the reservoir the first ten minutes were a feast of visual impressions – egrets wading at the waters edge, dazzlingly white against the green weed, the textures of sand and stone and feather. Then I began to think about more mundane things like food, shelter and a bath, and I climbed onto the bicycle and set off on the five-mile trek into the town of Wadi Halfa. An hour later I was still trekking and beginning to realise the enormity of what I had taken on. Specially designed to cope with all terrains though it was, the laden bicycle was sinking up to its axles in the soft sand, and I found myself pushing it more often than riding. Even pushing took tremendous effort and I was soon soaked with sweat. To make matters worse there was a bewildering choice of routes, with hundreds of tyre tracks criss-crossing the sandy waste. I'd follow what I thought was the predominant one only to have it peter out in a confused series of deep trenches where a vehicle had obviously got stuck and had had to be dug out.

When I did reach Wadi Halfa it was still not clear where I should make for. Low dun-coloured buildings were scattered about over a very wide area of brown sandy waste, without any coherent plan or pattern. It looked a most depressing and forsaken place, and for want of anyone to direct me I headed laboriously towards a jumble of railway lines. After a while a young man wearing a heavy tweed coat came up and asked me if I wanted to change money. He was an amiable youth called Matara, suffering from the cold in Sudan's only winter month, which produced temperatures of about 80° F. He had nothing much to do and when I told him I was looking for a hotel he escorted me for miles over the unlovely sand of Wadi Halfa. The best hotel – a cluster of little concrete cells and cubicles built around small dusty courtyards, planted with a few dry-looking plants – was perfectly acceptable but alas it was full. Then on to the second best hotel, which was of similar construction but with no plants and slightly less clean; it too was full. The third and final hotel showed just how desirable the first two had been, not that the management needed to worry, as they too had no vacant room. I began to wonder if I was being discriminated against as an unaccompanied female, until Matara explained the problems of Wadi Halfa to me.

The old Wadi Halfa was deep under water, together with its surrounding arable fields and date palms. This new place had no reason for existence other than being at the head of the railway and the nearest point to the drowned town. Most of the inhabitants of old Wadi Halfa had been resettled far away up the Atbara River but a handful had stayed in this desolate sandy waste, brooding on their loss. 'We could have any land for resettle; anywhere they would give us, but we love this place, this our grandfather land.' said Matara.

Actually his own people were comparative newcomers, he told me, the result of an Hungarian soldier deserting from the Turkish Army and hiding in this obscure corner of the old Turkish empire. He claimed there was a settlement of blue-eyed people known as the Hungarian village, but when I visited it later, I found only brown eyes.

General Kitchener built the railway from here to Khartoum in order to reconquer the country after the Mahdi had defeated General Gordon in 1884. The same antique line is still operating today with the same rolling stock. It is scheduled to meet the boat from Egypt and the suq lorries which cross the desert with passengers and goods from the scattered villages. In practice it is always breaking down, and nothing connects with anything and people simply accumulate in Wadi Halfa waiting for transport out. The Sudanese wait with the quiet patience of resignation, while the Europeans fume and fret in the belief that they can influence events.

Even to talk of something as technical as a railway in relation to the Sudan is to give a false notion of modernity. Sudan is the largest country in Africa, over a million square miles, and it is still mostly uncharted desert. There are no roads except for ones recently built in the east to link Port Sudan on the Red Sea with Khartoum, and a few miles of rough tarmac around an irrigated area to the south of the capital. The Nile has four more cataracts before Khartoum, which, together with innumerable shoals and sandbanks, prevent the river from being the highway it is in Egypt. Ten years of bitter fighting between the Moslem north and Christian south has reduced the country even nearer to the state it was in the 1870s, when its only link with the outside world was by camel caravan. Arriving in Wadi Halfa I could see what an ancient Moslem sage was getting at when he wrote 'God made the Sudan and then He laughed!'

There were several hundred people already camping among their goods in the sand alongside the railway lines. Their numbers were further swelled by my fellow boat passengers, now arriving in a fleet of Japanese pick-up trucks. Matara suggested we should go to the police station and get permission to use the 'special railway room' reserved for Europeans in such emergencies. On the way we joined up with my friends from the boat – all except Heinz, who cunningly hung about the best hotel until someone courteously moved out to make room for him. The bus people were waiting down at the jetty for their bus, so we started off on a positive note as adequately dressed Westerners. The police station was a small mud brick hut with a prisoner incarcerated in a flimsy cell begging for cigarettes. I gathered he was in on a charge of drinking alcohol, a serious crime in the Sudan where Moslem Sharia law, reintroduced only recently, had resulted in a horrid spate of amputated hands and feet for quite trivial offences.

The special room turned out to be the station platform, a noisome spot which even the camping Sudanese disdained. We had just decided to bivouac somewhere in the desert when Matara offered us the use of his 'hotel'. This was one of a ragged line of rickety hovels which formed part of the suq of Wadi Halfa. About eight foot square, it was built out of discarded pieces of railway sleeper, cardboard and sacking, with plenty of spaces for fresh air and light to pour through – very like the sort of den small boys knock together. One day Matara was going to turn it into a real 'hotel' selling tea like all the surrounding shacks, but in the meantime we were welcome to use it, and he would even spread some matting over the bare floor.

This shack became our centre for the next three days, though Judy and I were fortunate enough to obtain a bed in the best hotel the following day. After all this rough living, the cold-water showers in the bare concrete cubicles seemed the greatest height of luxury. The real joy, however, was flush toilets, the only ones I think in all that scattered town. I am not squeamish about such things, and I don't at all object to a reasonably clean hole in the floor type, or to a trek to the great outdoors. But no matter how far out into the desert one went in Wadi Halfa, there were always others carrying the distinctive and rather elegant metal water pots with long curved spouts which were used instead of toilet paper. The wide open spaces around Wadi Halfa were simply one huge open air lavatory. The only way to think of it, I decided was that the sand and the hot sun dessicated everything hygenically, unlike wet British parks full of the immoderate droppings of large overfed dogs.

I had no wish to linger in Wadi Halfa; it was bureaucracy once again that kept me there, and the difficulty of finding the way out. Some cyclists have simply followed the railway line, painfully bumping over the sleepers, seeing nothing at all but lifeless desert and relying for water on the maintenance stations along the way. This was not for me; I wasn't looking for a testing-ground. I wanted to follow the Nile and see the people who lived beside it, and have as pleasant a time as possible on the way. The problem was that the route didn't actually lie alongside the Nile but cut off through trackless sandy wastes, coming back to the river here and there. The first section known as the 'Belly of Rocks', is a notoriously difficult area that has undone many armies, including the British forces on their way to relieve General Gordon at Khartoum. Difficulties aside, I couldn't even find the beginning of this route out of Wadi Halfa, and I was reluctant to simply set out through the soft sand in a southerly direction hoping I would come across tracks somewhere.

All this worry about tracks was purely academic anyway as the district commissioner wouldn't even hear of me leaving Wadi Halfa by bicycle. I had to see him in order to get my travel permit and photographic pass – not an easy feat as breakfast comes mid morning in the Sudan, which means that offices are open only for very brief periods between meal breaks. The D.C. sat in his prefabricated office hung about with photographs of Old Wadi Halfa, and told me that wolves and jackals teemed in the arid wastes, just waiting to devour bicyclists. It was useless to argue that if there were such animals there they would probably be more shy of me than I of them. I wasn't altogether convinced of his grip on reality anyway, as he also told me that the war in the south was coming to an end and I would be able to bicycle safely all the way through to Uganda. The last I had heard the

SPLA were on the offensive and travel south of Khartoum was forbidden. The D.C. had his own ideas about this: 'At first we don't want to fight them, they are our brothers. But they hurt the people, shoot at aeroplanes. Women and children they kill. We have to stop them' – and here his eyes widened dramatically and he looked fierce and proud. 'Now we decide this thing, it is done. Rebels are forced back in the bush, trouble is no more there.'

The important thing was to get out of Wadi Halfa however I could, and then review the situation. I consulted various people in the suq and hoped I had fixed a ride out on a lorry. Mark and Judy arranged to come on it too, in order to see a little more of the country before flying out of Khartoum to Uganda. Tom, Andy and Heinz were going on the train when it came. The scantily-clad bus people continued to camp by the lakeside, waiting hopelessly for their missing transport.

Hanging about the hovels of the suq drinking glass after glass of tea was the order of things. The air was full of rumour, and nobody dared rely on anything. We took it in turns to keep an eye on the lorry and to find out the latest news of the train, which had apparently broken down several times and been derailed once. There was a false alarm when a train did come in with a great shrieking and whistling in the middle of the night but it was only a relief train sent up from Atbara and everything had still to wait on the Khartoum train, already three days overdue. In the meantime I was arrested for taking photographs and producing my newly-acquired photographer's pass had little effect. I was marched off, thinking I was about to join the alcohol drinker in his cell. Instead I was asked a lot of irrelevant questions and then released with vague mutterings about the inadvisability of taking photographs. Outside the station a man was waiting for me who whispered in my ear 'Sudan bad country, but you not worry, I am secret policeman.' The established order, I felt, was breaking up around me.

The train arrived on the fourth day and within minutes it was filled to bursting-point and the roofs were covered with a solid carpet of humanity. Our lorry had gone to meet it and came back loaded to the top of its very high rails with sacks of bullet-hard, dried dates. The bicycle was tied to the tailgate and Judy, Mark and I were told to climb up on top of the load, where we fought silently for sitting space with twenty-six bony Sudanese, all using elbows, hands and feet indiscriminately to secure their position. Five Sudanese women shared the cab with the driver and his mate: how this was achieved I cannot imagine, since I only saw them coming in and out when we stopped.

We moved off as soon as darkness fell, three lorries travelling in convoy in order to help one another at need. One of the men told us that the drivers always preferred to travel this section at night, as the details of the sand showed up better in the headlights. The lorries were all old high-wheeled Bedford ten-tonners with bald tyres, which made splendid desert vehicles. Their sides were built up so as to take the maximum possible loads and they were so top-heavy, it was a miracle to me that they didn't turn over. Their drivers were very skilful at maintaining them and at finding the firmest ground through the atrocious terrain, a matter of making endless split-second decisions about which tyre track to choose among many, in sand which was continually drifting and changing. The important thing was to keep moving forward; stopping normally meant a laborious digging out, and all vehicles in Sudan carried spades and mats as well as supplies of water.

Almost immediately outside Wadi Halfa the landscape changed dramatically. Hills rose up darkly against the starry sky and mysterious dips and hollows opened up in front of the headlamp beams. The lorry lurched over at alarming angles, first one way then another, threatening to dislodge us from our precarious perches. It grew colder and colder and we three huddled together under Judy's sleeping bag, which was the only one we could get at. Some of the men had bare feet, and many were only in thin shirts or light cotton gowns. They too tried to cuddle up close and get their feet under the bag. You couldn't blame them, but Judy was none too keen as she had no way of washing the bag, and planned to use it for some months. Apart from this, everyone was polite and friendly, passing around dates and nuts and other comforts. The excruciating pain of soft flesh being ground unrelentingly against the unyielding sacks vied with the cramps that afflicted my leg muscles and yet the savage beauty of the night scene was a compensation that I wouldn't have missed.

We stopped twice during the night, once at a 'station' which was simply a lean-to hovel, quite alone in the wilderness, half-open to the bitter air and housing a sheep and a goat as well as two men. The men roused themselves to make tea, boiling the water over a few twigs of thornwood. The second time we stopped, we were too stiff to climb down and stayed where we were. Someone kindly brought tea to us and then everyone vanished into the surrounding desert for a few hours sleep, while we shivered on top of the load. I suppose we slept a little too, because suddenly it was early morning and the stars were fading.

When the lorry finally emerged from the 'Belly of Rocks' and the Nile came into view once more, we were about sixty miles up river in a sparsely inhabited countryside of narrow sandy fields and stands of date palms, with small hamlets every few miles and the desert pressing in all around. I felt I had never seen anything so vulnerable as these small pockets of life cut off so completely from the rest of civilisation. Only the small communities on tiny specks of islands like St Kilda and North Rona, far off the north west coast of Scotland had achieved this degree of isolation and it was some time since life had been supported there. Suddenly I felt very happy to be where I was; the irritations of Wadi Halfa were all forgotten, and I knew I was going to enjoy the Sudan.

After a nourishing bean stew at the village cafe I felt full of energy and eager to get under way. The bicycle seemed to have travelled well and lost nothing more than some of its paint. It had been unrecognisable when we untied it from the tailgate, completely disguised under a thick layer of bright red dust. I cleaned it off as best I could, hoping that not too much had found its way into vulnerable bearings – in fact it had, but I was not to discover this for a long time yet. I then set about preparing the day's supply of water. Since reaching Wadi Halfa, this had been a necessary daily chore, as there was no longer any water which could be relied upon. All the water came straight from the Nile, a thick dark substance that was particularly rich in foreign bodies, especially gardia and bilharzia. Every drop I needed to use for drinking, cleaning my teeth or washing my pots had first to be passed through a special pump to remove these perilous substances. This pump was an ingenious Swiss invention and worked by micro filtration through a solid ceramic core. The only drawback was that where the water was as full of solid matter as this, it was tremendously hard work to force it through. The surface of the core would quickly clog and I would have to dismantle it, clean it and reassemble it maybe thirty times in order to filter half a gallon. The day's minimum requirement was a gallon and a half, so preparing water was a long and laborious process. The fact that I came back free of foreign microbes bore testimony both to the pump's efficacy and to my perseverance.

With all the water aboard the Agala was ominously laden down and I could no longer lift it. I said goodbye to Mark and Judy thinking they would pass me that day or the next when they had found another lorry to take them on to Khartoum. If the bicycle proved impossible to ride they would get the lorry to pick me up. I did not realise then that there were so many different tracks through the desert that it was as unlikely that I would see them again as for two small ships to bump into each other in the Atlantic.

To my delight I found that the sand seemed able to support the wheels for most of the time, once I had got the technique of keeping on moving no matter what. The terrain varied between stone, gravel, dust, sand that was like porridge to cycle through and sand that was as soft as talcum powder and impossible for anything. Riding required concentration and a lot of physical effort. When I hit a patch of the soft sand it was all I could do to haul the Agala through on foot, but fortunately such sections were infrequent. I was feeling well rested after my days of comparative inactivity, and happy to be moving along under my own steam in the right direction. The best thing was the weather which was still a mild 80° F; another month and it would start to climb to way beyond the 120° F mark, when such physical effort would be impossible.

I was following indistinct tyre marks in the sand that gave me the illusion of being on some sort of highway, but in fact from the moment I had left the little hamlet where the lorry had set me down I had seen no one, nor anything but sand. I stopped for a rest after a few hours, and all around there was nothing at all but rough stony desert, while at my feet a black armour-plated beetle scuttled away towards a low, bare bush covered with vicious spikes.

CHAPTER NINE

Getting Through to Dongola

I had now arrived at the point in the journey where all the equipment I had transported through Egypt would at last come into its own. The tent hadn't yet been out of its bag, and I was looking forward to sleeping in it for the first time. It was a very small tunnel-shaped tent with a lot of mosquito netting for coolness. Its hooped design would make it easy to pitch in sand, and its yellow colour would render it inconspicuous. The stove was also unused. I had chosen to bring a model that ran on petrol, which I thought would be the most easily obtainable fuel anywhere. In fact Sudan's limited transport operated largely on diesel and petrol was like gold dust, so it was as well that I had a reasonable supply with me.

My basic diet was to be dehydrated packet meals, mostly from Scandinavia, with solid sounding names like 'Beef Balls with Noodles' 'Stewed Meats with Rice' 'Macaronies with Sauce'. They did not claim like many restaurant dishes, to be 'lovingly sautéed in a marinade of exotic spices and gently grilled over charcoal to impart a subtle flavour, before being flambéed to a final perfection in luxurious armagnac'. I found that packet meals had one distinct advantage over such expensive titillations, namely that there was no possibility of getting them down at all unless I was absolutely ravenous. They therefore save greatly on weight, and were ideal for me, even if I did at times envy Victorian travellers like Sam Baker their Fortnum and Mason hampers borne on the heads of long lines of porters. With my Earl Grey tea bags, self-inflating mattress, slow-burning candle and other bits and pieces of travelling domesticity, I should be comfortable enough and I was looking forward to my first night of self-reliance under desert skies.

The first intimation that this cosily romantic picture was not going to become a reality occurred when I reached the next little hamlet by the Nile. Seeing me struggling with the Agala in the soft sand, two men came running from the fields to help me. They had no English and apart from the lovely greeting of 'Salaam Aleikum' – 'I greet you in the name of God' – my knowledge of Arabic had not advanced beyond simple nouns and two word utterances like 'Hinna Wayne?' 'Where is here?' But although these conversational gambits were soon exchanged and I learnt that 'here' was somewhere not shown on the map, the two men did not leave me until they had escorted me to a house where a frail-looking woman was tending a fire on the bare floor in a roofed-over corner of the courtyard. They indicated that I should sit down while the woman made me a drink, and then departed with friendly waves back to their fields.

The woman and I crouched on either side of the fire and smiled shyly at each other while she boiled water in a can, blowing on the handful of twigs to produce a flame. A pinch of tea was stirred into the boiling water and several spoonfuls of sugar added. The contents were then left to settle for a while before being carefully poured into a glass. While I was drinking this she was busy opening what I was sure was a carefully hoarded tin of sardines and mashing it up with some chopped onions. I was served this with some wafer-thin unleavened bread, and every time I paused she urged me to take some more. It felt uncomfortable to be eating the food of people who were clearly very poor by Western standards, knowing that there was no way I could recompense them, since to offer money would be the deepest insult. I carried a few pens and postcards of texts from illuminated manuscripts of the Koran, but these were very small tokens in comparison with such unbounded generosity.

It wasn't easy to leave. The woman wanted me to stay and sleep there, and she remembered a few English words she had learnt at school, telling me she was a new wife and had no children; but it was only three o'clock and I wanted to get some more miles behind me before nightfall. After that the villages were closer together and at each one I rode through the people came out smiling and calling to me to stop. I didn't dare do so or I would have made no progress at all and I developed the ploy of saying 'Dongola' as I returned their greetings and waved and rode on – I thought Dongola was the next town, but in fact it was about a week's ride away. No wonder the people looked puzzled as I brightly answered 'Dongola' to their shouted queries of where was I bound.

The villages varied little. There would usually be two lines of square, high-walled detached dwellings facing each other across a strip of soft sand, well clear of the precious arable fields. There were no windows in the walls, but only a pair of double metal doors painted in a decorative geometric pattern; the walls themselves were also painted sometimes, in watery shades of eau-de-nil, pink or blue but more often they were left sand-coloured. There were no gardens or fences, and they seemed more like small fortresses than houses. Infants playing in the sand before the doors screamed with terror when they caught sight of my white skin, and bolted away inside, howling.

A little before sunset, just as I had decided to set up camp, I rode through another village on the Nile's edge and shouted my usual 'Dongola', but the inhabitants who were sitting resting in front of their houses after the day's work, sent an English-speaking boy after me on a bicycle, who told me that it would be dark in half an hour and I had no choice but to come back and spend the night with them. It was very nice to be so much wanted and for the next hour or so I sat on a bentwood chair in the middle of the village street, drinking tea and answering the men's questions with the boy translating, while the shadows grew longer and longer until the sun was almost down – at which point it suddenly got so cold that everyone took up his chair and departed, and I was taken in through the decorated gates that the Agala had been wheeled through an hour before.

I don't know what they made of me. I think they thought I was a member of a third sex. The sleeping arrangements of the household were rearranged so that I had a room to myself – clearly the best room in the house with a garish modern rug hanging on one wall like a tapestry, showing a mountain scene done in fluorescent wools. There were two heavily shuttered windows looking in towards the courtyard and the sky was faintly visible through the flat roof of papyrus stems. A bed had been brought in from somewhere and the Agala had been placed carefully against one mud-plastered wall, like another honoured guest. I ate with the men in a more modern room with metal beds, head to foot all around the edge, the men reclining upon them on one elbow like Romans at a banquet. Above the beds, the room was swathed in tinsel streamers as though Christmas was being celebrated. I didn't learn the significance of this, nor did I get to see the women or their quarters, which opened off another part of the courtyard. All the bringing in and taking out of the dinner dishes – foul, boiled eggs and rolled up pieces of the wafer-thin flaky bread – was done by a young boy, and as soon as the meal was finished the men lay down full-length on their beds, which I decided was the cue for me to retire. I was given a hurricane lamp to light me to my room and the only thing I lacked was somewhere to wash. I never solved this daily problem in these parts: I think they probably wash themselves in the shallows of the Nile, which I certainly wouldn't have risked, because of the bilharzia and gardia. I made do, as I had to on many subsequent nights, with a rub over by flannel, using some of my laboriously purified water.

When I awoke next morning and began to get my things together I found a little old lady hovering outside with hot tea and biscuits. She pressed my hands between hers when I left and recited something which sounded like a blessing. I couldn't say goodbye to the men for although it was only just seven o'clock they were already hard at work in the fields. By ten o'clock the mid-morning breakfast was under way and as soon as I reached a village I was also made to stop and eat. This hospitality became the pattern of my days until I reached Dongola. Never once did I use the tent, and only rarely did I cook a dehydrated packet meal or brew up tea and whoever was entertaining me tried to make me feel that it was I who was doing them the honour.

The riding continued to be very hard, and I could seldom do more than twenty to twenty-five miles a day. The Nile, always somewhere to my right, was usually out of sight because cliffs and sand drifts forced travellers always to move inland. It was only where pockets of cultivation occurred that the route dropped back down to the river once more, and the sudden sight of it as I came round some stony outcrop and saw it far away below me, flowing through the dead land in a broad silver flood, seemed miraculous. I often felt I could have sat there for days just watching it flow past. The small settlements by the Nile's edge were also a moving sight, they looked so vulnerable in that savage landscape, with the dark green palm trees and the brighter green of new crops startling against the dry monochrome wilderness. Around these hamlets was always the sound of slow dull thuds, like heartbeats hanging on the air: they came from old Lister single-cylinder diesel pumps, still irrigating the fields after fifty years of service.

A few hundred yards away, and out of sight of the Nile, was a completely different, alien world, in which the dangers of getting lost and wandering around in circles were very real, particularly when exhaustion set in and the mind began to play tricks. Nowhere was there the smallest patch of shade. The sun was a constant menacing presence, drawing out the moisture from living tissue, so it was essential to keep covered up as far as possible – I was thankful that I had repossessed my sun-hat. Perspiration constantly ran down my face into my eyes, and where it dried it left a layer of salt behind to irritate the skin, and rot my clothing. My lips quickly became cracked unless I frequently applied special cream, as did the lining of my nostrils. Dark glasses were essential to protect my eyes from the glare of the sun on the sand. I had a fright one day when I found that the plastic side pieces had melted when a bottle of insect repellent had come undone in the handlebar bag. It had also damaged my flash unit and my torch lens and had reduced several pens to a sticky goo. After that I made sure the repellent was kept in an outside pocket on its own: but if it could dissolve plastic I wondered what it did to skin! The dark glasses had a rugged gnawed appearance but were fortunately still wearable. My only shoes were cycling ones with stiff soles to distribute the pedal pressure and perforated leather uppers to help keep my feet cool. They did their job excellently and lasted the whole journey, but I suffered badly with them in the desert as they kept filling with hot sand whenever I had to walk and haul the Agala through the soft places.

Having the sun directly overhead, or very nearly so, meant that direction was not so obvious as it is further north. I normally knew where south was, but I kept my compass pinned to my shirt just to check from time to time. Haboobs were a constant threat – blinding sandstorms that could descend without warning, blotting out everything in a choking cloud that could last all day. Not to have a compass to hand at such times was to court disaster. Even without an haboob, dust was a constant irritation, coating everything, and getting under my eyelids and into my nose – I must have swallowed pounds of it. Water became the most precious substance in the world and my waking fantasies were mostly about swimming in cold Scottish rivers, or lying in still deep pools under waterfalls. My daily quota of a gallon and a half of drinking water was adequate but not bountiful. I allowed myself a small drink every half hour by the watch and sometimes, when conditions seemed hard, I kept going by concentrating on the next issue of lukewarm liquid. Tea was a luxury I reserved for particularly bad days when I felt I needed cossetting; someone in Wadi Halfa had given me a handful of tiny limes, rock-hard and juiceless, but I added them to the Earl Grey tea bags and the result tasted wonderful.

For all its menace the desert was exciting and not without a certain austere beauty. Once, long ago, it had been a well-wooded, fertile place, the habitat of pastoral nomads and wild animals; now it was inimical to all forms of life except scorpions and the hardier insects. Yet each morning I set off eager to see more of it. It challenged something in me, something perhaps that I needed to wrestle with, and at the same time it gave a tremendous sense of peace and freedom. I could see why the holy men of so many religions had worked out their spirituality in such places. It wasn't just the absence of distractions, it was the absolute sense of reality, the coming up against the bare bones of life, that was the attraction; a feeling that if God was anywhere, He was here.

A little before sunset one evening I came down to the Nile, thinking how lovely it would be to camp alone beside it. For once I felt disinclined for human company and the struggle of trying to communicate. I had seen no one all day and was reluctant to let go the stillness of the desert. Only the need to replenish my water supply had prevented me pitching the tent out in the sands. As soon as I came in sight of the low, fortress-like houses, all blank-walled and inward-facing, I turned down a small path through the outlying fields, hoping to escape detection. It was a futile hope; I was spotted immediately and greeted in the usual friendly manner by some young men who were just finishing planting out beans. I said I wanted to camp by the river and one of them, Achmed, who had learnt English at school, thought that I was asking where I was and started to tell me about somewhere called Sulb on the other side of the river. It suddenly dawned on me that he was talking about the ancient temple of Soleb from where two peerless stone lions had been taken, which are among the greatest treasures of the British Museum. I had always loved these lions even when I hadn't cared for other Egyptian statuary, and I was very excited by being told that the temple they came from was just across the water, until I realised I had no way of getting across the river to it.

'You wish to go there?' asked Achmed. 'Tajil and I will take you now' – and in no time I was aboard a craft which looked as though it had been dug out of one of the pyramid boat pits. It was built of massive, roughly-hewn timbers and had a high square house amid-ships. The mast was immensely tall, and since there was a strong wind blowing, the gaff was unwound only enough to expose a small fraction of a ragged patchwork sail. Once again things had turned out not as I had planned, but infinitely better.

The sun was low as we glided across the mile-wide river, steering an erratic course to avoid sandbanks and shallows. There were few places where a boat could put in, and on the other side we had a two-mile walk through crops and date palms, and came to the temple only ten minutes before the sun set. It was all in violet shadow, with a rim of bright red around the roofless entrances where the sun flared briefly before disappearing. Very little remained – a few columns and inscribed walls standing on a mound in a field of fallen stone. Even so, in its remoteness it made as great an impact as any of the ruins I had seen in Egypt. Amenophis the Third had built the temple about 1420 BC, when Egypt was at the zenith of its power and spreading its influence far into Asia and Africa. The pharaoh was worshipped here as the manifestation of the god Amun, Lord of Thebes, and the ruins indicate how much more widely populated this wilderness was at that time. Near the bottom of a broken flight of steps lay a few fragments of a stone lion; it was still recognisably a companion piece of the two perfect ones in London, and finding it there felt like a link with home.

Sailing back to the east bank after this late temple visiting was my most lasting impression of the Nile in Sudan, and even at the time it seemed almost impossibly idyllic and unreal. The surface of the river was dappled with silver and shadow and riffled up in small waves among the beds of reeds around the islets. The reeds rustled like whispers in the wind, answered by the small watery splashes that the hull made moving through the water and the creaks of the gear shifting overhead as the great sail dipped. Achmed leaning on the long curved archaic tiller was like a figure from legend, with Tajil crouched silent and watchful at his feet. The boat sailed down a broad swathe of moonlight towards the far shore – a black edge with the stiff sharply-cut shapes of palm fronds against the stars. It was difficult to believe I was in the same harsh dry land that I'd been labouring through only a few hours before.

I slept that night in a small room in Achmed's house where someone had already put the Agala. We were way past normal eating hours and I was given a handful of dried dates to sustain me. I was so tired with the walk coming after the long day's struggle with the desert that I slept for eight and a half hours instead of my usual five or six. Before I left I gave Achmed my spare miniature compass, for I felt I had to mark such a memorable evening in the most appropriate way I could.

When I reached the very small town of Delgo a few days later, it seemed enormous after the villages. It had a hospital and people came to it from miles around, which was unsettling for the local populace, or so it was explained to me by the young district commissioner who plucked me from the middle of a group of unruly children who wouldn't let me pass. He put the Agala into his Toyota pick-up and took me off to spend the night at the hospital with his friend Ibrahim, who was the only doctor. Ibrahim had trained in Romania and was very unhappy about the conditions in his hospital; he had no oxygen, no refrigerator and electricity for only three hours a day. The buildings were old and dilapidated and far from clean. He confirmed that gardia and bilharzia were endemic in the area and said it was almost useless treating them when the root cause, dirt, was left untackled. There were only two patients in the wards – a child with bronchitis whose mother was told off by Ibrahim for cooking her dinner beside the child's bed instead of outside in the courtyard, and a new-born baby who had been born with its umbilicus around its neck but was doing well. Mother and baby were curled up together on a dirty striped mattress, the mother looking radiantly happy.

It was here I began to see the subtle distinctions of Sudanese men's dress; to show me round the hospital Ibrahim changed into Western shirt and trousers, which apparently conferred an enhanced status, and on his return he changed back into his cotton gellabiyah which he found cooler and more comfortable. Although I did manage to get a fairly reasonable wash in his house, nonetheless it was rather a squalid place with hardly any furniture other than a couple of beds and a few hard chairs. Ibrahim had been born and brought up in Khartoum and felt out of place in this primitive backwater. His enthusiasm for medicine had atrophied, and he no longer even cared about his own health and drank the torpid local water without treating it, though when he first came there he had been frightened to do so. His hopelessness was depressing, and I felt I had walked into something I would rather not have known about. Later the commissioner returned with a couple of schoolteachers, and they played cards far into the night. Before I retired and left them to it, I was introduced to one of the fruits of prohibition, a fierce home-brewed spirit, colourless like arak. One sip was enough for me – I decided it was lethal. I was to find this illicit liquor everywhere in the Sudan, and with nothing else available I grew quite to like it as it relaxed tired muscles wonderfully, though it always needed to be treated with extreme caution.

The following morning I got up at dawn and leaving a thank-you letter for Ibrahim I departed before there was anyone about, and rode for four hours until I came to the first village. It was a very poor place, but some old men said I must stop and eat some bread and date syrup, and they apologised that they had so little to offer. In every village I had found people who knew English. In theory all children attended school and were taught the subject. Sudan even recruited two hundred graduates a year from Britain for the purpose, though this also meant that Sudanese teachers could be released to teach in Saudi Arabia for considerably higher wages than those paid to the young British teachers. This emphasis on the English language meant that my lack of Arabic was less of a problem than it might have been. In this particular village, young people were home on holiday and able to translate and the men sat around me while I ate and told me how the old ways were changing, and how the young people were not eager to work on the land, which was a good life and full of peace, but wanted to ride in motorcars and rush away to the cities.

It was when I was entertained by women, however, as I was in the small town of Kerma that I noticed the greatest difference between the generations. I was taken home by a young primary school teacher called Aida, who lived with her husband, also a teacher, and his four younger brothers. Once the men had been fed and had gone off to play cards or dominoes with their friends, I was taken on a tour to meet Aida's friends. We passed in and out of a maze of houses and courtyards without once going into the street, as they were all linked together like a maze. Every so often we came to a room full of women and girls crowded together on beds and on the floor watching black and white television. It never ceased to seem totally incongruous – this highly technical piece of the twentieth century in mud brick Arab houses with no furniture other than beds and a few low stools. Where there was electricity, even for a few hours a day, television quickly followed. The twentieth century hadn't reached the kitchens to any great extent, however: everywhere women squatted on their heels on the floor, or on very low stools, blowing charcoal stoves into action. These stoves were mostly half-gallon oil drums punched full of holes, though sometimes there was a primus stove running on paraffin. I never saw a sink, though several people had a tap in their courtyards.

Meeting these women and girls was a real pleasure, and gave me some idea of the changes that were taking place in modern Sudan. The young women who were undergoing higher education seemed altogether surer of themselves than their gentler, more self-effacing mothers, though this may have been largely a question of language. They were eager to talk about the problems of Sudan, which they saw as being largely economic; even female circumcision was readily and openly discussed. It seems ironic that a country with such a scattered population and so few hospitals should subscribe to a practice that prevents women being able to give birth naturally at home. The custom goes back a long time, however, and is so deeply entrenched in the social pattern that an uncircumcised woman is considered socially inferior and thought to be undesirable to men; and although there is nothing to support it in the Koran, it has also assumed a strong religious significance. It is not something restricted to isolated pockets but affects at least 10 million women in Africa, and probably far more if the entire Moslem world is considered. Nowhere is female circumcision so sweepingly practised as in the Sudan, and although many agencies are trying to eradicate it, there is no evidence to suggest that they are succeeding. In fact, some recent surveys suggest that female circumcision might be on the increase as Moslem influence spreads southwards and social pressure is brought to bear upon new neighbours to conform to the practice.

Female circumcision takes place at around six years of age, and in its most extreme form all the girl's external genitalia are excised and the opening sewn up so tightly that only a tiny aperture is left. Apart from the obvious objections to this gross mutilation, there are distressing side-effects such as the retention of urine and a great risk of infections. Most importantly, though, the woman has to be cut open again each time she gives birth. There are less extreme forms of the operation, and many of these are performed in hospital on the grounds that since it is going to be performed anyway it is better that it should be carried out in hygienic surroundings with the use of some form of pain relief than be the work of a back-street practitioner, with the attendant risk and traumas.

None of the young women who discussed the practice with me condemned it out-of-hand or thought it barbaric. Their greatest concern seemed to be that it should be a matter of individual choice. Most said they wouldn't have it done to their own daughters if they could choose, but they thought the older women of the family would make them conform. The grandmothers together with the midwives, who carried out the operations as a matter of routine seemed the most responsible for perpetuating the practice. In fact, circumcision is the main source of income for the state-trained midwives. The curious anomaly is that female circumcision was officially banned by the Sudanese government as long ago as 1957.

I had already known about the circumcision practices of the Sudan before coming out, as there had been a lot of publicity about it recently, particularly in respect of the United Nations declaration on children's rights. What I was unprepared for was the level of acceptance among the younger, educated generation of Sudanese women. They were rather puzzled by some of our practices too, in particular not having to pay a dowry – a Sudanese bridegroom has to give between £3000 and £4000 to the bride's father, they told me, as well as supplying a house while the bride is responsible for the furniture. They were also very surprised that my husband had 'allowed' me to come on this journey on my own, and probably thought it was all in keeping with his not having had to pay a 'bride price' for me in the first place.

There was to be one more magnificent day of riding through the desert after Kerma. I went far inland on the advice of some people who entertained me to breakfast. The route cut off a great bend in the river and climbed up to a strange lunar-like plateau where jagged bare red hills rose up singly all around. There was one dead thorn tree in the middle like a surrealist painting. It seemed to be hung about with votive offerings, bits of paper and plastic mostly, and someone had lit a fire at its base and burnt a good deal of the trunk. Dead as it was it still exerted a tremendous attraction in the empty open plain and I stayed beside it for a while and brewed tea. Afterwards I rode on for hours over rock, which felt wonderfully firm under the wheels: it was like discovering the joy of bicycling anew after the days of exhausting progress through the endless miles of yielding sand.

CHAPTER TEN

Arrested in Dongola

Some miles before Dongola I came down to a wide flat plain where the sand became progressively deeper and softer until, after hours of exhausting pushing and heaving which gained me no more than a few hundred yards, I gave in and hailed a passing truck. The tough Japanese four-wheel-drive pick-ups – Toyotas, Mitsubishis and Isuzus – have cornered the market in this part of the world. Later on in the journey, when I drove one through another inordinately difficult terrain, I began to appreciate their merits. In the deserts of Sudan it was daunting to see how easily their large wheels and four-wheeled drive coped with the soft sand and dust that had completely halted my progress.

The truck that stopped for me was converted into a taxi, with curly wrought-iron stanchions supporting a roof of sorts to keep off the sun and a bench down either side. As many people as possible were squashed into it, together with the goods they were taking to Dongola market. Everyone cheerfully squeezed up even further and the Agala was pushed down the centre, where it was held upright by knees, sacks of vegetables, chickens, baskets of eggs and so forth. I was given a place on the end of one bench and two young men who had been dislodged perched precariously on the tailgate with their heads outside. It was not a comfortable journey as the truck slithered and bounced through the sand and the sharp parts of the bicycle dug into soft flesh. My fellow-passengers wanted to know what the various bits and pieces of the bicycle were for as none of them had seen anything like it, and they thought that it might be a motorbike. Trying to explain these technicalities to people with only a very little English while at the same time trying to prevent my head crashing against the roof of the cavorting truck was not easy.

There was a great bustle on the river bank where we were eased out of our cramped taxi and set down by the ferry, for many paths through the eastern desert converged here, and large numbers of people and vehicles were waiting to cross over to the regional centre of Dongola, on the other side of the river. A large wedding party arrived from somewhere by lorry, and all the young women hitched up their skirts and climbed down the steep sides, some singing, others ululating and one of them beating out a rhythm on a plastic jerry can. Like many of the people of northern Sudan they were remarkably attractive and also very varied in appearance, for the Sudanese are a mixture of races and their skin colour can be anything from a black so profound that it has a blueish tinge, right through every conceivable shade of black and brown to a sun-tanned beige. The Arab invaders of the seventh century had intermarried with the indigenous Nubians and earlier Ethiopian invaders, and as the dreadful slave trade with the interior of Africa was developed, Negro blood was also added in large quantities, for the Arab slave traders were in no way averse to sampling their merchandise. Unlike in India, where a skin is valued for its degree of whiteness, in Sudan there seemed to be not the slightest prejudice about colour one way or the other.

The women of the wedding party were dressed in bright shades of the ankle-length wrap-around gown which most women wore in these country places. Like an Indian sari, it gave them a classical draped appearance and was always accompanied by a long scarf called a tobe, which, as in India, the women wrap around themselves for modesty and with which they could cover their heads and faces when they wanted to disappear completely. These young women had no wish to hide themselves and were eager that everyone should join in their celebrations, including me. They drew the bride forward to show me the tracery of delicate patterns drawn in henna all over her hands, arms and feet and pointed out other details I shouldn't miss, like the large amount of gold jewellery and the pretty high-heeled golden sandles. Most of the other women had just the palms of their hands or their fingertips stained with henna, and also the soles of their feet. They drew me into their circle on the ferry and tried to teach me their songs and posed so that I could take pictures. When they climbed back into their lorry at the other side of the river they invited me to follow them, but I couldn't keep up for long, and there were far too many other novel sights to distract me from noticing which way their lorry eventually disappeared.

The town was not visible from where the ferry put in, so I followed everyone else along a rough track. On one side a man was ploughing a field with two large oxen – dark powerful animals straining eagerly forward and charging around each turning point at a great pace while the ploughman hung onto the handles, only just in control but looking as if he was full of pride and joy in his work. All the people were going to market with their produce, many of them crouched on donkeys and balancing very long poles which projected on either side with baskets and bundles of vegetables swinging from them; others walked with similar poles suspended from their shoulders: it all looked a little like a medieval woodcut, a slightly foreign scene from *Piers Plowman*.

Just before the town I came to a strip of tarmac, the first I had seen in 700 miles. It was fairly rough and potholed but it seemed the height of luxury, and I couldn't believe the smoothness and the lack of effort in riding on it. It only ran for a short way before degenerating into horrid sand again but while I rode on it I remembered some of the advantages of twentieth-century civilisation in a way that I had not when confronted by a lack of bathrooms and other amenities. I felt it linked me to my own world like the fragments of the stone lion at Soleb, so that for a moment, amid all the excitement of foreign travel, I felt a pang of homesickness.

Dongola itself wore a strangely displaced air. There was the usual corniche alongside the Nile, which was clearly the most prestigious road in town, with good stone buildings left over from British colonial days, and the luxurious tarmac surface. On the other side was a well-built parapet wall with elegant seats in front of it, but where, beyond the wall, the majestic Nile should have been flowing past, there was nothing but a wide, deep, dry ditch with a few allotments at the bottom. The river had deserted this particular channel, leaving the town with a few vegetable beds as its focal point. While I looked down at this prosaic prospect a young man in European clothes came up and addressed me in exceptionally good English. He said his name was Mustapha and that as I was clearly from England I must come and stay with his family, like all English travellers to Dongola did. I asked him if he had very many visitors and he said, 'Well, he had had two several years ago and it had been very nice to be able to practise his English.' To add weight to his invitation he said that the town's hotel was no place for a woman as it consisted of just one room where everyone slept together, and it was very bad for mosquitoes.

I accompanied Mustapha through the centre of town, where suq lorries, lorries converted into buses, pick-up trucks, donkeys and street-vendors blared and hooted, brayed and shouted, making a bewildering cacophony in the narrow hot dusty lanes and the crowded market places, colourful but hard to cope with after the quiet of the desert. The wide street which bisected the town had a hospital and about half a dozen pharmacies, in one of which Mustapha worked. Here too all was noise and bustle, with large crowds queueing to get into the hospital and lots of family groups sitting around having picnics. I could well believe that the six pharmacists were hard pressed to keep pace with demand.

The hotel was also on this street, and a quick look at it made me see why Mustapha thought it wasn't suitable, though I would have said it was a good place rather than a bad one for mosquitoes as there were lots of dank puddles around the overflowing water troughs for them to drink and hatch their eggs in. I had not been much bothered yet by mosquitoes in the Sudan as there was so little stagnant water about, but in Egypt they had been quite troublesome at times. Every Sunday I took two pills to help prevent me getting malaria, and once I reached Khartoum – where the risk began to increase dramatically – I was to add a different one, to be taken on Wednesdays. This was at the advice of British Airways who have a splendid immunisation service and keep a watching brief on most health hazards that affect travellers. Malaria, they told me, is so resistant to any form of prophylaxis that the only sure way to avoid getting it is not to be bitten by mosquitoes, which was why I was also carrying the plastic-dissolving insect repellent. I had a mosquito net bag to protect my face in humid jungle places where voracious biting insects were likely to be at their most numerous; it went over my hat and made me look like a bank robber in a new kind of sinister stocking mask. It had already come in useful when I was attacked by clouds of sand flies in the desert, but I couldn't possibly use it when there were people about.

The residential part of town, where quiet, uniform streets built on a tidy grid system turned blank, anonymous faces to the world, afforded a respite for the ears but was otherwise a depressing prospect. The living quarters of most Sudanese towns I visited had a sense of dereliction about them, a combination of the soiled, rubbish-strewn expanses of trampled sand, the crumbling mud-brick walls of the houses, and the complete absence of trees and plants. Nothing looked clean or sharp-edged; lines were always blurred, and colours were muddy and indefinite. There was little for the eye to focus on, or to hold the attention; everywhere looked alike and it was very difficult to find one's way or retrace one's steps. The sand dominated everything, and what was not actually made of sand was soon covered in a thick layer of it. Sudanese towns wore the derelict air of popular seaside resorts abandoned to their rubbish at the end of the season. It was completely different from being in the desert where the landscape had the pristine quality of a beach from which the tide had removed all traces of man.

Passing through the high metal gates in the wall of a Sudanese house was like coming out of a hot, over-lit and empty film set into an oasis of shade and coolness. The uniformity of the exteriors was not echoed within, and no two houses were ever quite alike. Mustapha's gates opened onto an immensely long open path. Just inside the gate was the lavatory, with a small door low down onto the street, convenient for removing the contents, as there was no plumbing here. At the end of the path was a courtyard, criss-crossed with washing lines, an open sink with a tap over it against one wall, and a mud-brick shower-room against another. An archway with a room on either side of it led into another long, narrow courtyard with a covered section in the central part, under which was a tall refrigerator, three metal beds, a washing-machine and a television. Two bedrooms and a kitchen were at one end of this courtyard, and a pigeon loft and a shed for the goat at the other. A few chickens were scratching about in makeshift confinement opposite the bedrooms.

On one of the beds a very large lady sat preparing vegetables. She had three deep parallel scars down each cheek, the tribal patterns once cut into the facial skin of every Sudanese child but now a fast dying practice. This was Mustapha's mother and she held my hand between hers while she recited a long speech of welcome in Arabic, which Mustapha translated as 'In the name of Allah I offer you anything that is in my power to give you.' Mustapha's sister, a plump young woman with a scarf tied around her head, sleeves rolled up to her elbows and a sacking apron tied around her ample middle, looked in this setting like a peasant in a Vermeer painting as she bustled about the yard with buckets of water, followed everywhere by a hopeful brown and white goat. There were also some children sitting on the beds; these were some of Mustapha's many nieces and nephews, for he was the youngest of several brothers, all of whom were married or out in the world. His father was a grain merchant, a small thin old man who fell asleep the moment any meal was finished and who like his wife spoke no English.

I was able to repay some of the hospitality I enjoyed here since Mustapha's mother was a confirmed smoker. Like all other smokers in the area, she was unable to indulge her craving, because there was a current severe tobacco shortage, and no one had had a cigarette for weeks. The moment her speech of welcome was finished, she asked me, via Mustapha, if I had a cigarette for her. It so happened that I was carrying a few to give away, and not knowing that they were like gold I gave her a whole packet. Such a gift annoyed Mustapha, who said it was much too valuable as cigarettes were changing hands on the black market at a hundred times their normal value. Also his mother would hoard them and keep them for herself whereas he would have shared them with his friends. Another packet restored harmony – which was just as well since I was to have Mustapha's room to sleep in, opposite the chickens, and judging from the amount of male clothing spilling out of two large cupboards and hanging on a long rack this could not have been very convenient for him. Like the doctor at Delgo, Mustapha spent much of his day changing back and forth between Sudanese and Western dress.

Lunch was served soon after I arrived, and I was honoured by being fed special bits by Mustapha's father. Luckily, Mustapha's father did not smoke, as my small potential goldmine was now exhausted. It was richer fare than I'd had so far in Sudan – a dish of stewed kidneys, aubergine, okra and foul. While the older people settled down to sleep off this meal on the beds in the courtyard and the sister, upon whom most of the burden of the household chores seemed to fall, started to clear away, Mustapha took me out to see Dongola.

After wandering around the featureless streets for a while a friend of Mustapha's appeared in a pick-up on his way to deliver some medicines in a nearby village. We went along with him so that I could meet a young girl who was supposed to be a famous fortune-teller. We waited about near her house on the edge of the desert, where a pump brought up an endless stream of sulphurous water from a deep pit about fifty feet down in the sand. Around the irrigated fields and old abandoned mud-brick houses, hordes of brown rats scurried to and fro dragging long stalks about and co-operating so intelligently that it was easy to forget what a menace they must be in this poor country. We left the place without seeing the fortune-teller – apparently it was not a good day for her – and Mustapha came to help me make enquiries about my onward travel instead.

From everyone I spoke to on the subject, I had gathered that the sand beside the Nile did not improve further on, and that there was no possibility of my riding through it. There were several alternative routes. The suq lorries and the splendid buses built onto suq lorry bodies went straight across the desert to Khartoum from Dongola, cutting off about four hundred miles. This was no use to me, however, since I wanted to stay with the Nile and see various things along the way. This would mean going almost full circle round the largest meander in the world, which after two hundred miles would bring me back further north than I was now, before turning south again. There was supposed to be a boat which went as far as Karima, just below the fourth cataract and if this was so, it would suit me very well. We spent a considerable amount of time and effort trying to find out about it but nothing, it seems, is ever more than rumour in the Sudan, and this boat was no exception. 'It might go tomorrow. It might not. It is in the hand of Allah.'

In fact the boat sailed two days later, and the intervening day I spent alternately in the clutches of the secret police and the uniformed police. I was taking photographs in the fruit and vegetable suq with the willing co-operation of all the colourful vendors when an oldish man with a tweed coat over his gellabiyah, the collar turned up around his ears, and with eyes like hard-boiled eggs on stalks behind his fancy dark glasses, started to interfere. 'You not do that, it is forbid,' he said, pushing me rudely. I produced the relevant photographer's pass, at which he looked most offended. 'I speak no English,' he lied as though denying some pernicious vice. I put my pass back in my pocket and tried to melt into the crowd. It didn't work; in no time I found myself being marched off by one of his minions. I wasn't frightened since I was sure it was all a mistake which my permit would rectify, but I was annoyed at the unnecessary interference and the spoiling of the friendly atmosphere. It was proving difficult to take the photographs I needed in any case, so when people had no objection to my recording them it seemed very hard to be stopped.

I was taken to a distant compound where I was questioned by various individuals who pored over all my papers, especially the passport, leafing through it again and again, in the hope I decided of finding something incriminating like an Israeli or South African stamp. As I knew there was nothing offensive in it and all my papers were in order I was still not worried, but simply impatient to leave the cream and green offices. Mid-morning breakfast time came around and as all the officers wanted to go off and eat I was released, though I was told I would have to return again after breakfast to see the chief officer. I was let out on bail, it seemed.

Mustapha came with me when I returned, in order to interpret and the whole farce was repeated, with my getting more irritated as the temperature outside soared. 'You visit many Arab countries,' said the 'chief' after he'd leafed through my passport for half an hour, going through from front to back and then the other way around. I said I had, and that in none of them had I been harassed by the police in this way. There was a muttered apology at this but no explanation and various other men sitting around the periphery went on firing questions about how I earned my money, where I lived and so on. I don't think any of them expected answers: they were simply giving tongue to show off their command of English or to bolster their sense of importance. After a while I ignored them and let Mustapha answer for me, and the whole thing fizzled out as they lost interest, and eventually I was told I could go. Mustapha said it had been useful for him as he now knew who the secret police in the town were; they had changed recently when Sadiq al Mahdi had taken over the government of the country from Nimiery. He seemed to think that the only function of secret police was to report on signs of disaffection among the populace, and that this current lot were stupid to blow their cover.

I had no sooner returned to the market, this time to buy fruit for what I hoped would be the next day's boat journey, when a young uniformed officer on a bicycle stopped me with a bellowed 'Who you are Missus? Where you going?' I was so incensed at being accosted by the law yet again that I decided I would ignore him in the hope he would go away. This was not a good idea, and by the time I had found Mustapha again to interpret, the young man had ground my metal watchstrap into my wrist in his determination not to lose hold of me. Once again there was a mile-long march to the police station but this time I was taken to the compound next door to the secret police. The uniformed branch, it seemed, had nothing to do with the secret variety, and denied that they even existed. I was in serious trouble, they told me via Mustapha, as I should have reported to the police on arrival: all travellers must report to every police station that they pass throughout the length and breadth of the country, and must get their travel permit stamped to show that they have done so. I managed eventually to persuade them that I had not known of this requirement and had not been told about it in Wadi Halfa. When I was finally released Mustapha thought it might be wiser if I didn't venture out alone again for the few remaining hours of daylight.

This was no hardship as what charm Dongola had held for me was now quite gone and I was eager to check over the Agala and do my washing in preparation for leaving the place. A quick trip down to the waterfront with Mustapha had revealed the welcome sight of a battered steamer drawn up against the ricketty jetty; with luck (or rather by the will of Allah) it would depart early the following morning. The bicycle certainly needed some attention. The chain was as dry as a bone and sounded very gritty, as did the cogs on the rear wheel. These cogs, which are of varying sizes to enable the cyclist to have different gears, are screwed onto a body which incorporates the freewheel mechanism, which although quite robust is the weakest part of the transmission. It is definitely not improved by dust and grit, ridiculous amounts of which had been finding their way into it recently. The chain was not as bad as it might have been because I had removed all the grease before leaving England and replaced it with a non-greasy lubricant which didn't attract dust. I cleaned both parts and applied a little more of my precious stock of lubricant. Afterwards I checked the whole bike over, helped by Mustapha's three eager young nephews, who thought it was wonderful. Inspired by the unlimited supply of water I washed all my equipment and scrubbed the panniers which were impregnated with dust; a waste of time really as something had only to be dropped on the floor or leaned against a wall for it to be just as permeated with dust as before.

The evening was spent with the family sitting on the beds in the courtyard watching television, all of us wrapped in blankets against the sudden chill of nightfall. Although the weather was getting noticeably hotter every day, the nights were mostly quite cool as it was still winter. There was an Egyptian soap opera on the television. The same instalment had been shown the previous night, and mother and daughter watched just as avidly as they had the first time round, cracking sunflower nuts the while with great efficiency. The goat kept coming over to watch too, peering closely at the action with intelligent quizzical eyes and then going round to stare at the back of the television. A cock stalked the hens around the yard chivvying them about so that now and again one would half-run, half-fly squawking across the screen, and the daughter would heave herself up crossly and shoo them all back down to the other end. The pigeons which occupied the ruinous dovecote swooped down to seize any morsel left by the hens, and a cat passed to and fro, a limp kitten hanging curled beneath her jaws as she moved her family one by one to new quarters.

CHAPTER ELEVEN

The Big Bend

I was down at the river bank very early the next morning in anticipation of the promised dawn start. In true Sudanese style, however, the boat stayed where it was until midday, when quite abruptly and for no discernible reason the captain decided it was time to depart, and several people in the process of negotiating the difficult access to the boat over the mudbanks and broken bits of planking were left behind. By this time the decayed charm of the ancient vessel had completely won me over and I hardly minded if we moved or not. The chief attraction was my accommodation. I had been given a first-class cabin, which cost me the equivalent of rather less than a pound a day. It was so luxurious for those parts that my temporary possession of it made me an enemy of one of the crew who had been turned out to make room for me. He kept coming in throughout the three day voyage to take away various items which he had hidden about the place – two cigarettes behind a mirror, a rolled up shirt and a large, chipped enamel bowl under the bed – and when there were no more of his things left, he came to harangue me about how unfair it was that I had the use of two bunks for the price of a single ticket.

The small cabin was one of eight forming a block on the forward section of the top deck but one. Behind this there was another block of ten second-class cabins which were only slightly smaller but without the advantages of a cracked sink, a chest of drawers in which the bottom of the drawers had disappeared and part of a mirror – a great shock this as I hadn't actually seen my face since Egypt and had been combing my hair and brushing my teeth from memory. There were hooks for clothes on my stateroom wall and a chair with three legs; there was even a tap fixed to the sink, which although it swivelled around freely through 360 degrees actually delivered water when one of the crew remembered to fill the tank on the top deck. A small wattage electric light bulb sometimes blossomed into dim life when the generator worked, but the bedside light – undreamed of luxury – did not.

Only one other of these first-class cabins was available for the public. The remaining six were kept locked, probably because they had fallen below the required safety standards – holes in the deck, wash basins hanging off walls and so forth. The shipping company was clearly conscious of safety requirements because before buying my ticket I'd been made to sign a paper absolving them from all responsibility should anything unfortunate befall me on the voyage. This was much cheaper than having to provide lifebelts or rafts and such like, but since the leather trade had denuded the Nile of its crocodiles (I had not seen a single one in 1,500 miles) I did not think there was much to worry about.

When I came aboard, one of the crew acting as steward took off the dirty sheet from the even dirtier straw palliasse on the lower bunk and replaced it with another equally dirty sheet. He also said I could keep the 'Oh so nice Agala' chained to the rails outside my cabin and later brought the 'headmaster of this boat' – the captain – to my cabin to shake hands, making me feel like a cross between a schoolgirl and a distinguished passenger on a trans-Atlantic liner. When I had un-packed my panniers, laid out my sleeping bag and arranged my possessions on the chest of drawers I experienced all the delight of the wanderer who has found a temporary settled base and can retire behind closed doors for a short while and cease to do battle with sun and sand and policemen.

In addition to the ten second-class cabins, some of which managed to house a large, active Sudanese family in their cramped confines, there was also steerage accommodation on a lower deck, conveniently near the galley. Here a traditionally temperamental cook produced quantities of bean stew and lentils on an enormous cast-iron range of such antique charm that it would have fetched a fortune at auction. There were 'hole in the floor' type lavatories on each deck which were sluiced down sometime in the day, immediately after which was the only possible time to use them. There was also a room in which a shower could be taken, but in practice this wasn't such a good idea as you came out rather dirtier than you went in. Both lavatories and shower room were, like my sink, dependent upon the good offices of the sailor in charge of pumping up the river water into the header tank – a man notoriously irregular in his habits.

Drinking water was also drawn straight from the river and set along the decks in tall pottery amphorae, supported in metal stands. These classical vessels were slightly porous and so kept the water cool but the water was full of all the endemic Nile bugs, especially gardia. Pots like this are used all over the Sudan, and I was interested to learn from a doctor that the water which dripped out through the bottom of them, and was usually thrown away, was almost 100 per cent free of gardia, the microbes having been filtered out by the layer of pottery. This was exactly the principle my Swiss water pump worked on, forcing the water through such a close-pored ceramic core that not even the smallest bacteria could get through. While aboard, I tried to collect water that had passed through the amphorae as it made the effort of pumping my daily supply so much easier, most of the clogging sludge having already been removed.

A huge barge was lashed on either side of the boat, each far larger than the boat itself, giving it a slightly pathetic look, like a tiny parent willow warbler trying to rear two fat cuckoo chicks. One barge was for mixed cargo, while the other was a sort of ark for the numerous crew and their friends, who lived a relaxed and carefree existence under a thatched roof, endlessly cooking up little meals on firewood, procured with much excitement and comment from ashore. Wood was scarce everywhere in northern Sudan, so every dead branch dragged aboard was a triumph for the boat and a loss for some Nile-side village. When the crew were not off foraging, cooking, or praying, they were lying around on the decks sleeping in the sun, and if the captain wanted anything done he had to lean out of his bridge window and blow lustily on a referee's whistle. Once aroused a violent verbal exchange would rage to and fro before the sailor would reluctantly move off to carry out his instructions. It was a very democratic little society which I felt would have quickly lapsed into complete anarchy had the captain not been patently more energetic than everyone else.

What powered the craft I never did discover. I think it must have been diesel, but I only glimpsed yards of shiny convoluted brass piping through the open door of the large engine-room behind the galley, and every time I tried to have a closer look I was shooed away by the intimidating individual whose domain it was. Had I really cared, I could have appealed to the captain about this as he became a friend of mine, frequently sending the 'steward' to bring me to the bridge with the invitation 'Headmaster of this boat he say you come'. But the 'headmaster' spoke no English and I never did discover the purpose of the summonses. I think they were simply intended to make me feel welcome. After I had sat for a while among the dozen men who were always there and had smiled at the steersman who worked very hard at the outsize wheel and liked to be admired for his skill in avoiding the endless sandbanks, I went happily back to my own concerns. At last I had discovered what the joys of a cruise were all about: doing nothing. The demanding journey from Wadi Halfa and the constant effort involved in trying to communicate, not to mention the arrests in Dongola, had all taken their toll, and I needed exactly what the trip offered – rest and quiet. I cooked up some of the dehydrated meals and caught up with my writing; otherwise I was content to simply sit and watch the unvarying panorama of sand and occasional palm trees of which I thought I would never tire.

There were two other British women aboard in one of the second-class cabins. They were two of the young graduates employed by the government to teach English in Sudanese schools, and unfortunately they were not in the least enjoying the experience. Since it was now holiday time, they were travelling around in the hope of meeting up with some other young British people to spend Christmas with. It was a little depressing being with them as their attitude to the country was so negative and they felt such a sense of grievance about so many things, in particular, the character of the young people they taught. They had not come out with any positive idea of helping in the third world or even because they were interested in teaching, but simply because they were tired of being unemployed in Britain and thought it would be nice to travel at someone else's expense. It was not the sort of motivation that was likely to be of much use in a country as poor and disrupted as Sudan, and it seemed to suggest that there was something seriously amiss with the selection procedures for these jobs. The only compensation the girls could see in being in the Sudan was the ready availability of 'bhang' or marijuana, which was cheap enough even on the pittance they were paid.

The three of us were allowed to use a small locked sun lounge on our deck, right up in the bows, underneath the bridge, and we spent long hours there, sitting in battered basket chairs from which it was necessary to extricate ourselves with great care to avoid being ripped by the many nails that were left exposed where the cane work had rotted away. I didn't think the boat would last for many more years; already its decks were thin and white with age, and the caulking was quite gone from between the timbers. There was no trace of paint left in most places and the crew were certainly not doing anything about maintenance. It was another left-over fragment of colonial days, like the diesel pumps along the river, the Corniche and the grid system in Dongola. It must have been especially built for this stretch of the river between the third and the fourth cataracts, a distance of just 150 miles – the 'garden province of Dongola'. Behind the sundeck with its broken wire insect gauze and wrecks of basket chairs was a perfect little wardroom beautifully fitted out in walnut. There was no use at all for such a piece of outworn gentility in the present scheme of things; nowadays meals were eaten squatting on the deck or seated on a bunk, and the wardroom remained a locked shrine to the foreign customs of the British, who had undoubtedly built it. It was a less enduring monument to conquest than other cultures had imposed upon this ancient cradle of civilisation.

At intervals along the banks there were the remains of the old Kingdom of Kush, fragments of masonry protruding from the desert like the tips of icebergs, indicating that vast ancient temple complexes and palaces were each year disappearing ever deeper beneath the sand. I saw none of them for I was no longer a free agent able to stop at will. I was tied to the rhythm of the boat making its slow way up river against the inexorable current, stopping only where it had practical business such as snatching up a likely piece of wood, dropping off passengers on seemingly deserted shores or discharging cargo at townships which were mere handfuls of dwellings, too small to be mentioned on my map. I didn't mind in the least; I had had my fill of ancient ruins in Egypt and nothing has yet been excavated in these parts to compare with the beauty of Soleb of the Lions.

The tide of Egypt had ebbed and flowed through this once fertile area in competition with the great civilisation of Meroe, whose capital, Napata, had been just below the 4th cataract. From this city, conquerors had on occasions marched forth and overwhelmed Egypt in their turn, founding new dynasties and leaving a foreign cast of features on statues of the pharaohs. The land must have been so much greener then, though even at that time, around 1500 BC, it had already begun its decline into desert. This part of the Nile had not flooded and renewed the fertility of the soil with yearly deposits of rich silt. As with other ancient sites of civilisation the ground had been worked until it was exhausted, after which the cultivators had abandoned it to its inevitable erosion. When the conquering Assyrians swept into Egypt in the sixth century BC, bringing the iron age to the entire Nile Valley, the vast amounts of wood needed to produce charcoal for smelting the new metal denuded the area of its trees, affecting local climatic conditions and laying open the soil to further erosion. Nomadic tribes have long since destroyed the last vestiges of the Meroitic culture as surely as their herds of goats, sheep and cattle, fighting for survival in the harsh conditions, have completed the destruction of the land. Sand has now obliterated all but the faintest scraps of cultivation and every year the desert continues to advance – the most terrible and implacable conqueror of them all.

Three days aboard the little ship passed like a dream. Long before I had time to grow tired of the confinement we had rounded the great bend of the river and were ambling around the sandbanks in a north-westerly direction towards Karima, where my battle with sand, dust and sun would begin again. We docked early in the morning, and Karima looked quite a sizeable metropolis after all the little one-donkey villages along the Nile. I made my way into the centre alongside the railway line – and that was enough to convince me that all my informants had been right. The sand was even worse than it had been around Dongola. It was the softest I had yet seen and more like grey talcum powder than sand; there was no way I was going to be able to bicycle through it.

I had been going to stay a few days at Karima and explore the Meroitic ruins, but after discovering that the weekly train was due to depart in a few hours I changed my mind. There was no other way of continuing along the course of the river, as the suq lorries sensibly cut straight off across the desert to avoid the next huge bend where the river found its southern course again. I didn't want to wait about for a week in a town which had few obvious charms, even assuming there would be another train running to schedule. A few days in the Sudan are enough to convince the traveller of the need to seize whatever transport is going in roughly the right direction.

I found out about the train from a middle-aged Scottish nurse named Lexa, who was funded by her church in Glasgow to work in the hospital in Karima. I met her because a man had plucked at my sleeve as I was struggling along with the Agala and had smiled at me and said something that sounded like 'Coadjer, coadjer'. He clearly expected me to go with him and seeing no reason not to I had done so, and he had led me to the hospital. This happens quite frequently in Sudan. People assume that foreigners – 'Coadjers' – want to be with other Coadjers and haul them off to where the resident foreigners live or work. This can be very useful for travellers and is seldom much of a nuisance to the expatriates, who say they enjoy these occasional glimpses of a face from home. Lexa assured me she was particularly delighted to see me as British women of her own age were extremely rare, and she pressed me to stay. We had breakfast together in a ward in the hospital where all the small patients were being fed by their numerous relatives. Every family was responsible for their own food, so the whole place was abustle with people running in and out with bowls and dishes and having animated picnics beside the beds. The children were all suffering from bronchial infections. In a few months, Lexa said, this would change and the wards would be filled with cases of malaria and acute diarrhoea as the weather grew hotter. In spite of the bronchitis, the children were at their healthiest in the winter-time and put on flesh, but as the terrible heat of summer gripped the land, their appetites declined, and when they contracted an intestinal infection the babies and smaller children dehydrated very swiftly. It was this that killed them in large numbers, and not the infection itself. Complications arising from female circumcision was another serious and year-long problem.

After breakfast we went to look at the baby clinic which Lexa had begun and which was now being run by Sudanese staff. Most of the work consisted of weighing the children as the clinic handed out supplementary food to underweight babies and toddlers, as well as running an inoculation programme and attempting to educate mothers in primary health care. In spite of the poverty of the mothers

1. The village of Gurna, by the Tombs of the Nobles.

2. The tribe in Egypt that robbed me of my sun-hat.

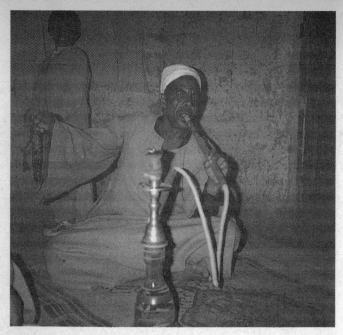

3. My friend Ibrahim, in whose house I feasted.

4. Between the Nile and the road: an unchanged land.

5. Renk: Shilluk mother and child.

6. Nyala: young girls watching with envy Vimto learning with the boys.

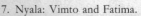
7. Nyala: Vimto and Fatima.

8. A vagrant boy at Nyala.

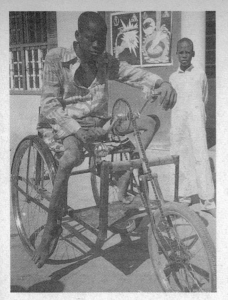

9. Sabah.

10. Renk: Michael, the little boy who didn't die.

11. Khartoum: street boy.

12. Khartoum: a young vagrant begging.

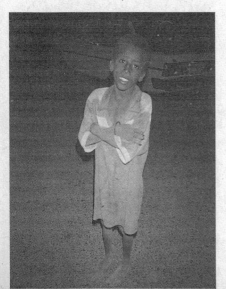

13. North Sudan: ploughing.

14. Renk: displaced Shilluk.

15. Juba: Mundari cattle camp.

16. Juba: Mundari cattle.

17. Juba: Mundari girl.

18. My porters on the Mountains of the Moon.

19. Luta Nzige – Lake Albert.

who attended the clinic there was never anything but rejoicing at a child being declared fit enough to be taken off supplementary rations. There were very explicit posters all around the rooms showing various horrible results of female genital mutilation, but Lexa said that as yet they were having very little effect, social pressure being far too strong for mothers to dare go against the practice. The Sudanese doctor in charge of the hospital was the only parent she knew of in the district who had refused to allow his daughters to be circumcised, and the price paid for this had been high. The girls had been continuously ostracised at school and there was no possibility of the family enjoying a normal social life in the town.

Lexa impressed me very much with the way she was able to stand back and let the locally-recruited staff take over. She obviously had a policy of not directly interfering or leaping in, even when something was being done less than properly. She aimed to become redundant as quickly as she could, she told me, by passing on her skills to others and building up their confidence at the same time. Later, when I had met lots of other field-workers, I came to see how rare a characteristic this was, and I felt that if only more foreign aid workers could acquire this skill there would be less resentment amongst the people they were supposed to be helping. It wasn't only a question of intention but of attitude too. Lexa had a genuine liking and respect for the Sudanese and believed she was among her equals, which was the opposite of how the two young graduates on the boat seemed to feel. What Lexa had to offer came from what she was as a human being; she was fulfilled enough in herself to be able to concentrate almost entirely upon the needs of others, which would seem to epitomise the ideal of Christian charity in its simplest and most direct form.

I cannot pretend that I felt very much charity, Christian or otherwise, during the next twenty-four hours, for I was far too engrossed in my own extreme discomfort to give much thought to anything else. Due to the reluctance of the railway booking-clerks at Karima to make out the necessary forms later than two hours before the train was due to leave, I was unable to buy anything other than a third-class ticket. Had I known what this meant, I should somehow have got myself onto the roof of the train with the non-fare paying passengers and braved the desperate cold of the desert night, for nothing could have been worse than being inside that railway carriage. Even getting the bicycle safely stowed in the guard's van had been an exhausting business. I had been reluctantly talked into letting the railway staff deal with it, and had just walked away when I happened to glance back just in time to see my faithful steed flying through the air, followed by a resounding thump and a cloud of billowing dust pouring out of a truck door. I tore back and managed to prevent a heavy refrigerator being heaved in on top of it. The truck they had thrown it into had been used for carrying cement and there were several inches of loose powder still on the floor which had broken the Agala's fall. Despite efforts to dislodge me I refused to budge after that and stayed around until the train had started. I also put all the panniers back on the bicycle to protect it should anyone else take it into their heads to use it as a projectile. As various officials, all vying with each other to be 'in charge', kept unloading and rearranging things I got pretty dirty before I boarded the train.

The third-class carriage had only the bare bones of seats; all the padding had been stripped off. There were drifts of sand and piles of dirt under the seats, and lavatories with no flushing mechanisms made their malodorous presence all too obvious between the doorless waggons. Every inch of space was filled with the tightly-pressed bodies of men, women and children so that initially I was thankful I had no luggage with me except for the handlebar bag containing my documents and traveller's cheques. But after only a very short while I realised how useful it would have been to have things like my sleeping bag, mattress and spare clothing, all now unobtainable in the locked and sealed goods van.

It soon became apparent that the train was going to average no more than ten miles an hour, and after two hours even this estimate could be seen to have been ridiculously over optimistic. The pattern of progress was a half hour's slow run followed by three quarters of an hour's rest. With nothing between me and the flat piece of hardboard I soon began to suffer agonies of cramp which after four hours or so became intolerable. There was no question of moving about to relieve the discomfort, since this would have meant walking over the tightly-packed bodies. Everyone else had had the forethought to bring shawls and bundles with them to pad out their places. As night fell the sudden drop in temperature added to the misery and in my thin shirt and trousers I began to seriously wonder if I should survive. Just as I had decided that this was extremely unlikely, succour appeared in the shape of a wayside halt where the train stopped and enough people left the carriage so that I could move my atrophied limbs and climb stiffly down after them.

The train stopped during the night at several wayside halts along this remotely populated stretch of the Nile and at each one the passengers stumbled out of the unlit, dust-filled carriages or climbed out through the windows into the desert night, where beautiful girls lit by the fitful flicker of resin-soaked flares crouched in the sand beside the tracks selling dates and cakes, and hot tea that was like the elixir of life. These were the only respites from the continuing misery which went on and on for eighteen hours, during which time we had travelled no more than 150 miles. The worst moments came just as it was growing light when everyone in the carriage except for me lay asleep on the seats or spread out on the floor under a thick coating of dust like hoar frost – not a pretty sight. My throat seemed to be full of the same choking substance, particles of it crunched between my teeth and I could see drifts of it in the folds of my clothes and covering my skin like a pall. I looked like something which had recently been dug up. Glancing down at my stiff, numb legs, I was horrified to observe my ankles swollen up to twice their normal size. It was the result of the prolonged comfortless sitting, I suppose, but as such a thing had never happened to me before I brooded darkly on whether I had contracted some horrible African affliction like elephantiasis. It seemed all of a piece with the miserable state of exhaustion into which I had sunk.

I crawled out of the train at the next stop which I think was Berber, though I was in such a daze I cannot be absolutely sure. I was consumed by the desire to find somewhere to sleep and to wash – especially to wash, for I felt that the dust had ground deep into the pores of my skin and that only a long soak in a deep hot bath would dislodge it. A likely occurrence, I taunted myself, a bath this side of Khartoum! I'd hardly seen a bath since I left England, and even cold showers dripping out of rusty pipes were luxuries. Somehow I had managed to push my preoccupation with water to one side long enough to concentrate on finding someone to unlock the luggage van and release the Agala. I didn't try to free it of its thick white coating of cement dust, but got on it and set off in the right direction – southwards. Then I found I was cycling along on tarmac instead of sand, which seemed so improbable that I'd given up trying to make sense of things and had just concentrated on turning the pedals.

After a long time, several hours at least, I found myself in a town of wide streets, and feeling that I could not go a yard further, I had asked someone where I could find a hotel and the person I'd asked hadn't said a word but had led me to a rather grand-looking building in a garden. At the door a small elderly man received me as though I had been expected and I was led off to a large shaded bedroom smelling of paraffin (doubtless for keeping the cockroaches at bay). There was a bed with one single clean sheet which later I found was the custom in the Sudan – and, unbelievably, there was a bathroom with both bath and hot water, and at that point heaven could have offered me very little more.

CHAPTER TWELVE

Angels Fulfilling Wishes

Luxuriating in the unbelievable comfort of my second hot bath, while at the same time being careful not to dislodge my waterproof torch which was stuffed into the plughole in lieu of a bathplug, I began to wonder about the identity of the person who had led me to this delectable place. I had not noticed any suspicion of wings under his gellabiyah, but guardian angels can take many forms and my particular one had been so very active on this journey that I was no longer surprised wherever and however he appeared. Never had his efforts on my behalf been more appreciated. I had already slept right round the clock and could now begin to appreciate the strangely unreal quality of this hotel, in which I was the only guest. The meals I ate all alone in the large dim dining room were ordinary enough and not particularly well cooked, but omelettes, stuffed peppers and cut and segmented grapefruit were dishes that I'd all but forgotten, and at this stage of the journey they seemed as miraculous as the bath. I was served by a silent little man who appeared whenever I showed my face in the dining room, carefully placing quantities of solid cutlery on a cloth which, stained and greyish though it was, had at one time been double damask. I was never asked what I wanted; food was simply brought and placed before me. Baths, tablecloths, made-up beds – even with only one sheet – towels and cutlery seemed so elegant and so at variance with what I had grown used to in the Sudan that my stay in what I understood to be the resthouse at Atbara was passed in a dream-like trance.

I used the time as far as possible in doing nothing at all but bathing and eating, and trying to rest with my feet above the level of my head, in order to reduce the swelling in my ankles. Even walking down stairs to the dining room seemed an effort, which made me realise just how exhausted I had become. It is all too easy to underestimate the demands of a journey like the one I was making. The unrelenting hard physical effort in a hot climate, inadequate food, the continuous strain of communicating in a foreign language and of being always 'on show' are all too often ignored; and of course they have to be to a large extent if one is to travel in remote places. The problem is knowing just how far one can afford to push oneself; if too much is demanded of the body or the mind for too long they have their own way of getting back by simply refusing to function properly. The lethargy I was feeling and the swollen ankles suggested that I needed a longer rest than the three days on the Dongola boat had provided. I could stay where I was for a day or two, eating well and putting back some of the weight I had lost, and this seemed the most sensible thing to do. But Khartoum was only a few days away if the friendly strip of tarmac continued, and in Khartoum there would be friends to celebrate Christmas with, and letters! The thought of mail has a powerful effect on travellers far from home, and has even caused several explorers close to death to drag themselves for months on end through dense jungle: it had a similar effect upon me. I would press on.

My decision made, I could at least relax and enjoy the rest of the day comfortably ensconced on the wooden balcony outside the paraffin-impregnated bedroom, with my freshly washed clothes and luggage hanging up to dry around me. The sky was full of huge brownish-red kites riding the wind in their eternal search for carrion; they had replaced my familiar companions of the desert, which were even more sinister-looking birds with dirty white plumage, yellow heads and black wing tips whom I had been convinced were following me in the hope that I would expire from sunstroke so that they could devour me. The balcony overlooked a half-ruined garden and here and there an unusual patch of bright colour flamed out of the ubiquitous dull ochre of the Sudanese landscape, where a few flowering shrubs had been tough enough to survive. Stones with traces of white paint on them still edged paths that had been laid out with military precision around dry bare expanses which had once been lawns, and there was a warped and cordless flagpole in the centre. Beyond the garden, the wide streets were lined with avenues of leafy trees and there were vestiges of pavements. The more the scene impressed itself on my mind the more it all seemed a touch *déjà vu*. Then I realised that I had in a way been there before and that the same ghosts were lingering in this oasis as stalked through the hill stations of northern India. It was the unmistakable aura of empire – tea and scones, croquet and chota pegs; and the sixty or seventy decaying railway engines I'd seen on the way in, all stamped 'Made in Darlington', were part of that not yet forgotten world.

Atbara had been General Kitchener's railhead for his Sudan campaign and the site of the first of his battles to avenge the death of Gordon and 'teach those damned Mahdiists a lesson'. No one who understood the situation could have really believed that the Mahdi's successor, the Khalifa Abdullah and his men, constituted a threat to the security of Cairo and the Suez Canal, though that was one of the reasons advanced for mounting the expedition. The real reason was that a proud and powerful nation had been made a fool of by a bunch of 'naked savages', and one of its heroes, General Gordon, had been murdered and his head paraded for the amusement of these same 'heathen fuzzy-wuzzies'. It was an act crying out for revenge, as was the 'damnable cheek' of the letter the Mahdi had subsequently sent to Queen Victoria, demanding that she submit to the will of Allah. Another avenging force of 10,000 men under General Hicks had already been wiped out by the Mahdi two years before the fall of Khartoum. Clearly it was high time Britain did its Christian duty in restoring the Sudan to Anglo-Egyptian rule, and when the land-grabbing in Central Africa began there was even greater public pressure to secure this sandy waste through which the greater part of the Nile flowed.

Thirteen years after the fall of Khartoum, Kitchener's considerable Anglo-Egyptian force was moving up the east bank of the Nile, along the route I had just cycled, and one of the Khalifa's emirs was entrenched at Atbara with 2,000 tribesmen, in the vain hope of stopping the advance. On Good Friday 1898, Kitchener engaged the emir's men with the full weight of his modern artillery and annihilated them. Of the handful who remained alive after the short engagement, one was the young emir himself, and he was chained and manacled and dragged along in front of the victory parade with camp followers pelting him with rubbish, while Kitchener sat on his white charger taking the salute and a young soldier named Winston Churchill made a careful note of the proceedings.

Having established his railhead Kitchener marched on to Omdurman and the decisive battle of the campaign. Here the Khalifa met him with his force of 50,000 tribesmen, placing his men where Allah had directed that he should stand – just across the river from the scene of the defeat of Khartoum, and well within the range of Kitchener's gunboats. The British force was less than half the Khalifa's, just 20,000 men, but whereas the Sudanese were armed for the most part with spears, Kitchener had Royal Navy gunboats, machine guns, rifles and a hundred pieces of artillery. No one thought much of the Khalifa's chances. Describing the battle, Churchill wrote: 'The whole black line that we had thought were bushes began to move. Behind it other immense masses and lines of men appeared over the crest; and while we watched amazed at the wonder of the sight, the whole face of the slope beneath became black with swarming savages.' It was a scene that would be re-enacted in a hundred romantic films – the thin red line in white pith helmets holding firm against overwhelming odds. But it had not been like that at Omdurman. The Arabs never reached Kitchener's lines, but had been mown down by the withering artillery fire pouring into their massed ranks. 'It was not a battle but an execution,' observed another eye witness. Within a couple of hours 10,000 of the Khalifa's men lay dead in mangled heaps on the sand and the rest was streaming in a general rout back to Omdurman. 'The enemy', observed Kitchener as he put away his field glasses, had been 'given a good dusting'. Only four hundred casualties were reported among the allied forces and most of those were put down to an unnecessary and unordered cavalry charge by the Lancers.

There followed a rather dreadful incident, reminiscent of a more barbarous age and not at all in keeping with Victorian principles of decency. General Kitchener rode up to the Mahdi's tomb in Omdurman and had the Mahdi's corpse dug up and flung into the Nile, after first cutting off the head for the purpose of turning it into an inkstand. Censure had followed from Queen Victoria herself, though not disgrace – his victory had been far too popular for that. The head was quietly reburied at Wadi Halfa where it has joined the same element as the body, since the cemetery is now several metres beneath the waters of the dam. Such maverick actions are long remembered and give colonialism such a bad name. They overshadow the slow patient work of breaking the appalling slave trade, trying to establish law and order and creating some sort of economic basis for the country's growth – work that had been going on for several decades before Khartoum fell and which was to continue as the 'white man's burden' long after Kitchener had gone down in a ship off the Orkneys in the First World War.

On the way to Khartoum I was planning to see something of the workings of a modern 'white man's burden' in the shape of a scheme called Green Deserts which was concerned with replanting areas of the Bayuda Desert with trees, using the labour of the pastoral nomads whose ancestors had been responsible for the over-grazing which had turned the land into the wilderness it is today. It had sounded a most exciting project when I'd first heard of it in England and now I'd had some experience of the terrain I was even more eager to see what miracle could make these deserts bloom again. I left Atbara fairly early, having still seen no one but the silent little man who had served my meals and finally presented the modest bill.

The sky looked dirty with an unusual sick yellowish light to which I did not give much thought at the time, as bicycling along the strip of tarmac with a very strong wind at my back was such fun. I crossed a ricketty bridge over the wide rocky bed of the Atbara River, the last major tributary of the Nile – though coming from downstream it was the first for me – and it marked the 2,000-mile point of the journey. Although it was only a trickle now, as soon as the rains fall in Ethiopia it becomes a strongly flowing river five hundred yards wide, bringing down the rich silt from the Ethiopian Uplands. The Nile itself, when I caught a glimpse of it over on my right, looked for the first time iron grey and unattractive in a flat light that robbed it of its sparkle.

At Ed Damer I tried out my Arabic with satisfactory results, procuring the services of an intelligent old man who came plodding around the sandy streets with me in search of the Green Desert people. By dint of questioning a succession of young boys my guide eventually discovered a sturdy vehicle in an alley with Green Deserts written large upon it. The house it was parked in front of yielded no response to our knocks and shouts, but neighbours appeared who told us that the truck had been broken for a long time – Green Deserts, it seemed, was no more. I was disappointed but not surprised, for it had been hard to believe that there were the resources available in this desperately impoverished land to tackle such an enormously difficult task. Multi-million dollar international aid to save ancient temples from the waters of a dam are one thing, but few people seem to be concerned with the less dramatic process of growing trees. Modern man is too busy creating new deserts out of the great rain forests and the Himalayan pine forests to worry about repairing the old deserts created by his ancestors.

There was nothing further to keep me in Ed Damer, so I gave my guide a few cigarettes and got on the Agala. But the old man stopped me bicycling off by hanging onto the carrier and I realised that he was worried about something that he couldn't convey because of the language barrier. It turned out that the sick light I'd been ignoring was a sign of an haboob – a dust storm – brewing up and he feared for my safety knowing, as I did not, that there was only a desert track leading to Khartoum. Some more young boys were questioned and I was led through another series of streets where he knocked on a set of high pastel-painted gates, which looked no different from a hundred others, but when opened they revealed an Englishman with long bare legs which he made a futile gesture of hiding, one behind the other, as though he had been caught indecently dressed – which of course he was by Moslem standards.

Having missed one development project I found I had stumbled upon another – not such a coincidence I discovered later, since nearly every white face in the Sudan is engaged in some aspect of aid. David and Julie were both nurses and professional aid workers who had first come out to East Africa the previous year in response to the famine crisis, and had had a harrowing three months in a refugee camp with children dying like flies all around them. Now they were employed as a husband and wife team by one of the smaller charities (or 'agencies' as they prefer to be called these days) to carry out primary health care work in the Atbara River area. They were just packing up to go to Khartoum for Christmas and offered to take me with them as they thought the condition of the track was far too difficult to bicycle on. They had a four-wheel-drive Toyota, and said that even in that it was touch and go in places – they never travelled without spades and mats for digging out, and copious supplies of water for lengthy break-downs. I accepted their kind offer gladly and David and his Sudanese driver loaded the Agala carefully on top of the piles of luggage, all of which was firmly lashed down with a spider's web of ropes. Julie in the meantime took me on a tour of their house and garden.

It was a typical small Sudanese dwelling, rather primitive and enclosed by a high wall, with separate little rooms built into a courtyard, making charming odd corners and angles – except that all the walls were painted white and plants grew in profusion in a few small beds, something seldom seen in Sudanese houses. It made a tremendous difference, for where the natural material was everywhere the same dull mud-brick hue, the eye forever craved colour. I'm sure that this was the main reason why people liked my bright red Agala so much, and why the Sudanese painted their gates with the brightest paints they could lay their hands on. But nothing made such a pleasant difference as plants and trees; it was as though they visibly added moisture to the dry atmosphere, making everything seem a little less dusty and arid. Julie said she could grow most things successfully in the small patch; it was just a question of frequent watering and shade, for the earth itself was fertile enough.

It was in this garden that I first saw the inconspicuous little bush, rather like privet, from which henna is produced, without the use of which, applied to the tips of her fingers and the soles of her feet, no Sudanese woman feels properly dressed. Sudanese women, no matter how poor, have many beauty practices which I hadn't seen before, like smoke baths, where the woman squats for hours over a fire laid in a hollow in the floor of her house, with her tobe draped over her like a tent; it is said to soften the skin and impart a burnished sheen to it. Bodily hair is not considered attractive and is removed with homemade depilatories made of lemon and sugar. Afterwards per-fumed oils are rubbed into the skin; no two fragrances are ever alike as each woman makes her own from pounded leaves and flowers, and the recipes are closely guarded secrets.

We left Ed Damer after lunch with the idea of camping near the ruins of the royal city of Meroe, but with the haboob really beginning to blow up, making me glad I wasn't on the bicycle, we made for Shendi instead. It at once became apparent why there had to be so many cords around the luggage, for the car leapt and bucked in the deep sand and fell with sickening thuds into the sudden dips and hollows, while the steering wheel looked as though it was perpetually trying to wrench itself out of the driver's hands. Some of the hollows had been made by camels rolling on the track like horses and scratching their woolly backs against the sand to rid themselves of parasites. The driver seemed particularly drawn to these hollows as if by magnetic attraction, hitting them at considerable speed. I didn't think he was nearly as good as other native drivers I'd ridden with further north, and I supposed this was because it wasn't his car and so it did not matter to him if he damaged it. It wasn't David's car either, though he was concerned that after only six months' use it needed major repairs. The springs had already been strengthened, but when we reached Khartoum it was discovered that one was totally broken, something that came as no surprise to me after suffering two days of barbaric bone-shaking.

David was very interesting on the whole subject of modern aid and I could not have met up with anyone more helpful in explaining its workings to me. He had chosen his field carefully and saw a career in developing countries as offering exciting prospects for promotion. He had started by reading Aid and Development as a degree course at university and then gone on to do his practical nursing training. I had always thought of aid as a finite thing, there to deal with a specific, fairly short term need, so David's view of it as continuing far into the twenty-first century was a novel concept to me, and one I found disturbing – not that I found it easy to grasp complicated ideas while bouncing around on a pernicious track with strange pieces of the ancient ruins of the royal city of Meroe looming up alongside out of the dust clouds. I'm afraid I took in no more than a fraction of what I was told about the philosophy and structure of this new boom industry, and it marked the beginning of a confusion that became ever more clouded the closer I became acquainted with it in the Sudan.

As field workers, David and Julie were aware of the politics of aid without being directly involved in them. Their job was to try to impose practical changes upon the attitudes and customs that underlay the terrible problems of sickness, poverty and ignorance, and they were well aware that this was a slow process. They also knew that the native workers they employed to help with the inoculation programmes and with the clinics they were attempting to set up would prefer to have the equipment, the transport and the money to run things themselves in their own way. A continuous sense of dissatisfaction was built into the work because of the paucity of what they could hope to achieve in their enormous area of operations, with the very limited resources at their command; nor did the realisation that this was inevitable really help. Even with the little they had, they felt they were frustrated at every turn by the sheer physical difficulties of the terrain – its immense size, terrible heat, non-existent communications and the lack of roads.

Comparing their job with Lexa's at Karima I could see how much harder and less rewarding it was bound to be, and how essentially different. Lexa had so much more contact with the people she was helping; she spoke their language and her sphere of operations enabled her to have a close relationship with the people she was teaching. Being funded directly through her church back home, she was able to appeal directly for anything she needed, saving months of frustrating delays. David and Julie, on the other hand, had even greater freedom in that they could identify the needs of the area for themselves, but with everything, especially the problems, being on such a huge scale, they had little continuing contact with the individuals they were trying to help, seldom seeing the same people twice. And working through interpreters must have caused major difficulties and reduced their effectiveness. Altogether, while I admired their intentions I wouldn't have wanted to take on their jobs.

We reached Shendi in the early evening, shaken about and bruised by the drive. The light, which had brightened up a little in the middle of the day, was once more grey and evil-looking. It had turned suddenly very cold, and with the ferocious wind blowing the top layer of sand through the air, together with a miscellaneous assortment of rubbish, Shendi seemed without charm. David and Julie had friends there with whom they were proposing to stay – a couple with two young sons who had had something to do with Green Deserts but now worked on another forestry project. We found the house easily because it had a solitary tree outside it, protected from marauding goats by a brick wall built around its trunk to a height of about five feet. If it required this much effort to grow a single tree in northern Sudan, it was not difficult to see why there were so few of them about. I was doomed to find out nothing more about the forestry projects in the area however, as the friends were laid low with a combination of hepatitis and malaria, and so with typical Sudanese generosity we were put up instead in the home of friends of the driver.

Our hosts were an Egyptian family, merchants who had lived in Shendi for years. That they were able to accommodate four chance guests in their small house with absolutely no fuss and every sign of welcome was one of the continuing wonders of life in the Sudan. Where the driver went I don't know, but a room with three beds and a wardrobe was made over to Julie, David and me. we were all so tired from the drive that after a shower in the mud-brick shed in the yard where a modern washing machine was housed we went straight to bed, helped on our way by a generous measure of local fire-water.

Within an hour of leaving Shendi the next morning, we were lost. It was the strangest thing; one moment we were ploughing along an obvious track with hundreds of imprints of wheels all around, and the next we were in virgin sand with only our own tyre marks stretching out behind us. We had been following a compass course, choosing from the plethora of divergent tracks that presented themselves every hundred yards or so. We'd hit one that had simply fizzled out, the wind having finally obliterated all trace of it. At first we were not worried. We steered a little to the west and the track wasn't there, so we looked for it over to the east and it wasn't there either. It showed just how easy it is to get hopelessly lost in the desert, as I had found out for myself in the deserts further north. On a bicycle things happen more slowly and I had normally found it possible to pick up a lost track again before it was gone forever. It was not so simple by car; travelling faster the difference of a degree or two could make a world of difference to the direction and we might now be miles away from both the track and the Nile. There was no serious danger as we had two compasses, and if all else failed we would simply have to go west until we came to the river. The worst that could happen would be mechanical failure or getting bogged down in impassable sand, with no likelihood of passing traffic to assist us if necessary.

For several hours we cast about in a trackless waste. Occasionally we passed nomads' camps, which looked cheerless derelict places of one or two multi-patched tents with an old vehicle or a motorbike parked alongside and piles of junk half covered in sand, but with no one around. Once or twice we got into an area of scrub and thorn trees, from which it was not easy to extricate ourselves without damage to the car. It was after one of these sorties that David decided to backtrack – which did get us into a rather dangerous situation because the haboob started blowing again, covering our tracks, and the first time we could see further than just a few yards beyond the bonnet we found we had driven into the middle of some military manoeuvres and were on a firing range with red flags, scores of army trucks and hundreds of armed soldiers milling all about us. They were not over-friendly, and we wasted no time in getting out of there.

Eventually, in time-honoured tradition, a lone figure loomed up out of the clouds of dust, swaying on a tall camel, his flocks of goats and sheep all around him and only his eyes visible through the cloths swathed around his head. Once he had understood where we were trying to get to, he made his camel kneel down and came and drew a map for us in the sand.

After that it was plain sailing. There were one or two heart-stopping moments, when the wheels spun uselessly in superfine sand, but with a judicious use of the four-wheel drive we got back onto a well used track which David and Julie recognised. After a few more hours of punishment on an atrocious track with furrows several feet deep we hit a hard corrugated surface of quite unmitigated ferocity, which David tore along at great speed in order to get to the end of it before dark. With nightfall upon us, absolutely exhausted and with sand and grit once again clogging every pore, we gained the strip of battered tarmac which would bring us into Khartoum.

CHAPTER THIRTEEN

Khartoum

Khartoum sprawls its ungainly acres over a flat sandy plain at one of those singularly significant places on the earth's surface – where two great rivers meet. The Blue Nile, sweeping down out of the heights of Ethiopia, executes two wide flamboyant turns before meeting the White Nile, whose own precipitous fall from the great inland seas of Africa has been somewhat tamed by the long passage through the swamps of the Sudd. From one of Khartoum's bridges the two rivers can be plainly seen flowing together northwards side by side, their waters not yet combined and one side clearly darker than the other. For me the point marked the parting of the ways; from here onwards I would be following only the course of the White Nile.

'Why you stop here?' asked a military-style policeman each time I got off the Agala to enjoy the tremendous prospect: 'It is forbidden to stop on the bridge.' And he would make a small, almost imperceptible jerk towards me with his rifle to show he was not joking. I would have liked to have taken a photograph but even if I had not been aware that all bridges are regarded as military secrets, photographed only by spies, I was in any case growing increasingly nervous about producing my camera anywhere in the Sudan. The attraction of the place was so strong however that in spite of the policeman I returned there each day I was in Khartoum to ride across the broad expanse as slowly as I could. The Blue Nile is quite as wide here as the White Nile and when it floods in late summer, bringing down quantities of rich silt – the 'gift of the Nile' from the Ethiopian highlands – its force is so great that it holds back the flow of the White Nile, which then follows with its own flood a month later.

It is hard to believe that there was no town here at all until the Turkish-Egyptian invasion of the early nineteenth century established Khartoum as a trading post for the iniquitous slave traffic. There are now three large cities at the confluence, each one spreading far back into the desert from a different bank of the two rivers. The original

Khartoum was destroyed by the Mahdi and was begun again under Kitchener's administration at the beginning of the century. The comfortable Edwardian buildings were laid out in a rectangle beside the Blue Nile, their streets intersecting in the pattern of the Union Jack – this was supposed to make it easier to defend, but seems like an ultimate statement of colonialism. All the large houses of Kitchener's Khartoum have become government offices, except for the Grand Hotel, whose marble terrace on the Corniche I found was the most pleasant place to sit and sip a lemonade and escape for a while from the heat and dust of the rest of the city. Started as an industrial centre by the British in the early part of the twentieth century Khartoum North lies across the water, a horrid place but with a waterfront lined with lovely defunct paddle steamers. The Mahdi's city, Omdurman, lies on the west bank of the White Nile and is the most colourful and interesting. All three are growing like wildfire with the influx of refugees and the general drift to the cities caused by the recent years of drought and famine.

'A more miserable, filthy and unhealthy place can hardly be imagined,' wrote Sir Samuel Baker of Khartoum in 1862, when he arrived there with his wife for the first time. I wondered what he would think if he could see the three large towns now. Samuel Baker had been a good deal in my mind since I'd crossed the Atbara River, which he had been the first to explore and map, solving in the process the mystery of where the life-giving silt came from and why there were two yearly floods. Of all the Nile explorers he was the most colourful and endearing, even if Queen Victoria had disapproved of him. Florence, his second wife, had been the cause of the Royal disapprobation. A widower of comfortable private means, with a family of daughters left in the care of his sister in England, Sam Baker was travelling in Central Europe when he came upon a young Hungarian girl, seventeen years his junior, up for sale in a Turkish slave market; and moved by pity he had bought her. As he was en route for his Nile venture at the time he had taken her along too, and during the course of their passage to the source of the Nile Florence became his '*chère amie*'. After surviving a succession of extraordinary Boy's Own adventures, the two eventually returned to England, and went through a marriage ceremony, and lived happily ever after. However, trial marriages were not at all the done thing in Victorian England, nor was being so careless as to have a past like Florence's, and these factors together with Florence's open admission that she had donned male clothing in the desert and been mistaken for Sam's son, weighted the scales heavily against their social acceptance. That the Bakers were received nearly everywhere, even by some members of the Royal Family, shows in what esteem African exploration was held at this time. Only Queen Victoria herself remained implacably of the opinion that they were 'not suitable'.

I don't think Khartoum would have suited the Bakers any better today, and I can't say I liked it much either. I found the whole complex very confusing and got lost all the time. It was no use people telling me that it was all very logical and built on a grid system, for apart from Old Khartoum I found it all looked so much the same that there was nothing memorable to latch on to, so what with avoiding the craters in the road and trying to survive Khartoum's free-booting driving style, I never knew where I was and could find myself completely lost a hundred yards from where I was staying. This was out by the airport, in 'embassy land', which was the newest area of the city. Memorising national flags and the emblems on gates was the best way of getting about here, as street signs did not exist.

It was a strange area, combining tasteless affluence with squalor. The houses were large, block-like and modern, but although they were all different they somehow lacked any character. Their broad expanses of walls were painted in a variety of garish pastel shades and many of them were swathed about with barbed wire, like indigestible, armoured wedding cakes. Four-wheel-drive Toyotas or Land Rovers – the status symbols of the expatriates – were parked in front of every house. At night they were taken inside, behind the high locked gates where a night watchman slept on a string bed, presumably ready to spring awake should an intruder get through the defences.

The streets themselves looked as though they had been used for tank manoeuvres: the pavements were ripped to pieces and the roads were all craters and hummocks, with almost no sealed surfaces anywhere, so that the air was always full of swirling dust. Every street had at least one large litter-strewn gap, like a missing tooth, where flocks of goats climbed the flights of exposed stairs to find shelter from the sun on the open concrete floors of the half-built structures. Chai ladies squatted on the ground with their stoves and kettles to serve tea to office workers from the embassies. Other large unpaved open spaces served as bus stations and market places or simply as playgrounds for the wind to blow the rubbish about. The city cried out for water: a profusion of fountains and lakes would have made it bearable, but all it had was an occasional burst sewage pipe flooding a road and providing a happy breeding ground for swarms of mosquitoes.

Khartoum was full of expatriates, most of whom were running aid agencies, of which there were over a hundred. Conversations were largely unintelligible due to the plethora of abbreviations – 'DEBESCA's having a party tonight for the CRITCH lot. Everyone from LODDY will be there and all the FITSA people.' The terrible famine crises were over for the moment, so many of these agencies were trying hard to justify their existence, while the Sudanese government was anxious to reduce the number of foreigners in the country without losing the immense sums of money involved. Britain, in any case, seemed to be pulling out of many of its commitments. The Sudan Club, where the British expatriates were busy rehearsing their annual pantomime, was loud with the complaints that this withdrawal was producing. Bill, who was the prime mover of the dramatic production, was one such malcontent. He was employed by the ODA – British Overseas Development Association – and enjoyed a standard of living he could never have achieved back home. His three children were being educated at private schools in England, and he had a couple of servants and a Land Rover, but most of all he was a big cog in a small wheel, and he was very bitter about having to give it all up. 'They'll never get anyone else to put in the amount of extra I do here,' he said, which I am sure was true for he drilled the cast of the pantomime from early afternoon to late evening, until tempers were at breaking point and the air was taut with jealousies and injured pride.

It was an inward-looking community that gathered each afternoon around the small swimming pool and thronged the bar, where only soft drinks could be sold but where sausages and chips and other nostalgic British fare provided consolation for the absence of a pint of bitter or a g and t. Not that people were totally deprived of alcohol; there was plenty available for those who had a contact with someone in the diplomatic – and this seemed to include just about everyone, for

I visited few expatriate homes where drinks were not on offer. Khartoum, I thought, must be a trying place to live in the intense heat of summer, but otherwise it seemed an unexacting, comfortable sort of existence and not in the least exciting – certainly not the kind of ambiance that Samuel Baker would have found stimulating. Just as the Sudan Club had been moved from its previous prestigious quarters to its present more humble premises, so the people who represented Britain in Sudan had changed from those who were here even twenty years ago. It was a more prosaic and less colourful scene now, where the long slow decline of British influence seemed to be in its death throes and where the departure of those with higher ambitions was symbolised by Jack's progress up the Beanstalk to the refrain of a forgotten popular song.

My main task in Khartoum was to find a way of continuing my journey, and this was not easy. I went first to the British Embassy to find out the current political situation and they issued me with an official warning to the effect that all British subjects were being advised not to go anywhere near southern Sudan or northern Uganda. The SPLA effectively held all the south below Malakal and were infiltrating northwards as far as Renk. Fighting had also broken out again around the Nile area of northern Uganda. Unofficially I was told that my only possible hope would be to fly into Juba, where a skeleton staff of aid workers had remained behind on the British compound when everyone else had been pulled out. From there I might be able to get through to Uganda on a food convoy returning from the beleaguered city on the one road that was now de-mined and open – but, of course, it would be strictly against their advice.

As I had anticipated problems, I was not really dismayed by this assessment of the situation. That there was any road open out of Juba, and that relief lorries were getting through, was excellent news; for the last few months the town had been completely cut off except by air. I had no intention of taking stupid risks, but having come so far I was not prepared to give up without a try; if there was any road open in roughly the right direction, I intended to go on it. The thing to do, I decided, was to get as far south as I could by bicycle, and when I could get no further I would return to Khartoum and try to fly to Juba to take a closer look at the situation from there. The situation changed from day to day and nothing could be gained by dwelling on the frightening stories of journalists being blown up by mines and civilian planes being shot down by the SPLA.

I left the Embassy with one new worry. They had asked me if my visa to Uganda was in order, and when I said that I thought visas to Uganda were not required for British nationals they told me they thought they were. No one could confirm this, which seemed very odd for an embassy in a neighbouring country: what after all are such places for? As it turned out, this was an excellent thing because in my wanderings around 'embassy land' I came across the Ugandan embassy and after finding out from a charming Oxford graduate that I did not need a visa I persuaded him to write me an official letter explaining that I was a harmless writer travelling by bicycle to the source of the Nile, to whom any assistance rendered would please the Ugandan government. After several visits to remind him I received this 'firman' which turned out to be a document of great worth, without which I might well have been shot.

The problem of getting a travel permit from the Sudanese authorities was not nearly so easy. It was a laborious and soul-destroying task. Eventually, after many days of hanging around for hours in dreadful smoke-filled offices with everyone spitting copiously, I was allowed to purchase an expensive permit to bicycle to Kosti, a hundred miles south, and was given a vague promise of a travel permit to fly to Juba if I could produce an air ticket. This was a poser, as there had been no official flights operating to Juba since the SPLA had shot down a passenger plane over Malakal earlier in the year. I had been hoping to hitch a ride on one of the private cargo or aid flights, which don't issue tickets. I had been warned that these small planes flew in at thirteen thousand feet and then dropped down like a stone so as to minimise the chance of getting hit by a rebel missile. It was not a nice experience, I gathered, but I wouldn't mind that as long as I wasn't packed off straight back to Khartoum when I got there because my papers were not in order. The governor of Juba was, in any case, supposed to be suffering from *folie de grandeur* and applied his own rules, which were not reckoned to be either consistent or rational. He had already expelled an Oxfam worker and a European priest for some trumped-up offence, so there seemed to be no real way I could ensure a trouble-free passage. Once more it would have to be a matter of chance.

Having put out feelers with the air-freight people I could do no more about Juba for the time being, and I decided to head off on my trip south a few days after Christmas. I wanted to combine the ride with seeing anything I could of aid development projects in the field, and with this in mind I contacted Oxfam whose Oxford headquarters had been very helpful about briefing me before I came out. Finding anything in Khartoum was a miracle. There were no directories, the phone hardly ever worked, and addresses were usually just PO Box numbers, so it could take days of misdirection to find the place one was looking for. When I did finally track down Oxfam I was not best pleased at being told rudely over the telephone by the director to get lost, as he was having a few days off and there was no one else there to provide information. However I think my guardian angel was at work again in another unlikely disguise, because I went to the office next door instead and presented my *bona fides* to UNICEF, who subsequently proved very helpful in solving my travel problem. They liked the newspaper articles I had been writing and thought we could be mutually beneficial through a project concerning vagrant children with which they were currently concerned, and an appointment was arranged for me to meet with their director when I returned in a week's time.

It was such a delight to be on the move again after a frustrating week of kicking my heels in grimy offices that I almost enjoyed bicycling through the unlovely industrial outskirts of Khartoum. My route led along one side of the Gezira, the area between the Blue and White Niles, which has a reasonable irrigation system and grows Sudan's important cotton crop. The fields were bare at present, endless brown surfaces with not a blade of anything growing. The road seemed to go on for ever, with the faithful African wind still blowing strongly from the north – I remember thinking that this was the only journey I'd ever made where there was no need of the ancient Irish prayer 'May the wind be always at your back'. I covered fifty miles in almost no time and arrived at Jebel Aulio, where I turned west to come down for my first sight of the Nile since leaving Khartoum. There was a dam here built by the British in the 1930s. It seemed on a very human scale after the mighty Aswan Dam, and had a lock for shipping to pass upstream, with small gardens planted among the machinery. The whole place looked for all the world like Teddington Lock on the Thames, but when I got onto the dam wall itself the similarity ceased because of the staggering width of the lake that had been created. Being close to such quantities of water after weeks in desert places felt like a miracle.

I stopped on the causeway to cook up one of my dehydrated packet meals and a small boy with two flat silver fish he'd just caught came and sat silently by my side looking hopefully at the bubbling pot. When he judged it was ready he slipped down to the water and washed his hands, giving me to understand that he expected to 'fuddle' – an old Sudanese custom meaning to share. It was 'Mince Beef with Macaronies' and as I had only one spoon I dropped dollops of the unsavoury-looking concoction into his hand. I thought his palate would be too unspoilt to cope with monosodium glutamate and all the other additives, but he seemed to enjoy it better than I did. He 'fuddled' my orange too and then immediately made off with his fish, which was polite, for if he had hung around it would have meant he expected more.

On the way back across the lock I was invited to spend the night at a nearby army camp by three young officers who were strolling by. It was a large training camp and they had only recently come there after graduating from the military academy at Omdurman. Their next posting would be to the jungles of the south to fight the forces of John Garang and his SPLA, and they were not looking forward to it. They were full of youthful idealism and convinced they were fighting in a just cause but, they said, Garang had superior weapons and the terrain on his side. Fighting in the jungle was not something for which they felt they were equipped, and their losses were always heavier than those of the rebels.

They went to a lot of trouble to make me comfortable in an empty room with a sagging bed and a broken cardboard ceiling. One of them put what was probably his own sheet over the stained cotton mattress and I was escorted by torch to a spartan washroom, cockroach-infested and with no door. They kept apologising for the poor state of everything, saying they were only a poor country, but I was perfectly happy and delighted to be with such pleasant young men. However, a major turned up in a little while and the Agala and I were whisked off in his pick-up to spend the night at his house. I would have preferred to stay where I was, especially as the major's wife was away in Khartoum, but I had no say in the matter. After putting some pink flowered sheets on a bed in an inner room and making me a grapefruit drink in a liquidiser the major disappeared for the evening. I was left alone in an odd concrete house with four interconnecting rooms, an exposed corrugated roof, and with walls painted a bright jade green, which looked particularly virulent under the neon lighting. The place was a mess, the walls festooned with cobwebs, small piles of debris and cigarette butts all over the bare cement floors, and most of the furniture piled up in the two unused rooms. I wondered how long the major's wife had been gone. I was also faintly intimidated by sinister armour-plated black beetles strutting around the debris, stalking cockroaches that looked quite sylph-like in comparison.

I was away bright and early the following morning, having slept wonderfully well. I hadn't even heard the major return, so I must have felt safe. He showed me a snapshot album before I left; most of the pictures were of his wife and small son, but there were others of fellow officers killed in the south. It was a 'terrible war', he said, 'too terrible to talk about. After a few months down there if you were not killed you were thin and ill. It was too dreadful to think of going back but you had to go, it was your duty.'

The novelty of riding on tarmac had worn off and I found the price paid for the speed and ease of it was too high; lorries and buses tore past with reckless abandon leaving clouds of choking dust in their wake, and by the roadside the corpses of cows and sheep which had fallen victim to them lay with their bones showing through the gaping holes pecked in their drum-taut skins. The wind, sensing my smug complacency of yesterday and the absence of prayers for its continued favour, had swung round to the west, and when the road also turned in that direction there was nothing at all in the flat plain to check its force, and riding into its gritty teeth was hard unpleasant work. The only features in the flat bleak landscape were the occasional hovels selling food to the passengers of passing buses. When I stopped at one of these to eat boiled eggs and foul, a boy who was standing beside me as I made notes in my journal displayed his literacy and knowledge of

English by telling me I had written the wrong date – actually he was wrong, but for a while he had me worried.

I grew so weary of the featureless plain that I decided to cross the river and spend the night at a town shown on my map as Ed Duiem. When I reached the banks of the Nile I thought I had come to another dam because the river was still like a huge lake, but it was only the back flow from the dam at Jebel Aulio, piling up the water seventy-five miles further south. To cross to Ed Duiem there was a car ferry, a small boat with a piece cut out of the side through which the cars were coaxed and bounced and not at all improved in the process; it carried just two vehicles at a time on the twenty minute crossing. There were half a dozen young girls in bright clothes and jewellery, carrying large flat baskets on their heads. They had been selling packets of sunflower seeds and such like to bus passengers on the tarmac road – a round trip of six miles – and were now returning home with many bold, flashing glances at the young local males. They were Felata girls, a type of gypsy whose culture encourages their young to pay their way from an early age. Unlike other Sudanese girls, they are expected to be able to go about without male protection.

I spent the night at the home of a Dutch couple to which I'd been taken by some local people on the boat. It was the cleanest house I'd seen in the Sudan, though it was just a traditional Sudanese house with a courtyard and rooms off. They had a young baby and they were determined that it was going to remain healthy, so they had spent a couple of weeks before moving in filling in all the holes in the plaster and scrubbing and painting. The result was really very pleasant without it being pretentious or putting them on a level far beyond that of their Sudanese neighbours. They were employed by the UN International Labour Office which is concerned with people's working conditions worldwide. Bas was instigating a labour-intensive drinking water project and his wife, Wil, was conducting a survey among the women to see what sorts of things they would most like to learn when the schemes were set up there. Solar cooking was on offer and seemed to be creating interest, not surprisingly really in a place where natural fuel other than cow dung is almost non-existent.

Over supper they told me about their work. The problems of the area were quite grave, although only a short time ago it had been a fertile region with a reasonable rainfall. The old people, said Bas, could remember when fish had been caught in the wadis which had been full of water for half the year but now were just desert. There were too many cattle overgrazing the land and not enough trees and hedgerows to form shelter belts to break up the country and defeat the erosion. Drinking water was the single biggest problem, for in a hundred-kilometre stretch the rainfall could vary from nothing at all to four hundred centimetres a year. Wells were always caving in, and in the rainy season children drank from puddles on the ground and got sick. Ten kilometres from the Nile there was no water, so much of the villagers' resources were spent walking back and forwards over large distances carrying every drop they needed from the river. The area Bas and Wil were working in was small enough for them to be able to see results, and already Bas had one irrigation canal in operation and some wells dug; but he said it was just a drop in a very large ocean of poverty and neglect, and that it was difficult to feel very optimistic about the future of Sudan unless there was a drastic re-thinking in the West.

CHAPTER FOURTEEN

Southwards to Renk

There were about eighty miles of rough track to Kosti on the west bank of the river, and after making enquiries I thought there was a good chance of getting through on it, even though traffic seldom went that way now that there was the new tarmac road on the east bank. It was too far for one day's ride but I would see much more of the country and the people than by continuing on the easy way through the featureless plain. When a traveller has been steadily pressing on for a couple of months and the ultimate destination is still very distant there can be a tendency to hurry unnecessarily, losing sight of what the journey is really all about, but I was being so curtailed in how far south I was allowed to go that I had no trouble remembering that every mile was precious.

I did not regret my decision for a moment, for the route led me through a uniquely fascinating area of rough, dry scrub country, where the square mud-brick Arab houses were beginning to give way to round, conical-roofed grass huts, and the racial mix of the Sudanese Arabs was replaced by a people who were more completely Negro. It was like entering a new country, the beginning of what Churchill had called 'the real Africa'. The villages I saw varied in prosperity, depending on how close to the Nile the path led me; those near the water had plenty of tall shady trees and a greater proportion of Arab-style dwellings and even an occasional tea house. Those furthest away were small grass hut encampments, squashed closely together behind a thorn hedge. Everywhere, scores of children with water containers made from ten pound tin cans rode their donkeys to and from the Nile, invisible somewhere over to my left. Most donkeys and children were nervous of me, probably because they saw few white people and certainly none on a bright red bicycle. They were ragged, skinny kids, and not a few were crippled or had some other deformity, but when they were not startled, they seemed full of life and would smile and give friendly waves, and occasionally one or two would run beside me for a while.

All the problems Bas and Wil had told me about the night before were apparent, especially the over-grazing, the lack of water and shelter belts, and the erosion caused by these things. Within a mile of any village I was off the Agala and pushing it with difficulty, even though most of its load was back in Khartoum, for the ground had been reduced to a dry dust bowl by the staggering numbers of goats as well as cattle that milled about in large herds. It was not all a trial by dust, for at one point I rode into an irrigated patch that crossed the track, broke through the crust, and began rapidly to sink. I just managed to snatch off the panniers and throw them onto a firm bit of ground ahead before the Agala and I were knee-deep in thick squelchy mud. It was a difficult scramble out, and a lengthy process scraping off the glutinous stuff.

There were no offers of hospitality in any of the villages, which was so unusual for the Sudan that I think it was a good indication of how poor the region was. There was a pull-in for trucks about half way, though I can't think that it did much business since I had seen only two trucks all day – both had been old high-wheeled Bedfords, full of people, and both had stopped to make sure I was all right. The pull-in was a series of little open-fronted booths built out of grass matting, with further mats on the floor to sit on; there were about a dozen of them, and fierce competition ensued for my custom. I went into one that served only tea and when I made signs that I wanted to eat, a man went off and brought me a bowl of something that tasted so foul I couldn't eat it. When I rejected it, the man was obviously worried that I wouldn't pay, though I did of course and then he rapidly demolished the contents of the bowl himself with every sign of enjoyment. It was not a restful stop as all the local boys came to stand and stare, edging forward as close as they could get, while the chai lady and several older males tried to chase them away.

In spite of the difficulties of the track and the amount of walking I had to do I still made very good time, so that just before nightfall when the fiery plumed sky was beginning to flood with violet shadows, I was not far from Kosti and could see its lights twinkling in the distance. I had thought to wait until dark and then spread the sleeping bag under a bush, but the closer I got to Kosti the more frequent and poorer the villages became, and as night approached the atmosphere seemed to become suspicious and hostile. Menacing-looking dogs began to patrol around outside the perimeter of the thorn hedges with hackles raised, growling as I passed. I was definitely not keen on bedding down in such surroundings – and suddenly I remembered that it was New Year's Eve and I felt a yearning to 'first foot' in the New Year with some of my own countrymen. This meant getting to Kosti, and so I increased my efforts; but darkness won easily, overtaking me while I was still in the bush. Had an Isuzu pick-up not stopped to offer me a lift I would have had a hard time getting anywhere, since unbeknown to me the Agala had just picked up a vicious thorn in its front tyre.

Kosti looked the height of twentieth-century sophistication, with solid buildings, a railway and street lighting, but it was not so large that 'coadjers' could remain unknown in it. I was taken straight to the home of two young British teachers, both called Jane, who were on contract to the Sudanese School service. Committed young people, they were very different from the contract teachers I had met on the Dongola boat. The Janes' year in the Sudan had convinced them that they wanted to make a career of teaching and they planned to return to Britain to become properly qualified before coming back for another spell. They received a fellow countrywoman dropping in out of the blue as though it was an everyday occurrence, and I was given just ten minutes to down a cup of tea before they, two friends who were staying with them and I were picked up by car and whisked off to a New Year's party – fairy godmother stuff I decided this time, rather than the guardian angel, though I did think she might have done something about my travel-stained appearance before summoning the pumpkin.

The house we were taken to was owned by an American transport company and was huge and luxurious for those parts. It was also under-used as the company had rather shrunk in the present troubled times, with only half the country to operate in. We were all going to sleep there after the party because it was easier than getting everyone home again. Before the party began wonderful things like baths and quantities of food from a giant freezer were organised for the house guests, and there was so much of everything that for the first time in weeks I felt adequately fed.

There were many nationalities at the party, including some rather lugubrious Finns; in fact it was the most international New Year I had ever celebrated. There were no Scots, however, so there was no Robbie Burns and no first footing, but there was enough alcohol, both the locally made gut-rot and the illegally imported kind, to get everyone mildly merry, and there were ancient Beatle tapes to supply the necessary nostalgia. It was a long night as different nationalities wanted to see the New Year in when it was twelve o'clock in their own countries – which were all later than Sudan time – and there was not enough of anything alcoholic to last that long. Most of the people present were Irish, from an agency called CONCERN, and among them were two nurses running a feeding station 150 miles further south, at a place called Renk. As casually as if they were inviting me to tea, the nurses, Claire and Joan, suggested I might like to go with them to see the place when they went back by Land Rover in the morning, and almost as casually I accepted, for I was beginning to get used to the way that things were falling uncannily into place on this journey. I'd spent so many frustrating days in Khartoum being refused permission to go further south than Kosti and yet here I was being given the chance to get on another 150 miles. Only one journalist to my knowledge had been allowed into Renk in recent months, and he had been so incensed by the time and trouble it had taken to get the travel permit that his entire article had hardly mentioned Renk but only the difficulties in getting there. He had been particularly bitter, I remembered, because after all the trouble he'd gone to no one had asked to see the precious permit. Since I had no permit I was going to have to rely on things not having changed.

In the morning I wasn't sure it hadn't all been an alcoholic dream. The Irish had vanished and the four young teachers were fast asleep and looked as though they might stay that way for a long time. I wandered around in the garden watching four ridiculous baby storks stumbling about in their precarious nest, which was swaying around high in an acacia tree while the parents kept a watching brief from nearby, their long pointed beaks following the huge predatory kites circling endlessly round. I was called in after a while by the African cook to eat another cholesterol-rich, non-Moslem feast of sausage, eggs and bacon from the immense freezer and by the time I'd filled up any remaining hollows, one of the Janes appeared to take me back to her house.

There was ample time to mend the puncture and clean the residue of thick mud from the Agala while I waited for the Irish nurses to collect me. Eventually when it was two hours past the promised ten o'clock start Jane took me to CONCERN's house where we found all the members of the agency having an Independence Day lunch – Sudanese independence, I believe, not Irish. Apart from the organiser, all the CONCERN personnel seemed to be volunteers, experts in various fields working for a pittance for a limited period of time. Their quarters were certainly not luxurious, and they were clearly making considerable sacrifices in their standards of living to work out here – which was more how I had imagined aid in Africa than what I had seen in Khartoum.

We set off in a Land Rover piled high with blankets. A young Sudanese called Mousa was at the wheel, for foreigners are not allowed to drive in this area. We crossed a huge, white aggressively modern bridge, totally incongruous, in the empty, primitive landscape, and almost immediately there was a giant white cube of a building rising out of a sea of sugar cane, which was appropriately the sugar refinery of Kenana. All the other schemes for making Kosti into a modern industrial centre have been shelved for the moment, so these two solitary and uncompromising structures looked particularly odd and out of place in the wilderness – like a Dali painting. There were two police checks before we turned south towards Renk and at both I tried to look unconcerned, though my palms were sweating with the worry that I might be asked for my travel permit. Only the car's papers were checked, however, and no interest was taken in the passengers.

The road was atrocious with great drifts of dust and deeply rutted places where one or other side of the vehicle canted up at an alarming angle. There were several occasions when we nearly rolled right over, Mousa fighting to regain control after taking a corner too fast. We were in something of a hurry to get to Renk before dark otherwise we would be made to wait all night at a police post. It was hot, much hotter than Khartoum, and the huge herds of camels and cattle that occasionally moved over the immense expanses of scrub land became fragmented, broken images, insubstantially wavering through the heat haze like dreams of lost Biblical tribes. The country was dramatic, beautiful even, though on no human scale. Great rocky jebels reared up abruptly from the plains with not a hint of a bush or a blade of grass growing on them – castles of stone from which the vultures kept a lookout.

Once out of the White Nile Province and into the Southern Province the police checks became more frequent and we began to see many abandoned villages. Some of these had been burned by the army because of suspected S P L A infiltration, while from others the people had fled in panic when the two forces had opened fire on one another. We saw the Nile only once when we stopped at a small town on its bank for some refreshment. It was a quiet friendly place where the people were very black and the women did not wear a tobe. I had become so used to seeing all the women in Sudan swathed in this long cloth that it wasn't until I noticed these southern women walking so freely that I realised what a restricting garment it is. Everyone wore rather less in these parts and it was nice to see that legs no longer had to be hidden under long robes or trousers.

The police checks reminded me of the Bakers' journey through these parts and their constant problems with corruption, exploitation, inertia, and insolence. I wondered if it was so very different now. Slaves were no longer lying manacled in sheds by the waterside, waiting for the slavers' transports and hurriedly pushed out of sight when the interfering white man appeared, but the underlying disregard for the sufferings of others was still just as apparent, as was the divide between north and south, between Arabs and the others.

When we came to a checkpoint, we always stopped; Mousa turned off the engine and we sat with tight placating smiles on our faces until one of the lounging guards condescended to drag himself to his feet and stroll slowly towards us with his gun. Sometimes they felt too tired to do more than wave us on from their chairs, but if any of them spotted the blankets, they gathered around like jackals. Having admitted that she was the one in charge, Joan would be marched off to be subjected to twenty minutes or so of wheedling, argument and veiled threats in an attempt to relieve her of the blankets. She always tried to explain that they were for the poor and needy southerners. But this cut no ice with the guards, for they too were poor, and people from the south were not really people to them; they were non-Moslems and potential rebels, so why waste blankets on them?

We made it to Renk just before nightfall and I had time only for a fleeting impression of a small Nile-side town surrounded by a huge number of small grass-hutted villages before we arrived at the ramshackle house in the town which CONCERN rented for its workers. The only other Europeans likely to be in town were some Poles who did perilous crop-spraying from World War 11 aeroplanes. They were not around, however – which was a pity as they also filled the water tank for the nurses. I wouldn't have liked to live for long with no water and no electricity in those temperatures. In fact there was electricity, once a diabolical generator had been started, but the noise of it was so dreadful that no one could bear it for long. There was also a cook-cum-general factotum, a local man who produced indifferent meals but in such primitive circumstances that complaint was not possible. My respect for the Irish who not only coped but worked extremely hard in these conditions, and stayed cheerful with it, grew with every hour I spent in Renk.

I was awoken while it was still dark by the Moslem dawn call to prayer somewhere very close and I lay in the already hot little room slowly taking in the fact that I was now in an uneasy frontier town. Formerly a sleepy little Nile-side town of no importance, Renk had become the present limit of government influence. Beyond it to the south the SPLA held sway, living in the bush and fighting a guerilla war with sophisticated weapons. All the major Nile-side towns like Malakal, Bor and Juba had been effectively cut off for some time; barges coming up the Nile had been blown out of the water, ending the Nile's role as the main highway between Kosti and Juba. When the SPLA also shot down a passenger airliner over Malakal, communications with the area between Renk and Juba had virtually ceased, as had all the multi-national, multi-billion dollar projects for materially improving this part of the world. One scheme, the building of the 220-mile-long Junglei Canal, which would drain the Sudd and provide enormous quantities of additional water, had been not far short of completion. It is unlikely that it ever will be finished, as the hugely expensive trenching machine has been destroyed by the rebels and what has already been cut is slowly filling up with sand again.

The satellite villages around Renk are the temporary encampments of Shilluk people who have been driven north in their thousands as the government army pursues its policy of clearing areas that might aid the SPLA. The Shilluk lived in tight-knit farming communities and had been settled in their Nile-side territories since the sixteenth century. They had a religion in which the Supreme Being, Nyikang, maintained the harmony of earth, sky and river and brought the rain each year to defeat the ruin threatened by the sun – in this desperately hot part of the world the sun is seldom seen as a beneficent deity. The Shilluk also believed in divine kingship with the king as the manifestation of Nyikang, and this has had a very unifying effect on the tribe and helped them to survive during the centuries of Arab slave trading. Since the mid-18th century, missionaries set up schools and hospitals in Shilluk territory and converted many of them, until in 1963 the Sudan government expelled all missionaries from the south as part of their attempt to unify the country under Islam. Though many Shilluk are Christian many more follow the old beliefs.

Before breakfast we went to the feeding centre which was housed under two open-sided marquees by an abandoned hospital building. A stream of eager, smiling little black children were making their way there, struggling along as fast as they could, carrying babies and toddlers scarcely smaller than themselves and stopping occasionally to try and hoist their little burdens higher onto non-existent hips. They were all from the temporary Shilluk villages round about, but it was quite a walk for some of them. Babies between six months and two years old are most at risk among displaced people. Back home, with a wide variety of foods available there is no problem, but here once the babies are weaned they cannot thrive on the unpalatable dura wheat which is all they can get, and they die in large numbers. A feeding station identifies the children most at risk by applying an internationally accepted height to weight ratio, and so throughout the day hungry children have to be turned away because they are not yet in a poor enough state. Once accepted on the scheme, the child and the person who brings him are fed a sort of nutritional porridge three times a day at the centre, returning each day until they have put on the required weight. Unlike refugees, these displaced Shilluk people were receiving no government aid at all. What CONCERN had seen as a temporary problem was not improving and while I was there it had been decided to reorganise the centre on a permanent basis.

The first child in the queue on this particular morning was a newcomer called Michael, not quite two and almost comatose in his mother's arms. He was in a state of advanced emaciation, with the skull-like head of an old man and limbs that seemed as brittle as a bird's. His vastly swollen stomach was covered by a T-shirt with a grinning cartoon rabbit on its front, in obscene contrast to the skeletal child. His mother had the saddest face I'd ever seen and for a while it was all I could do to stay where I was and not turn away to spare myself the humiliation of weeping. It is strange how nothing seen on television or read about is really anything like being face to face with the actual scandal of a child dying of hunger. It is impossible not to feel a profound sense of guilt and shame just by being there, well-fed and healthy. Claire put her arms round the mother and said she would try and get her baby admitted to hospital so that he could be fed by tube. The woman didn't understand the words but the warmth and comfort got through and she tried to smile, and I think that was the hardest moment of all.

Within an hour every space under the awnings was packed with a solid mass of black humanity, concentrated on the red plastic bowls filled to the brim with thick yellow goo. Plastic spoons flashed up and down as fast as they could go, and eyes never strayed from the bowls for a second. Little boys and girls of five or so were spooning the mixture into the younger ones, whose faces were soon covered with the stuff, with flies crawling thickly all over them. The porridge was prepared in enormous cauldrons by some Shilluk women, recruited from among the displaced people. They were lovely with the children, filling every bowl as full as they could and rejoicing at the amounts eaten. Some of the bigger children tried to secrete porridge in old bottles and tins to take away with them but this was discouraged because of the very real danger of food poisoning in the insanitary conditions everywhere. For the same reason they were made to use spoons, whereas they would all eat with their hands at home.

The whole area around the tents was an open lavatory as the children did not use the latrines provided and it was impossible with present resources to enforce hygiene. Now that it was to become a permanent station there were plans afoot to fence the area, convert the unused building into dining rooms and organise some educational activity for the children between meals instead of their just sitting there. Some of the present cooks could well be nursery assistants, I thought; especially one beautiful young woman called Elisabeth who, when she wasn't doling out food, always had some small child or other on her knee while she sang softly to it, 'One, two, three, Jesus love me; two, three, four, he love you more.' The Shilluk women dote on their babies and can think of no greater joy than producing more of them. While Claire and I sat with the cooks, helping to sift the weevils out of the flour, Elisabeth softly touched each woman's stomach in turn, informing us proudly 'She three month, four month her, her maybe have two' amid the proud conspiratorial giggles of the others.

I could not estimate how many displaced Shilluk there were in the villages around Renk, tens of thousands certainly, but no one had any real idea. In their flight to Renk they had tried to remain in their original village groupings, which was obviously of great importance to so tight knit a people who, even in adversity, had maintained a sense of harmony that was very endearing. They were also a particularly attractive people physically: slender and graceful with beautifully poised heads and a traditional tribal scarification that seemed to enhance their appearance rather than otherwise. It is very like that of the Dinkas' – a horizontal line across the forehead 'beaded' at intervals by having ashes rubbed into the incision.

A man called Jude who was employed by CONCERN took me to visit some of the nearer Shilluk villages. Jude was of the same tribe but had been at college in Malakal until it was closed down by the government, after which he had gone to Khartoum to continue his education. After graduation he was unable to return to his home because of the road blocks, so he was waiting at Renk for an opportunity to get back and take up his post as a lay worker with the Lutheran church.

Most of the Shilluk were living within extended family groups, with three or four huts inside a wattle-fenced area. The small round huts were beautifully made but completely bare of all possessions except perhaps for a few flour sacks, cut in half for sleeping on. The nights can be very cold at that time of year, and the blankets we had brought were no more than a small drop in this huge ocean of need. There were few people around as most were out on the endless task of trying to find some means of surviving. Many of the women walked each day to distant woods to gather sticks to turn into charcoal for sale in the suq. The men did any work they could, but only in harvest time would they have a chance of a few weeks steady employment bringing in the cotton, sugar or dura crops. A large number of younger men were engaged in transporting water from the Nile to sell in town. They used home-made carts, really just painted oildrums on wheels, and could hope to earn about thirty pence for a long day's work, half of which went to the owner of the vehicle. Renk had once had piped water, but the system had long since broken down. I saw several young boys making remarkably detailed model cars and lorries out of old tins, the separate pieces held together by wire threaded through nail holes punched round the edges. They took many hours of patient work and were sold for a few coppers.

When we were in one compound, talking to a man who was mending a fishing net, an old dishevelled woman rushed screaming at me with her hands curled like talons ready to strike. Several members of the family caught her before she reached me and led her away. She was mad, the man told Jude, and had been that way since they had fled from their home six months ago – she must have associated me with the enemy in some way. While we talked several other people drifted in and Jude said they wanted to tell me 'their story' and after they had done so I could only wonder that more of them had not lost their reason. 'We tell you these things,' they said, 'because we know you are a journalist and you want to know the truth; if the government knew we tell you these things they would maybe kill us. We put ourselves in danger to tell you these things. When people ask us why we are here we say it is because John Garang ate up all our cattle. We say this but it is not true. John Garang did not eat up all our cattle. He took only some. Then the army came and they say we help John Garang and they drive off all our cattle and chase the people out and while the people run, the army shoot at us. Many we leave dead, many small ones, women and men also, many. Then the army slaughtered our cattle. We come here with nothing in our hands; everything we have left behind in our villages. We had everything there; even those who were poor had fish in the streams and mangoes growing wild in the forests. Our people have not known hunger till now. The government cares nothing for us. We are Christians; better for them if we and our children die. The only hope for us is to have our own country. We hope for this.'

Before I left Renk I went with Mousa on a tour of the town itself. The centre was solidly Arab, with the police barracks, the bank and the houses of an important few surrounded by a high wire fence that could be locked and guarded at night. The rest of the town and the villages of the displaced Shilluk had no protection in the event of an SPLA raid. I was told that there were frequent SPLA infiltrations, and that when the army heard of one, they brought up artillery and shelled the village despite the fact that it was full of people.

Apart from a few streets of run-down Arab houses, like the one rented by CONCERN, the rest of Renk consisted of traditional African family compounds, a woven perimeter fence sheltering six or seven grass huts, the goats, hens, cattle and a few dogs. There were some larger compounds, and some where a red flag on a tall pole indicated that home-brewed beer could be drunk there, while a white flag denoted that spirits were on sale. Down by the river, where the town's vegetables grew, huge barges lay rotting and gathering weed; it was well over a year since they had been in use, since the day the SPLA had blown a string of barges out of the water, cutting the main artery of the country at one fell swoop. Nothing moved on the water now, except for a pump working perpetually to fill the oil drums of an unending line of water carriers.

Coming back I stopped to photograph some smiling children squatting in the dust beside the little piles of fruit and vegetables they were selling, and immediately a drunken policeman came up and started to threaten me with his baton. I had been given an upgraded camera pass in Khartoum with my photograph in it and 'Press' and 'Special Permit' written large on the front; it even claimed I could shoot ciné film, but it didn't impress this uniformed bully. Probably he couldn't read anyway. Remembering that I had no permit to be there, I climbed back into the Land Rover before he tried to arrest me.

Before I left Renk next morning I returned for a final visit to the feeding centre, and there against all expectations was little Michael, still too weak to sit unaided but slowly spooning food into himself

with such grim determination that once again it was all I could do not
to cry. The adults and the bigger children pointed to his efforts
proudly, looking as delighted as though it was their triumph, which I
suppose it was really – another of their number had survived for
another day.

CHAPTER FIFTEEN

Back to Khartoum

The huge, rubbish-strewn open space was full of ancient sagging buses, but few were functioning and it was impossible to find out what if anything was happening in the milling crowd. The unplanned visit to Renk had left me with precious little time to backtrack the three-hundred-and-fifty-miles to Khartoum in time for my Monday morning appointment with UNICEF, since I'd reached Kosti only late on Saturday, battered and bruised from the appalling Land Rover journey. Even on a tarmac road, the remaining two-hundred-miles against the wind was far too much for one day's ride. A bus was the only solution – except that transport had now been added to the long list of Sudan's 'temporary' shortages, so much so that the military had just commandeered sixty large United Nations lorries that had been trying to get through to the besieged town of Wau with much needed food supplies. I'd learned this from the aid people at Kosti, who were all greatly concerned by the implications, especially as it was rumoured that the army had loaded up the lorries with weapons and had driven them south to an unknown destination. Against this my own worries seemed trivial, though it made the waiting no easier.

After several hours of fruitless enquiry and agitation, a friendly bystander pointed out a Khartoum bus. The driver was sensibly keeping out of trouble by selling the tickets through a window of the locked vehicle and a great crowd of bony Sudanese men were agitatedly jumping up and down below him in competition to buy them. I tried waiting my turn but I was just pushed out of the way, and hampered as I was with my bicycle I couldn't compete. Then I spotted two young men from CONCERN who were also supposed to be going to Khartoum and I thought they might leap in and get all our tickets, but they were much too shy. There was nothing else for it; giving the machine into their keeping, I burrowed into the scrum on the principle of 'when in Rome', and was rewarded with three tickets and one for the Agala.

The young men repaid my sportive efforts by helping to haul the bicycle up the ladder to the top of the bus and also by letting me sit between them on the broken back seat, which was more comfortable than sitting next to a Sudanese as the Irish boys were better padded. It was a hot tough journey back to Khartoum: with the bus packed to more than twice its official capacity, and with the Sudanese men having no inhibitions at all about taking more than their fair share of the space. We had the opportunity to expand a little when there was a police check for rebel infiltration and all the Sudanese men had to get out of the bus and line up, but as there appeared to be no rebels among them, just as many got back on again and we soon lost our advantage under their remorseless boring techniques.

My anxieties about getting a flight to Juba were resolved as soon as I was shown into the director's office at UNICEF. 'Why not fly with us?' said Cole Dodge. 'We're taking our plane down there next week, there's plenty of room for you and your bicycle.' It wasn't as casual as it sounded I realised, for he had photocopies of my newpaper articles in front of him, and clearly he thought I might be as useful to him as he was being to me. The scheme he thought I might like to look at – the rehabilitation of vagrant children – was one which deeply interested me; before I left England I had heard about the thousands of young homeless boys roaming the streets of Khartoum, and had already decided that I would try and find out more about them if I could. UNICEF were flying a Norwegian psychologist out to a town on the Chad border the following day to see a part of the scheme in operation, and Cole Dodge thought I should go along too. I jumped at the chance of seeing another part of the Sudan, even though it would leave me just a few hours to get some idea of the background of the problem. Not for the first time I realised that Americans operate on a different time-scale to the British. I was however to have the assistance of a local employee called Sadiq to help me 'get orientated'.

Sadiq rushed me from office to office, to shake hands with a variety of people whose function I had no idea of, but all of whom had American accents and gave an overwhelming impression of eagerness, like football cheer leaders. The all-important 'fixer', however, was Sudanese. He arranged all the travel permits for the agency and needed my passport for the flight schedule. He could get documents through in a few hours which would take anyone else days to obtain; he said it was simply because he dealt with a different government department to the one I had to use. This was probably true, but it was only a fraction of the story, and I was beginning to realise that without a fixer no agency or business could function at all in the Sudan.

I came away with my head in a whirl and I had no time to collect my thoughts before I was hurried to a raw new building which I was told was 'Sabah' or 'Morning' which was a refuge for the Street Boys.

My first impression was of a courtyard bursting at the seams with tough-looking, ragged boys and youths, whom a couple of men armed with long sticks were trying to keep in order, quelling the acrimonious fights and scuffles that constantly erupted as the boys collected plates of food doled out from a large black cauldron. The place seethed with angry, hurt young people bristling with rebelliousness and suspicion, and I could feel waves of resentment directed at me, or rather at what I represented – a stranger from a world of privilege, who was seeing them in such humiliating circumstances. Then I began to notice that many of the boys lacked hands and limbs, and a horrible suspicion began to grip me. 'Dear God, surely not?' Even under the recent hideous application of Shariah law, whereby the hands and feet of convicted thieves had been amputated as a punishment, they surely couldn't have done such a thing to these children? The idea was so awful that I thought I was going to faint. I'd spoken aloud without realising it and Sadiq said in a matter of fact way that some of the boys were old enough to have been so punished but that probably all these mutilations were accidental, not deliberate. The boys had been crippled while running away to Khartoum, falling from the roofs of trains in squabbles or while asleep and getting some part of themselves crushed beneath the wheels.

Sadiq thought there were about 20,000 homeless boys aged between seven and twenty living rough in Khartoum, but there could well be more. Now that the immediate famine crises in the Sudan were over, many aid agencies were beginning to address themselves to the problem of homeless children, and some seemed to be leaping in with instant solutions. Given the amount of rivalry that existed between the various agencies and the need for them to justify their existence, there was a real danger of a free-for-all, with no co-ordination of effort or building on what had already been achieved. No one was more aware of this danger than a charismatic Yugoslav woman called Blanka whom I met at Sabah. She had been at the forefront of the problem, and knew more about the whole subject than everyone else I met put together.

Blanka is a practical, energetic person in her mid fifties, who has lived in the Sudan for thirty years after marrying a Sudanese she met at university. Twenty years later, with her three sons practically grown up, she found she needed to do something about her rather stultifying life, for the restrictions placed on females in a Moslem country are seldom easy, especially for a highly educated Western woman. Her husband's salary as a university professor did not enable her to return to Yugoslavia for the annual visit which she felt was her life-line. So at forty she decided to brave the opposition that independent female action is certain to arouse in such a society and do something to help herself, and after much thought she opened an ice-cream parlour, the first in Khartoum. It was an immediate success and gave Blanka far more than mere monetary independence. It also brought her face to face with the problem of the Street Boys.

The ice cream drew the homeless boys like flies, and they hung around long enough for Blanka to become aware of how desperate their plight was. They were not only hungry, in rags and often needing medical attention, but equally in need of psychological support, education and training. At first she gave them food and sometimes clothes – though these they often sold straight away – and tried to get them medical help. Slowly, some of them learnt to trust her and to talk to her about their lives and problems. The plight of the older boys tormented her most and still does. 'The cute little ones make out by begging,' she told me. 'But sixteen is not an attractive age. They learn not to hold their hand out any more because they know they'll be refused. I see such boys withdraw more and more into themselves until they become desperate.'

A few years ago, when the results of the drought and famine had dramatically increased the numbers of vagrant boys, Blanka realised she could not cope alone with the problem any longer. One day she came across a youth lying in an alley with a leg so gangrenous that no one could get near him for the smell of it. Somehow Blanka got him into her car and drove around and around Khartoum with a handkerchief pressed to her face, trying not to vomit while she searched for a doctor who was prepared to help. She found one eventually, but her trial wasn't over by any means: as she then had to hold the boy tight in her arms while the doctor sliced away at the rotten flesh, trying to find enough healthy tissue to avoid an amputation.

After that it was Blanka's turn to hold out her hands and, as sometimes happens when a need is made known, various individuals and local voluntary aid groups came forward to help. The first priority was for a centre where the boys could find temporary refuge from the life of the street, somewhere away from the ice-cream parlour which was beginning to suffer from the boys importuning the customers. The money for it was raised just a year ago and Sabah opened its doors; as Blanka says, 'It is a place that gives the boys a little space to take stock of the situation.'

It also gives them their first opportunity to learn to trust again. Watching Blanka with these tough streetwise youngsters was to see a transformation come over their closed faces. They thronged about her smiling and laughing, eager to talk and be cuddled or to have an arm about their shoulders. They visibly relaxed and became children again. Sabah was one of the best things I saw operating in the Sudan and yet its security was extremely tenuous. Its only funding were casual gifts of a few thousand dollars raised here and there, and it had absolutely no fixed income. The best it was currently hoping for was that UNICEF would underwrite its expenditure for the following year.

Because the children talk so freely to her, Blanka, with her training in psychology, has been able to build up a detailed picture of what drives the boys from their homes and what their lives are like on the streets. There are two sides to their flight to the city. On the one hand there is the break-up of families and the upheaval of whole communities in the drought and famine, with the attendant weakening of social values and interdependencies. Absentee fathers have had to seek work elsewhere and are often never heard of again, mothers move in with another man, and hostilities and resentments result – any or all of these things can drive a boy from his home.

On the other hand there are the factors which draw the aspiring youngsters to the 'golden cities of infinite promise'. As in many disadvantaged countries, the cinema in the Sudan is flourishing and shows an abundance of cheap imported films, with frequent changes of programme. Most of these films glorify a tough urban image of overt material values, with an emphasis on the martial arts and on grabbing what you can get. These 'dream palaces' become reality for many boys, with film characters replacing the absent father or whatever male figures they would once have modelled themselves upon. They begin to want to live the dream, and they talk over the idea with their peers. Normally an older boy provides the catalyst that finally decides a child to run away; often they go in groups, with an older boy in charge. They believe the streets will be paved with gold – indeed there is a story about a boy who on leaving the station at Khartoum, saw a banknote lying on the ground but left it there because he was sure there would be lots more lying about whenever he needed them.

Once in the city their lives follow an inevitable and brutish pattern. It is impossible to find work, apart from an occasional portering job in the suqs. Most have to beg and many become thieves; some start off that way, organised into stealing gangs by the older boys. Few of them stay clear of the police for long and when they are caught they might well spend a considerable time in prison before being sentenced to fifteen lashes, after which they are back on the streets. At one time police policy was to round up all the street boys in a certain area, load them onto lorries and drive them hundreds of miles into the desert where they were dumped, but they always found their way back and now there are too many to make the exercise worthwhile. There is a lot of sexual exploitation too, and many boys are terrified and develop phobias about rape. Apart from time spent in a cinema, there is no safety, no let-up from perpetual fear and harassment and they are too scared to sleep in case they are attacked. In consequence, most of them roam about all night and it is small wonder that so many of them are accident prone and are always wounding themselves. Solvent abuse has recently also become a problem, even among very young boys.

Sadiq took me to see one of the first schemes to rehabilitate a handful of this army of lost boys. It was at a technical school where, after normal college hours, when the students had left, twenty ex-

Sabah youngsters had the use of the workshop facilities. They had just completed an eight-month course of basic education combined with technical training in carpentry, electronics or engineering, living together in simple housing, learning to cook, to wash their own clothes and generally maintain themselves. When I saw them they could have been any group of normal well-motivated teenagers, interested in what they were doing and able to work with only a minimum of supervision. It was hard to believe that eight short months ago they had been like the suspicious, hostile and anti-social boys I had seen at Sabah. By any reckoning it had been a very rapid re-socialisation and based on principles totally opposed to 'a short sharp shock programme'. They had had the chance to regain their self-respect, and they seemed to have grasped the opportunity with both hands. I could only hope that others would be able to find a similar break.

The psychologist Magne Raundalen was being flown to El Obeid and Nyala to prepare a report on the whole problem and to see the schemes which were being originated for the runaways back in their own communities. I was grateful to be included on the trip and given a bird's eye view of Western Sudan, but I couldn't help thinking that he had an impossible task. Even the most eminent expert must be at a disadvantage if he speaks no Arabic and had never visited the country before, and has less than a week to find out what Blanka's long years of patient listening had discovered. To add to his problems Magne was suffering sunburn, having come straight from the snows of a Norwegian winter to the tropical climate of the Sudan.

We flew out of Khartoum airport at 5 a.m. in a little Piper Aztec 6-seater. It was my first flight in so small a craft. It seemed far too fragile to be taken seriously, so it was with a feeling of disbelief that I found myself airborne, with the White Nile far below – a red molten river that changed to sparkling gold as the sun climbed out of the eastern horizon, flooding the grey desert with light, and revealing a pattern of square dead fields and dry wadis and the straight swathes of what passed for roads. It was hard to believe that anything ever grew down there, and I wondered whether the recent years of drought had not finally killed this harsh habitat. No one on the plane had any idea. Sadiq had not long finished his education in England, and knew little about his homeland outside of Khartoum. Because of his foreign upbringing, many of his countrymen did not believe that he was a Sudanese. The pilot was an Italian who had been expelled from his home in Ethiopia along with other foreigners; the Sudan was his place of exile, and he did not care for it. Magne was heavily engaged in paper work. To everyone on the plane except me the journey was merely a boring passage between the two points and they lacked the traveller's curiosity about what lay in between.

Soon the strange, bare, root-like branches of baobab trees were reaching up towards us and we were coming down over the ancient capital of Kordofan. El Obeid was the first town to be taken by the Mahdi and the place where General Hicks' 10,000 men had vanished like a shadow. Sudanese inefficiency struck at once, for there was no one to meet us. Suave and unruffable, Sadiq found a taxi, and we were soon bumping over the potholes into the centre of town, passing on the way the sixty commandeered white UN lorries, with military personnel swarming all over them and a heavy guard with weapons at the ready. The taxi driver told Sadiq to warn us not to stare at the trucks as the army was sensitive about them.

More inefficiency revealed itself when it was discovered that the people Magne was supposed to see in El Obeid were just leaving for Khartoum. 'Never mind,' said Sadiq, urbane as ever, 'we shall have breakfast.' A very nice breakfast it was too, taken in a dusty but leafy garden and consisting of a tasty liver dish cooked with fresh coriander, foul, fish and eggs.

Sadiq then suggested a stroll around town while the pilot refuelled the plane. This turned out to be a mistake because Magne, being unused to attitudes in the Sudan, started to use his camera, and in no time we were surrounded by a hostile crowd. It would probably have been all right had not Magne said, 'Please don't punish me, I am only an ignorant man.' This incensed the ringleader, who decided that Magne must be a spy or a saboteur, and that it was his duty as a citizen to arrest him. We had no time for arrests if we were to make Nyala before nightfall, so I fished out my camera pass – Magne didn't even have one – and Sadiq showed our UNICEF travel passes and we both made suitable apologetic and placatory noises, after which they let us go, though we were followed all the way back to the airport. There was one more narrow escape when Magne flashed out his camera again to try to photograph the hijacked UN lorries which would undoubtedly have landed us in a cell for some considerable time had he been spotted. I never saw the lorries again, nor did I hear if they ever got to Wau.

It was hot and very hazy flying on to Nyala, with the visibility down to a few hundred yards. The pilot kept consulting maps and losing height to try and find out where we were, but it all looked the same – endless flat, dry desert marked out in rectangular fields, with an occasional round village which appeared quite lifeless from the air. There were no navigational aids at all at Nyala, not even radio, so it was just as well that the pilot's compass reading was accurate, for we came in over the dirt runway just as the fuel gauge was registering empty on both tanks.

There was no one to meet us again nor was there a taxi. As Sadiq had led a privileged and sheltered life, it was up to me to prove my worth and hitch a lift into town. Sadiq decided that the radio message announcing our visit must have gone astray, and that we were not expected and had better see about a night's lodging, so the person who was giving us a lift took us to the town's hotel. It was called The Warm Welcome – 'A big joke,' explained our guide, 'it doesn't have air conditioning, you see? Yes? Ha Ha.' Joke or not, it was full and we were trundled off to the town's rest house, which was primitive and picturesque, with lots of men relaxing in *semi-deshabille* in dusty gardens and courtyards. It was also full, but while we were there we somehow caught up with the people we had come to see. The radio message had not in fact gone astray, they had merely lost track of the time and were now rushing around to try to find us accommodation.

We were eventually put up in the VIP rest house which was ex-British colonial and rather suburban, with the unlikely and certainly unnecessary adornment of a tiled fireplace. The building had once been surrounded by a fine garden and the magnificent trees which remained were thronged with black birds the size of crows, with immensely long tail feathers and a soft fluting call. It seemed delightful after the heat and dust of the desert. We were housed in the annexe, and had the water and the electricity been working it would have been one of my more comfortable billets in the Sudan. It was now about 6 p.m., and the idea was that we should return to Khartoum the following morning at about 10 o'clock which seemed to me absolutely crazy after coming so far and seeing so little. I said as much but could see that it found no favour with Magne who had his tight schedule to keep and seemed more able than I at picking up the information he needed at lightning speed. The pilot came to my aid however by stating that flying conditions were such that we must leave before dawn so as to get to Khartoum while visibility was still reasonable. Since it was out of the question to leave at four the following morning we would go the morning after and spend a day at Nyala.

A small child called Vimto after the fizzy drink which is very popular in the Sudan made Nyala memorable for me. She and her sister Fatima were Felata girls who hung about the rehabilitation centre, picking up an education of sorts together with the returned runaway boys. Fatima was about ten, and her sister was two years younger; both girls were pretty, but Vimto was dressed as a boy in shorts and T-shirt. This was unheard of for a Sudanese girl, and the teachers were deeply shocked by it. Vimto wasn't in the least bothered; she said those were the clothes her mother put out for her, so she wore them. Her mother also sent her out to beg and Vimto had built up a regular clientele, whom she visited just once a week on a regular basis and from whom she never came away empty-handed – which was not surprising because she had that indefinable quality of charm which is universally recognised and which few people are proof against. I would have adopted her on the spot were such a thing possible.

That these two little girls were there among the boys helped to pinpoint the attitude that exists towards women in the Sudan. There are no girl runaways, for example, because for a girl to be left to roam the streets is shameful to the community as well as to the family; it is also against the tenets of the Moslem faith, which lays upon men the duty to protect these 'weaker vessels'. No matter how hard pressed a family is, it will probably be prepared to take in a needy young female relative, whereas with today's weakened ties and straitened circumstances, a boy is more likely to be left to fend for himself. Only the Felata tribe has a different attitude to their daughters, allowing them much more freedom of movement and expecting them to contribute in some way to the family economy from a young age. The headmaster of the scheme, who seemed to me a most caring man, confessed that he encouraged the two girls to come to the school not so much because he felt they would benefit from the education but because he simply couldn't bear to see them wandering the streets, it 'broke his heart'. When Fatima and Vimto were doing their lessons amongst the boys I saw several small girls with babies balanced on their hips looking enviously at them through the open classroom door.

About twenty boys had been returned to Nyala from their lives on the streets of Khartoum, and Magne questioned them through an interpreter. Only one boy said that he thought he might one day go back there, the rest were adamant that it was 'a bad place', and the stories of what their lives there had been like, were very much as Blanka had told me. They had seen awful things and now they wanted to forget them and be safe. On so short a visit it was difficult to see what the scheme was doing for them, as it was not yet properly off the ground and was all a little ad hoc; but although the funding for it seemed minimal, the children were fed and some attempt at classes was under way in the decrepit premises. There was no compulsion for the boys to attend and they could leave whenever they wished. They stayed only because they wanted to, and perhaps because of this an atmosphere of growing trust and confidence could be discerned. I spent a long time working with a group that was trying to mend their clothes; they were desperately ragged to the point where some of the older boys were barely decent. Influenced no doubt by the cinema, clothes mattered to them a great deal, and hardly any of them wore a traditional gown. A few of the older boys helped the younger ones but they hadn't attained the level of co-operation and confidence that I'd seen in the technical school project in Khartoum and there was still a lot of jealousy and rivalry. The smaller boys struck Kung Fu poses all the time and had an insatiable desire to be photographed and given attention. Sadiq and I also came across some of the boys away from the premises, stoned out of their minds on glue-sniffing. Nonetheless there did seem to be a framework there whereby the young vagrants could be absorbed into the community again.

Most of the boys returned to their families in the evenings and we visited some of their homes and talked with their mothers. Like Renk, Nyala was surrounded by little satellite villages of round grass huts, though nothing like as poor; they were the homes of people displaced by drought and famine, as well as by the general world-wide drift to the cities and many of the occupants had been there long enough to count as locals. They were Sudan's shanty towns and much more attractive to look at than most shanty towns around the world, though probably no easier to live in. We were invited inside, ducking low under the small round entrance. In each hut there would be at least two string beds to sit on, shared between up to twelve people at night. A plethora of small belongings and a few pots and pans hung in nets on the walls. They were more like children's play houses and could only function properly as family homes with the addition of a fenced-in compound, which the poorer houses, those of the one-parent families, often did not have. Once outside his door a child from such homes was literally on the street.

I couldn't help feeling that the masters who were taking us around, though both delightful people, took rather a superior, hectoring tone with the mothers, lecturing them about what they should be doing for their children. Many of the women claimed that having their son back made no difference, as he spent all his time down at the centre, contributing nothing to the family: he was just another mouth to feed. These women had been brought up to take a subservient role in society, and suddenly they were having to assume the duties of both parents; no wonder they couldn't cope. Deserted by their husbands and struggling alone against overwhelming odds, many had found that the only way to make money to feed the family was by brewing native beer to sell in their huts. Some of them were doing this when we called: had we been the police, they would have been arrested immediately, and the children left to fend for themselves. So the teachers scolded and lectured them and told them that they should sell vegetables instead, and the women looked more dejected than ever. It was all very sad, and it seemed to me that there were already far too many women selling vegetables in the suqs of the Sudan. What gave me just the faintest hope of a different future for the down-trodden women of this country was the small, determined Vimto setting a totally new precedent, hanging in there somehow with the boys, trying to get herself the sort of education that would one day make her a doctor.

CHAPTER SIXTEEN

Dropping in to Juba

Khartoum was a dead city at night; by eight or nine o'clock, everything except the cinemas had closed their doors and the streets were given over to roaming bands of predatory dogs and a few fierce cats. The vagrant boys, whose plight I wanted to photograph to illustrate my articles, were hard to find. They had mostly gone to ground inside the cinemas or in a warren of hidden places where I could not find them. Sadiq drove me slowly through the dimly lit streets in his large white Mercedes – which seemed grotesquely opulent in the run-down city – and a few young boys emerged from the shadows around the smaller hotels to beg from us, under the impression that we were a couple of rich tourists. One boy was in an awful state from solvent abuse. His hair was reduced to tufts and he was so emaciated it was a wonder he could stand; Sadiq tried to persuade him to go to Sabah, but he seemed too dazed to take anything in.

I wanted to see where some of the boys slept, for I could not believe that they all roamed about all night. Sadiq thought that a few of the older youths slept around the central police station – ironically the one place where they felt safe. Sure enough, there were rows of pathetic human bundles lying pressed against the walls, wrapped in bits of cardboard. Very discreetly, so as not to wake them, I took one solitary picture and moved on. Almost immediately a hand reached out of the gloom, removed the camera from my grasp and revealed itself as attached to a policeman, who without a word proceeded to march us off. 'Malish,' breathed Sadiq, a word which covers all events in the Sudan which can't be helped, from having your head blown off to tripping on a banana skin. This time I couldn't really complain: I had taken a chance, knowing full well that the subject and the location would be sure to earn official disapproval. Had I realised that the film UNICEF had found for me, all twelve rolls of it, was too stale to be of much use I would not have been so upset. As it was I felt sick about losing the pictures, for even if they gave me back the camera I thought they would be sure to keep the film. About twenty of the boys, including the one I had photographed, were woken by the policeman and made to get up. Protesting their innocence and rubbing their eyes pathetically they were led off with us as incriminating evidence. It was a highly embarrassing procession, but at least the police station was mercifully close this time.

As a mere woman I was not expected to say anything in my own defence, but simply to wait patiently while Sadiq, convinced as ever of the rightness of our cause, argued the case. He must have done it very well because for the first time my photographic pass was accepted as valid authorisation, and although we were told we shouldn't use a camera near a police station, they agreed that I had a perfect right to take photographs, and my camera was returned complete with its film and a greasy thumb print across the lens. Sadiq said he had been most shocked by the hostility the policemen had expressed towards foreign aid organisations; he said the police had warned him not to get involved with them as they were usually a cover for other less innocent operations.

What few charms Khartoum possessed – other than its people – had grown quite thin by the time of this latest arrest, and I was more than ready to get away; but in the two days before I flew to Juba however, I still found I had a multitude of things to do, and when I wasn't stalking around after pictures, I was getting my notes in order and finishing off letters and articles. After Khartoum I couldn't hope to be near a postbox or a telephone again for some considerable time, nor was I likely to meet a returning traveller who could take a message for me. Like the Victorian explorers before me, I anticipated being out of touch for a long while – always assuming that I did succeed in getting through and wasn't bundled straight back to Khartoum again – a fate that had also hung over the head of my hero Samuel Baker when he and Florence had set off on this stretch at much the same time of year in 1862.

I wrote mostly beside the small swimming pool in the garden of the Sudan Club against a background of pantomime rehearsals, the stage directions of which rang out ever more stridently as the day of performance approached. The athletic bearded person who was playing the fairy in a pretty pink tutu was coming in for some particularly caustic comments, as the director urged him to go for buffoonery and the obvious laughs, while the fairy had pretensions to something more restrained and graceful. It was all as far removed from life outside the club walls as it was possible to imagine. Only very early in the day did Africa impose itself on the anglicized scene. This was when I went swimming while it was still dark, and as the first hint of morning lightened the sky and began to bring out the heady garden scents, a bulbul bird took up his customary perch on the rim of an empty Coca Cola bottle, his small grey body quivering with the intensity of the marvellous song he fluted out into the swift pink dawn.

On the last Friday I turned my back on Khartoum, expatriates and vagrant boys and went across the Nile to Omdurman to see the Dervish dancing. It was rather a popular affair that took place on some open ground near the shrine of a local saint, whose body had been recovered from the river in a miraculous state of preservation some centuries before – an event which had inspired the devotion of this mystical sect of Islam. It was a bleak area of unkempt, dusty Arab cemeteries and tented shanty villages of unrelieved squalor. Large numbers of Dervishes, mostly clad in green and red gowns and tall pointed hats and armed with antique weapons, were all supposedly dancing themselves into a state of religious ecstasy with the aid of a native orchestra. By far the most inspired was a little, plainly swathed old lady who was defying the rules by dancing around among the resplendent men. Women participants appeared to be tolerated as long as they remained static in a small out-of-the-way corner, in much the same way as they were expected to behave in a mosque. The masters of ceremony were stouter than the rest, wore the most elaborate costumes, and tried to impose some order and form upon the highly idiosyncratic dancers, all of whom seemed to prefer to do their own thing, very much like the pantomime characters at the Sudan Club. Several of these august personages tried to capture the little old lady as she flitted past, her arms lifted and hands fluttering in ecstasy. But even with her face raised heavenwards, stamped with an unseeing and rapturous expression, she still managed cleverly to evade their clutches by judicious weaving, and perfectly timed twistings, just out of the reach of their outstretched arms.

My final night in Khartoum was spent cleaning and oiling the bicycle. I dared not go to bed in case I didn't wake in time for the 4.45 a.m. take off. I changed the tyres, washed the panniers and went through every piece of equipment several times to make quite sure that everything was as ready as possible for the rugged journey ahead. I was slightly bothered by the freewheel block which was entirely silent when I spun it instead of making a pleasant clicking sound. This ought to have alerted me to the fact that the mechanism was so full of impacted sand and dust that the pawls which engage in the ratchets to make the thing operational were barely able to connect. Just a little more dust and it would cease to function altogether which would mean that I could pedal away for all I was worth without being able to move the bicycle forward one inch. For some reason my brain refused to recognise the full implication of this lack of clicking, which was just as well really, because the only way I could have dealt with the matter was to take the block off the wheel, and in order to save weight, I had not brought the necessary tool for doing this. By remaining in ignorance I was at least spared the worry until the evil hour.

All my dark fears and anxieties about the fighting and the general mayhem and the unpredictability of officialdom in the south, were temporarily forgotten in the excitement of setting out. It was still night as I rode the Agala through Khartoum's ruined streets for what I hoped would be the last time, and I was thankful not to run into one of the notorious roving packs of savage dogs. We took off in a De Havilland Twin Otter, a powerful roomy twelve-seater which lifted effortlessly away from the dark ground and soared upwards like an eagle towards the stars. There was a sort of Dan Dare atmosphere aboard from which I felt excluded: five men were on a mission and I with my bicycle was the odd one out. There was a doctor who had been contracted to UNICEF for a year to assess the immunisation needs in the south and who had been kicking his heels in Khartoum for seven months, unable to get there. There was an office organiser in much the same situation and a strange young man who had drifted around the world since leaving high school, and who was now employed as an expert on vagrant boys. He declined to share his expertise on the grounds that he didn't talk to people like me, so I didn't learn what role he was playing in the proceedings. The European pilot was brilliant and temperamental; I felt he had never quite got over the disappointment of missing out on World War 11 and was relishing practising enemy avoidance techniques in the current political scene. Cole Dodge wearing a funny hat, was leading the expedition and acting as co-pilot.

The object of the mission was to find out if it was possible to set up operations again in Juba. UNICEF had pulled out at the same time as most other agencies, because of fears of the SPLA advance, leaving Oxfam and a consortium of smaller agencies to minister to a growing number of displaced people. Now the idiosyncratic governor of Juba had written to UNICEF begging them to return, saying that the needs in the area were serious and that there was no longer any danger from the SPLA. After the recent trouble there had been between Oxfam and the same governor, leading to the expulsion of an Oxfam employee on a charge of aiding the rebels, there seemed to be more than a touch of triumphant rivalry aboard the UNICEF plane.

There was a slight hiccup when we landed in a small field in the Kordofan Mountains to refuel and the hand pump blew a gasket, showering everything with petrol for many yards around and causing the pilot to throw an impressive display of temperament. I thought if we were stuck there I would take my chance and quietly cycle on, since I did not think I could bear to return to Khartoum again. However, American competence with things mechanical sorted out the pump and we were airborne again within the hour and beginning our ascent to 13,000 feet.

Below us the path of the Nile and the unfinished Jonglei Canal unfolded like a map. In the distance, in the middle of the lifeless brown of the desert, the largest swamp in the world – the great Sudd – beckoned, deliciously and innocently green, dwarfed by our height into a park-sized pleasaunce. Landscape has no true reality from an aeroplane, it isn't in the least like being at the same height on a great mountain range where there is a relative scale to things and nothing is robbed of its true perspective. It seemed incomprehensible that Sam and Florence Baker had been marooned for months in that green place, among claustrophobic reeds and towering elephant grasses, trying desperately to cut a channel for their boats while facing mutiny, murder and mayhem. Somewhere down there, after surviving an attempted midnight assassination, Sam had written proudly in his journal, 'Florence was not a screamer, a touch on my sleeve was considered sufficient warning.'

The Bakers had had frightful problems trying to get through southern Sudan. The country had been part of the Turkish empire and under the corrupt governor, Mousa Pasha, it had sunk to its lowest point. Sam Baker, who loathed him, wrote 'He combined the worst failings of the Oriental with the brutality of a wild animal. During his administration the Sudan became utterly ruined; governed by military force, the revenue was unequal to the expenditure and fresh taxes were levied upon the inhabitants to an extent that paralysed the entire country.' It was against the interests of such a regime to allow people like the Bakers to discover the horrible excesses of the illegal slave trade along the upper reaches of the Nile, and every obstacle had been placed in the way of their leaving Khartoum. I could see many parallels in the Sudan of today.

The journey I was making this morning had taken the Bakers months by boat. Added to the horrors of 'winding slowly through this wretched labyrinth of endless marsh, through clouds of mosquitos', the entire native population was hostile, due to the years of the depredations of the slave trade. Hunting buffalo and hippopotamus were Sam's only consolations, together with his never-failing interest in everything about him. He discovered a fish that blew itself up to huge proportions when taken out of the water and used its dried skin to mend the stock of his rifle, where 'it became as strong as metal when dry'. He thought hippo meat very superior, especially for making mock turtle soup, and decided that boiled head of hippo 'throws brawn totally in the shade'. There were many times when I envied Florence such a travelling companion. I would gladly have put up with the mosquitos, the claustrophobia and any other discomforts to be travelling down there in the Bakers' tracks and I was full of regrets for the herds of hippos, buffalos and the crocodiles lurking in the reeds which I would now not see.

A clash with authority occurred as we were flying over this deceptively innocent-looking swamp. Cole Dodge asked me if I had succeeded in obtaining my travel permit. Rather mystified, I pointed out that my name appeared with those of the other passengers on the travel document, of which we each had been given a copy. This seemed to upset him: 'The deal was that you should get your own,' he said. As I was unaware of any 'deal' and as it was his own organisation that had arranged the whole thing without my asking them, I put his irritation down to stress. Later, I decided he had suddenly thought that if anything unfortunate befell me, he might be held responsible for transporting an independent female bicyclist into a tricky area – Americans being always so worried about hostages. I told him that the Sudanese authorities had no objection to my coming to Juba, and I had in any case to register with the police on arrival. He did not seem in the least reassured by this and told me, in rather bullying tones I thought, that I would have to fly back with them that night if there was any suggestion of my being unwelcome in Juba. I wondered whether it would constitute an international incident, equal perhaps to the return of Jenkins' Ear, for a British national to be hauled off protesting to Khartoum by an American, representing what I had thought was a United Nations organisation; but being outnumbered I said nothing.

I had been told that the De Havilland Twin Otter was the right sort of plane for coming into Juba, tough enough to take the plunging corkscrew descent that left my stomach trying sickeningly and unsuccessfully to catch up with the rest of my body. The idea was to get down from 13,000 feet where we had been shivering for the last hour in the cold thin air, and onto the runway in as few moments as possible, so presenting the minimal target for any guerilla force that might have its heat-seeking missile operating in the area.

My stomach was still in knots and my ears ached abominably as we taxied to a standstill, and the door swung open to reveal a waiting committee. 'UNICEF comes back to Juba in triumph,' crowed one of the party gleefully. Cole Dodge sprang down first and I unloaded the bicycle, keeping discreetly in the background. Even so, someone came forward to greet me. 'She's not with us,' said Cole Dodge. The smiling black man didn't hear him and shook my hand warmly. 'She's not with us,' repeated Dodge, 'she does not have a pass.' 'No problem, we will facilitate,' said one of the men, clearly thinking he was doing Cole Dodge a favour. 'But she doesn't have permission to be here. She is not with UNICEF,' repeated Dodge with obvious exasperation. Looking puzzled by now, the official asked me my name and nationality. As soon as I produced my passport his brow cleared and he was all smiles again: 'No problem,' he repeated, 'the British are welcome here.' He must have thought he had been witnessing a little tribal jealousy, the sort of thing that had been the *modus vivendi* of these parts since the dawn of time.

I went straight to the British compound where I found three local employees of the British Council holding the fort. One of them, Davey very competent at dealing with bureaucracy, and within half an hour my passport had been expensively stamped by the Juba general registration office and I was legally in residence behind rebel lines, deep in the heart of Eastern Equatoria. So far so good.

I had only had time for the most cursory impressions, but even so there seemed little of the tense atmosphere of a heavily beleaguered town which I had expected from the briefing at the British Embassy in Khartoum. I had been advised to contact Nick Stockton who was in charge of Oxfam's operations in Juba; he was not 'holed up' in the compound, as I had been led to believe, but had an office half a mile away. So much for British Intelligence. He gave me a completely different picture of the current situation, and one which was much more encouraging for the traveller.

'Can't put you on a convoy, hasn't been any need of such things for weeks,' he said. He looked a youthful twenty – which was surprising, as he was at least half as much again and had been bearing a tremendous weight of responsibility for a long while. He reminded me of a district commissioner at the turn of the century carrying the 'white man's burden' in some remote and troubled corner of the British Raj. 'There's a lull at the moment, the SPLA can't operate easily in the dry season and the road through Yei is open and de-mined as far as the border,' he went on. 'All the other roads out of Juba are closed and still mined and there are reports of fighting in and around Nimule, but just at present I see no problems for you on the Yei road as far as Uganda; from there on, you'll have to take local advice.' I left him feeling that I had been given a gift, for the journey was again a reality, with the promise of a great deal more freedom of movement than I had anticipated. I had also gained the heartening impression that Nick Stockton did not regard my travels as a nuisance, as was the case with so many weary consular officials and professionals, who felt I was 'treading on their beat'. His attitude seemed to be that it was important that independent travellers, especially writers, should also see what was going on in the troubled areas of the world, not only those who were intimately involved.

As I was riding back to the British compound, I noticed a curious metal and concrete tower at the crossroads in the centre of the town. It was a signpost with arrows pointing to places whose names had excited me since the idea of a journey to the Mountains of the Moon had first taken shape. It was odd and thrilling to see them written there so casually, black on white, ideas no longer but real places, with distances to underline their reality – Nimule, Kampala, Yei, Torrit, Gulu, Yambio. Because the road was closed, I wouldn't be able to follow my original plan of keeping close to the Nile and making for Nimule and Gulu and so up to Lake Victoria, where Speke had at last seen his belief in the source of the Nile justified by the waters of the lake tumbling out northwards over the Ripon Falls and where, in the delight of his discovery he had named both lake and river for his queen and, hedging his bets, had called the Falls after the nobleman who had funded his expedition.

Instead I would have to make a wide sweep westward to Yei and then turn south to the tiny border crossing of Kaya – a backdoor approach, close to the border with Zaire, with the additional safeguard of a quick escape into that country if necessary. If all went well the route would bring me back to the Nile at Pakwatch, where Samuel Baker had discovered Speke's Victoria Nile flowing into another great lake, which he was the first white man to set eyes upon and which he romantically named Albert after Victoria's Prince Consort. From that point the river sets out on its 4,000-mile journey to the sea, with the combined weight of both great lakes behind it.

I was musing on all these wonders ahead, and checking the route on my map, when a military type of vehicle skidded to a halt and a voice said, 'There she is!' It was Cole Dodge, still in his funny hat, and the rest of the UNICEF mission hurtling back to the Twin Otter. 'Are you properly fixed up?' demanded Dodge sternly. 'Oh yes,' I said cheerfully, 'no problem.' There was a slight, uncomfortable pause before he let in the clutch and continued on his way. Suddenly I saw how I must appear to them, and how I had inadvertently dimmed their glory – some damned woman with a bicycle creating an impression so totally at variance with their daring *sortie* over rebel territory.

CHAPTER SEVENTEEN

A Town Under Siege

Juba is another especially significant place, marking the last navigable point on the White Nile. From here the river alters its character dramatically as the land begins its steep upward thrust towards the high Central African plateau. The rolling savannahs giving way to rough slopes and terraces down which the young river plunges and boils, through narrow gorges and over waterfalls, gathering the momentum that will carry it on to the distant sea.

A triumphant John Speke had walked out this way in 1863 after his successful expedition, and it was just across the fast flowing river from Juba, in Old Gondokoro, the infamous slavers' post, that Sam Baker met up with him and was given copies of Speke's maps, together with the welcome news that there was still probably one more vast lake left for Baker to discover. Eventually the spot became established as the capital of Southern Sudan, but the modern town has turned its back upon the Nile and is built at some little distance away on higher ground, to avoid flooding in the river's annual twenty-foot rise.

After the flat barren deserts of northern Sudan the undulating red earth and the exuberant vegetation of Eastern Equatoria came as a welcome relief. Magnificent, glossy-leaved, tall trees crowded in all around, bushes burgeoned in a riot of colour and in the distance to the south, the lovely shapes of the Imatong Hills rose up out of the early morning mists. The relief was an illusion, however: after half an hour in Juba I found the humidity sapping my energy far more than the dry desert heat. Sweat trickled interminably down my neck and forehead, and ran in rivulets across my back without ever drying; it was an effort to move about much or to concentrate on anything, and when I wrote the ink smudged from the wetness of my hand. Conditions were not so very different to those described by Sam Baker, even to being surrounded by hostile forces – except that the hostilities were further off than in his day, in spite of what the media had led people to believe.

The extraordinary false reports, broadcast by the BBC, of a rebel takeover of Juba, which had led to nearly all the foreign aid workers being withdrawn, had come about because of the Mundari fleeing south. The Mundari are pastoralists, cattle people, very like the Dinka who are the largest of the thirty or so tribes which make up the South. But whereas the Dinka are extremely warlike and form the largest part of the SPLA including the leader of the rebels, John Garang, the Mundari are more interested in preserving their ancient way of life. The Mundari had fled in their thousands from their lands south of the Sudd, before a sudden assault upon them by the SPLA. As the waves of frightened, naked people poured into Juba with their great herds of cattle, many of which stopped to eat the thatched roofs off the houses, a general panic had ensued, exacerbated by the attempts of the police and the army to restore order. With rifle-shots ricochetting around and the panic-stricken cattle stampeding through the dark streets, panic and confusion had continued unabated for several hours. The local BBC contact had assumed the SPLA was attacking and had built up the story with accounts of the airport being overrun and of fighting in the streets. The result was that the need for aid increased enormously with the influx of all these thousands of displaced people, but there had been almost no one left to minister to them.

In fact the rebel forces had never come within five miles of Juba, Nick Stockton told me. The town had been entirely cut off by road, and there was the ever-present threat that John Garang would move up his sophisticated missile launcher that could knock any approaching plane out of the sky, so that only private aircraft were prepared to risk flying in. But although Juba had been virtually isolated for months and supplies had at times been very scarce, there had never been any danger of an SPLA takeover, nor had imported beer ceased to flow. The rebels would find it far too costly to capture a town which maintained a permanent garrison of government troops I was told, especially as there was no way they could hope to hold onto it afterwards. The SPLA operated from hidden bases deep in the bush near the eastern border and in the dry season it was difficult, Nick said, for guerilla forces to operate far from these hideouts because there is not sufficient water for them, and since the farmers burn all the scrub to encourage the new grass to grow, there is not enough cover either. SPLA targets were small towns and villages where they could take the food and clothing and other things they needed and get away again quickly.

All this helped to explain why Juba was so different from how I had imagined a town under siege would be. I had expected it to be desperately overcrowded, instead it appeared almost deserted. The central part of the town was a place of wide streets, with buildings set expansively in gardens, and although nearly everything was falling apart, it had the space to do so unobtrusively and the rampant vegetation covered up a lot of the sores. Nearly all these crumbling edifices were administrative offices, schools, churches, a hospital and aid operation centres and many were empty because of the evacuation of their personnel. Even the rackety downtown area was muted and shuttered, for there was little trading except for the sale of food, which took place in the market. Most of the people lived around the outskirts, in picturesque clusters of grass huts, which were easily repaired or replaced. There was very little rubbish lying around because the poverty was such that anything discarded was snapped up at once. Fuel was in very short supply, so the streets themselves were pleasantly free of anything except people and bicycles. It had a certain charm, not unlike that of an unremarkable French provincial town sleeping through a long hot summer's afternoon. The huge area of crowded tents, where the 20,000 displaced Mundari struggled to maintain a bleak existence, was outside the town and hidden by a dip in the ground.

The British compound where I put up for a modest charge, was simply a collection of identical prefabricated huts within a wire perimeter fence, near the airport. Each hut had a few bedrooms, a living room, a kitchen and a bathroom and was furnished in an anonymous, Home Counties boarding-house style, with no concessions to the steamy tropics other than the mosquito nets smelling of dust which hung over each bed. Without electricity to turn the fans and provide cold drinks, and lighting for the twelve hours of darkness, they were ill adapted to Equatoria; and it seemed ridiculous that with all the sunshine available, no use had been made of solar power except to provide hot water.

One of the huts was the office of the British Council, who had run education programmes in the area before the evacuation. Another was the guest house, which I had to myself, as the first visitor in nearly a year. The rest were being minded by some of the few aid workers still in Juba, operating either with Oxfam or CART – the Combined Agencies Relief Team. The compound was not a restful place, since it was patrolled all night by bare-footed, scantily clad men, armed with bows and arrows, who sluiced themselves down at intervals at a tap just outside my window. The nights were hot under the mosquito netting so I kept the windows open, and the high-pitched chatter of these watchmen mingled with the drunken jollity coming from the Juba Hotel just across the road, where Arab traders – who somehow managed to continue to trade by circuitous routes – made merry with local police chiefs and high-ranking army personnel in the secluded garden arbours of the decayed ex-colonial building. A week before, I was told, the guards had shot at a thief with their bows and arrows, and in the morning had followed the blood spoor and found a young man dead in a nearby overgrown garden.

The handful of aid workers were hard pressed and desperately overworked but they found time to talk to me and show me around their projects. Nick Stockton impressed me very much. He had been holding the relief operation together for a long time and seemed to be worn paper-thin; he was also two years overdue for leave but I doubt he could have handed over to anyone else even had it been possible. He knew his way through the web of corruption that spread over everything in this part of the world and had learned how to tread a delicate path and always be one step ahead the whole time, so as to get the aid to the people for whom it was intended. Living perpetually in a state of imminent crisis had in a curious way become a necessity for him; it was when he was finished with the office for the day that the strain showed, mostly in the fact that he couldn't stop talking. I didn't mind this in the least for it was then he was at his most interesting, singing the praises of the cattle people who were threatened with extinction by war, cattle fever, famine and the pressure of progress. Nick had travelled a great deal among these people before the present troubles and had grown to admire their way of life to the point where it had become a passion. It also made economic sense to him, to try to maintain the balance that had been achieved between man and the land for so long, and he had little patience with schemes to drain the swamps and impose a modern system of agriculture upon it.

It would have been difficult not to feel sympathy with Nick Stockton's ideas about these pastoralists after visiting one of the Mundari cattle camps with a vet from Durham called Mel, who was carrying out treatment for East Coast cattle fever. About a hundred magnificent looking cows and bulls were assembled in a clearing in the bush for him to inspect. The large powerful animals had huge thick branching horns, some of which had been carefully trained from calfhood to grow in a particular fashion. The Mundari were a tall sinewy people who wore little but necklaces and bracelets and they made a perfect foil for these heroic cattle, unconsciously creating classical tableaux like reliefs on Etruscan vases.

Apart from the strikingly beautiful scenes, what emerged most strongly in the camp was the feeling of co-operation; it was essentially a very happy place. The harmony was apparent in the interaction of people but also in the Mundari's relationship with their animals. Their mutual interdependence was obvious, for the well-being of each species was entirely dependent upon the well-being of the other, but there was something there much stronger than simple survival. It made me realise something of what we in the West have lost through our exploitation of the animal kingdom. The Mundari cattle are far removed from the dehorned, denatured creatures of our factory farming methods; and the Mundari clearly love them and are proud of their character as well as their strength and beauty. They love their children too, but there was no interference from the men as the boys learnt courage and respect, dodging about between those tremendous horns and accepting the well-placed kicks with which the cows punished the inept, nor did I see a boy retaliate with temper or a blow.

I was fortunate to have had the opportunity to visit the Mundari in their natural habitat, for even in a year or two such scenes may well be a thing of the past. For I have no hope that the few people who feel like Nick Stockton will be able to do much to preserve the pastoralists. They stand in the way of what the dominant part of the world sees as progress, just as the Red Indians, the Australian Aborigines and the South American Indians were thought to have done, and like them I think their way of life will inevitably be destroyed. The destruction is in fact already far advanced and their innocence has already been undermined. Both sides in the struggle for the south have been accused of arming these people, who until the present conflict had possessed nothing more lethal than bows and arrows. Among the various gourds and primitive implements hanging from wooden hurdles in this camp I saw one of these modern automatic rifles. It was openly displayed, a grimly technical horror in a setting which had almost nothing else of the twentieth century and it seemed to symbolise the end of an era.

According to Nick Stockton there was also a military push in progress which would prevent these people from gathering at their traditional cattle pens along the Nile, which would lead to the death of thousands more cattle by cutting them off from their seasonal feeding grounds. Every day MIG fighter planes took off from Juba airport, flying low over the Mundari territory, destroying the villages and anything else that might give aid and shelter to the rebels.

The contrast between the Mundari with their cattle and those who had already been in the refugee camp for a few months was very depressing. The rate at which they had lost their physical condition and become apathetic and defeated was probably much faster than would have happened with more sophisticated people. They had no coping mechanisms for a life of inertia, and of living on handouts in crowded tents, and none of the helpers was very hopeful about their long-term prospects. If they were prevented from returning to their territories in the next month or so, it was feared that they would no longer have the will to do so. Odile, the small, deceptively frail-looking French nurse who was coping almost single-handed with the supple-mentary feeding centre, was growing daily more worried even about their physical survival as more babies and young children needed help and as the risk of epidemics soared in the hot, crowded, insanitary conditions. When the rains started in a month or so, the whole site would turn into a sea of mud, and to be under canvas then did not bear thinking about.

There were a few unco-ordinated attempts to provide some distractions for the camp people. The most depressing one I saw was a women's self-help group funded by UNICEF, where a large Ugandan lady was teaching a group of women to sew. These Mundari women are bare-breasted and apart from their jewellery they wear little except brief, beautifully made beaded aprons, though the older women sometimes wrap themselves in a sort of cotton sarong, or wear a cloth around their shoulders. They have a facial scarification across their foreheads, in the manner of the Shilluk and are also scarred concentrically around the navel with raised patterns like living mandalas, and they are as proud and warlike as their menfolk. Seeing them sitting dejectedly at the feet of the Ugandan, stabbing their fingers clumsily with the unfamiliar needles in an attempt to make voluminous cotton knickers reminded me of the least sensitive aspects of the Victorian missionaries.

A great deal more pleasurable was the Food for Work project which Linda, an Oxfam worker, had organised. Linda was a forestry expert who had been contracted to improve the fruit trees in the Mundari villages, but since she couldn't get on with this work in the present political situation, she had acquired some prime riverside land in Juba and was growing vegetables, using a very large workforce so as to get as many women as possible involved in the scheme. There were not enough tools for everyone, so half were always resting in the shade playing with the children while the others were doing a little leisurely watering or delicately wielding hoes. No one could claim they took the work very seriously but, as Linda said, it got them out of the camp. They certainly seemed happier by the river, the older women smoking their elaborate pipes and taking swigs from the watering cans while the banter swung to and fro.

The result of even these half-hearted agricultural efforts were amazing. I had never seen such vegetable munificence. Root crops like yams were dug up, packed as closely together as if they were ready for market, while low bushes bent under the weight of large purple globous aubergines. It was difficult for someone like me, coming from a cold northern country to see how there could ever be famine in this fruitful land; nor could I understand why fruit and vegetables were so much more expensive in Juba's market than in Khartoum.

An American called Gordon Falconer who was working for Episcopal Church Aid explained this to me, for he was very much concerned with the price of vegetables. He was one of those youthful middle-aged westcoast men who seem to be blessed with far more energy and enthusiasm than is quite fair and who are able to fire other people with their ideas. He operated from a house that was as ethnically furnished as was possible, and so had all the character lacking in the British compound huts. Being among locally made tables, chairs, mats, bowls, carvings and so forth made me realise how alien to the culture were most of the buildings and interiors of Juba – quite unnecessarily so, as the local products were cheaper and much more attractive than most of the imported stuff. It also seemed right that aid workers should try to support and encourage local craft and industry.

The whole Sudanese north – south conflict was, to Gordon, a matter of pure economics, a war to maintain the huge profits which the Arab traders make out of the produce of the southern people. The Arabs buy direct from the individual small farmers and sell at profits in excess of 400 per cent, and according to Gordon the whole of this trade cartel is run by just four Khartoum families. His solution was to encourage the local farmers to band together into co-operatives to market their own produce, with the object of both reducing the price of food in the shops and making bigger profits for the growers. Most of these farmers were desperately poor and had no transport other than bicycles, so support was being provided in the shape of loans to get the schemes started; there was even talk of constructing a cycle path along the hundred miles from Juba to Yei. Gordon's economic strategies seemed very much in keeping with modern liberation theology and I wondered if he feared a knife in the back some dark night, the reward for people elsewhere working on similar lines against powerful vested interests. I never had the chance to ask him this, but I think there simply wasn't time for him to be afraid.

The place to go for a little necessary relief from the serious problems of life in Juba was the Greek Club which was the centre of the town's night life for expatriates and for the few black aid workers who could afford the expensive drink, which had never failed to be flown in throughout the siege. The Club was like the Africa of the thirties I'd read about – a run-down saloon with a garden darkly lit by a few flares, huge thatched umbrellas on tall poles, cicadas stridulating into the velvety throbbing night, and beer and spirits flowing freely. It was run by a frail, old-fashioned Greek called Jerry and his slightly younger friend, Kostas. Jerry had come here via Ethiopia and Egypt and goodness knows where else. He had a fund of stories and innuendo about bar life in Cairo during the war, none of which I heard to the end because of the general clatter and the mixture of strange accents.

'You have hippopotamus in the Thames?' someone asked politely, and before I could answer, Jerry brought another round of beer and said, 'Me I never drinks the stuff, thanks God! My doctor he tell me when I come here forty-one years ago, Jerry, he tells me, drink the whisky, drink the gin but don't touch the beer, and me, ha ha, I am still well, thanks God!'

It occurred to me that now that I was in the south, where legs were not considered objectionable, I could have exposed my knees without fear of giving offence, and I wished I had brought a pair of shorts with me for bicycling. Then, when I was shopping for fruit and vegetables in the market, I noticed a line of twenty young men sitting idle at their sewing machines in front of the row of little tin shacks that sold material and I decided to support local enterprise and have a pair of long shorts made. In a land that grows superb cotton, it seemed sad that most of the materials for sale were imported synthetics but I found some cheap plain blue stuff, agreed on a modest price for the work and twenty-four hours later I picked up the finished garment. They made a tremendous difference to my comfort, especially cycling uphill, and I wore them daily for the next two months, washing them out each night to remove the day's accumulation of dust and sweat. Before I flew home I donated them, still quite intact, to a local charity.

The next thing was to attempt the tricky business of getting an exit visa to leave Sudan and a permit to travel to the point of exit – two concerns that had been worrying me for many weeks, and had added to the growing burden of uncertainties that besets a traveller in modern Africa. Apparently only the all-powerful governor could facilitate my passage and I had a letter to him requesting his help, written by an admirer of his in Khartoum, which was to be delivered via the admirer's brother who was in the Military Intelligence Service in Juba – nothing and no one could be approached directly in Africa it seemed. It was a rather cringing epistle, which began, 'Your Excellency, my apology for not writing your full name which I know, but I fear a spelling mistake in your name. I do not like to blunder with a national character like your goodself. We all admire your valiant efforts. God bless you.' It then went on to complicate the issue by putting in a plea for the brother's advancement. It was also full of holes where the typewriter had stamped right through the thin paper.

As it happened, my arrival in Juba corresponded with the governor's departure for a conference in Khartoum so I did not have an opportunity to present this document and see what effect it had. Instead fortune had provided Davey, the British Council's local fixer, who had already dealt so successfully with my permit to stay in Juba and was cautiously optimistic about obtaining the other two documents from the governor's stand-in.

Apparently Davey had used my various letters of recommendation to good purpose and had had no problems until it somehow got out that I was travelling by bicycle, at which point the iron fist of bureaucracy had hammered on the desk in angry disbelief, and the man behind the fist, Brigadier Nicola Obwoya Cazaro, chief of internal security, had demanded my immediate presence in his office. By the time Davey had located me some hours later he was a worried man, for the Brigadier did not take kindly to being kept waiting. Davey rushed me off to him on the back of his small motorbicycle to save time – the fact that he was able to obtain fuel, which was like gold dust, showed what a resourceful man he was. Before we went in he intimated that all might not be plain sailing: 'You want to go to Uganda, so better you not argue with this man; normally we do not have so much trouble from him.'

I was glad of the warning because the Brigadier started straight in, shouting angrily at Davey, 'Why you not come before? Why you keep me waiting? I am not so sure I can do anything for you now.' Davey kept his gaze on his shoes and said nothing, so I saw it was up to me and stepped in quickly with a humble apology which seemed to mollify him somewhat. After a short preamble about a visit to England which he had not enjoyed, the Brigadier began on the matter in hand with all the charm of a pile-driver banging in a stake. 'How you expect to come to Yei?' he demanded in heavy hectoring tones, emphasising his words by thumping his large fist on the desk. 'Don't you know it is over one hundred miles? How you expect to do that on a bicycle, huh?' I pointed out as tactfully as I could that I had already come several thousand miles by bicycle and was still well and safe and not at all lost. He ignored this and regarded me with a deep and undisguised disdain. 'You are a woman,' he informed me unnecessarily. 'A white woman,' he added with disgust. 'It is not suitable for you to travel by bicycle.

You will be robbed by the villagers and I cannot one hundred per cent guarantee your safety.' Since he had such a low opinion of bicycles, white women and the local populace, I could see that meekness was indeed the only course and I thanked him politely for his solicitude on my behalf. 'Of course I wouldn't dream of going by bicycle if there was the least danger. Certainly not! I would arrange for self and bicycle to travel on whatever truck was prepared to carry us out of Juba.'

Out of the corner of my eye I could see Davey regarding me with a new respect, but I was more interested in the travel documents which were now being flamboyantly issued as my reward for bolstering the Brigadier's ego. It seemed unfair that I should have to pay so highly in monetary terms as well.

CHAPTER EIGHTEEN

Through Eastern Equatoria

I left Juba at noon, unaware until then of how strong a sense of claustrophobia there had been in that hot, tightly cordoned town. The feeling of being trapped was further aggravated by an army of minor military officials who exercised their self-importance by delaying departures for as long as possible. In deference to Brigadier Cazaro's wishes I was not even attempting to go out on my own two wheels, but was to travel with an Oxfam mission until Juba was out of sight, after which I would take my chance. The three people organising the small convoy rushed around with permits and passports, controlling their irritation with increasing difficulty as the sun rose higher and the officials found fresh causes for delay. Twenty young Sudanese men and women sat in the four vehicles clutching their bright, newly issued blankets and chirruping excitedly like a sunday school outing. It was the first expedition of Oxfam's newly trained nutritional survey teams and the first opportunity for most of them to get out of besieged Juba for nearly a year.

One of Oxfam's roles in this mad world, in which one half suffers from food mountains while the other half faces starvation, is to monitor food availability in areas known to be at risk of famine. In this way it is hoped to pinpoint serious shortages before they reach a crisis state. As no one had been able to do any of this work in southern Sudan recently there was some urgency about getting on with the survey, for even in the towns signs of malnutrition were so commonplace as not to excite notice anymore. Because tribalism is so strong in the south, Juba's administration had little sympathy for any aid work in the outlying districts. 'Charity begins at home' was their working motto, and there was considerable and continuing resentment that Oxfam's goods and vehicles were not confined to more parochial uses.

We got away after four hours delay, mainly because by that time officialdom had itself become bored and overheated. I stayed with the truck as far as my first night's stop so as to be sure of arriving with plenty of time in hand. It is nearly always a good rule for a traveller to reach shelter before dark; here it was essential. We had travelled at speed on the appalling road as the convoy was also anxious to make up for the long delay and reach its place of safety before nightfall. Twice we had to stop to retrieve items of equipment torn from their lashings as our wheels hit projecting rocks or crashed into the worst of the deep potholes. After a very few miles I felt exhausted by this battering, and was thickly covered with brick-red dust – to be other than first in line was to drive permanently in a dense choking haze. Even so, when I was eventually dropped off at Lanye Vocational School I was glad we had hurried because it gave me the maximum time in this delightful place.

I was immediately put in mind of a European monastery in the Dark Ages, for the school served much the same function in an area where life was seldom much above the level of subsistence. Centuries of depredation by the slave trade had debased the culture so that life in general, and farming methods in particular had not advanced much beyond a very primitive stage. The Lanye school's primary aim was to train young people in agriculture, carpentry, simple engineering and home economics, but it also saw its role as initiating new and better methods of farming and home economy and improving by example the life of the people round about. It was entirely run and staffed by Sudanese, and although it received some funding from overseas, it operated on a shoestring budget. Nonetheless it had initiated fish-farming, and the rearing of improved stocks of chickens and pigs; and it was training oxen to plough, something never before seen in these parts. Everything was, of necessity, low cost and low technology, but this was a positive advantage as it meant there were fewer economic barriers to imitation. The storage of grain was a case in point; traditionally, grain is placed in miniature round huts set on stilts but the rats run up the stilts easily and devour a considerable proportion of the harvest. Lanye's solution was to produce a similar little hut but with a kind of metal coolie hat around each stilt which totally foiled the rodents.

Among the sixty students at the school, building their own simple dormitories and workrooms as part of their course, were some girl students. One of them had produced a baby during her year and it had become the focus of the home economics. 'Never', said Thomas

Kedini, the principal, 'has one small child received so much care and attention, or been bathed so many times in one day. She is the cleanest baby in all of Equatoria.' The atmosphere sang with enthusiasm and hope; even when Thomas took me on a tour of the fields to show me the many crop failures, the optimism didn't waver. 'We learn for next year,' was the comment on anything that had proved less than satisfactory. There was rejoicing at the newly established pineapple patch where, among the straight military rows of spiky blue-green foliage, a single pineapple raised its stiff, heavy head in solitary splendour, as though it was gracing the gate pillar of a stately home. 'Three we have had,' said Thomas; 'one we have feasted upon and one someone broke in and stole, but this one we guard very fiercely.' And he laughed with such good humour and enjoyment of life that I was suddenly conscious of how sad I had been feeling about this country until now.

If Thomas had raised my spirits, with Elias I entered a world of eccentric delight, far removed from the sordid power struggles, the poverty and the corruption all around. Elias was the inventive mind in charge of the Appropriate Technology Department, which was a cross between the ingenuity of the Flintstones and the genius of a Leonardo. All the innovation around the place seemed to be Elias's province. It was he who had trained the oxen, invented a more efficient charcoal stove, an improved blacksmith's bellows, a maize husker, roofing tiles and a specially balanced box on wheels capable of transporting very heavy loads. 'Look, it takes even me,' he said, leaping into it and directing his immensely tall thin assistant to pull it along; but the assistant, perhaps realising how like two small boys playing with a home-made cart they must look, was too helpless with laughter to oblige.

Each ingenious invention produced by Elias or the boys on his course looked a little like an Emmett cartoon, for everything had to be made out of any old bits and pieces that could be found in the impoverished environment. It was more a case of 'make-do' than 'appropriate' technology, but each invention clearly gave Elias the greatest satisfaction. 'The principal is right, very appropriate technology, yes?' he said, running his hands lovingly over one beloved brain-child after another. He treated me with the respect due to a fellow enthusiast when I told him that I had designed my bicycle, a machine for which he had conceived an immediate passion, which had further endeared him to me. It was when we were deep in the subject of bicycle construction and the possibility of making a bicycle trailer for farmers to take their produce to market, that I realised the strength of Elias's genius: he had absolute confidence that he could do anything at all he put his mind to.

His current favourite invention was what he called his VIP or Ventilated Improved Pit, a superior type of non-flushing lavatory that was designed to obviate the health hazards, the smell and the cockroaches which are the bane of tropical loos. One of his more solid constructions, it was rather an elegant building, like a small native round house, spacious within and with a large tin chimney protruding through the thatch. According to his enthusiastic and lengthy explanation, which I didn't understand, its products would be rendered totally non-toxic and very useful as a fertiliser.

Darkness had fallen while we were still deep in technicalities, inspecting ring wells by torchlight; and we would probably have continued for hours had I not been summoned to supper in Thomas's old and unluxurious bungalow, which had once been a missionary's house. We were served a meal of school-produced eggs, chicken and cabbage, cooked by the girls on the home economics course, who also carried in the dishes with some degree of ceremony but were soon giggling with a mixture of embarrassment, pride and enjoyment at Thomas's banter. One of the anomalies about the school was that whereas girls were encouraged to lay bricks and learn engineering, equality did not yet extend to the boys learning to cook.

After supper, some bishops who were having a convention on the campus dropped in for a visit and the conversation turned to an SPLA raid that the town of Lanye had suffered a few weeks back, which was related in hilariously graphic detail. About a hundred heavily armed but almost naked rebel soldiers between the ages of fourteen and twenty had emerged suddenly from the bush and taken over the town for three days. They had instructions to kill no one as the SPLA were anxious to restore their tarnished image, so there were only about seven casualties, mostly policemen who had offered resistance. The raiders were after food and clothing and people were made to strip and hand over their clothes at gun-point, even the priest. Disappearing guerillas were seen making off into the bush attired in long petticoats and women's dresses; one was even said to be sporting the priest's surplice round his hips as he danced out of sight.

The school had fared less well, for many of the pupils had taken to the hills, and this had angered the young rebels. They had shot the locks off the doors and generally roughed the place up, as well as denuding it of all its stores. Sadly they had also shot at the trained oxen. They had succeeded in killing one, which they had barbequed over a blazing fire, but the other three had fled wounded into the hills.

Humour was perhaps the greatest asset of Lanye; it was certainly the only one not in short supply, and it was achieved at the expense of no one. They laughed with rather than at people, somehow turning humour into a Christian virtue as well as an art. There was no outright condemnation even of the SPLA, though they were unanimous that John Garang was as great an enemy to the people of the south as the northern government. Given their tolerant attitudes, it was strange to hear them echo the belief that the real problem of southern Sudan was tribal jealousy. 'If we could work together; if we could produce one leader who all would follow, then we could stand up to the north and we would win with no fighting,' said one of the bishops: 'but until that time we have no hope.'

As I was taking leave of the gathering to be escorted to the round thatched hut where I was to sleep, Thomas slipped me two cans of beer in a plastic bag, whispering that I should not let the bishops see as they had a very presbyterian attitude towards drink. Before I turned in under the rustling straw I had the privilege of trying out Elias's VIP; it was definitely the most superior and commodious loo I met with in those parts.

The bright red road went much better next day on my own two wheels; and the bicycle – which I no longer thought of as the Agala now that we were out of Arab lands – felt as if it had at last come into its own, the tyres gripping the dirt and rock with equal sureness and swinging over the undulating tracks with ease in spite of its load. I felt that an entirely new country was opening up to receive me, a world of dense glossy green vegetation, with occasional shafts cut through it that gave glimpses into half-hidden little settlements and fleeting impressions of people's daily lives. On my left hand, nearer now, the big hills towards which I was heading gave a promise of coolness to come. There were plenty of people about; most looked poor and ragged, but contrary to the Brigadier's expectations no one made the least attempt to rob me.

Bicycles were very much in evidence. All were in a shocking state of disrepair, many with only the rudiments of brakes and pedals and some whose tyres were just scraps of rubber lashed onto the rims with string. Most of them were used simply as a means of wheeling goods along, including huge bundles of timber, sacks of root vegetables and great stems of bananas.

Part of the sense of freedom I was so consciously enjoying was because of the scarcity of motor vehicles, though when one did appear, roaring belligerently from within its dense clouds of raised dust, it came on as fast as its engine allowed, bucking and plunging over the awful surface as though all the demons of hell were pursuing it. Every other bicycle on the road fled in terror into the bushes but I tenaciously held my ground to the fury of the drivers who had a Toad-like attitude to other road users, and it was very much to my own peril and discomfort – but it is hard to break the habits of a lifetime. Nonetheless, I reached Yei without serious accident and delivered myself once again to officials, who processed my documents with another impressive display of labour-intensive time wasting. The tired scraps of low grade paper were already showing signs of disintegration, after being inspected at several army posts in the fifty miles between Lanye and Yei.

The Episcopal Church Aid compound where Gordon Falconer had offered me the loan of his 'tukl' was on the far side of town and riding through to it I had an impression of wide, broken streets, ugly brick buildings and two very large churches. As in Juba, there was a plethora of abandoned foreign aid centres, like the British Overseas Development Aid compound, where a collection of much-needed road-building machinery sat lined up in neat yellow immobility behind a chainlink fence. The population seemed to be divided evenly between Catholic and Protestant, and the shiny-faced school children who thronged the streets were dressed in either green or blue to denote which camp was providing their education. The uniforms were in varying degrees of raggedness but the children mostly looked reason-ably nourished and were undoubtedly the privileged ones, for although Sudan claims to have compulsory education, this is far from being the case. When I stopped because a boy had scored a slight hit on my shoulder with a stone, some other children from the rival organisation also stopped, and a superior-looking boy in a smart blazer said smugly, 'They are not nice; they come from the Protestant School. We would not do this thing to a madam, we know it is not polite.' Not having been hurt over much by the stone I laughed out loud at this little gem of a speech, which I fear somewhat puzzled the child.

Gordon's tukl was a very attractive large thatched native round-house with three rooms and a miniature version of itself at the rear where one washed in a tin bowl with water carried in by bucket. Its only drawback was that the electricity, which was generated by solar energy, wasn't working and at night the cockroaches moved in early and took over the kitchen with such determination that I was intimidated and left them to it. They were huge shiny beasts, rearing up in confrontation when caught in the dim light of the hurricane lamp and moving around with the speed of racehorses. They lurked under and behind everything, including the lavatory, which was sited in another miniature tukl, and was certainly not a VIP. When I raised the round wooden lid which covered the pit, even larger glossy brown cockroaches came charging forth into the air waving their feelers in furious challenge, which caused me to bang down the lid again, flattening the few aristocrats who had taken up positions on its underside. The others then scurried back down, temporarily bested, and I kicked the corpses in after them in the hope that they'd demolish their dead companions before attempting another sortie.

With so little reason to keep me on the compound I accepted with alacrity the offer from James Lo, the young Sudanese project manager, of a trip to the UN Club, which had both electricity and cold beer as well as a cool garden setting in which to enjoy them. We were immediately joined there by a number of local men who were working in aid, or who had been employed in agencies which had been discontinued. Apart from aid there is almost no outlet for the talents of educated southern Sudanese, and not unnaturally therefore they welcomed a chance to harangue a rare Western visitor on Britain's perfidy in pulling out the ODA. 'We know now who are not our friends and we can change you for others just as easily,' said one with hostility. I tried to disclaim responsibility for my country's real or imagined wrongdoings and asked them to explain what their grievance was, because I had little understanding of the complicated situation.

What emerged was a catalogue of betrayals and let downs in which everyone present joined including my host. It was clear that the bitterness went very deep. They felt that under British administration they had been taught to accept a different set of values and having embraced them, they had, in 1952 with Independence, been thrown back into a situation of hopelessness under the increasing Arab domination of the north. They were convinced that the SPLA raids had been used merely as an excuse for Britain to pull out of its aid commitments. 'You can see for yourself there is no danger here,' they said, 'the first opportunity was seized for the West to take away its aid.'

The anger of these politically conscious men crackled through the tropical night like forked lightning and their pent up resentment and frustration was like a tangible presence. Things I had come across only in the most tenuous way, as innuendo and rumour – debts to the World Bank, the use of International Aid to make more money for the countries originating the aid, the cynical exploitation of minerals and other resources under the umbrella of aid – were here real and burning issues and it made me feel ashamed of my ignorance and naivety. 'We are just as much slaves as when the Arabs sold us in chains,' said one: 'our master now is Mr World Bank; it owns us all. You know how they talk about us? We are "servicing our loan". With every single thing we produce and own we can just manage to "service" this debt, which means we pay only the interest and our children and children's children will still be "servicing" this debt to Mr World Bank in a hundred years from now. We will never be free while we have the West for a friend.'

The next day I was taken to visit a village where the struggle for sheer physical survival absorbed most of the available energy. It was a small village that two years ago had set up a co-operative with a small loan from ECA. Agriculture is still relatively new in Eastern Equatoria; until a short time ago the people were mainly pastoralists like the Mundari and growing crops was a supplementary occupation carried out by the women in the settled period of the year just after the rains, when they would grow only as much as their immediate needs demanded. Now the cattle have gone and crops like millet and dura are their staples, but they haven't made the transition to efficient farming. The ECA loan had enabled the village to build storage sheds for their crops and buy up any surplus from the surrounding villages, instead of them selling it to the Arab merchants. People could bring a basket of grain and be paid on the spot or, if they preferred, they could become members of the co-operative and wait until the accumulated harvest was sold, when they were likely to receive more money for their produce.

Apart from the new cement-floored, rectangular storage buildings, the village was a cluster of small round huts with deeply overhanging thatched roofs and lots of little thatched storage houses on stilts of which Elias would not have approved, as they were not rat-proofed. The plastered mud walls of the houses were decorated with simple outline paintings of flowers and patterns; and it was all very pretty and reminded me a little of parts of Switzerland years ago when things were much more primitive than today in the higher Alpine villages. Most of the adults were out in the field but there were one or two women with round-eyed babies in a loose cloth sling on their backs, and some young boys sitting under the eaves of the huts making model trucks from the newly harvested millet stalks. Like the tin trucks of the Shilluk children, these trucks were beautifully made and very detailed, showing a high level of skill and observation. There is clearly no shortage of talent in this part of the world, only the lack of opportunity to develop it.

I was interested to know how much difference the co-operative had made to the village's economy, but I think it was too early to tell. The problems they face are formidable, flying as they do in the face of Arab vested interests. Travel especially is absolutely ludicrous. A curfew lasts from about 5.30 p.m. until 8 a.m. the following morning, although if the soldiers at the road blocks decide to, they will stop a vehicle at around 4 p.m. and make it remain where it is all night.

Permits are necessary even to travel a couple of miles, and seem to be designed to discourage all movement. A driver often has to report to a post miles from where he is going and leave his pass there; after he has finished his business he has to retrieve the pass before returning to Yei, all of which can more than double his journey. Getting anything to market under this system adds enormously to the cost, especially with petrol having to come all the way from Kenya. Again and again I was told, 'The British started it. They isolated us. They started the travel permits, and the Arabs have just carried on the system.' I fear this is no more than the truth, even if it was done to protect the south from Arab exploitation.

I had lunch with a young man who had come out with us to instruct the co-operative in simple book-keeping. He spotted some friends who were sitting in the shade under a lorry, preparing a large salad of tomatoes, cucumber and oil in a plastic washing up bowl. I was invited over and after we had poured water from a bottle over each other's hands, we all tucked into the salad together, dipping bits of bread into the bowl. I had shared so many meals like this in Africa and they had all felt special, even a little holy sometimes, like being at a communion service – 'We being many are one body because we all share in the one bread'. Sharing this particular meal with three light-hearted young men, sitting in the dust under a lorry, felt especially blessed and I think it was more than just the open-handed sharing. It probably had a lot to do with the feelings of guilt that travel in this part of the world brings. In the light of such poverty I couldn't help feeling a sense of shame at coming from a life so immeasurably more materially privileged – a life moreover that I could return to whenever I chose, while they were trapped in a perpetual struggle for the bare essentials of existence. Under such conditions, their generosity towards me seemed an act of pure graciousness, but without such encounters, where for a while I felt I was accepted into their world on an equal footing, it would have been a derelict journey.

CHAPTER NINETEEN

Into Uganda

I approached the border with Uganda with more trepidation than I had ever felt before. Even friendly frontiers create tensions, taking the traveller from a country that has become familiar into a strange environment where money, language and customs are all different, and a period of disorientation is inevitable. But with Uganda these ordinary trivial anxieties were overshadowed by fears of a much darker nature – so much so that if the road had suddenly been closed I should have felt a certain relief to temper the disappointment. I was about to enter a land which for the last twenty-five years had been the playground of one megalomaniac ruler after another; where torture, arbitrary killings and wholesale massacre had become commonplace. It was a country where the army had preyed openly and rapaciously upon the civilian population, casually eliminating people on the merest whim as though they were of no more significance than flies.

There was now a new president who had been in power for less than a year and whom the Foreign Office in London had pronounced a 'good chap'. His name was Yoweri Museveni and he had been several years fighting in the bush in order to wrest power from Milton Obote. The grisly excesses that Museveni's eventual takeover uncovered, revealed to a horrified world that Obote's second period in office had resulted in even more killings and torture than had been perpetrated during Idi Amin's bloody reign. Could even the remotest semblance of normal civilised behaviour have returned after so recent a history of out-and-out barbarism? This was the thought that kept gnawing at me, rather than the embassy's warning about renewed hostilities. Fighting is a confined affair by and large, a local event that one can skirt around, but a brutalised, debauched soldiery manning those notorious road blocks was something else, and of that I was undeniably afraid.

Partly because of the fear, I enjoyed my final day's ride through the uplands of Eastern Equatoria as though it was my last, relishing every detail with senses sharpened by thoughts of danger. It was not a good

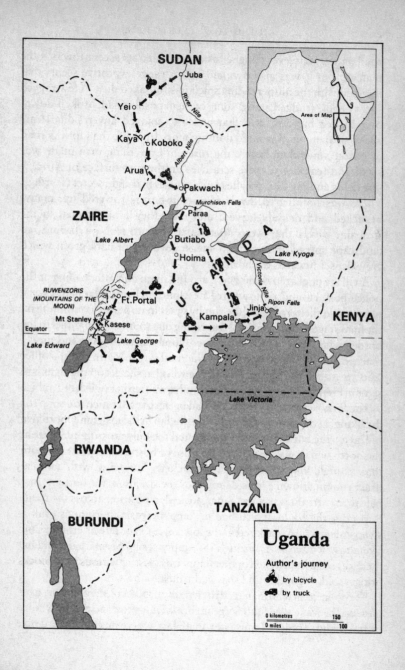

SUDAN

Juba

Yei

River Nile

Kaya   Koboko

Arua

Albert Nile

Pakwach

ZAIRE

Murchison Falls

Paraa

Lake Albert

Butiabo

Hoima

Lake Kyoga

U G A N D A

Lake George

RUWENZORIS
(MOUNTAINS OF THE
MOON)

Ft.Portal

Victoria Nile

Ripon Falls

Kampala   Jinja

KENYA

Mt Stanley   Kasese

Equator

Lake Edward

Lake Victoria

RWANDA

TANZANIA

BURUNDI

Area of Map

Uganda

Author's journey

by bicycle

by truck

0 kilometres   150

0 miles   100

road and it grew ever rougher as it continued its ascent towards the plateau. But it was also overlaid with strange evocative scents that mingled with the all-pervading smell of sun-baked dust. A few ragged silent people trudged along, some of them pushing sad, broken-down, over-loaded bicycles, and that at least removed any residual fears about stray mines. I wanted nothing more from life than for the road to go on unwinding before me forever. Everything man-made was small and temporary, mere scratches on the vast surface of Africa – tiny fields and toy-like, fragile round houses in rough, secret clearings. There was nothing to dwarf nature; the trees towered up, many-branched and densely leaved, and even they looked small in the widening vistas that were opening up before me – a rolling red landscape spread about with a sparse covering of dark green which grew denser towards the horizon.

A village appeared somewhere around noon and after calling at the police-post, I found a café where I ate a lunch of liver and tomatoes on a plank table sheltered from the sun by grass mats before continuing on the final stage to the frontier. I was riding due south now, parallel to the border with Zaire which drew ever closer on my right hand until I reached a point where one side of the road was in Zaire and the other side was still in the Sudan, and all the wooden shacks on the right had signs in French while those on the left were written in English or Arabic.

The forty-seven miles from Yei had been covered much too soon for my liking. I had come to the end of the Sudan in the insignificant village of Kaya – the backdoor into Uganda and the only crossing-point from the north which was not closed because of hostilities. It was no more than a single long street lined with racketty buildings, with an open drain running down each side towards the stream at the bottom. Just before the stream was a metal bar, locked in position across the road. Beyond it the route, which had become increasingly ruinous took a steep upward turn, dark red in the low angle of the late afternoon sun, like a raw wound torn through the empty scrub. Seeing me standing there, a young man jerked his head towards the barrier and the wooden bridge, said, 'Uganda', and spat in the dust.

The policeman who managed the lengthy process of stamping my exit pass said he was called Staff Sergeant Francis Gordon and that he would be my friend. Tonight I must stay in a place where he could guard my safety 'in case of trouble, only of course there will be none, for this is the Sudan.' I had to wait until he had changed into 'civvies' in order he said to arrest someone who must not know he was coming. 'All the worse for him,' he said darkly, tapping the side of his head mysteriously with his forefinger. He dropped me off at my 'safe place' on the way. It was the most awful dump, a 'hotel' made up of a row of small shacks, like run-down prison cells, with tiny windows high up in one mud-plastered wall. Mine was distinguished with a door on which the word 'Toelet' was still decipherable. I demurred rather at this sign but was told that the 'toelet' had been moved elsewhere and that this was only the door; I must not worry myself. There was just room inside for the bicycle to squeeze in between the sagging remains of an old iron bed and a wooden chair without a back, on which reposed a stump of candle. Beneath the bed was a rich collection of cigarette butts, bits of plastic and insect corpses.

Later, having a glass of tea with some Arab traders who had called to me to join them as they sat cool and elegant in their long white robes in front of their shop, I learnt that my 'hotel' was owned by the chief of police, who always made sure his staff took travellers there instead of to the better establishment up the road. The place seemed full of rumour and I could see they were ready to tell me more of the goings-on, but were put off by a fat, totally unclad man who had come and sat himself down close behind me – Moslems being always so very upset by nakedness.

I didn't meet the police chief who owned my deplorable lodging but I received a call from his second son, a would-be smooth and urbane young man called Cosmos, who invited me to come and drink a beer with him. Cosmos was a Moslem, as was his father, who somehow managed to square Allah's ban on alcohol with owning the only bar in Kaya. Seated before a litre of commendably cold and quite palatable lager, poured for me with voluptuous ceremony by an elaborately dressed young lady, I began to suspect that the bar was also, if not exactly the town's brothel, then at least a *'maison de rendezvous'*. It was a good deal more attractive than my 'hotel' however, and on closer acquaintance, Cosmos proved to be an appealingly ingenuous young man, anxious to discuss all things Western and with a craving to get to England or, better still, America. He moved his shoulders about constantly in a sort of yearning sympathy with the schmaltzy pop music that another elaborately adorned young lady fed onto the tape machine.

When I had finished my beer, which had gone straight to my head as I had not had any supper, Cosmos pushed his untouched bottle towards me, saying, 'I am Moslem, I do not drink this. I am only keeping you in company.' At that moment one of the young women came up and whispered something in his ear and he visibly paled several shades. 'My father is coming, if he finds me here he will be very angry,' he said in tones of panic, and bolted. There was only one other customer in the small bar and while one of the girls hovered around him, the other came and poured out Cosmos's beer into my glass, practically sitting in my lap while she did so, laying her arm along the back of my chair and slowly stroking the back of my neck. I began to wonder exactly what I had got myself into and in my confusion and desire to extricate myself, I polished off the second beer in haste.

Feeling distinctly unfocussed I made off into the pitch-black street, struggling to remember the way back to the noisome little cell. I had not taken more than a few tentative steps before I heard a whisper, and there was Cosmos with a shaded torch, somewhat subdued but determined to do his duty and see me safely home. 'My father knows I was in the bar. He is very angry with me,' he told me sadly. 'He is going to send me back to our village.' I tried to feel sympathy with what he clearly regarded as a harsh punishment, but the thought of exile from a 'half-horse' town like Kaya simply refused to make sense.

Kaya is at a considerable altitude and is very cold at six o'clock in the morning, at which hour I had decided to cross into Uganda. All my paperwork had been completed the night before and my 'friend', Staff Sergeant Francis Gordon, had assured me he would be there to unlock the barrier and see me off. He was not, nor had he appeared by 6.30. The usual large number of unemployed Sudanese menfolk were hanging about the police post, anxious to interfere in anything that might provide a welcome diversion. They were quite sure that I had no business to be going into Uganda and did their best to prevent me leaving, so that it was nearer seven before I was at last able to squeeze round the metal bar – the key had been lost – and start off across the bridge and up the steep earth slope that passed for a road.

The fear which had struggled all night to rise to the surface was by now a tight knot in my chest, making it difficult to climb the hill. Sharp spurts of panic kept shooting across my mind, and the only way I could keep them at bay was to concentrate hard on something else. I tried to work out how the huge lorries I had seen the day before had managed to negotiate this appalling strip of ground, which had been ploughed into deep furrows and craters and looked suitable only for tanks and 'all terrain' bicycles. In the distance ahead I could see a long stationary line of these lorries, and as I drew nearer to them I could also make out figures with guns very much in evidence milling energetically around the vehicles; the confrontation I had been dreading was about to happen. The lump in my chest moved upwards and as it did so I was suddenly aware of the cool touch of the jet amulets that I had attached to the strap of my passport pouch inside my shirt. I hadn't imbued the three small charms – a cross, an anchor and a heart, representing faith, hope and charity – with magical properties as such, but at that moment they reminded me of all my friends back home and of their prayers for my safety, and with the thought my panic subsided somewhat. I was still afraid, but I didn't feel quite so alone any more.

The soldiers gathered round me, their eyes wide with a mixture of astonishment and delight. They were dressed in a motley array of military garments eked out with the odd civilian touch – a pair of bright green shorts under a long heavy greatcoat, a battered trilby hat above a battledress. They were all young, some of them no more than twelve, and a few little boys of seven or so. All had mills bombs and hand grenades in their belts and carried heavy automatic rifles in their hands. They made me feel I was an unexpectedly welcome parcel which they were not sure how to begin unwrapping. They jabbed at my different panniers with their rifles, chanting 'Open, open', barely able to contain their impatience. I hadn't planned what I would say or do when I came to my first road block, but it seemed to me that there were far too many things in my bags that these ragged young soldiers might covet. Once they had started to root around in the panniers there was no knowing where things might end. So instead of undoing the tricky buckles, I hauled out my pouch and handed the oldest of them my passport, saying firmly, 'I am a special VIP and I have an important letter from your government which says that I am very welcome in your country.' This produced a lull in the proceedings and when the document I had been given by the Ugandan embassy in Khartoum had been read aloud there were smiles all round and little murmurs of welcome. One or two of the younger boys were disappointed at being denied the chance to inspect the contents of my bags, but I couldn't really take them seriously in spite of their weapons and I shooed them off as I would any other twelve-year-old nuisances.

My fear had been largely dispelled by this first encounter with Uganda's soldiery, though I remained distinctly nervous – children with grenades do not inspire peace of mind. There were heavy concentrations of troops for the next five miles or so and I passed through several road blocks where each time my VIP act and my letter saw me safely through.

After a while I stopped hunching my head down into my shoulders at the thought of stray bullets, and began to take a more active interest in my surroundings. I was now in the country that an ancient legend had supposed to be the earthly paradise from which four mighty rivers flowed, which brought fruitfulness to the whole earth. It was a depressing introduction to Paradise, and quite definitely post the Fall. The land looked as potentially rich and fruitful as the legend claimed, but it had returned to scrub and presented a bleak, unpeopled aspect. Every house I passed was a gutted ruin – its roof, windows and doors and every scrap of anything that was removable were all gone, leaving only a brick or stonework shell standing starkly in the grey light. I passed two small churches and they too were bare, stripped skeletons overgrown with weeds.

With no supper and no breakfast inside me and a lot of energy being burned up, my thoughts were turning more and more to food. I had no local currency and I did not think anyone in this ravaged land would have anything left over for strangers, assuming I ever came to a habitation. There was nothing to do but to cycle on and it seemed a very long fifteen miles before I arrived at the small township of Koboko, the first place in which I saw houses with roofs and people walking about. I stopped a young man to enquire about food and with a gentle courtesy he directed me down a turning to 'the Fathers'. This turned out to be a huge Verona Fathers mission school, one of the largest in Uganda, with a prestigious reputation, and with not a single roof left on any of its many buildings. Father Dino fed me on avocado pear, cheese, pineapple and marvellous restorative coffee and told me of how the place had been looted and gutted three times since 1979. Each time the fathers had fled to Zaire, and each time they had come back to a scene of desolation, after which they had set to and built up the whole edifice again.

'Who takes all these tin roofs?' I asked, mystified. 'Ordinary people.' Father Dino replied, 'The economy of the country is totally destroyed; there is nothing coming in, nothing being made. One piece of roofing tin is worth six months of a man's salary – where there are such things as salaries! What a teacher earns in a month wouldn't buy a bunch of bananas. People are surviving here as best they can; leave a place empty and there will be nothing left in a day or two; the temptation is too great. People will risk even shells and bullets to stay behind and loot a neighbour's property.'

I continued on my way with a large pile of Ugandan shillings in my pocket, which Father Dino had exchanged for a few of my dollars. There were more people about now and the trickle grew into a stream, mostly animated, cheerful women going to market with their produce on their heads – bundles of greens and baskets of strange heavy prickly jackfruit, pineapples, lemons and bananas. The women wore long, bright dresses, many with puffed sleeves, full skirts and bodices buttoning high across ample bosoms – a style introduced by the missionaries at the turn of the century and still very much in vogue. Sometimes the women called a greeting but usually they broke into loud cackles at the sight of me – from which I gathered that women did not normally ride bicycles in Uganda. I didn't in the least mind being a figure of fun: it was so wonderful to hear laughter and to see people going about the normal business of life.

There was another Verona Fathers mission conveniently sited for lunch, to which Father Dino had directed me and where I was warmly welcomed and fed on delicious spaghetti. This mission was a hospital, the only one for miles around, and although the last military raiding party to pass through a year before had wantonly smashed up the operating theatre, it had not been looted as badly as Koboko had been and was serving the area again. It was in a beautiful setting of spacious well-tended gardens, and I was tempted to accept the fathers' kind offer to lodge there that night; but I was anxious to get on and instead I pedalled on through the heat of the day to the town of Arua, where I had been invited to stay with the parents of the two young Americans, Mark and Tom Hooyer, with whom I had shared the dirt floor of the shack in Wadi Halfa.

With time pressing, it was galling to find that I had to kick my heels in the regional capital of Arua for a few days, waiting for the end of the independence celebrations which marked one year of Museveni's administration. I needed the necessary entry stamp in my passport and the office would not be open until the festivities were over. The wet season was only a few weeks away, when the dirt roads would become quagmires and travel would be almost impossible. If I was going to reach the Mountains of the Moon I needed to keep moving. I was also anxious to communicate with home and let my husband know I was safe: something I had not been able to do since leaving Khartoum, and which I now found would not be possible until I reached the capital, Kampala.

I made the best of things by arranging for enough money to see me through Uganda and in servicing my dust-encrusted bicycle. With Uganda's economy in tatters, changing money was a matter not of banks but of the street. Hard currency was worth more than fifteen times the official rate and everything was calculated on this 'street rate'. My changer was a man called Matteus who came complete with a teaplate-sized badge on his chest which read 'The Lord is My Shepherd', so I was assured of being in good hands. For my hundred dollars I received exactly one million Ugandan shillings – in Kampala I would have received half as much again – and although it was a heady notion to be a millionaire, stowing the huge stack of notes away safely created quite a problem. Matteus made me pay an additional fee for his services in the shape of lending an ear to the long, long story of his 'conversion to the paths of righteousness', which was closely inter-woven with impassioned biblical exegesis, so I was not sure which was which and lost the thread early on.

There was more impassioned preaching the following morning at the tin church to which I went with my hosts. It was a very presbyterian service, with a young black preacher giving his first sermon. He took as his text the story of the woman with the bloody flux and he backed up his theme with extracts from just about every book of the Bible. Once again I found it difficult to follow the argument, but this time it was because of the strong, ripe smell of closely packed humanity filling the hot little church. With water, electricity and most other services out of action, the reek of unwashed bodies was not really surprising.

A loop of surfaced road about half a mile long ran round Arua and it made me realise how lucky I was that most of the other roads in the country were in such a ruinous state; for it was a killing ground, where any young man who could get his hands on a vehicle came to see how fast he could go before he crashed. My hosts, John and Ihla Hooyer, had only recently suffered a tragedy there. Two years before they had taken in a young girl, an unmarried mother with a small baby. They had grown very fond of them both, and had come to regard the little boy as their own grandchild. John used to take the toddler for rides on the back of his bicycle, and one day one of these suicidal youths had swept into them, killing the child instantly and landing John in hospital on the critical list. He had been suffering from awful headaches since the accident and just after I left he flew to Nairobi for a brain scan which revealed a blood clot on his brain. Fortunately it was removed successfully, but nothing of course could bring back the child.

The public celebrations of Independence mostly consisted of two-hour long speeches by the district administrator and other dignitaries, all in military uniform. They were not unlike the sermon of the previous day except in their subject matter, and were so unbelievably tedious that those not imprisoned on the podium drifted away to more agreeable pursuits, taking their bands and dancers with them. Private celebrations centred around strong drink, to judge from the numbers of men reeling down the gutters of Arua as I left the following morning with my newly stamped passport. One man was loudly and tunefully singing 'God save our gracious Queen' which seemed an oddly colonial sentiment.

Over the next few days I rode for long hours through a green, hilly countryside, my musing on Uganda aided by the soothing hypnotic turning of the pedals. My fears of a violent and barbaric race had been quickly dispelled, for the people had proved to be perfectly friendly.

And while it was only too clearly a tragic and ruined country, the bizarre aspects of the mad court of the Red Queen were more in evidence than its underlying menace. There was no shortage of charm and humour, and with so much apparent gentleness in the national character it was difficult to see how the sickening events of cruelty and rapaciousness had come about.

The most lethal hazards I had to face came from the road itself, where all sorts of nasty surfaces had to be negotiated, from sudden patches of soft sand to scatterings of gravel which lay treacherously along the top of narrow slippery ruts of sun-baked clay. I was only 200 miles now from the equator and the weather was growing progressively hotter and dust permeated everything. Food was proving a continual problem and all I found to buy was a little pile of limes from a farmer. I couldn't live on limes, and was wasting away in spite of being a millionaire. Most people seemed to be living by barter since money had lost its meaning.

It was neither the road nor hunger that all but ended the journey however, and I remain convinced that only a miracle prevented an ignominious *finale*. I was pressing hard on the pedals going up a steep slope, when suddenly all resistance ceased. The bicycle came to a halt, and the pedals spun round as freely forward as backwards. What I had feared for some time had happened: the freewheel was so choked with dust that the pawls had slipped out of the ratchets.

Within minutes several concerned Ugandans had gathered round from somewhere and after studying the problem had all quickly come to the same conclusion – there was nothing to be done without the special extractor which I had left at home. There was unlikely to be anywhere that I could get hold of such a highly specialised tool, probably nowhere in Africa. Disaster for the sake of saving a few ounces of metal! I felt ashamed of having been so short-sighted, but most of all I felt bereft at having my marvellous freedom of movement taken from me in one fell swoop. There was nothing for it but to wait for a lorry that could take me and the maimed bicycle on the long journey to Kampala. I could have sat down and wept.

I don't remember praying for a miracle and I wonder at my gall if I did do so having been so remiss, but something made me put a foot on the pedal again a little while later, and I found to my joy that the pawls were once more firmly lodged in the ratchets. Some time after that I came by a precious tin of penetrating lubricant with which I was able to flush out some of the accumulation of sand and dust, and I had no more trouble with it. As I write this some five months later, I realise that I have not yet taken off the freewheel to investigate the miracle.

Each night found me the guest of some religious body, like a traveller in medieval Europe. Like them I had no choice, as there wasn't anywhere else, but I wouldn't have wanted it to be otherwise, since each stay assumed a special significance. One night I stayed at a former leper colony, which was now a general hospital; on other nights I stayed with Ugandan nuns of different orders, each convent directing me on to the one ahead. They were simple places, often very poor, and there was no false modesty about accepting my contribution towards the cost of feeding me.

A place called Nebbi stands out in my memory because the nuns there were at such pains to serve me and make me welcome. They swept and garnished the ugly little concrete cell where they housed me, hanging sheets at the window in lieu of curtains, and they washed my sweaty stained clothes and ironed them by moonlight with a charcoal iron. Without enquiring what religion I professed (if any) they drew me out onto the verandah to join in the evening reciting of the rosary and afterwards took me into the chapel for four Hail Marys for my safe arrival and for the success of my journey. Perhaps it was their prayers that saw me through the bizarre and frightening incident which befell me the next day, at the spot where once again I came to the banks of the White Nile.

CHAPTER TWENTY

Bullets in Paradise

I came to the banks of the Nile at the dilapidated bridge of Pakwatch, where the river, having rushed and tumbled its way headlong down the 250 miles of falls and rapids from Lake Victoria to join the waters of Lake Albert, has turned a ninety-degree corner and taken up its northward direction again. It is only a few miles below Lake Albert and the quantities of moisture ascending invisibly from the vast expanse of water had changed the look of the land entirely. In fact land had ceased to have any significance. It was a scene of air and water only, of limitless space and a marvellous light with the bloom on it of something primeval and eternally fresh. The sky was like an opalescent shell casting a pink glow into the sparkling blueness of the upper air, and was reflected back onto the dancing silvery surface of the mile-wide infant river. Far away to the west, so faintly etched as to make them seem of the same elements, was the soft grey outline of a range of towering mountains.

I would probably have remained at this vantage point for a long time had it not been for a line of soldiers who squatted watchfully on their heels along the rotten planking of the bridge. In their stiff heavy uniforms, trailing their clumsy weapons in the dust, they seemed as alien as the bridge itself in that primitive, ethereal place. They did not need to remind me that people who linger on bridges are regarded with the deepest suspicion. Once across the bridge and rolling down the shallow incline on the other side, I felt no such inhibitions about gazing my fill, which was how I came to pass the rusty upturned wheelbarrow which constituted an army road block, and at which I was meant to stop.

The first intimation that I had committed a grave error was the look of fear on an old woman's face as she gestured at me with flapping movements of her hands to go back. In the same moment I realised that the grunts behind me, which had been rising in pitch and volume, might have something to do with me. As I turned round I saw a soldier bearing down fast towards me, his rifle aimed at my middle and his finger trembling on the trigger. His face was contorted with anger and his shouts had by now become screams and bellows of rage; it was clear that he was preventing himself from firing only with great difficulty. Realising what I had done I hurried back towards him and even as I was taking in the situation, it came to me that here at last was the other side of things – the root of the fear I had felt in crossing the border. It was my first encounter with the terrifying violence that had ruined this land.

I think I realised straight away that the soldier was, in a curious way, as helpless as I was, and was possibly just as frightened by his own anger. He knew he shouldn't shoot me and would be in grave trouble if he did, but he clearly had an enormous urge to pull the trigger because I had so greatly offended his sense of self-importance by ignoring the barrier. He tried to dissipate his anger by humiliating me instead, and screamed at me to pick up my bicycle and put it on my head and carry it back to the wheelbarrow. 'You have to be punished,' he kept shouting.

The mind is a curious thing and many-layered, and probably one is never more conscious of this than in situations of acute danger. I was aware of how close I was to being killed and was deeply frightened and could hear myself apologising over and over again, doing my best to placate the man and calm him down. At the same time a part of my brain was debating the absurdity of his order to carry my bicycle on my head – an impossible feat, I decided, quite apart from which I could barely lift one wheel off the ground as it was so heavily laden. I almost laughed aloud at the picture it conjured up, and even to save my life I knew I wouldn't dream of even pretending to attempt it. Fortunately there was another, more sensible layer in overall control that was intent upon getting us both back to the barrier and the comparative safety of the other soldiers whom I could see waiting there. Once I could lean the cycle against the rusty wheelbarrow and fish out my papers and the magic letter, I knew all would be well. But I had no idea of just how terrified I had been until the other soldiers told me to calm down and be quiet and I realised I was still apologising over and over again, the words tumbling over themselves in their eagerness to get out. I told the soldiers that it was their fault because they had frightened me so much and they said they were sorry for that, and suddenly the incident was over and we were all friends, except for the first soldier whose chest was still heaving and shuddering with suppressed emotion.

It was here that the famous Murchison Game Park began. I had doubted whether I would be allowed through it on a bicycle, and at first the soldiers were all for forbidding my passage: 'Too dangerous. Lions, big animals, chomp chomp. They eat you up.' Then they decided that I must have a gun with me, which explained why I wanted to go through a game park, and they concentrated on trying to get me to declare it, telling me (untruthfully) that I was allowed to travel with a gun, only I must show it to them. Then, quite suddenly, they simply lost interest in me as a Suzuki pick-up drove up, and they waved me on through. 'It is not dangerous,' said one, 'you go.' I went in haste, before they could change their minds again.

At first there was a lot of military movement on the road; I saw at least twelve large army lorries, each with a perfectly dressed miniature soldier of seven or so, preserving a stern unsmiling demeanour as he posed on the steps of the cab. They were all going off to the east towards Gulu, where fresh outbreaks of fighting had been reported, and once I had turned onto the narrow sandy path which ran south through the park towards the Victoria Nile, I had the place to myself – except for whatever might be lurking in the undergrowth. After the recent confrontation I was only too glad to be alone and could not worry over-much about being attacked by wild animals.

Every mile seemed an extra bonus now that I had had my first thrilling glimpse of one of the Nile's great sources. I felt I was in a momentous place, the centre of things, and to have got this far gave me a tremendous sense of achievement. All that planning and those long dusty miles had finally led to the point where I was riding alone on a bicycle through this almost legendary game reserve, part of the rumoured paradise that had remained hidden from the rest of the world until barely a century ago. It felt like the height of good fortune just to be here, even if the stories were true of Amin's troops having shot most of the game.

The only animals I saw were large water buck bounding away with long extended leaps over the open ground, and gazelle which seemed to hover in the air as they made off. There were also a few African storks and one very large pacing bird with a long pointed beak. I was very lucky to see anything because a short way into the reserve I heard firing and came across a large army truck stationary in the middle of the path with the soldiers fanned out all over the place shooting for the po*. I made sure they knew I was there before I approached them; I wanted no more near encounters with a heavy calibre bullet.

After that I saw no one and I pressed on hard in order to make the shelter of Paraa before nightfall. I often had to walk because of soft sand, and the sweat poured down my face past the headband that was meant to stop it, but even so the feeling of a deep joy and contentment kept growing. The landscape had changed again dramatically from the lucent watery scene of a few miles back. Here it was like being on the roof of the world – another limitless expanse, but this time of hot dry brown plains that went on and on into far blue distances; an heroic landscape, charged with energy and with a slight undercurrent of menace. It was a landscape that threw out a challenge. 'This is Africa,' it seemed to say, 'this is what you travelled so far to find.'

A further hour's riding over this high and open sun-burnt plain brought me to a place where the scrub began to grow more plentifully and where the first sign of man appeared – the incongruous carcase of a crashed plane, one of Idi Amin's military toys I learnt later. After that the track began to descend steeply and I hurtled and slithered down it, the wind drying the sweat on my face until I came finally to the banks of the Victoria Nile at Paraa, just as the light was beginning to go, and the air was loud with the snorts and grunts of hippopotami.

I doubt if I could have afforded to stay at the prestigious Paraa Lodge when it was a hotel set in sweeping lawns, with wide views over the water. Now it was only a shell of a place I was welcomed by the caretaking staff for the price of a bottle of beer. Because it was so isolated, it had been worth no one's while to make off with the roofing tiles, and even the doors and windows were still intact. Inside there was nothing left, not a stick of furniture, no water, no taps, no light, not even light switches. It had been picked as clean as a tree in winter.

I was given a room on the first floor and was not too badly off with my inflatable mattress, my cooking gear and dehydrated food. I was brought a bucket of the thickest, greenest water I had ever seen and once more blessed my filter pump. I was also supplied with a glass jar of paraffin, with a rag stuffed into it for a wick. It all had the satisfactory feeling of an African safari, enhanced by the thousands of bats which suddenly peeled off the upper balcony as the sun finally vanished. It was a magical place. All night the chorus of grunting hippopotami rose and fell and when I went out onto the balcony and shone my torch into the blackness, it picked out the form of a huge elephant, not more than fifteen feet away, ambling through what had once been flower-beds.

At this higher level the Nile has nothing of the serenity and purpose with which it passes under the bridge at Pakwatch. Here it still reflects the huge turmoil of the Murchison Falls which are only about twelve miles up-river and which were my next objective. The easiest way to reach them was by boat, and the launch which served this purpose was tied up by the ferry, its engine gone, its windows and dashboard looted; clearly no one would be going anywhere in it for quite a while. There were no other boats. Another way was to trek through the park, a distance of about thirty miles. Roads had once led there, as it had been a feature of the park to walk beside the Falls and gaze down on them from above. I gathered that the park rangers had been recently issued with a Land Rover and would be pleased to take me over the now ruinous overgrown paths if I was prepared to pay the high price of the petrol. I would have happily paid twice or even three times the amount asked for as it was inconceivable to make a Nile journey and miss out the Murchison Falls which have been described by Mr Rennie Bere as 'the most exciting single incident in the Nile's long journey to the sea'. To my fury however, after first agreeing a price, the head ranger turned his back on the deal and refused to take me. He knew he was wrong but he was in love with the vehicle, his first in a very long while and he spent his time going up and down the road in it, his wife beside him nodding gravely to the few passers-by. He was not going to get it scratched on the overgrown tracks. 'Bring me a letter from the head warden in Kampala,' he taunted me. 'When he orders me to take you, you come back.'

There was nothing for it but to cross the river and at least my luck held there, for the ferry had been out of action for days, and broke down again after making this single journey. After a long sandy haul up out of the river valley, I came to the old road to Kampala, which was disused now, with the bridges down and already returning to the bush. If I went that way, I would get to the track that led to the Murchison Falls. I had a big tussle with myself about it: wild animals – buffalo, lions and elephants – were a real danger in this now totally unfrequented part. There might be still worse, for there were reports of many guerilla bands holing up there and living on the game. I went a little way down the tree-grown road, but caution triumphed in the end and I turned back and slogged along the newly opened dirt road that ran down into the Rift Valley alongside Lake Albert – Sam Baker country.

At some point in the hot and humid afternoon, cycling slowly along the sandy valley floor in a dry, unpeopled area, marked on my map as an elephant and hippo sanctuary, I saw a Land Rover approaching with a couple of white men in it. My drinking water had been used up some time ago and the lake was far away and had no visible route to it. I waved to the car to stop, in the hope that they might be carrying something to drink and would spare me a little. They were the first white people I had seen in a week, and almost the only people I had seen all day. They were missionary workers for the Church of Uganda, pink, plump young men, perspiring freely and in a hurry to get to Pakwatch before nightfall. Having stopped they decided to take the opportunity of tying their roof rack load down more securely, tossing me the odd remark over their shoulders as they did so. I could hardly believe my ears when they told me that they had water but none to spare, as they would probably need it themselves. They had no interest at all in me or in what I might be doing alone in a remote part of the Rift Valley and I could only hope they made more use of the Christian virtue of generosity with the people they had come to help. I went on feeling very much the poorer for having met them.

I rode on and on through the empty hot landscape. It was the toughest day of the journey so far and I could begin to appreciate something of the hardships Florence and Sam Baker had suffered when, nearly dead with malaria, hunger, thirst and general weakness and exhaustion, they had finally made their way to the edge of the lake. By the time I reached the place where the road started to climb steeply up the almost vertical escarpment of the Rift, I too was exhausted and knew I couldn't make it. There was only one other choice; a small track ran down to the shores of the lake at a place marked on the map as Butiabo. I turned the wheels in that direction and let the bicycle carry me gently down the four miles. At the end of the track I rolled to a halt in a square of rough unkempt huts made up of bits and pieces, with ragged people standing about in front of them. Everyone stared and a few of the younger women giggled. I said, 'I have to stay here tonight, where can I go?' Immediately a young man came forward and said formally, 'I am in charge here, my name is Gracious, come with me.'

He took me to his friends, Frederick, the fisheries officer of Lake Albert, and his wife Rose. At first I thought the rough building was some sort of works office; a decaying single-storey brick structure, taller than its square base – like a slightly over-sized sentry box, it looked as if it had been left over from the period of British administration. We sat outside on oil drums and bits of boxes and Rose made tea, boiling the water in an old tin on some twigs on the ground. After some whispering, a beautiful young man called Godfried was sent off with some money clutched in his hand and came back with four biscuits taken from a packet of 'plain tea biscuits' and wrapped in a bit of old paper. It hit me like a blow. It wasn't delightfully *al fresco* and casual: this was the grim reality of how Ugandans were forced to live in the state to which their country had been brought. These were educated, urbane people – Frederick was a Ph. D, who had read for his doctorate in Japan, Godfried his assistant was an M.A., and Rose was about to qualify as a teacher. There were two tiny rooms inside that nasty building, in one of which Frederick and Rose's mattress just about fitted on the floor. The other room had an oval table and a heavy desk without its drawers. There was nothing else; it was all that remained after the years of fighting and looting. That they were prepared to share this poverty with me was another of the moving experiences of the journey.

I hardly dared ask where I could wash but when I did, Frederick suggested a swim in the lake, and we all five went out in an ancient flat-bottomed punt. Godfried, like a young black Apollo, punted superbly with a bent branch making up a song as he went about being a slave to Frederick. 'I am the boy, Man Friday my name,' he yodelled. Once past the tall reeds that grew around the stinking black contaminated ooze of the landing place, we shot out through the reed-grown margins of the lake and were at once back in the enchanted world I had glimpsed at Pakwatch. Rose and I were landed at a clean little beach while the men poled off discreetly around a headland. For an hour I swam about in the soft warm water or lay on my back gazing up at that pearly pink translucent sky, watching jewel-bright kingfishers hovering overhead, fishing the shallows in company with stately herons and a host of other birds. I thought I would like to stay there forever, and almost had to be dragged out by force. As we towelled ourselves dry Rose looked at my white body with dark brown arms and legs beginning with abrupt precision where shirt sleeves and shorts ended. She laid her own arm against mine and said, 'One month more and you are a black woman like me.'

We came back to the smelly landing place as the pink and purple shadows of early evening were changing to a dramatic red, slashed through with dark grey and sharp yellow bands. Rose sat there topless in the cool breeze, her heavy shapely breasts causing no embarrassment to the three men – such a completely different attitude to that of the other two countries of the Nile.

Supper was a dish of sweet potatoes and the bony salted and dried mudfish which are a speciality of the lake and enjoyed only by those who have acquired a taste for them. I made myself eat and drank quantities of beer which was my contribution to the meal. We ate in the light of one small home-made paraffin lamp and when it was finished we talked on in the darkness and drank local firewater. Like most people in Uganda, Frederick and Rose had a need, a compulsion even, to talk about the traumatic experiences that they had been through. In this out-of-the-way place the opportunity to tell their story didn't happen very often.

According to Rose, Uganda had sunk into barbarism from the moment independence had been achieved twenty-five years ago. She was the first to tell me that she thought Uganda was morally decadent, and had no hope unless Britain came back to restore order. It was the saddest thought I heard expressed in that country because it made me feel that they had given up hope of a solution. I was to hear the same sentiment repeated on many occasions. This first time I demurred, and Rose launched into a passionate speech to defend her view. 'Three times we were looted. They came with bombs and guns. If you had a child sleeping in a room inside, you would leave him and just flee. You would run with seven children and arrive with just one; the others would be left lying dead by the roadside. The prisons were full. They would come and gouge out people's eyes, cut out their tongues, crush their testicles between stones like they were castrating a bull. Between Hoima and Kampala they left the skulls lying all along the road so people should know what happened here; some have a rope still around the neck.'

Frederick was quieter but more embittered. 'There would be thirty or forty road blocks between here and Kampala,' he said, 'and at each one the soldiers would demand money and they would be just as likely to shoot as not. A man left home not knowing if he would return. "Sit down," they'd say to some and to others, "You go," and you knew those who were left sitting were finished. There was nothing you could do. I had everything in this house, now I have nothing. When I came back last time there were just three stones on the floor for a fireplace. They have been terrible times; people should know what we went through.'

They had borrowed a mattress from somewhere to make me a bed, balanced on the oval table and the desk, so as to be off the floor and clear of the rats. But I didn't sleep much, partly because all night the thunder rolled around the lake and sheet lightning flared across the sky in tropical extravagance, and partly because I was so disturbed by the testimonies I had been given that I sat up to write them in my journal by the fitful light of the storm. For most of the rest of the night I lay there wondering what would happen to this country. Compared with what I had been told about life under Obote and Amin I would have thought that there were now clear grounds for hope; at least the arbitrary shooting at road blocks had stopped, as I could testify. I had put this point to Rose and Frederick and they had agreed but were not overly impressed. 'That is one thing Museveni has done, he has got his army under control, now let us see what else he can do.' They had been through too much to believe that the new regime could undo all the tribal jealousies and bring about a total change in the nature of Ugandan leadership.

The next morning was shimmering and fresh after the storms, and I climbed out of the Rift Valley with impressive ease on the only reasonable tarmac surface I came across in Uganda. The view from the top was of the whole immense lake as Baker had seen it, 'like a sheet of quicksilver', with the 7,000 foot peaks soaring up beyond it, away in Zaire, quite clear now across the sixty-mile expanse. I thought of what Frederick had told me about the lake, to which he seemed to have an almost mystical attachment. He could not bear he said to hear it called Lake Albert. Its name since ancient times had been Luta Nzige, which means Death of Locusts. It was so called because the great marauding swarms of voracious insects which harried Africa came always from the west and they could not fly the whole width of the lake without landing. As there were no islands they came down on the surface and were drowned. 'Death of Locusts,' he said musingly, 'I don't know if it is true but certainly there are never locusts on this side, only human ones.'

Before I turned my back on the scene I tried to get a glimpse of my objective far away to the south beyond the limits of the lake. The Mountains of the Moon are about two hundred miles from this point as the crow flies, twice that by road. Elusive peaks, their snow-capped tops rise to over 16,000 feet and yet they are as often as not invisible, wrapped in shrouds of mist and cloud. Even the great explorer Stanley doubted their existence, until one day to his great surprise he caught his first glimpse of them. 'I saw a cloud of a most beautiful silver colour, he wrote, 'which assumed the proportions and appearance of a vast mountain covered in snow.' I wasn't so honoured but there was a long way to go yet.

CHAPTER TWENTY-ONE

The Mountains of the Moon

The first person I saw on the plateau as I turned my back on the lake and rode away around a corner was a soldier strolling along the narrow dirt road between the tall hedgerows. He was quite alone and dressed in a well-fitting camouflage uniform, a gold cross showing up brightly in the vee of his open collar. As he came nearer his magnificent white teeth parted in a broad smile. He was casually tossing from hand to hand as he walked a live grenade, and at once the surreal quality of Uganda was back with its underlying current of menace.

Fortunately for my peace of mind he was the last soldier I was to meet for a long time. The route towards the Mountains of the Moon led over such minor little ruined lanes that for days I did not even see a single vehicle. The area had suffered badly from the attentions of Obote's army over the last few years when they had been hunting for Museveni, who comes from these parts and was thought to be hiding out here. But although my way bordered the notorious Hoima Triangle with its piles of human skulls that Rose had talked about, I saw nothing of that. I journeyed instead through a closely inhabited, fruitful plain, a domestic landscape where steep little hills produced naturally small fields and created close private places – cabins hidden among tall sugar cane, women hoeing in a chattering congregation behind a sheltering curtain of trees.

There was always a sparse but endless stream of walkers, on their way to and from market, with many little boys crouched in the shade by the sides of the road, selling cane juice to them as they passed. Probably because of what had happened to them – and it was said that there was no family here that had not lost at least one member in the massacres – there was often more than a hint of reserve in their manner towards strangers. The children and the women too seemed much warier than elsewhere and if I came upon them suddenly they appeared absolutely terrified. Some of the men would relieve the tedium of their walk by such conversational gambits as 'How are

YOU? I am ALL . . . RIGHT. How is your journey?' or 'How are you Sir? How are you feeling going up that hill?' or 'Why are you riding that bicycle? Is it not tiresome for you?'

They always delivered these pleasantries on the steepest part of the hill where it was difficult to summon up breath to answer them; I felt sure that they were aware of this, and that it was all part of their sense of humour.

The nights and the early mornings were pleasantly cool, but once the sun was well up above the horizon the heat was fierce. What made it bearable was the fruit that was available everywhere, an indication of the unfailing fertility of the 'pearl of Africa' that had enabled the population to survive the total breakdown of the country's economy. 'Put a broom handle into the ground of Uganda and it will send out shoots' the saying went. Pawpaws and bananas became my staples and the acid sweetness of pineapples quenched my perpetual raging thirst, aggravated by the dust of the road, as nothing else could, though after a few days of eating a whole pineapple at a sitting, my lips and the inside of my mouth were split and I had to have a day of abstinence. I tried jackfruit instead for the first time, after persuading a small boy to show me how to tackle it. It is an enormous melon-shaped fruit, a shiny greenish-yellow and covered in spines like a sea urchin. Inside, a white pithy substance is studded with large translucent seeds like lychees, and it is these which are eaten. I was not so impressed as to try it again. I preferred the passion fruit – hard little brown-skinned globes with a wonderful astringency that went well with pawpaw.

The road surface was even more awful than usual, very heavy vehicles having cut it into deep, narrow trenches during the last rainy season. It required the utmost concentration and I fell off the bicycle several times, especially when spectacular butterflies – yellow, blue, black, white and paisley patterned – danced suddenly before my face, or when the flame trees and the blue jacarandas distracted my attention. Clothes and skin began to show the inevitable scars and stains of the hard journeying, but my increasingly disreputable appearance did nothing at all to dampen the welcome I received in the convents, which continued to provide most of my nights' lodgings.

One such resting place was in a particularly beautiful setting, on top of a high spacious hill with fine old trees, lawns and vistas all laid out so much in the style of an eighteenth-century English park, that I was convinced that it had once been a colonial farm. The first building I came across when I had struggled up there was a low stone barn filled with local village children sitting on long benches, beginning a catechism class. Sister Justinia had been instructing them on how they must receive visitors, so even in my stained shorts and sweat-soaked shirt I was a useful object lesson and was seated on a stool while the children put on an impromptu concert to welcome me. I soon forgot my embarrassment and sat there feeling like royalty, while the young musicians enthusiastically cleared away the benches and gave a concert of traditional songs and dances, a small girl of nine beating an accompaniment on the drums. They all seemed most tremendously talented. The nuns here were also running a primary school and a dispensary, financing their projects with the proceeds of a farm and a banana plantation, but the heart of the place was a home for forty-five little orphans whose families had been destroyed in the last wave of killings.

Once, when I was settling down by the roadside to eat my midday fruit a man insisted that I come into his garden, where he set out a table and chair for me under the shade of a tree and brought a plate from his tiny cabin for me to eat off. His wife and his young family, standing around wide-eyed, all appeared adequately nourished but were very ragged and there were several umbilical hernias among them. No one had more than a few words of English, so not much was said but the man cut me a pineapple from his garden and try as I might he steadfastly refused to accept any payment for it. I found this sort of generosity from the traumatised people of Uganda even harder to bear than in the countries further north.

Contacts with fellow Westerners were more problematical. I was kindly invited to stay on several occasions with American missionaries of the 'born again' variety. I know of no religious group that is as one hundred per cent certain of its claim to salvation, but it was not their complacency that I found difficult so much as their life style in relation to the people they were attempting to convert. The material differences were so great that it seemed to make a nonsense of the message, unless God was meant to be seen as firmly on the side of the affluent. For their part the missionaries were hurt and puzzled by the way the Ugandans received their evangelising, which centred on a film of the life of Jesus which they took around to show in the villages. They told me that it was a very moving film with a good commentary in the local dialect, but that at the point where Jesus is nailed to the cross many of the audience started to titter or break into loud laughter. It had never seemed to occur to them that the film might be at fault, or that white actors portraying the story through an unfamiliar medium might come over as hysterically funny, or even that this might be their way of coping with an excess of emotion, they could see it only in terms of something lacking or wayward in the Ugandan mentality.

Still they were kind enough to me, and only once was I challenged about my own position *vis-à-vis* 'salvation' – by a minister I had not taken to, and who I felt was quizzing me more in order to display his superior position than to have any real dialogue. He did this at the dinner table in front of a number of Ugandans who were employed in mission work and who kept up a sycophantic chorus of 'Just so brother, praise Jesus'. After repeated attempts on my part to side step I told him that I thought theology was far too important a subject to be bandied about at mealtimes, which was not what is expected of a guest.

One Western Christian institution about which I had no such reservations was a hospital in the beautiful foothills of the Ruwenzori Mountains, just a few miles from the equator to which I had been invited by a doctor I met in Arua. He had suggested I came up there to borrow the gear I should need for climbing the Mountains of the Moon. The staff at Kagando Hospital worked hard and lived very simply; they had ample opportunity for practising the faith they professed in the busy daily life of the wards and operating theatres and they left evangelising to others. I rested a few days there, recovering from the long ride, sitting for hours on a ricketty verandah watching yellow weaver birds refining their extraordinary nests that hung in the trees like a bumper crop of some strange fruit.

I didn't decide to actually climb the Mountains of the Moon, until I got to Kagando. All the way down to the equator, bicycling parallel to the range, I had hoped to get a sight of their snow-covered peaks, but not once had the veils parted; all that could be seen was the lower 3,000 feet and it was difficult to believe that the mountains existed at all. They were hidden in a sort of haze of moisture, thickened by great quantities of smoke that rose up everywhere from the burning of the land in preparation for the rains. I could see why so many early explorers had missed the enormous range altogether and I realised that if I wanted a closer acquaintance with Ptolemy's 'eternal snows which feed the lakes that are the source of the Nile' then there was nothing for it but to make the long haul up to around 14,500 feet, where the snows began.

By far the hardest part of the enterprise was organising the supplies and the porters. It was like mounting a full-scale expedition and without the help and advice of some of the doctors and nurses who had already made the climb I doubt I would have raised the necessary energy to embark on the venture. After they had kitted me out with warm trousers and several sweaters, they sent me off early one morning with two burlap sacks, an assortment of heavy cooking pots, cutlery, metal plates and mugs, and a panga – a heavy curved chopping knife that was ideal for clearing a path through the jungle but was just for the porters to cut firewood with. The porters I was to discover later, never did more than was strictly necessary for survival. I was also lent the official handbook of the Mountaineering Club of Uganda – a publication of colonial times, portraying a rather different state of affairs from today, but containing the list of necessities that was still *de rigueur* for climbers of the Ruwenzoris. The mountains were so taxing, it claimed in the opening pages, that even fit young men could not hope to make the exhausting ascent and carry their own equipment; porters were essential. The staff at Kagando thought I should need three porters; actually I managed with two, but not knowing this beforehand I set about shopping for a week's supply of food for four people.

The taxi dropped me at the market town of Kasese and with the help of a man who rushed forward with a home-made wheelbarrow, I set about buying the necessary stores. With all commodities so scarce I decided to eat what the porters did – a great mistake. Their ration was one dried and planklike mudfish per day, and exactly laid down quantities of sugar, tea, groundnuts, curry powder, milk powder, cigarettes and casava flour. To the twenty-four mud fish and quite ridiculous quantities of the other items, I added a few extras like some onions, to prevent scurvy and some bananas for energy. Nothing could be purchased without lengthy bargaining, sometimes to the point of hysteria. Here in the south money had slightly more meaning than in the north, but even so the street price for my dollars was so ludicrously high compared with the official rate that it was hard to take the bargaining seriously. Nonetheless one was obliged to for the sake of people who lived here on a permanent basis – nothing annoys residents more than tourists who inflate prices by paying way above the going rate.

At last the two burlap sacks were filled to the point where I could no longer lift them. As a result I had no option but to agree to the price of the only taxi that was prepared to take me on the next stage – a price that turned out to be just over twelve times what it should have been and as a final insult the wheelbarrow man quadrupled his original quote. If all this sounds as though I was seriously robbed, I can only say it certainly seemed so at the time, but like everything in Africa, it was relative. The whole expedition of a week's duration cost less than 100 dollars to mount, but there was of course a good deal of that strange thing called 'principle' involved.

If I had thought that I was already worn out by all the haggling, I was mistaken; it had only been a warm up, the real work was yet to come. The starting point for the ascent is the Mountain Club Hut at the village of Ibanda, high in the foothills among the elephant grass. The man in charge looked me over and decided I was fit enough to manage a fast six-day circuit with just two porters, selected it seemed to me on a purely *quid pro quo* basis – to whoever would tip the most for being chosen. I was given Silvano, a thirty-year-old man with a protruding navel, and Hezron who was younger and shorter and looked as powerful as a sumo wrestler. My sacks were tipped out and everything was sniffed, tasted, counted and weighed. I had made one serious mistake by buying a vast quantity of casava – a rock-like, unshapely root vegetable, instead of casava flour, so we started the bargaining on the cost of replacing this. Wages were no problem as these were laid down; Silvano was to get rather more than Hezron on the debatable grounds that his knowledge of English was greater.

Once that had been agreed, the real work started. Part of their wages (sanctified by tradition) was a sweater and a medium weight blanket each, and as both these items were supposedly unobtainable, cash had to be agreed upon instead. They had a good ploy which was to state magnanimously that they would 'forgive the price of the sweater' and demand an astronomical sum for the blankets instead.

Four hours later, after the monumental bargaining session had resulted in a compromise, or rather in total capitulation on my part since time was on their side, we set out fast to make the first stage before dark, climbing through the elephant grass and bamboo jungle on overgrown paths that had not been re-cut since 1962. Once the haunt of elephants, lions and other big game, only the occasional monkey now hooted in the depth of the dense forest. 'You hear?' asked Silvano, the 'interpreter'. 'Good meat' – making it clear where the other animals had gone. The walking was as tough as anything I had ever done, precipitous, wet and slippery, with all sorts of creepers and barbed fronds reaching out to tear and scratch – how useful that panga could have been, instead of being firmly stuck in Hezron's sack. Sharp broken stumps of bamboo were nicely poised to inflict savage wounds, and the dense undergrowth was claustrophobic and humid. The bare splayed feet of the porters found a surer grip than my borrowed sneakers, and since they were respectively twenty and thirty years younger than me, I suspected that the going was easier for them even with the heavy sacks which they were carrying suspended from banana fronds around their foreheads.

By five we had reached a welcome clearing in which stood the aluminium shell of the first mountain hut. It must have been comfortable before its wooden lining, bunks, stove, door and windows had been looted, but being so close to the equator it was not too cold in the open with a reasonable sleeping bag even at 9,000 feet. The porters had no such provision however, which was why part of their wages had always been a blanket and a sweater. Silvano and Hezron had each only a thin sweater and shorts, their long trousers had been rolled up and placed in the sacks together with their shoes, ready to don again just before they returned to the village. They had extracted enough money from me to buy several blankets, claiming that such rare commodities were available in a shop nearby, and they could not set out without them. When we reached the first shelter, however, I was told that they had had to give the money to their wives instead. 'We have to pay for school for our children,' Silvano pleaded to explain their perfidy. They busied themselves with the panga, assembling large quantities of firewood to keep a fire going all night in another, lower aluminium shelter. Here they would sleep, curled around the cooking fire, their feet and legs in the empty burlap sacks.

But first we had our meal, which was prepared with all the excitement and sense of adventure of a couple of young scouts. Each day many hours would go into the preparation of their food and I often had the distinct impression that the trip was organised more for their benefit than for mine. They selected their fish carefully, slapped it vigorously between their hands till it fell to bits and then mixed it with water, one of the onions and curry powder and set it to cook vigorously on the fire. The white and innocuous-looking casava flour was added in handfuls to boiling water and stirred with a huge specially carved wooden spoon about a yard long, the only piece of equipment that remained in each of the huts. The stirring required the efforts of both porters and the end result was a rubbery opaque purplish-grey substance, the consistency of plasticene, that tasted as vile as it looked. The porters ate huge quantities of it, pulling off bits and moulding them briefly between their fingers before pressing their thumb firmly into the centre to form a little cup shape. This they dipped into the fishy broth, and tossed it into their mouths, champing away happily as they prepared the next morsel. The fish fragments were sucked off the bones with a great deal of ecstatic slurpings. I told myself grimly to persevere with my own portion as there were six more days of it, but after tea had been prepared and served – all floating tea leaves and lumps of undissolved milk powder – I decided it was not my palate but their lack of culinary skill that was at fault.

After supper it was smoking time for Silvano, though not with the cigarettes I had provided, they had been left at his home on the way. Instead, home-made tobacco was produced and rolled up in bits of the old brown paper that had been wrapped round the fish. The smell was terrible and I made sure I kept upwind of him. While we relaxed around the smoky fire and the silent Hezron roasted groundnuts, I learnt that Silvano was 'a failed Catholic'. 'I needed another wife and so I failed,' he said, 'and now I need another wife because I have too much land and only five children.' We had met one of his children, a boy of ten who was playing truant from school to go fishing. Silvano had said he was very angry, but had then tried to give the boy some of our stores so he could sleep out in the forest. I asked him how he kept the peace between his two wives and he said it could only be done by building them separate huts which was expensive, like education – looking hopefully at me in case I was moved by the story and offered to help.

I soon discovered that most of Silvano's conversations concerned his needs. Some requests he put directly. 'Mama,' he would begin, 'Mama you have those hooks in your country with the shining silver bits the fish like?' No affirmative was needed, he would continue immediately, 'The ones that have the three hooks we need. You will write me a letter to tell me you have sent them.' At other times he began with a thought-provoking preamble appropriate to the occasion, such as when I was peeling off my sodden socks before the fire: 'Mama, our babies when they are just born are of a colour like your feet; God has not been fair to the blackman.' This would be followed after a suitable pause for reflection by a request for some commodity to make up for God's partiality.

In the morning both Silvano and Hezron complained of having been fearfully cold during the night, and although this hardly seemed reasonable under the circumstances, I somehow felt responsible. That day we climbed to 11,500 feet, having first crossed a foaming river from which the bridge had long ago vanished. Most of the time we ascended steeply through bamboo and stinging nettles, lianas and dense brush. The creepers caught in my shoes, pulling open the laces; they got tangled in my hair and snatched the stick out of my hand, so that for much of the time I wondered what I was doing there paying good money to suffer. But then the view would open up on magnificent peaks, soaring high above great secret valleys thickly hung with rain forests. Squalls of rain scudded over the tree tops, with the edges curling up into marestail plumes and evaporating in the warm upper air. Red hyacinths, pink roses, trees hung with exotic ferns and mosses ravished the senses with their exuberant abundance. Higher still, towering fifteen foot spikes of giant lobelia and spongy giant groundsel thirty feet high rose out of the weird bogland in prolific abandon – strange plants, the stuff of science fiction, their stacked leaf bases all containing quantities of rain water, to tip over anything that brushed against them.

At 13,000 feet the going was harder in the thinner air. Even at this height it was still a world dominated by water and plant life. I climbed continually mired to the knee, sometimes plunging into a bog hole up to my thighs. Like the porters I wore shorts but whereas mine remained wet but still intact, Silvano's were no longer even remotely decent and he reluctantly had to don his precious long trousers, which were already split from waist to ankle when he started out – so much for having two wives to do the mending. The requests seem to come thicker with each upward foot: 'Do you have tablets to stop my children coughing?' 'Will you make pictures for me of my family?' 'Can we not keep the cooking pots and the panga.'

Certain jealousies developed about who carried the most and Silvano, who smoked incessantly, could never keep up with the strong abstemious young Hezron. He took his revenge by trying to discredit Hezron. 'That one, he is eating all the milk; there will not be any for your tea, Mama.' Nonetheless there was never any serious dissension; nor was I worried – like some of my Victorian forerunners – that the porters would slope off and leave me to my fate.

The climax of the ascent came on day four with the crossing of the Scott Elliot Pass at 14,500 feet – the additional 1,500 feet of Mount Stanley revealing its ice bound flanks for brief moments through the swirling cloud on our right, with Mount Baker to our left. Mount Stanley had almost been named Mount Gordon Bennet after the proprietor of the *New York Herald*, which financed Stanley's journeys, but later all the peaks were called after Africa explorers and climbers. The sudden glimpses of the summit ridges kept me from dwelling on my various miseries as we climbed steeply towards the head of the pass, first through forests of the weird giant lobelia and giant groundsel, and then up the even steeper final scree slope. We had climbed the mountain too fast for me to acclimatise properly to the altitude; and I felt nauseous and had an acute headache and a bad bout of diarrhoea. I was also wet through and totally disenchanted with the slipping and sliding progress through the bogs.

Only on the screes and in the saddle of the pass did the muddy ground give way for a short while to rock, where it was my turn to feel at home, while Silvano and Hezron found the going difficult on bare feet. It was a dramatic place with the ice fields on either hand and the sun coming and going in fitful gleams, while the clouds rushed up from below, surging over us like insubstantial express trains. All mountains are tremendous at this height and no two are ever alike or ever the same again; it is never easy to leave them after such a struggle to get up there. The porters didn't like it at all and were all for pressing on down quickly to the next hut at 13,200 feet, and leaving these stony heights to the spirits that Silvano firmly believed were resident there. Seeing me placing a stone on each cairn we passed which marked the route, he went out of his way to do the same and probably thought I was placating these spirits. It wasn't fair to keep the bare-footed porters hanging about and they would not have left me up there on my own. Had I been alone I would have probably stayed there for a long while, aches and pain forgotten, while I waited for the clouds to draw apart again and reveal other brief gleams of glory.

The camp below the pass was almost as magical as the pass itself. It was on the edge of a small round lake, the other side of which lay in Zaire, and although it was very cold, with rain clouds closing it in on all sides, beautiful little shining green malachite sunbirds with yard-long tails sipped nectar from the giant lobelia spikes. There were also marvellously shaped black birds with long tails and scarlet under-wings, swooping low over the water. Graciously the clouds lifted for an hour to reveal blue skies and a ring of high distinctive cliffs, with the sun shining on their streaming flanks and on the 'eternal snows'. It marked the final point of the journey, the realisation that I had been to the Mountains of the Moon. I thought of all the various names given to them – the Ruwenzoris, 'That Which Strains the Eye', 'Place of Eagles'. Of them all, 'Mountains Where the Rains Fall' seemed the most appropriate.

CHAPTER TWENTY-TWO

Epilogue: The Murchison Falls

Many people told me that I had not reached the ultimate source of the Nile. In the hills of Barundi, they said, there was a pipe trickling out water and near it a German had built a small pyramid to commemorate all the Nile explorers, which proved it must be the true source. Others laid claim to different sites. I didn't argue with any of them, for I had not been on that kind of journey and I was not a geographer. The Nile has a multitude of sources, as befits so great a river. Hundreds and thousands of acres of ice and snow drip and trickle and gather into streams that eventually find their way into the great lakes – as Ptolemy knew without ever going there. Which of these infinitesimal trickles is the highest or the furthest south will always be a matter of conjecture, and compared with the immense quantities of rain water which fall on the surface of Lake Victoria these other sources are of minor importance anyway. The real source of the Nile is that great inland sea which John Hannay Speke glimpsed all those years ago before dying in tragic circumstances, while Burton who was so much more persuasive in his manner but totally wrong in his views on the subject tried to demolish Speke's claim and advance the case for Lake Tanganyika instead.

I had the worst experience of the journey when I went to pay my respects to Speke's memory at the place where the Nile really begins, where the waters of Lake Victoria start their exit through the Ripon Falls. The visit began pleasantly enough. A friendly policeman had escorted me to the Falls, ruined now by being incorporated into a hydro-electric scheme. He took my photograph standing by the plaque which seemed to have been used for target practice. It didn't matter much that it was indecipherable as I knew what it said about being at the spot where the Nile began its long journey etc. and it didn't matter for the photograph because the policeman had a finger over the lens when he took it so it didn't come out anyway. It was all a bit of a non-happening really and very soon I went in search of a hotel for the night in the town of Jinja which has grown up at this northern end of the lake. I found what appeared to be a very decent place, right on the lakeside, an ex-colonial building with pretty balconies and what had once been lovely gardens. The clerk at the desk said Queen Elizabeth had drunk tea there when she came to open the dam, so even if had I worried about such things I would have thought I was staying somewhere reasonably respectable.

There wasn't much in the way of amenities in the hotel – no water, no carpets on the bare wooden stairways, and not even milk for tea. But there were copious supplies of beer and other alcoholic drinks and when I went to bed at 11 p.m., fairly tired after the day's cycling and sight-seeing, the bar was throbbing with revellers very much the worse for wear. 'Don't worry,' the barman told me, 'we close the place at twelve.' By twelve the noise had reached fever-pitch and the continual clatter of stiletto heels on their way to the only loo in the place, which was opposite the door of my room was driving me demented. By 1.30 I thought I was demented and, sleep being impossible, I went down to see if the bicycle was still all right.

I asked the barman when he thought the party would be over. 'No party here, we're just guests having a good time. Don't you like it?' asked a sharply dressed man lurching over to me and blowing tobacco smoke in my face. 'Not much,' I said: 'I was trying to sleep.' It would have been wiser to have given a softer answer.

There followed one of those sudden ominous hushes and then bedlam broke out. My attitude had been seen to be critical, and they were not in a mood to put up with it. I had touched some raw nerve and unleashed a latent hostility; clearly there was going to be a reaction. I decided to depart swiftly and discreetly and on the way back to my room I picked up the bicycle and took it in with me. There was a few moments grace and then came the almighty clatter of a horde of people charging up the bare stairs, calling out as they came, 'Where you white woman? Come out of there sister, we going to pull you apart.'

The room was in darkness, which stopped them for a while. I heard them trying several doors along the corridor, but after a while they gathered outside mine and in the dim light from the corridor which shone through the fanlight I could see the knob turning – and then the door shook and the calls for me to come out were renewed. They did not stay long and when I heard them retreating downstairs again I set about barricading the room as well as I could in case they returned. There was not a lot I could do, as there wasn't much furniture. My main fear was that they would find their way onto the balcony that ran along the whole front of the hotel, and from which a flimsy door and window led into my room.

They came back at intervals throughout the night. Sometimes a group of high-pitched women's voices would threaten and taunt, sometimes it was men. There was one man who came alone, silently, and whispered through the keyhole, 'Woman open the door'; that was the most terrifying of all. I never answered but sat still and silent on the edge of the bed, sweating in the dark, closed, airless room. I tried to make my mind a blank, but the words of T. S. Eliot's 'Ash Wednesday' kept running continuously through my head, like a medieval litany – 'Although I do not hope to turn again, Although I do not hope, Although I do not hope to turn . . .'

The intervals between the footsteps on the stairs became gradually longer, and at some point just before dawn there was a great revving of engines and drunken shouts and several cars roared away from the hotel. I knew then that it was all over but I was too drained to feel any sense of elation. A couple of hours later my breakfast was brought; the waiter murmured an apology about there not being any milk for the tea, but no mention was made of the night's disturbances.

Back in Kampala I thought a great deal about the incident. The city was struggling to restore itself and clean up the mess of years of fighting. Even so, every night I went to sleep to the sound of rifle fire, and there were almost daily reports of vehicles being hijacked by armed men posing as soldiers – the soldiers from the various different armies seemed to have kept their guns and uniform. Several Europeans were killed when they didn't surrender their vehicles quickly enough. Every building I visited seemed to be pockmarked with bullet scars or to elicit some tale of horror – like the university, where in a single night three hundred young men had been thrown to their deaths from the top-floor windows by Idi Amin's henchmen. Yet all this violence seemed so at variance with the general atmosphere. Almost all the Ugandans I met were such overtly friendly, gentle people: 'a soft race', someone had said of them, and that seemed to me a good description. Only in the hotel at Jinja, and when I had aroused the soldier's anger at the wheelbarrow at Pakwatch, did I see the other side of the coin and experience for myself something of the contempt for human life that underlay the violence, and was also a part of this ruined paradise.

It was time to leave Africa, to return home and let the various experiences of my travels shuffle gradually into place. I was quite ready to do so, except for the feeling of something important left undone; the nagging sense of disappointment that I still felt about not having seen the Murchison Falls. Without at least a glimpse of 'the most exciting single incident in the Nile's long journey to the sea' there seemed to be a yawning gap in my own journey. With a week to go before departure I decided to make one last attempt to get there. Remembering what the arrogant warden at Paraa had said about bringing him a letter, I went in search of the director of Uganda's game parks.

The office took a good deal of tracking down because telephones didn't work often in Kampala and there were no directories, but I found it eventually, and had the good fortune to arrive there when the director was in his office. Mr Ssemwezi was a large, fatherly man who seemed passionately devoted to Uganda's national parks. He listened attentively to my story about how I had come all the way up the Nile, and seemed altogether in sympathy with my burning desire to get to the Murchison Falls. When I told him about the soldiers shooting at the water buck in the Murchison Park, I thought he would weep, but on hearing the account of how the warden wouldn't take me to the Falls his grief turned to anger. 'That man is a thorn in my side,' he said. 'He does not reply to my messages. I have sent for him to bring the Land Rover here but he ignores me.' Things looked hopeful I decided, with Mr Ssemwezi only too eager for me to see the Murchison Falls and to 'Tell the world about it and what these perfidious soldiers are doing shooting Uganda's remaining animals'. I thought he might arrange for me to be driven down there. Alas, his anger was as much due to frustration as to the various perfidies. He would take me himself right now, he said, except for the fact that there were no other vehicles in the whole of the Uganda national park service; the solitary, single Land Rover was ferrying the chief warden (acting) and his lady up and down the road at Paraa on the wrong side of the Victoria Nile.

I certainly hadn't time to make it there and back by bicycle before my flight to England, even if I was allowed to get through, and with reports of increasing fighting in that direction it was unlikely that I would. It looked like I'd drawn another blank. More out of habit than with any real hope of needing it, I asked if he would write a letter instructing the warden to take me to the Falls in case I somehow found a means of getting there. This he did, jumping at the chance of doing something positive and of having a possible courier to deliver an order to his recalcitrant subordinate. In addition to telling the man to get in touch immediately, the letter gave firm instructions to get me 'At all cost and without delay to the Murchison Falls, accompanied if necessary, by two armed rangers.'

I spent the next thirty-six hours visiting every agency I could think of that might have a vehicle going via Paraa. I would have paid anything within reason, but money was of no use. There were no vehicles to hire and no form of transport at all, other than a lift with someone. When I had exhausted every avenue of enquiry, and had just about abandoned all hope of ever seeing the Murchison Falls, I had the good fortune to meet someone who said simply, 'Why not take my truck?'

I started off the following morning while it was still dark, stalling once as I eased the unfamilar vehicle through the perimeter fortifications that surrounded all Kampala houses in the vain hope of keeping out the thieves. Then I was off through the series of gigantic linked potholes that stretched for the 350 miles to my destination. I had had only the most cursory of instructions in driving the four-wheeled-drive pick-up, because the anonymous American who lent it to me assumed that anyone white and over the age of twelve could drive anything and I hadn't wanted him to change his mind by expressing any lack of confidence. It was pouring with rain when I left so I couldn't gauge the depth of the potholes, but at least I became familiar with the windscreen wipers.

By the time it was light I had reached the last of the road blocks before the turn-off for Masindi – Sam Baker country again. I had had no trouble at any of the others but as I slid gently to a halt, a soldier pretended that I had nearly run him over. It was only a simulated anger in order to make me take his girl friend back to her village, which lay on my route. He need not have bothered as I would have taken her without the charade. Once off the main road I was into a glutinous mudbath, with water up to the axles in places. I drove with extreme caution but the Toyota seemed to handle very well, so I took it a little faster as there was every need to press on. No sooner had I dropped off the soldier's girl friend than a young man asked me to give his mother and sister a lift. With transport so scarce in Uganda I felt I could not refuse, but it did seem to be taking things rather too far when they started to throw into the back, the complete contents of a small house – two beds, chairs, chickens (alive and dead) and various bundles and baskets. With every bump the women shrieked and banged on the sides of the truck. Then I got into a skid, and while I was struggling to get us out of it, they launched into a cacophony of shrieks and ululations, and tried to jump out. When I finally brought the vehicle to a halt I decided I couldn't cope with the additional distraction nor could I be responsible for other people's lives on such a perilous road, and unloaded the women with their beds, bundles and hens. For their part they seemed only too happy to escape from what they plainly regarded as a dangerous lunatic.

I got into another skid on a particularly muddy hill and the offside wheel slid neatly into a ditch. A large party of men and boys came roaring out of a village to help. All the vehicles went off the road here, they said and I wouldn't have been surprised if they'd dug the ditch specially for this purpose. It rose up to the level of the road again in about twenty yards and the men pushed the truck along to this point, demanding baksheesh with the disarming remark, 'We are many.'

There was one last road block, and at this one the young soldier was slow, and I was tired and impatient to get on. 'I have to check you,' he said. 'Even myself, I am having to be identified, there are terrorists everywhere.' 'What nonsense,' I said incautiously. 'Is there any way I could be mistaken for a young black terrorist?' Instead of taking offence, the soldier roared with laughter as if I had made a good joke, and he waved me on my way with a 'God be with you.' There were no more delays after that. The sun came out and soon I was pressing on along a dry road. By midday I was down in the Rift Valley again at the point where the missionaries had refused me water, and I suddenly thought of how much more I had seen of the country by doing it on a bicycle. But today though speed was of the essence, and I would be able to cover in an hour what had taken me seven times that long, pushing my bicycle through the soft sand.

By 1.30 it seemed as though there might just be time to make the Falls that day. I had been planning my tactics as I drove, and everything hinged on not having to go in search of the chief warden. There was a rangers' post at the entrance to the park, two hours before Paraa, and if I could pick up my escort there we could go straight to the Falls. If I had to go down to Paraa and cross on the unreliable ferry it would take another day at least and I could even be marooned on the wrong side of the river. There simply wasn't time for that. Accordingly, I was pleased to see several men lying on the ground, taking it easy as I reached the dilapidated huts which marked the entrance. They were persuaded to read the director's letter, and after a certain amount of hesitation and discussion about their not having any rifles, the fact that we needed to make an immediate start if we were to get back by nightfall decided the issue; a man called Julius climbed aboard and we were off on the last stage.

It was hard to believe that any vehicle other than a tank could have made it, for the way was almost completely obliterated. It was like driving through virgin bush. Saplings had sprung up along the track and in forcing a way through them, a hub got stuck against the trunk of one of them and the whole truck heaved up and the door handle skinned my arm from elbow to wrist. In places Julius had to go ahead, on foot. But the compensations for such slow painful progress were many, for we saw a great deal of wild life in this undisturbed place. There was a great variety of birds, all new to me, and a family of five warthogs, three of them very young, all of them making off in single file with their ridiculous stiff little tufted tails held bolt upright, quivering with indignation. Great herds of buffalo grazed undisturbed, and two huge sentinel bulls raised wary heads not many feet from where we inched past. In one rare flat place a flock of exotic geese walked towards us in a curved sweeping line cropping the grass rapidly as they came. All sorts of deer appeared, but my favourites were the small antelope which stopped for a moment to regard the truck in trembling bewilderment, before making off with marvellous heart-stopping leaps.

When we were half way down the final slope to the river and could get the truck no further, I manoeuvred it around and tried to climb out. I had been driving continuously for ten hours but had been so buoyed up that I didn't realise how exhausted I was until I found my knees were trembling too much to walk. Fortunately there was a can of luke-warm cola in the cab and that raised the level of my blood sugar again.

I could hear the roar of the Falls from the truck and I would have liked to have waited and approached them slowly, drawing out the anticipation, but there was no time. All the really important places on this final section of the journey seemed to have been taken at the gallop and the Falls were no exception. We came straight down through the woods to the upper section of them, the thunder growing louder all the while.

The river doesn't so much fall over Murchison; it hurls itself through a long rocky cleft, which confines the tremendous force and volume of it for a furious four hundred yards of raging tumultuous energy. The pent up mass leaps in ever greater waves, seeking an escape, only to crash back against other waves rising beneath them. Great plumes of water reach a height where their tops break away in spray fine enough to form a rainbow over the chaotic magnificence. At the end of the cleft the water does fall, dropping in a long straight line to the wide flat river below but this is not nearly so spectacular. What impresses here is the long view of the wide, placid, sun-sparkling river beyond the fury of the Murchison Falls.

I had, I suppose, only a brief two hours there, certainly not long enough to become used to the place or for it to lose the edge of its wonder. As Julius began urging that it was time to start back, and I tried to linger on for a little while longer, I thought of how hard it had been to get there, the energy that had been expended. Had it been worth it? There is no answer to such a question. Travel is for its own sake. If an answer was needed it was to be found in that long expanse of sunlit water far below, turning lazily around as it settled down and concentrated its energies to make the long, long journey through Africa, down through the way I had come.

Equipment

The bicycle I chose for the the journey was an eighteen-gear 'All Terrain' machine which I designed myself and which was built by Evans Bicycle Shop, The Cut, Waterloo, London. It was constructed from Reynolds 531 tubing and had a particularly 'tight' frame, short in the chain stays and steep in the head angle, which made it a good climber and very lively. It performed excellently on all the atrocious roads of my journey, only baulking at the talcum powder sand in the worst of the desert places.

Tools and spares for the bicycle consisted of two inner tubes, puncture repair kit, essential lightweight spanners, an adjustable spanner, a link extractor, a pair of pliers, and a spare tyre.

My luggage was carried in Karrimor's Kalahari panniers, which stood up well to sun, sand and floods and to being scraped along the ground when I fell off or when the bicycle was thrown about on alternative forms of transport.

The photographs were all taken on an Olympus XA camera, which as always, survived a great deal of abuse. The film used was Kodachrome Professional 64 asa.

My survival equipment included a Mayfly tent by North Face, a Thermarest self-inflating mattress, a Caravan down sleeping bag, a Katadyn water filter, an Optimus Climber petrol stove, water containers, Novia dehydrated packet meals, a Tekna Lithium torch, a compass, a seven-bladed penknife, waterproof matches, a slow-burning candle and a dog repellent spray (unused).

I was vaccinated against hepatitis, cholera, meningitis, typhoid, para-typhoid, rabies, yellow fever, polio and tetanus.

My medical equipment consisted of antibiotic tablets, vitamin pills, malaria preventative tablets, treatment for diarrhoea, headaches and fever, plasters, antiseptic cream, sutures, insect repellent, suncream, lip salve. But the most important item was the Katadyn water purifying pump mentioned above which provided safe drinking water and brought me through some of the most disease-riddled areas of Africa without contracting anything nasty.

Additional necessities were Michelin Map 154 (cut in half) 1/100,000 series which covered almost the whole of the Nile from the delta to the source, several notebooks, pens (for use and for presents), postcards of extracts from the Koran from the British Museum for presents, traveller's cheques, needle and thread, pieces of string and safety pins and sunglasses.

© Bettina Selby London 1987

METROPOLIS

New York as Myth, Marketplace and Magical Land

JEROME CHARYN

'Brilliant', said *Newsday* of Jerome Charyn, 'a contemporary Balzac', while the *Chicago Tribune* called him 'a realist of the urban nightmare'. Now he turns his keen novelist's eye on a phenomenon as elusive as it is alluring – New York, New York, a city, like its inhabitants, with no firm roots.

In *Metropolis* Jerome Charyn, whose parents both passed through Ellis Island, searches for the 'history' the city loves to hide: he spends the Fourth of July with Mayor Koch, invades secret Mafia country in Brooklyn, attends opening day at Yankee Stadium with Mickey Mantle, mixes with the homeless in the Bronx, investigates a sex palace in Times Square, meets the man who lit up the Empire State Building and the man who built Radio City Music Hall.

Jerome Charyn knows New York as well as anyone and better than most, and this is his personal paean, as endlessly fascinating as the city itself.

0 349 10010 1   NON-FICTION   £3.99

THE
PANAMA
HAT TRAIL
TOM MILLER

Panama hats don't come from Panama; they are made two countries away in Ecuador, in South America. Tom Miller travelled there to find the origins of the hats. Learning how a Panama hat is made and marketed – from the harvesting of raw straw in the middle of a jungle to the purchase of a finished hat in a store in San Diego – is more than a travel adventure and a cultural study; it is also an off-beat lesson in the workings of world trade. How is a hat, sold for seventy cents by the peasant who had painstakingly woven it by hand, eventually bought for thirty-five dollars? Why do the impoverished peasants have little knowledge of this – and less interest? Tom Miller perceptively and personably leads us around the old Inca Empire, across the equator, through American foreign policy, and along one of the least travelled and most remarkable trails in the world –

'A lovely little gem of a book. THE PANAMA HAT TRAIL is part reportage, part travelogue, and all pleasure; it is rewarding and entertaining on many counts. It is filled with lively anecdotes, pungent asides, vivid scenes and – best of all in a travel book – delightful characters . . . a pleasure on every page of the journey' WASHINGTON POST

0 349 10018 7   NON-FICTION   £3.99

An Unfinished Journey

SHIVA NAIPAUL

AN UNFINISHED JOURNEY comprises the last writings of Shiva
Naipaul before his death in 1985 – six articles and the beginnings of his
projected book on Australia. All the pieces are rich and vital, fine
examples of Shiva Naipaul's determination to harass the issues which
troubled him and demanded his attention: his search for his own identity –
within his family and within the world, his utter contempt for racism of
any kind and his fascination with India and the so-called 'Third World'
and, not least, his energetic yearning to understand mankind. AN
UNFINISHED JOURNEY is a memorial to a great writer and a
celebration of his art.

This collection of pieces is magnificent . . . beautifully written, utterly honest,
and curiously uplifting. And I should not forget to say that it is also often very
funny' LITERARY REVIEW

0 349 10009 8   NON-FICTION   £3.50

ZOO STATION

IAN WALKER

BERLIN   For most of us, the word whips up images of decadence, a dangerous *melange* of artistry, politics, and design extravagances; red-gashed mouths in smoky nightclubs, gaudy and melancholy. But qualified by 'East' and 'West' those images merge and disappear.

IAN WALKER lifts and separates the two zones, revealing Berlin as it is today: a two faced city where every single thing is mirrored and echoed in an undeclared war of buildings, cars, clothes, flags, food, music and street-signs. Drinking and dancing, talking to friends, exiles, ex-prisoners, and runaways, he shuttles in between communism and capitalism, a regular commuter on the smugglers' express . . . in awe of the faceless power of the Wall, yet crashing through it with addicted frequency.

'Will raise a pang of nostalgia in all who have fallen under the city's spell'
Daily Mail

0 349 10045 4   NON FICTION   £3.99